T0203464

HOUSE OF FRANK

HOUSE OF FRANK

KAY SYNCLAIRE

Published by Ezeekat Press, an imprint of Bindery Books, Inc., San Francisco
www.binderybooks.com

Acquired by Jaysen Headley

Edited and designed by Girl Friday Productions
www.girlfridayproductions.com

Cover illustration: Barry Blankenship
Cover design (paperback): Paul Barrett
Cover design (hardcover): Charlotte Strick
Image credits (hardcover): Piano keys ©La corneja artesana / Shutterstock; sheet music ©Svetlanaprikhnenko/Dreamstime.com

ISBN (paperback): 978-1-959411-66-6
ISBN (hardcover): 978-1-959411-88-8
ISBN (ebook): 978-1-959411-67-3

Library of Congress Cataloging-in-Publication data has been applied for.

First edition

*For Joy, the woman who gave me life and
a deep love for storytelling.
And for my sister, Donna. And all the stories
we have yet to tell the world, together.*

"Smile, my boy. It's sunrise."

—Teddy Roosevelt, as portrayed by
Robin Williams in *Night at the Museum*

CONTENT WARNING

This book contains portrayals of grief, death, mentions of death, the death of a child (off page), the mention of suicide (off page), minor ideation of suicide, and mental illness.

PRONUNCIATION GUIDE

Arboretum: ar-bore-ee-tum
Beelzebub: bee-el-zi-bub
Evette: ee-vet
Fiona/Fi: fee-oh-na/fee
Frank: fr—Do you really need this?
Hilde: hill-dee
Ignatius: ig-nay-sh-us
Kye: k-eye
Marionette: mary-oh-net
Morose: mor-rose
Oli/Olivie: oh-lee/oh-liv-ee or oh-liv-ee-eh . . . If you're feeling
    fancy
Phil: f—I'm not doing this one either
Saika: s'eye-kah

TWO YEARS AGO

"Sing for me," you whisper. "Please."

The words squeeze out of my throat like an ocean funneling through a straw. You close your eyes and hum. A tear curls around the smile on your face as I end on a warbly note.

You break the stillness with a soft chuckle, eyes still closed. "Oh, that was lovely, Saika. Though you hate the man, you still sing one of Father's favorites."

I slip the silk glove from my hand and hold yours in a warm embrace.

"I should count myself lucky." You hold up our entwined fingers. "My little sister is embracing me with her bare hand. This must be a momentous day."

"Fi, please." I look away to stop the ache encroaching on my throat. A sob threatens my chest, and it takes everything within my power to stuff it down. I have to show you that I'm handling this alright.

"Do you remember your promise, Sai?" Your grip on my hand is weak, but I feel your urgency all the same.

"Of course."

"And do you still have the star?" Your pale eyes drift down to the gold locket around my neck.

I hold it up, a tiny pendant hanging from the thin chain. "I haven't let go of it. I never will."

"And you know where it is, yes? You haven't forgotten—"

"I'm not a child, Fiona. Of course, I do. Ash Gardens is just outside the city."

"Look for the bright red door."

I pull back the curls from your sweaty forehead. "I promise, I will bring you there."

My chest aches. And suddenly it takes one look into your eyes for me to break completely. I weep at your bedside, clinging to you. For as long as I live, Fi, I will never let you go.

CHAPTER ONE

Remnants of old paint chip from the large front door. The color is more maroon than bright red. I expected to see something really fantastic. Like a castle, perhaps. With manicured lawns. Staff waiting to greet me at the door.

But the truth is, the famed Ash Gardens isn't as polished as I was led to believe.

Rain pelts over the weathered and aged wood. I note scorch marks on the top level. Works of an Architect witch who did repairs. I can hear our father's voice stating he could have done a better, more seamless job. The haughty old man.

Vines and flowers thread up the sides of the house. A wide veranda rounds the front, complete with a porch swing and a comically tall rocking chair. Potted plants decorate the steps and hang from the banisters, getting much-needed water from the rain. A pair of muddy work boots is thrown haphazardly by the door.

The ad I was given said that Ash Gardens was only a short distance from the last train stop away from the city.

I inhale and release. It's fine. I'm glad I walked. It builds character. After an hour-long train ride and an entire morning trudging through the rain, my feet are aching and my socks soaked through. The heels of my clunky boots are sinking into the squishy, wet grass. I grip my umbrella in one hand, swinging my suitcase in the other.

Inhale, release.

A voice calls from above, "Do you think she's petrified?"

I look up to the windows on the second floor of the house. A cherub sits on one windowsill, eating a melon slice. Another cherub with light brown hair sits in the opposite window, munching on grapes.

"She's probably half-baked," the cherub says. "You know, take one step. Breathe. Take another. Breathe. Blink."

"Hey, you're doing fine." The brown-haired cherub eats a grape. "Everyone knows how to walk and breathe."

"I'm not half-baked," I call up, squinting to keep drops of rain from going into my eyes.

The melon-eating cherub shrugs. "Could've fooled me. You've been putterin' around in the rain for ages."

"It hasn't been ages." Though it certainly feels like it. I scan them. Coarse, curly hair covers their naked chests. "And where are your clothes?"

"We're cherubs, love." He takes a heaping bite of his melon. "It's our birthright to be shirtless and free."

"Doesn't seem like you flew from the train stop." The brown-haired cherub inspects me. "Where's your broom?"

My brow twitches, but I force a smile. "I'm a witch bound to earth, I'm afraid. I don't own a broom."

The melon-eating cherub breaks out into a laugh. "Mer, have you ever heard of a witch without a broom? Strange thing, isn't it?"

My mouth twists into a frown. "If you must know, brooms

are terribly expensive. And to fly one is a waste of energy and magic."

"Yeah, I'm sure." He takes another bite of his melon.

"Still," the other cherub says, "it's a far walk. You must be hungry. Here." He plucks off a grape and tosses it toward me. It misses me completely, and the three of us watch as it hits the wet ground and rolls into the mud.

"Alright." I climb the steps, wipe my feet on the mat, and ring the doorbell. It doesn't work. I knock instead.

As I wait, I tug on the trim of my headwrap, making sure it hasn't slipped back during my strenuous journey here.

I feel the slightest tremble beneath my feet. A large, dark silhouette appears through the hazy glass above the door. I note the outline of horns and tall, massive shoulders. My breath stills when the door swings open.

I'm met with a smile full of many sharp teeth. It's a beast. My first speculation is that he must be a minotaur, but he's all fur and paws and stands on his hind legs. I've never seen a creature like him before.

"Hello, how can I help you?" the beast asks. His voice is so resounding and full that I can feel the vibration in my bones. He's wearing a beige knit cardigan. Tufts of reddish-brown fur poke out from his collar and his sleeves. Reading glasses hang from his neck, and he looks at me with small, yellow eyes. He looks so well put together. I'm not sure if I should feel ashamed of myself.

"Good afternoon. My name is Saika." I hold out my gloved hand, and he nearly crushes it in a handshake. "Is this Ash Gardens?" I ask, wincing. "I've heard about the arboretum sanctuary and—"

"Oh, of course." He steps back to allow me passage. "Come on in, Miss Saika."

I glance over my shoulder. A storm is quickly moving in. Rain hits the ground even harder. Swollen, dark clouds are rolling through the gray sky, blanketing the distant mountains. I won't be going back to the train stop even if I wanted to. I turn back to the beast and step through the door.

From the outside, the house looks unassuming and quaint, but the foyer feels grander. I gaze up at painted turquoise clouds and white stars surrounding a massive chandelier high overhead. It twinkles brightly, illuminating the entire foyer. A woven maroon rug (same old color as the door, mind you) runs from the front door to a winding staircase.

"Here, dear, I'll take that." The beast holds out his paw expectantly, and it takes me a moment to realize he's waiting for my umbrella. I'm so distracted by the house, I apologize as I hand it over.

"My name is Frank." The beast holds his massive arms politely behind his back. "Welcome to my home."

"Oh, this is your home. I thought this was the arboretum sanctuary." I pull a scrap of paper from my cloak pocket. "I received this ad about two years ago, so it's quite old. Let's see here: 'Ash Gardens is just a short distance from the last train stop. We are an ash sanctuary that is home to one of the largest arboretums in the country. Once you see the bright red door, you'll know you're home. Just ring the doorbell and—'"

"Ask for Frank," the beast finishes with a smile. He waves at me. "Hello, I'm Frank. And you are correct. This *is* Ash Gardens. The arboretum is in the back. But I live here as well. My wife and I ran the arboretum together until she passed on." He sets his eyes on me. "What brings you all this way in the rain? Do you have ashes you'd like to plant?"

"No," I answer too quickly. Instinctively, I hold my suitcase behind my back.

Frank pauses. "I'm sorry, I didn't mean to . . . um."

I don't know what's wrong with me. I made up my mind the moment I booked my train ticket to Ash Gardens. I came here to uphold my promise.

But you see, words can become so difficult when your mouth dries up and a familiar tightness tugs in your chest. I fall quiet, my hands gripping the handle of my suitcase.

Frank waits patiently. And suddenly, I feel horrible for taking up so much of his time.

I regain my composure. "I apologize. As you can imagine, it wasn't easy making my way here. In fact, it took me some time to even book a train ride all the way out to the countryside. The truth is, I do have someone's ashes to bury. It's just . . ." My cowardice silences me again.

He nods as if he understood the words I did not say. He smiles, his sharp teeth—intimidating at first—seem almost pleasant now. He lays a heavy paw on my shoulder. "It's never an easy journey to lay someone to rest. I fully understand, Miss Saika."

I swallow the lump in my throat. "Then what do I do?"

Frank looks me over. I can't tell if his small eyes are ghosting over my damp headwrap or my gold locket resting against my clavicle. I masquerade a cough, tucking the chain back inside my cloak.

He sighs and sets my umbrella in a bin near the front door. "You'll be stationary for a moment, so I can show you around Ash Gardens once the ceremonial meal finishes next door."

My eyes widen. "Are you hosting a ceremony right now?" Oh, I was so careless. I was so preoccupied scrounging up my courage to get here that I didn't even think about if they'd have availability. "I'm terribly sorry. Of course, you'd be busy. I should've called." I step back toward the door. "I can return tomorrow. What an improper thing to do. Turning up this way. Have I no manners? My mother would've had my head if she knew I showed up like this. Unannounced."

I reach to retrieve my umbrella, but a gentle paw stops me. "Miss Saika," Frank says, with a hint of amusement. "It's quite alright. The ceremonial meal is nearly over. Besides, it's raining. Possibly heading into a full typhoon by the looks of it."

We both look through the hazy glass over the front door. The very thought of walking back out there to the train stop sends shivers up my spine.

Frank notices. "You've had a very long journey. And although I'm sure you're quite determined, I hear it's no fun flying in the rain."

"I didn't fly. I walked." Noticing his wide-eyed silence, I quickly explain. "I would have flown, but I don't own a broom. They're awfully expensive. Terrible waste of magic as well." I chuckle, but Frank doesn't laugh.

Frank blinks his small, yellow eyes. "Oh, I'm so sorry. I didn't realize. Walking must have taken you all day. You must be exhausted."

"I'm fine. Honestly, I can return once you have availability." My hand grips the door handle, but Frank stands firm.

"We have a vacant room." He points toward the winding staircase at the end of the foyer. "A room on the third level. You can rest until tomorrow. The storm will probably last the night."

"I couldn't possibly—"

"Please. How could I allow you to go back out there when there's a place for you here?"

My arms are so tired from lugging this suitcase all morning. My legs feel like noodles, bending anywhere the wind blows.

And right now, the wind is blowing toward the promise of a warm bed.

"Of course, I'll pay you for your hospitality."

"Nonsense." Frank's smile takes up his entire face. "I'll show you to your room, Miss Saika."

I'm slow to move, and Frank offers his arm. He waits patiently for me to take it.

Resting against him I can feel his warmth, and strength, and softness. "It'll only be for the night. I promise. Then, we can talk about the burial tomorrow?"

"Planting ceremony. And of course."

He directs us toward the staircase. Beyond the foyer, I spot a wide brass double door that reaches to the ceiling. It's embossed with the silhouette of a horned beast on one side of the door and the silhouette of a woman on the other. Their lips meet in the middle where the door opens.

Frank catches me staring as we climb the steps. "That is my wing of the house, where my wife and I lived together."

"Judging from her profile, your wife looks lovely."

"Oh, she was." He shoulders more of my weight, but still allows me the dignity of walking. "Ash Gardens wouldn't be what it is if not for her."

"It is an impressive estate. It's amazing that you run it all by yourself."

Frank chuckles, and it rumbles through his chest. "Oh no, I could never." We continue up the steps. "I've employed staff, and they live here as well. There's quite a few of us. I'll be sure to introduce you."

"Where are they now?" I glance around the stairwell as if I'd see one of them lurking in the dark corners.

"Serving the family downstairs. After the ceremony in the

arboretum, we invite the bereaved back to the house for a home-cooked meal together."

"That sounds lovely." I can't help but think about my own family. It will only be me at the burial. I wonder if Frank will still offer a meal and sit with me out of pity. How depressing.

Frank has to duck his head a bit as we head farther up the stairwell. After a quick glance down the hall, I notice that the doors on the second level are also short. I'd probably have to duck to go inside any of them. But once we finally enter the third level, the ceiling height returns to normal.

"Was that last story shorter?" I take a break at the landing to catch my breath. I fear I'm about to fall over.

"Oh, yes. Our resident Architect witch designed that level for our small friends. Let's see, there's Evette (she's a light fairy), an elf, and twin cherubs."

I groan. "I met the cherubs briefly. When I arrived."

Frank nods knowingly with a smile. "Merry and Morose. I assure you, once you formally meet them, they'll grow on you."

"They were just very chatty." Fatigue is slowly seizing my legs. If I stand for a moment longer, I may never move again. "I'm ready to see the room."

"Of course." Frank leads me down the hall. "On this level, there are only two rooms. Our Nature witch stays in the room across from you."

"How many witches work for you?"

"Two," he says proudly.

"And you've managed to snag an Architect and a Nature witch? You must compensate very well."

"On the contrary, I can't offer very much. But what I *can* offer is a safe place to stay when you have nowhere else to go. All in exchange for some help around the estate, of course."

We stop in the middle of the short hallway when the door on the right clicks open. A young woman with a long braid backs out cautiously. She closes the door gently.

I glance up to Frank's perplexed face. "Is that the Nature witch?" I whisper.

"No, she is not," he whispers back.

The woman turns around and is startled by our presence.

"Oh!" She jumps and clutches her chest. "Mr. Frank, what a pleasure to see you again."

Frank smiles tightly. "Pleasure is mine. I hope you found the ceremony last night both comforting and healing."

"Oh, it was. I'm sure my grandmother's ashes will grow into a magnificent tree. If you're wondering why I'm still here"—a blush dusts the woman's cheeks—"it was late last night, so Oli was kind enough to allow me to stay with her."

Frank clears his throat and nods. "You don't have to explain anything to me. Oli can be quite hospitable."

A crash of thunder rolls over the house, and we all glance up to the ceiling. The house creaks and groans.

"Thank you again for the beautiful ceremony." The woman smiles uncomfortably. "I'll be heading out then."

Frank blinks. "Oh, are you sure? The storm—"

The woman shakes her head. "I've flown in worse weather. Have a wonderful evening." She takes off down the hall, pulling down the hem of her dress.

"Seems like you're fond of hosting guests." I doubt my words make the moment any less awkward.

He directs me to the other side of the hallway. "Now, I think you've had enough delay. Your room at last."

The bedroom feels warm and inviting. It has a vaulted ceiling, and thick, long curtains are tied beside the huge window looking out to the estate. A smaller window faces the back of the house. I try to look out at the backyard to snag a peek at the arboretum, but I can't see anything but the storm raging beyond the thick glass.

Two tall bookcases stand on either side of the bed with willowy vines and plants on their top shelves. I shuck off my damp cloak and hang it on the coatrack. "Oh, Frank. This is absolutely divine."

Frank stays in the hallway and sets my suitcase inside. "I'm happy it's to your liking. There's a bathroom down the hall to your left. I'd also like to invite you to dinner at six. Evette makes a delicious chicken and potatoes."

My brows rise. Chicken and potatoes is my favorite meal.

I came here with one goal in mind, but instead I'm taking this room, taking this bed, taking Frank's hospitality. Before he can go, I stop him.

"Wait." I go to the coatrack and rummage through my wet pockets. "Allow me to pay you for tonight. This is far too much charity. I haven't even used your services yet."

Frank analyzes me for a moment. He shakes his head, and his mane ruffles around his shoulders. "I have no need for your money, Miss Saika. Have a good rest. I'll see you soon." He doesn't allow me to respond. The door closes behind him. I resist the urge to chase him down and force him to accept my money.

A bedside lamp sets the entire room in a warm glow, and I'm ready to plop on the circular bed, its soft velvet pillows beckoning me. But I cannot sleep in my travel clothes. My socks are cold and wet. The hem of my dress is lined with splotches of mud, threatening the deep blue paisley rug that covers the wooden floor.

I begin to unravel my damp headwrap. I loosen the lace on

my corset. Breath returns to my lungs as gravity sets everything to where it ought to be. I pull off my boots, expecting to find my wand hidden inside, but it isn't there. "Damn it. Where did I put it?"

I snap open my suitcase. My clothes spring out like a jack-in-the-box. Shame on me for using a shoddy spell to overpack it. As I scoop up my clothes, I find my wand in the mess, but I also come across a square silver frame.

It's a picture of us. You're wearing that fancy red dress our mother forced you to wear, and as protest, you scowled the entire day. And when it came time, she asked you to smile and pose with me. And my, did you pose.

This is easily my favorite picture of you. You're cross-eyed and toothless, but your smile is so big that I thought your lips would split. And I'm laughing beside you, my tongue hanging from my mouth. Our mother was so angry with us for ruining the picture, but we didn't care. You made me laugh that day. You always made me laugh, Fi.

I place the silver frame on the nightstand beside my bed. I kiss my finger, then touch your face with my fingertip.

I find the clear jar filled with sparkling dust and gently place it beside your picture.

I love you, Fiona. I'm sorry it's taken me so long to bring you to Ash Gardens. But a promise is a promise. I made it. I'm here. And tomorrow, I will finally lay your ashes to rest. After years of cowardice, I owe this to you. And so much more.

CHAPTER TWO

A crash of thunder wakes me with a start. My arms feel like lead, and my legs aren't much better. When I slide them over the bed, I do so with much effort. My joints are stiff and achy. I wish I hadn't walked the entire way from the train stop.

The room has become dark. Lightning flashes beyond the windows, and the wind beats on the glass. The lamp on my bedside table is off, and when I pull the chain, it doesn't turn back on. Electricity must be out.

I run my hand underneath the mattress until I find my wand tucked between the sheets. I need to enchant some light. I remember the first time you showed me how to do it, Fi. Though, I wonder how well it will translate with an incantation. I suppose I'll have to try. I think of the words and give the wand a twirl.

"I cannot see. I have no sight. Turn this darkness into light."

My locket warms as the tip of my wand fizzles. It sputters until golden light illuminates the room, then falters, and I bang the wand against the heel of my palm. "Useless junk." The light returns.

The clock above my door dings six times. It's only six o'clock. It feels like I've slept for ages. I must've been really exhausted. I retie my loose headwrap and head out of the room.

The hallway is as dark as my room. A few candles have been lit at the end of the hall. The curtains have been drawn to block out the storm. It's quiet, but as I near the stairwell, the din of conversation and clinking silverware echoes from downstairs. The distant smell of food pulls me closer.

I hold up my illuminated wand. The top step creaks as I peer down. I'm not afraid of the dark, Fi, but I can't deny just *how* dark it is down this stairwell.

"Oh, my love, that's quite a waste of an enchantment," a silky voice says above me.

Coming down from the fourth level is an older woman wearing a black gown. The sleeves of her dress are long and translucent. Her silver hair is pressed in layers and sits past her shoulders. She holds a candle in her hand, and the soft glow casts upon her sharp jaw and catlike eyes.

Seeing her, I hide my wand behind my back, vigorously shaking it until the light fades. I slip my wand into my boot, and she chuckles.

"Oh, there's no need to hide that. It's okay if you're a wand user." She's a tall woman, and she towers over me. "We all have to start somewhere."

"Yes, I suppose we do." I hold out my hand. "Good evening. I'm Saika."

She stares at my silk gloves before shaking my hand. "I'm Hilde. I live on the fourth level."

She seems to struggle to pull the train of her dress around to the next flight of steps, so I offer my arm.

She smiles at me. "Well, Saika. It appears the storm has knocked out the electricity. Won't you accompany an old lady downstairs? I'm not as spry as I used to be."

"Of course. It sounds lively down there."

"They must be setting up dinner. Let's head down while you tell me a little about yourself."

Introductions. I think I'm good at those, Fi. I've had loads of practice.

"Right, well. I've come to Ash Gardens because I'm having a burial tomorrow." Hilde raises a sharp brow. "Oh, not for me. It's for my sister. She asked me to bury her here, and I've put it off for such a long time. So, here I am. And Frank was gracious enough to allow me to stay the night since there's a storm."

"Love, you may be staying for an entire week then. It's always storming at Ash Gardens." We walk down the flight of steps together, her candle guiding our way. "Frank's told me a bit about you."

What's there to say? We've only just met. "All good things, I hope."

"Of course. He isn't the house gossiper. That would be my job." She laughs.

I smile awkwardly as I slide my wand farther down into my boot. She watches me with a curious eye, and I panic. "It's to help me focus my magic," I explain.

"I know what wands are for." She pats my arm good naturedly. We reach the bottom of the steps in the dim foyer. Candles are lit near the front door. Orbs of yellow and white light are suspended in the air. The chatter is louder, spilling out from the next room.

In better lighting, I notice that one of Hilde's eyes is milky white and devoid of color. I try not to stare when she glances down at me. "You seem apprehensive about using our services."

I open my mouth to speak, but she stops me. "Frank has been doing this a very long time. Your loved one will be in good hands."

"I don't doubt that. But it's a strange concept, isn't it? I've never heard of burying ashes in the ground to grow a tree. It's peculiar."

Hilde shrugs. "We are born from the earth, and in death, we become it. It's not all that peculiar, love."

I still think it's a rather bleak way to mark the end of life—burying ashes. But this is the way you chose, Fi.

Conversation from the dining room echoes louder, and it grabs our attention. Hilde perks up. "Oh, they started dinner without us. Those bastards."

Oh my.

She pulls me along, surprisingly with a firm grip for a lady of her age. Off the foyer, we enter into the dining room and I'm met with the savory smell of rosemary chicken. There are also hints of sautéed onions and sweet pepper with an underlying aroma of fresh baked bread.

The food is laid out on a long oak table illuminated by candles in brass holders. A lace runner completes the table, and above us are more of those yellow and white orbs of light bobbing against the ceiling. The dining room has artwork similar to that in the foyer painted on the ceiling—romantic depictions of the heavens with swirling clouds and bright stars.

At the head of the table is Frank. His chair is far larger than anyone else's. He grins widely when he sees us. "Saika, thank you for helping Hilde down."

The soft chatter stops, and I feel the curious eyes of two cherubs and a fairy roaming over my face. They search my posture, and the way Hilde is still holding on to me.

"I don't *need* help getting down, Frank," Hilde says as I help her to a seat. The train of her dress gathers at the foot of her chair. "I'm perfectly capable of getting around on my own."

"It may be easier if I install a lift between the levels, Hilde," Frank persists. "If you'd just let me—"

Suddenly, everyone at the table lifts their wineglasses away from the lit candles. With a soft whoosh, the candles roar brighter. Large shadows dance in the corners of the dining room.

The flames return to normal, but poor Frank hadn't moved his glass fast enough. Steam rises from his wineglass, the liquid bubbling over. I nervously take the empty seat beside him.

"When are you gonna learn? The hag doesn't want to be treated *like* a hag," one of the cherubs says.

The two cherubs sit side by side. They eat in unison. Drink in unison. Wipe their mouths in unison.

"Don't say that about a lady," the brown-haired cherub scolds. Up close, I notice that he has dark freckles sprinkled over his face. They dust his naked chest and his bare shoulders. "Hilde, I'm sorry about him."

"No need to apologize." Hilde smirks. She fans a cloth napkin onto her lap. "Just a bit miffed, isn't he? He's an angry little guy." She pours herself a glass of wine.

The angry cherub scrunches his face. "Now, listen here, you—"

"I'm sorry, Hilde, if I offended you." Frank offers a placating smile. "Everyone, I would like you to meet Saika." He gestures a paw toward me, as if everyone hasn't already been watching my every move. "She stopped by this afternoon, but the storm is keeping her here for the night."

"Hello, everyone." I smile warmly, and they respond with varying nods of acknowledgment and return to their dinner. I wish I had stayed in my room and sat in the dark until sunrise. It's a chore sitting through polite dinner conversation while trying to reveal as little about myself as possible. If only I could have dined alone. Or with you, Fi. But I'm too far gone now, and the latter is just plain impossible.

"I'm Merry." The freckled cherub who'd come to Hilde's aid smiles. "The rude one is my brother, Morose."

Morose scrunches his face again and drops his fork. "Why do I have to be the rude one? Why can't you be the oblivious one? Or the annoying one?"

Before another argument starts, the fairy beside Morose speaks up. "My name is Evette." She's wearing a purple knit dress with a turtleneck. She has short coils of hair smoothed back with matching purple pins. Unlike the rest of us sitting at the table, she has her own tiny one on top of ours. Her place setting is miniature, filled with minuscule amounts of food. "It's a pleasure to finally meet you, Saika." Her voice is light, yet loud. And when she speaks, her entire face glows.

"The pleasure is mine, Evette."

"That's Phil beside you," Evette continues. Before I can ask what she means, the fork on the plate beside me rises and cuts into a chicken thigh. And now that I concentrate, in the flickering candlelight, I see the glimmering outline of a hand.

I've never met a ghost before. It must take an immense amount of power to enchant a soul to stay within our world.

"Pleasure, Phil." I glance down the table and smile at Hilde pouring herself another glass of wine. "It's a pleasure, really, to meet you all. I don't mean to intrude on your dinner tonight. I assure you that tomorrow, I'll be off as soon as I can."

"So soon?" Evette asks. "You haven't even met Oli yet. Maybe I should go get her?"

"She'll be in later. I've told her that it was time for dinner, but she insists on working through the storm." Frank looks at me apologetically. "Everyone here is a hard worker, and Oli, our

Nature witch, takes her tasks seriously. As does Ignatius. He's an elf who . . . Oh my, Ignatius." His eyes ghost over, and he leaps from his seat. He takes an empty plate and loads it up with food.

No one else is alarmed. In fact, Hilde helps him by scooping up more food. "You know that elf loves his potatoes."

In the next second, Frank hurries out of the dining room, the floor shaking a bit as he runs.

"Is it just me, or is Frank forgetting about Ignatius more and more?" Merry asks as he chews on an ear of corn.

"It's not just you." Hilde sits back in her seat. She lights the end of a smoking wand and inhales deeply. She blows smoke away from the table. With a wave of her finger, the cloudy air dissipates in seconds. "He's been a bit . . . preoccupied?"

"I think he's just gettin' old," Morose says.

Evette crosses her arms. "He's not. He's spry for a beast of his age. I think." She looks at me. "Don't mind them. Ignatius is a recluse. He never leaves his room. So, Frank forgets to give him his meals from time to time."

"I didn't know dining in my room was an option," I whisper. I didn't mean to say that out loud, and judging from the following silence, I may as well have shouted it. They all look at me with a scrutinizing gaze.

"I'm very tired, is all. It's been a long day of travel." I smile, and they return to their food.

"Saika," Evette says, "Ash Gardens is a really great place. Whosoever ashes you'd like to plant, they will be in very capable hands."

I cut into my chicken and take a bite of the juicy meat and sautéed onions. It's heavenly, Fi.

"This chicken is very good." I try to change the subject, hoping we can leave this conversation.

"I'm glad you like the food." The glow around Evette's face simmers as she picks at her potatoes.

I feel like I'm the rude cur in this situation. I think I should apologize—for what, I haven't the faintest idea.

Thankfully, our attention gets stolen away by the sound of the front door opening and closing. Wind whips all the way into the dining room. The candles flicker from the breeze.

Evette grins and flies up from her seat. Her tiny wings flutter as she loads a plate with a heaping serving of food. I'm tempted to help her. The ladle and serving forks are large in her hands. But she fills a plate up with food without faltering.

"Woo, nature's healing!" a voice echoes into the room and then I see her. A woman appears through the threshold, dressed in black and sopping wet. Water drips off her body, and it leaves a puddle where she stands. "Oh, it smells amazing, E. Thank you."

Her canine teeth gleam, sharp and white. She has dark skin, and in the low light, I mistake it for brown. But as she steps closer to the table (tracking water, mind you), I see she's actually purple. And those aren't just long canine teeth. They're fangs.

Hilde holds up her hand. "Where do you think you're going? Dry off."

The woman sighs and waves a hand over her head. A tiny cyclone of air spins in her palm, and she trails it over her body. The water dries up immediately. Her dripping wet curls puff up until they settle into a dry cloud of hair around her shoulders. "This takes so long, you know," she groans to Hilde.

"I don't care."

She picks up her voluminous hair to dry the back of her neck, revealing her pointy ears. "You just want to see me touch myself, don't you, Hilds?" She laughs.

"Please, Oli. People are trying to eat." Hilde takes another long drag from her cigarette.

Finally dry, Oli settles in the seat at the end of the table. She confounds me, Fi. Her purple skin, her pointy ears, her fangs. She's a magic user, but she doesn't use spells or any special elixirs to enchant. So then she's a witch. Clearly. A Nature witch like Frank had said, but why does she look so peculiar?

Her eyes land on me for a brief second before Evette sets her plate in front of her. "Thanks, E." She focuses back on me, an amused smirk on her face. "And who might you be?" she asks. She tears into her chicken.

"My name is Saika." My voice cracks. "Pleasure to—"

"That's unfortunate. What a fuddy-duddy name. It's so serious." She chuckles. "You're from the city, aren't you?" She takes one glance at my silk gloves and grins wider, her fangs gleaming in the candlelight. "A fancy gal?"

My brows tighten in a glare. "And what is your name?"

She takes a sip of her wine and tilts it toward me. "Olivie, but friends call me Oli."

"Oli, if you could stop for one second," Hilde says tiredly. "When will the electricity work again? Will we be in the dark the entire night?"

"Well, I did what I could for the generator. I even tried to siphon some electricity from the storm, but I don't think my magic is strong enough. I'll try the generator again in the morning. Until then, we eat like our ancestors. In romantic candlelight." She lifts her glass, and Evette happily clinks her tiny glass with Oli's.

"Damn these storms." Hilde blows out a puff of smoke.

"So." Oli turns back to me. "What brings you to Ash Gardens?"

How strange would it be if I were to pick up my plate and

make a mad dash for my room and eat the remainder of my dinner in the dark?

"I received an ad." I swallow. "And I have ashes to bury."

"Ashes to plant," Evette offers. "Like planting seeds. And something beautiful will grow from them."

It's a lovely sentiment, but it dredges up the image of you on your deathbed, stuffing the ad into my palms. *Take me here, Sai, you said to me. Don't scatter me in the wind to be forgotten. I want to be planted. I want to become something beautiful.*

My heart aches at the memory of your voice, and I take a sip of wine to ease it. The table grows far too quiet for my liking. Your spirit, your touch, ghosts over me, and I feel silly for even putting myself in this predicament. *I* came to Ash Gardens. *I* enacted the plan to finally lay you to rest. I should've known that there would be a time when I'd have to speak about you again.

The floor shakes slightly, announcing Frank's arrival back in the dining room. "That elf gets stranger and stranger as the days go by." He smiles when he sees Oli. "Welcome back. Have you met Saika?" he asks, but his voice sounds garbled behind my drowning feelings.

I'm having serious thoughts about abandoning dinner altogether, retrieving my suitcase, and heading for the first train out of here, damn the storm.

I thought I'd be ready to talk about you, Fi, even if just in passing. But it's taking everything within me to keep an even-keeled smile.

"We've met." Oli quickly changes the conversation, thank the stars. "By the way, Frank, we need a new generator. It may have finally given out on us."

"Can't Hilde make a new one?" Merry asks. "It's a structure, ain't it?"

"I'm an Architect." Hilde takes a sip of her wine. Her food has hardly been touched. I suppose her diet consists of smoke and wine. "I'm a designer. I cannot simply *make* a generator. I'm not some tinkerer."

"It's fine." Frank lifts his paw. "I'll gather some money to get a new one. In the meantime, do you think you can try to get it to work?"

Oli shrugs. "I'll give it another try. But if we have another big storm like this, I'm not sure if the damn thing'll hold up."

"Please do what you can."

As dinner goes on, I realize it's not so torturous. We eat in idle chatter. Frank discusses tasks that need to be done around the house and I'm only sat quietly, trying my best not to disturb their dinner.

After eating, everyone gives a hand to clean up. I try to gather up the dirty plates, but my legs still thrum with pain. Frank notices my sluggish movements and approaches me.

"Miss Saika, please. You don't have to do this. Why don't you go upstairs to rest?"

"You've housed and fed me today. And if you won't take my money, at least take my help." I push past my exhaustion and stack dirty plates, but he places a gentle paw over my hand.

"Will you sit with me for a moment?" he asks.

I follow him from the dining room into the parlor. A fire is already going underneath a portrait of a young witch with wavy orange hair so long it touches the floor. The color complements Frank's fur, and he's holding her in the portrait, caressing her face.

"That is my wife, Kye." He steps up to the mantel. The light from the fire glows on him. "She's planted in the arboretum, too."

"I was right." I stand beside him, admiring the scene. "She's absolutely gorgeous." She's wearing a silky green dress with a lace collar that covers her neck. Frank's gaze on her, though intense, is one full of love. Kye stares out at the painter, her wide-set eyes hopeful and inviting.

Frank nods. "She was quite a looker. You know, when we started Ash Gardens, I wasn't sure if it would work. Kye was a Nature witch. It was her idea to take one's ashes and plant them to make an arboretum. So when she passed, we took a lot of care with her research and outsourced magic users to carry on her work. I'd love to show it to you tomorrow."

I settle into an armchair. My legs throb, and I massage them gently. "I'd never heard of Ash Gardens before my sister told me about it. She . . . she wanted this to be her final resting place."

"I see." Frank sits in the armchair opposite me. "Would you like to tell me a bit about her?"

The fire warms half of my face. The cushion beneath me is soft. I'm perfectly sated from dinner. The storm still roars distantly beyond the walls of the house, but it feels like a pleasant chaos. And unlike earlier, the memory of you feels more like an invitation than an intrusion. I step into the world where you once existed with an assurance that—yes, you are gone, you are no longer here, but oh, how good life felt when you were. You once existed. And those moments with you still exist. And that is what I share with Frank.

"Fiona was very loud." A smile finds its way onto my face. "Very opinionated. It got us into so much trouble when we were younger. Like most girls from the city, she became an adventurer. When she became of age, she took to the seas to find purpose."

"How exciting. Did you follow in her footsteps?"

"Oh, I tried. I emulated a few of her quests as a way to keep her spirit alive. But her spirit was far too bold. Seafaring isn't for the faint of heart, therefore, it isn't for me."

Frank offers a gentle laugh.

I sigh, thinking back on a slew of memories. "One thing we did share was a love of music and stories."

"Do you still love them?"

"Do I still love them?" I blink. I suppose I hadn't thought of that. Music and literature have always been a joint affection. We *both* found them to be a part of us, Fi. We both used the arts as a line that connected us in a way that reality could never.

And once you passed, I think that line became severed.

"Well, it's been ages since I've played . . ."

"You play an instrument?"

"I'm a Music witch. I can enchant anything to play music, though piano is a favorite of mine."

"What luck." Frank rises to his feet. He crosses the room to a piano near the window, masked by a quilted dust cover. I'm not sure how I missed it coming in. "I'd love to hear you play something if you're up to it." He pulls off the cover to reveal a gleaming black piano.

It takes very little coaxing to get me to play anything. You know this, Fi. But in this moment, I'm hesitant. I cross the room, mindlessly twiddling with my locket. My wand is still in my boot, but I don't pull it out.

When I sit down, Frank backs away, settling himself by the mantel. He looks up briefly at his wife. I lift the fallboard, and my silk gloves slip over the white keys.

I press down, and I'm whisked away instantly. I play a major chord that turns into many, and soon I'm closing my eyes, feeling the weight of the keys. A hum comes alive in my throat as I play a familiar tune.

One of our father's favorites, you remember it well. I once sang it to you at your bedside.

The melody wraps me, kisses my forehead, and twirls me into our childhood living room. You're singing and playing the piano. Our father is spinning me, and the flames from our fireplace dance along. They twirl and dip and spin to the lilt of the song, and I copy their movements. Their energy is warm on my face.

Then you join me in a dance, and we're entangled, becoming aflame and alive.

I suddenly open my eyes and the black piano sits before me, no longer making any noise. I stare at my trembling hands as tears slide over my cheeks.

I wipe my face and gaze at Frank, where he stands speechless by the fireplace. His mouth is agape. His yellow eyes are crested with tears also. "You didn't use any magic for that, did you? I didn't see you enchant the piano. That came from you."

I smile. "I suppose after being so used to enchantments, I may have learned a thing or two."

Frank tilts his head, considering something for a moment. "What an amazing gift you have. It would be my absolute honor to plant your sister's ashes and make her death into something beautiful."

Tears prick my eyes. Your voice echoing once again, *I want to become something beautiful.*

"That's what Fiona wants."

Frank leans back on the mantel, folding his cardigan over his body. "It seems you two were quite close. Did you only have each other?"

I wonder if this is his own way of asking if it'll only be me at your burial tomorrow.

I clear my throat. "We always had each other, yes. Then she got married and had twin girls, and then it was the five of us for a while. When she died, our parents held this grand memorial in her honor, and apparently it was one of the biggest gatherings in town."

"Apparently?" Frank raises his bushy brows. "You didn't go to her memorial?"

"I . . ." I blink, running my silk-covered finger along the fall-board. I gently close it. "It wasn't because I didn't want to."

It was because I was forbidden to attend.

Frank nods, and we stew in silence for a moment. He sighs. "I see. Well, it is getting late. Perhaps we should both get some rest. We have an eventful morning tomorrow."

My legs wobble a bit when I stand up. Frank assists me out of the parlor and back into the foyer. We part ways. I start up the steps as he heads toward his side of the house. "Thank you for dinner. And for listening to me talk about Fiona. It's been a while since I have."

"It's my pleasure, Miss Saika. Have a good night."

The trek up to my room is a short but strenuous one. More orbs of light glow in the stairwell and in the hall. When I open the door to my room, there's a candle burning on my bedside table. Your glittering ashes and picture sit under the warm light. My suitcase is still a mess on the floor, but I'm so exhausted that I don't bother cleaning it up.

Also on my bedside table is a green clay mug filled with dark liquid. The name Hilde is painted on the rim. It sits on top of a note.

Enchanted tea to heal exhaustion. This should fix you right up.
 —Hilde

I nestle into bed, sipping the hot tea and letting the enchantment nourish my body back to health. I'm going to need all of my strength tomorrow. Because, Fi, after all this time, I'm finally burying your ashes.

A soft viola plays from across the hall. It's distant, but unmistakable. Ordinarily, I'd complain about the noise so late in the night. But as the tea works its magic, and I grow sleepier by the second, I'm not really bothered by the melody. In fact, it lulls me into a gentle sleep.

CHAPTER THREE

I'm sat in the middle of a field, peeling oranges while looking up at the twilight sky. Hues of purple and pink bleed together in soft harmony. And from that heavenly canvas of wispy clouds and streaking light, a barrage of shooting stars suddenly passes through. I swallow the rest of my orange to free up my hands. And with a wave of my wrist, I stretch my fingers toward the sky.

The star parade comes and goes, but one of the stars stutters to a halt. I struggle to pull in my hand and the star follows the motion. It wars against me, pressing to follow its family of stars. But then its resistance snaps like a dam breaking loose, and the star plummets to the earth.

"I did it!" I shout. I rise to my feet, following its path. "Fiona! Fiona, I did it!"

The star collides with the field, and the high grass blows back from the crash. A gust of wind rushes over me, and I choke on the dust.

I thought you were near me, Fi. Or at least, at some point, you were beside me, but when I look over my shoulder, you aren't there. "Fiona?" I call your name, but you don't answer.

"It's fine, I'll get it for you." I hike up my dress and jog down to the star. It's buried in a crater in the middle of the field, smoke rising to the darkening sky. I hold my breath, anticipating the noxious fumes that usually accompany stars, but when I breathe, I don't choke.

In fact, as I come closer, I smell heat. Or something akin to burning coal.

I reach the bottom of the crater and search for the star, but it's not there. In its place is a jagged slab of stone sticking up from the ground. Words are etched into the stone, but I don't need to get any closer to know what it says. I can make out your name from where I stand.

My knees grow weak, and I collapse. "I was too late. I'm so sorry." My chest aches with sorrow, but no tears come. When I glance down at my hands, I realize my gloves are gone. And even more peculiar, my palms are glowing bright like the sun. They burn, growing hotter and hotter, but the pain keeps me fixed in silence.

Your voice washes over me like the low tide. *Saika, what did you do?*

I look for you, but you aren't there. I want to tell you I'm sorry. Don't be angry with me, Fiona.

But my mouth is sealed shut, and I'm caught, staring in wonder as my hands give birth to a fallen star.

The dream ends, and my eyes open to the vaulted ceiling of the bedroom. Wooden beams reach down to the long, rain-sprinkled windows.

I close my eyes again, resting in the memory that's disguised itself as a dream. My fingers touch the chain around my neck.

We found this fallen star when we were just little girls. We nearly passed out from the toxic gas, and you almost burned your hand clean through trying to pick it up, if I remember correctly.

That day changed everything for us, Fi. It was our special secret. We'd heard rumors of the power fallen stars held, and we didn't want to mess up the opportunity of a lifetime. So we tucked it away. At the time, nothing in our lives needed the magnitude of power that a fallen star would've granted us. We were content with the life we had.

Of course, we would've opted for better parents. Ones who loved us more. Ones who didn't pressure us to live a life they'd specifically designed for us. Ones who wouldn't cast out their child for making a mistake . . . but the star is only a power source. It doesn't create miracles.

Eyes still closed, I fiddle with my locket. The metal chain slides across my fingers. I esteemed this star too highly. As if it provided a way to turn back time and grant life again. And because its power is so absolute and holy, I didn't think it would have any repercussions. I thought stars falling from the sky would be free tender to pay for all our problems to go away.

Where on earth did I ever get that notion, Fi?

My eyes open when a strange buzzing sound zips by my ear. I'm startled by an orb of light. Some part of me thinks that I've lost my mind. The star has slipped from my dream into reality.

But this orb of light has a familiar voice. One that I heard last night. "I'm sorry if I scared you."

It takes me a moment to get my bearings after being disoriented. I glance over my circular bed. The blue paisley rug on the wooden floor. Your picture and ashes on the stand beside me. And the small light fairy hovering above my face. Right. All things seem to be in order.

"I'm fine." I grunt as I sit up. I fix my headscarf, relieved it hadn't slipped off while sleeping. "Evette is your name, yes?" How did she even get in here? I should cast a protection spell against light fairy intrusions.

Evette nods. "I'm sorry, Miss Saika. I just thought I would check on you. It's midday, and Frank was worried."

"It's midday?" I look at the clock above the door. It's half past noon. I rub the sleep from my eyes. "The burial! I've overslept—"

"It's fine." Evette smiles. She flutters back, and I see that she isn't alone. Outside the door is a floating tray with tea and toast. Phil's translucent body shimmers in the doorway. He's wearing a bowler hat. "I brought you something to eat since you missed breakfast."

"Thank you, but it's alright, I'll be right down." I hop out of bed, and Evette nods. She turns back into an orb of light and flutters out of the room. Phil still stands there, holding the tray.

"Come on, Phil!" Evette's voice calls from down the hall.

Phil stands for a few seconds longer than is to my liking. Then he slowly turns away, and the tray bobs out of sight.

I close my bedroom door and sigh. I click open my locket, and a soft light pours from the shell. The picture of our parents stares back at me, their faces stern and unhappy. Sometimes I forget their picture is even there. I'm more focused on the tiny fragment of our fallen star, and I'm worried how dim it's getting.

I don't know how much power is left. I need to refrain from casting enchantments. Because if this light goes out . . . I'm not really sure what will happen. I close the locket shut.

After getting dressed, I grab Hilde's mug and head downstairs.

On the first level, Hilde is standing in the foyer. Her silver hair is no longer pressed, but in tiny coils that bounce when she turns her head. She mindlessly fusses with her sleeve as she gazes out the front window. She doesn't notice me until I'm passing through.

She whips up a smile. "'Morning, love. How was that tea?"

"I feel loads better, thank you." I hand her the empty mug. "How about yourself? You look forlorn."

She dabs her eyes with an embroidered handkerchief. "Oh, yes, I'm alright. Sometimes I get thinking about life, and it causes me to reflect. You realize how finite it can be once you've gotten to my age."

"I know what you mean."

She scoffs. "How could you possibly? You're still very young. There's still much for you to learn about the world."

"Young. Old. We all experience life whether we've had lots of it or very little."

She grins and folds her arms. "My, Miss Saika. You're quite the philosopher, aren't you?"

"Oh no. Any wisdom I have is from my own foolhardiness."

Hilde laughs. Today she's wearing an emerald-green dress with a bejeweled neckline. Her black boots match the color of her sharp nails and makeup. "You keep surprising me, Saika. Will you be having lunch with us?" she asks. I follow her into the dining room.

"I don't know. I was supposed to have the burial this morning, but I overslept. Have you seen Frank?"

"He's out in the garden." We cut through the dining room and enter the kitchen. Sunlight filters through half-circle windows, lying in thick strips across the wooden floor. The smell of cinnamon bread baking overwhelms my senses.

"I'm on meal duty today," Hilde explains. She goes to the sink and quickly washes the mug I returned. She leaves it to dry on the counter, joining a collection of name-painted mugs. Her name is by far the one most on display, but a few others are hung up as well, ones belonging to Morose, Merry, Oli, and even Phil, the ghost, which I think is a bit silly.

Hilde crosses the wide kitchen to the wood-burning oven and pulls out two loaf pans. She places them on the countertop. Vines and leaves are expertly etched into the loaves. She catches me staring and smirks. "Of course," she intones, "you may have some."

I look at her milky white eye. "You can read minds."

"Feelings," she corrects. "It runs through my family, this gift. Or curse, depending on who you're asking. My aunt resented it, but I actually find it helpful."

My cheeks warm. "You can discern every emotion then?"

She raises her brows, her right eye running me over. I stew in the silence until she laughs, shaking her head. "Not all the time. Only when they're quite intense."

"Ah." I chuckle nervously, looking over the loaves. "Well, I'll try to tamp down my hunger. These look and smell delicious."

"My baking skills aren't as good as Evette's, but when it boils down, it's all science and a bit of magic."

I nod. "Makes sense for an Architect witch."

She smiles. "How is it that you understand me so well?"

"My father is an Architect witch. You two are a bit similar— though, I think you're a lot more smiley."

Hilde cackles. "I don't think anyone has ever described me that way, so thank you." She wipes her hands on a towel. "Now, I'm about to finish making lunch. Will you be joining us?"

I fumble with the hem of my gloves. "I should speak to Frank first."

She eyes me curiously. "You're still apprehensive, aren't you?"

"No." I feel like I answered too quickly. "I simply overslept. I haven't rested like that in, well . . . ages. I didn't mean to wake so late."

"Well, when you go out there"—she points toward the glass-paned double doors leading to the outside—"and you see the arboretum for yourself, I want you to remember one thing: the planting of the ashes isn't an ending. It's a beginning."

She waves her hand, and the glass-paned doors open to the backyard. Warm air flows into the kitchen, the curtains flapping beside the doors. "Go on. I'm sure Frank is waiting to see you."

I venture out into the garden, but I stop at the sight of syca-more trees bounding the arboretum. Their leaves blow gently in the wind, and for a moment I close my eyes, tasting the buzzing enchantment coating the breeze.

Before the arboretum are multiple plant beds and trellises in the garden. Trees heavy with fruit stand along manicured paths.

One of the cherubs hovers before a bed of flowers, sprinkling them with water. He's still shirtless, but it's my first time see-ing his tiny wings fluttering vigorously to lift his pudgy body. He grins at me, and his cheerful attitude and freckled face assures me which cherub this is. "Good morning, Saika."

"Good morning, Merry."

"Did you have a restful sleep?"

I move to his side, eyeing the petunias bobbing under the weight of his watering. "Perhaps the best I've had in a very long time." I take in a breath of fresh air, and my body becomes re-laxed. There are enchantments at play. I look toward the entrance of the arboretum. It's a towering wooden arch laced with vines and flowers. The magic emanates from inside.

"So that's the arboretum, is it?" I ask. "Is this garden en-chanted as well?"

Merry laughs. "I wish it were. Then maybe we would've had a better harvest this season."

He sets his watering can down. "But I do my best to make sure everything is growing healthy. We take what we need for our meals and for the ceremonies, but the majority of what we grow gets sold at the market in the city. Morose handles all of that, though."

"It's a good system. Unfortunate about the harvesting, though. I . . ." I almost offer a bit of magic to help the garden along, but I remember our waning star. I can't afford to be careless right now. ". . . I'm looking for Frank. Have you seen him?"

Merry points across the yard to the cellar. "He's been down there all morning." The cellar doors are open, and I see the tips of Frank's horns poking out.

I pass by lemon and cherry trees to get to Frank. He comes up the cellar steps, wiping his furry brow with the back of his paw. He grins when he sees me.

"'Morning. Or perhaps I should say *afternoon*."

"I didn't mean to sleep so late. It's been a while since I've had such a comfortable bed, plus drinking Hilde's tea put me right to sleep."

"You drank tea from Hilde?" He hums. "Well, I'm glad you enjoyed it." He sighs as he looks down into the cellar. "And don't you worry about the ceremony. I've been trying to fix this confounding generator all morning."

"Oh, should I return once everything is in order?" I suggest. "You may need some more time to—"

"Miss Saika, it's alright." He laughs. "There's no need for you to delay. We can plant the ashes now if you'd like."

"Now?" I blink. "As in right now?"

"Unless there's a reason you'd like to delay."

I'm slow to answer. "No, there's no reason to."

Frank watches me intently. He gazes toward the vine-wrapped arbor before settling back on me. "Before we begin, would you first like to look inside the arboretum?"

I can't find a reason to say no, so I answer without realizing. "Of course."

The closer I get to the entrance of the arboretum, the more I feel its pull. Its magic is electrifying, yet soothing. It calls me near, promising to wrap me in warm arms.

We stop before the entrance. When I gaze through, there are tiny translucent glimmers drifting this way and that. "This is a portal."

Frank nods proudly. "The arboretum exists outside this realm. A design by my late wife and her colleague. He was a Research and Agriculture witch. He helped Kye create the arboretum. She wanted to create a place where the dead can continue to grow and live well after they're gone." He looks over at me. "Are you ready to head inside?"

I have to be ready. I nod and he walks in first. His wolfy tail swishes gently as he disappears through the arbor.

I hold my breath as I pass through the portal. When I come out to the other side, the air is cool on my face. Wind tinged with magic gently blows through the arboretum.

I lift my head to see the towering, magnificent trees crowding the sky. There are smaller sycamores like the ones from outside, but they're shades of green, white, yellow, and red. The chipped bark covers the ground in dried pieces that crinkle under our feet. There are massive, strong evergreens, their aroma sharp and refreshing. I note the vastly varying trees all in full bloom. It seems unlikely that they would survive being planted together.

The arboretum is a kaleidoscope of vibrant shades of blue, and orange, and white, and gold. Spruces with gradients of yellow. Evergreens that aren't very green. Willows with long, flowery purple hair blowing in the wind. Pines that bear striped and multicolored pine cones. They make up an entire colorful forest that goes miles back, and I feel swallowed inside.

It's also become starkly quiet. I feel an absence of pressure. The ache that I carry in my shoulders and my jaw relaxes. The air is sweet and calm. I feel like I could lie on the ground and sleep for hours, the magic surrounding me in a sweet balm.

"I think Fiona will like it here," I say.

"After what you've told me about her, I think she will, too." Frank stops before a sequoia with rich orange and red leaves. He runs his paw over the bumpy bark. "Not all of the trees in the arboretum are derived from ashes. We have a balance of natural and magical trees to help keep this enchanted garden thriving."

I gaze up at the large sequoia, my throat feeling a bit tight. "And where will Fiona be buried?"

"Planted," Frank corrects gently. "And I'll leave that to you. Oli will mark it so she can dig up the site later." He turns around, looking through the trees. "She's in here somewhere, tending to the ashes we planted yesterday."

I don't know how I can pick a place to bury you. I wish Frank would handle everything. I wish I could just hand him your ashes, and he'd just do the damn ceremony. I don't even have to be there to see it. I'd even pay him extra to handle it on his own.

Which is what prompts me to make a suggestion.

"If it's alright with you, perhaps . . . perhaps I can leave you with the ashes and you can bury her for me?" My eyes mist at the thought of dropping you here and running off, but I blink back the tears. This option works for both of us, Fi. You'll finally have your resting place, and I don't have to be around to see it. I don't know why I hadn't thought of it before.

"I have no need for a fancy ceremony or a meal or anything like that. It'll be only me anyway, and how depressing would that be? Sitting in your grand dining room all alone?" I chuckle sorely.

Frank looks absolutely gobsmacked. "You don't want to stay for the ceremony?"

"It's not that I don't want to stay." I twist the hem of my gloves. "I just . . . I have places to be. And I want this to be taken care of quickly."

He squints, analyzing me. "Why?"

"I'm sorry?"

"Why do you want this done quickly? From what you've told me, your sister meant a great deal to you. Part of the arboretum experience is witnessing the birth of her afterlife. I'd hate for you to miss it."

"Birth?" I ask. "You're burying ashes in the ground. It's marking an end. It's death."

"Miss Saika." He lifts his paws to the surrounding trees. They hum and sway in the breeze. "Does any of this feel like death to you?"

I swallow. I don't see how burying you means the start of a new life, Fi. It's foolish. And it isn't fair to give such ridiculous hope. "Placing her in the ground means . . . it means she's never coming back."

Frank raises his brows, as if he's just gotten an answer to a question he didn't even ask. He softly kicks at the ground. "Are you somehow waiting for the circumstances to change?"

I blink. "What do you mean?"

"Whether you plant her ashes or not, it doesn't change the fact that Fiona is gone. Are you waiting for the curse of death to be lifted? Are you waiting for some kind of miracle to raise her from the dead?"

"Raise her from the dead?" My blood runs cold, and I feel sick suddenly. "No, I'm not . . . I know she's . . ." I look away from him. "I know that Fiona is gone. Nothing will change that fact."

He sighs. "Saika, I'd like to be candid for a moment. I think you *want* to be here to plant your sister's ashes, but you aren't being honest with yourself."

I snap my head toward him, my face tight with anger. He looks at me with those sympathetic yellow eyes, and all I can do is ball my hands into fists. "You have *no* idea what I want." My voice shakes. "Or who I am or what I'm feeling." Tears cloud my eyes. "I have no problem burying my sister. I'm just . . . I need to get going. I've already spent too much time here. I have places to go. Adventures to have."

"And where is your next adventure, Saika?" he asks softly. "Where will you go from here?" Frank stares at me, and I nearly faint from his pity. I wish he'd stop looking at me like I'm some train wreck. I'm fine. I can bury you anytime I want, Fi.

But adventure is calling me. *Your* adventures. And isn't my time best spent living as you did? Not sitting in this place clinging to the shape of your memory.

It took some time, yes, but I did my part. I came to Ash Gardens like you asked. I inquired about the burial. You never said I had to stay and watch you . . . watch you go into the ground.

I'll go. I'll find something else to snuff out this ache in my heart from you leaving me.

But when I look at Frank to tell him this, the words crowd my mouth. And instead, a cry bubbles out, and I whisper, "I can't do this."

Before he can respond, I turn on my heels and hurry back

toward the entrance. Tears blind my vision, and I angrily wipe them away.

I bump into Oli on my way out, knocking a bucket of water from her hand. It splashes onto the ground.

"Whoa!" she yells. "Excuse me—" She stops when she sees my tear-streaked face. "Shit, are you alright?"

I ignore her and pass through the portal. My vision blurry, I cut across the garden, pass through the kitchen, make my way up the steps, and find the comfort of my room. And behind my closed door, I break down into a sob. My heart is so wet and heavy, it feels like I can't breathe.

CHAPTER FOUR

Dear Jonathan,

I'm sorry that it's been ages since we've seen or heard from each other. I'm sure the girls have grown unrecognizable by now. I didn't mean for it to be this long or for me to be as distant as I've been. It's just

It stops there. Frustration gets the better of me, and I tear the letter up. The ripped pieces fall onto the desk, and I sigh deeply.

Even if I send this letter off to your husband, I doubt he'd even believe it was me. I haven't spoken to him since you died, Fi. And for me to speak to him now, asking for him to come to Ash Gardens, and bury you in my stead . . . he'd respectfully decline. That man loved you too much. Of course, he'd respect your wishes.

After your memorial, he stole your ashes from our parents and sent them to me, knowing how upset they'd be if I had them. He knew, as well as I did, how adamant you were about me being the one to bury you.

Still, if I wrote to him and pleaded, maybe he'd come like a knight in shining armor.

I plant my face in the crook of my arm. Who am I kidding?

I've used up too much of Frank's hospitality already. I should just pack up my things and leave your ashes on my bedside table.

Tiny knocks echo on my door, and I recognize Evette's playful pattern.

"Saika, it's me." Her voice is muffled behind the door. "I didn't know if you wanted to come down for dinner, so I brought it to you. Hilde also sent you a slice of cinnamon bread. She said you wanted some. I'll leave it outside your door."

In my mood, even Evette's chipper tone sounds dim. I wipe the redness from my eyes and open the door. "Oh, you're up." She smiles.

"Thank you for bringing me dinner." I take the tray. "Goodness, it's heavy, Evette. You didn't have to bring this up for me."

I set it on my desk, on top of my failed letters to Jonathan. I discreetly cover them, hiding them from Evette's wandering eyes.

"I don't think you've eaten today." I haven't. "And I wanted to make sure you were okay, especially after . . ." She stops. "Um, well, I just want you—"

"Especially after what?" I ask.

She opens her mouth and closes it again. Starts, then stops. "He can be blunt sometimes, but Frank means well. He's great to talk to about things. He's helped me a lot. He's helped all of us. I just want you to know that."

Evette's words are like a wake-up call. I've been hiding out in this room all day, too ashamed to face anyone. I shouldn't have gotten angry with Frank in the arboretum.

"If that's the case, I'll give him a chance. Thank you, Evette."

Light ebbs from her face, and she bows. She flutters out only to stop at the threshold. Before I know what's happening, she zips toward my face and hugs it with her full body.

Has a fairy ever hugged your face, Fi? It's very awkward try-ing to pat her back. Do I tap her shoulder with the point of my finger?

Evette eases away, gazing at me shyly. "Take your time with dinner. I'll see you in the morning." And then she zips out, for good this time.

I sigh, glancing at my dinner tray. Hilde made potato and leek stew. I pick up the slice of cinnamon bread, its sugary aroma still strong. Under the plate is a note that's hitched a ride on the dinner tray.

> *I'm sorry that I've upset you. I assure you it wasn't my intention. You aren't obligated to do any-thing—planting your sister's ashes or otherwise. We'd still be happy to complete the ceremony if you choose to leave.*
>
> *But if you'd like to stay, you are welcome to for as long as you need. And this house will be yours as much as it is mine. You have the freedom to make your own decisions, Saika. That is essen-tially what Ash Gardens is all about.*
>
> *Sincerely repentant,*
> *Frank*

Damn it, Fiona. I've messed up again, haven't I?

I eat dinner in solitude (the stew is divine, Fi. Hilde added scallions and a pinch of dill. I think you would've liked it), and I go out into the hall.

The electricity is still out, so the hallways are lit with stick candles and a few orbs of light. As I go down the hallway, I pass by framed pictures of various people and creatures on the walls.

Upon inspection, I see Frank's wife, Kye, with her wavy orange hair flowing down her back. She's in many group pictures. One with her family, it seems. Others with a school where she's wearing a gold lion insignia on her uniform. I recognize it as the crest from our sister school in the north. It's a very prestigious school, Fi. But Frank said Kye ended up only being a Nature witch. She hadn't chosen a sector of magic.

There's an old picture of Kye and Frank in front of Ash Gardens when there were only three levels. They're standing outside in the front yard, Kye encased in Frank's arms. Proud and happy.

As I continue to the stairwell, I see the wallpaper is yellowed and peeling near the baseboards. I kneel to it. Maybe I can use a little enchantment to keep it from . . . no. I can't. I have to reserve my magic.

The floorboard creaks, and I look up to a little bowler hat floating in the air. In the low light, I see Phil's translucent body.

"'Evening." I stand to my feet. "I'm looking for Frank. Do you know where he is?"

Phil's bowler hat tilts up and down. Then, slowly, he ghosts down into the dark stairwell. Against my better judgment, Fi, I follow him.

We descend in the darkness until we reach the dimly lit foyer. Phil glides past the dining room to another massive double door. It creaks, opening to a wide library.

Candles are lit, and gentle rain dusts the long windows. Bookshelves cover the room's walls. Thick curtains are tied off to the side, giving a hazy, rain-streaked view to the dark outside.

Frank is sitting in a tall armchair that I'm sure was specifically designed for him. He has a book in his lap, but he pulls down his reading glasses when he sees us.

"Saika. Phil." He nods.

Phil doesn't join me inside. He tilts his little bowler hat and bobs off.

"'Evening, Frank."

Frank sets his book aside and takes this moment to pick up his tea. "Would you care for some?" he asks.

"If it isn't too much trouble." I join him, sitting in one of the muted yellow armchairs arranged throughout the room.

He prepares a cup of tea for me as I watch the rain trickle down. I thank him when he hands me the tea, and he settles back.

"It really does like to storm at Ash Gardens." I take a sip. The lavender is warm and soothing.

"It wasn't always like this." He gazes out the window with me. "The weather has been taking a bit of a turn lately. I . . ." He blinks. A crack of thunder echoes outside. "I forget what I was going to say."

"It's alright." I set my tea down. "I want to apologize for earlier. I didn't mean to storm out of the arboretum. I didn't mean to get upset with you. You didn't deserve that. You've been nothing but kind to me since I've shown up."

"As I mentioned before, Saika. It's not easy laying someone to rest. I can't begin to imagine how it feels to depart from a sister. I've only had the great displeasure of departing from my wife. And I fear I still haven't let her go."

"Why should you?" He lifts a gentle brow. "She was a major part of you. Letting go of her would mean letting go of a piece of yourself."

He smiles, amused. "I suppose you're right. Is that how you view your sister?"

A small smile crosses my face, and I try to hide it behind a sip of tea. "Sometimes I speak to her. It's like she's here. A part of me."

"Does it help?" he asks.

"I'm not sure if *help* is the right word." I blink as I think about you. "It's more like a comfort. As if she isn't really gone."

"I know exactly what you mean."

I look over at him, and he's gazing at a portrait of Kye that sits on a bookshelf. "After she died, Kye's memory used to follow me wherever I went. In our bedroom. In the garden or the arboretum. Her presence, although only in my mind, carried me through dark times."

He sips on his tea. "In any case, grief has peculiar effects on us all."

Heavy wind hits the windows, rain splatting against the glass. Water begins to drip from the sides of the panes. It falls onto the plush blue carpet in quick drops.

"Damn it all," Frank mutters. He gets up and grabs a towel from a neighboring window. He places it under the glass. "These windows keep leaking. I thought Oli fixed them."

I watch him as he presses the damp towel, and it soaks through in seconds. I feel terrible sitting here, having access to magic and keeping it to myself. One little spell won't hurt. I take a deep breath and slip the wand from my boot. I speak in a whisper so he doesn't hear.

"It's storming, and it's a cold night. So, heat these windows and seal them tight."

My locket warms against my neck as my wand shoots out a light. It startles Frank, and he steps out of the way. We watch the windows seal themselves up. The water stops dripping.

"Oh, thank you." He sits back down. "I thought you were a Music witch."

"I am." I safely tuck my wand back into my boot. "Witches are all technically born as Nature witches because we have the ability to enchant the natural world. We go to school to study a sector of magic like Music, or Architecture." I stop to think. "Your wife, Kye, didn't choose a sector. Did she always want to be a Nature witch?" I ask. "Didn't she want to hone her magic and become something more?"

He seems a bit surprised. "You know, I'm not sure. I never asked her." He strokes the fur on his chin. "I think she was happy studying whatever pleased her. She loved the idea of non-witches using magic through spells and potions, so she studied them, too." He sighs. "She liked the idea of everyone being on equal ground, much like the arboretum. No matter who you are, witch or no witch, you'll always be welcomed here."

I swish the warm tea in my mouth, pondering. "Do you believe we are all born equal?"

"I think the altruistic answer would be that we are. But we know life is quite unkind sometimes, isn't it?" He finishes the rest of his tea and stares into the empty mug. "I'm the only beast of my kind, Saika. I've never met another who looks like me. And I always wondered what a beast like me is destined to do." He smiles distantly. "And I found it in Kye, and in Ash Gardens. I believe I was born to love. It's the only course that feels natural to me."

My fingers cradle the half-empty mug in my hand. "I don't think I have anything to love anymore." The weight of my words pushes me over the edge, forcing me under rushing water, but Frank pulls me back up.

"You will. You will love again. You will love people, and things, and food, again. Even that piano you play so well. You'll love that, too."

I swallow the sob pounding in my chest. "How can I? There's no room for anything else. In my mind, she's still here. In my heart, she's still here. But that isn't enough. I want to hear her. I want to see her. I want to laugh with her." I shake my head, cursing myself for allowing a few tears to fall. I wipe them before Frank can see. "And I want to bury her ashes . . . I just don't know what's wrong with me."

We sit in silence for a moment before he gets up to pour himself another cup of tea. "Do you still plan on leaving? We can handle the ceremony if you still choose to go."

"I got your note."

I'm not sure what to say, Fi. But more than that, I think I'm tired. Since coming to Ash Gardens, it feels like my life has come to a screeching halt, and I'm forced to look the reality of your death in the face. I have no adventures or harrowing travels to distract me from you. Is this why you asked me to bring you here, Fi? Did you know that your death would send me into a spiral, and coming to Ash Gardens would force me into a stasis?

I can't return to our parents, and I'm too ashamed to see Jonathan and your girls again.

I have nowhere to go.

Frank takes in my silence with a gracious sip of tea. "However, if you choose to stay, I have an offer for you."

I wipe my eyes. "An offer?"

"I have a need for an extra pair of hands. Evette is our resident chef. She handles our ceremonial meals. Merry works the gardens and Morose sells the produce. Hilde handles our many major house repairs. And Oli takes care of everything else, from the house to the arboretum. But as you can see . . ." He points to the window I just fixed. Water is starting to seep through again. "I need more help."

"You need someone to do labor. I am but a simple Music witch."

He chuckles. "You are anything but simple, Miss Saika. Your melodies last night touched me. I felt Kye's arms around me. I could hear her voice. And it was all without a single enchantment."

I smile. "You're buttering me up so I'll work for you."

He laughs, patting his knee. "I mentioned before that I can't offer much. But I can offer you a safe place to stay." He looks at me. "Would you like to work for Ash Gardens, Saika? Until you have the courage to plant your sister's ashes. Or until your next great adventure. Whichever comes first."

I blink. I didn't see that coming. "It's a lot to consider." I pause. "Do you mind if I think on it tonight and answer you in the morning?"

Frank smiles as he stands to his feet. He picks up our empty mugs. "I wouldn't have it any other way."

Later that night, I light a few candles around the clawfoot tub. On the shelves are jars of purple petals, and when I open them, I'm pleased to smell lavender. I sprinkle a few on top of the water.

My foot slips into the warm water, and I nearly cry. I unravel my headwrap and pat the short patches of hair on my head. When I pull my hand away, my heart sinks at the clump of loose black strands on my fingers. Sighing, I roll up the hair and toss it to the floor.

I take off my silk gloves and scrutinize the loose, age-spotted skin on my hands. I flex my achy fingers, the joints clicking. I submerge my hands, and the rest of my body, into the warm water.

Exhaling, I think about Frank's offer. To leave or to stay, that's the big question, Fi.

I sink farther into the tub, letting the fragrant water reach the crook of my neck. In the silence, all my mistakes suffocate me. It seems about right. It's my penance for the way I've been behaving. Like a coward. I can't even make myself stay to place your ashes in the ground, Fi, the easy job that it is.

You've entrusted me with an important task. I stood by your bedside, clutching your hand in mine, and told you I would do it.

But I've spent the last two years avoiding it. I've carried your memory around along with a sack of my belongings, hoping that once I've walked in your footsteps, I'd be okay with burying you. But how can I be?

You honestly expected me to come here and dump you in the ground and move on to my next great adventure. But what if I don't? Will you haunt me until your ashes are finally laid to rest? Or will you continue to be a growth on my conscience, a void in my mind that I speak to, but that never answers back?

You're so very selfish, Fi. Don't you see how this is ailing me, body and spirit? You expect me to move on from this unscathed. But I can't. I don't even want to. There is no next great adventure without you.

I don't have an ounce of your courage. There's no way I can stand on two strong legs and face your husband and children again. I can't go back to the city to see our parents. I don't want to go back out to sea. There's nowhere for me to go, Fi.

Do I go with you? Do I follow you like I always have since we were girls? You've always set the path for me, and whenever I was lost, I simply followed the groove of your steps in the sand.

As a teenager, you cut your hair, and I cut mine a week later. You liked musical enchantments, and I studied my piano to play you songs. You were an adventurer and lived passionately. So, the moment you died, I took a small sack of my belongings and ventured out into the world.

Everything you did, I followed because you are my sister. But I can't emulate you now.

You died, Fi. There's no trail left for me to follow. It's gone. You're gone.

A familiar burn greets my throat, and my eyes water. "I can't do this, Fiona."

I slink down into the water, submerging my head. And I sit in the dark silence. Stewing, my mind emptying, and so is my heart. I want to be with you, Fi. There's nothing left for me here. There's nothing left for me to love.

My chest kicks. My lungs yearn for air, but I hold myself down. I grip the sides of the tub, forcing myself to stay under.

Is this how it felt to take your last breath, Fi? Were you desperate to hang on, or did you simply let go?

My hands slip from the edges of the tub, and I lie back in the water. My eyes are still closed, and my head is getting dizzy.

A bit longer.

Hold a bit longer, I tell myself. I need to feel how you felt.

Then, a warped sound reaches my ears. It's tinny, yet familiar.

I burst from the water, and I gasp for breath. The sound is much clearer now. It's coming from outside the bathroom.

It's a viola.

The melody is beautiful, gently bobbing in the air.

I scramble from the tub and hastily cover myself while opening the door. As I tug my gloves on over my hands, I pause in the hallway, dripping wet, and realize that it's coming from the room across the hall. Once I tighten the tie on my robe, and readjust the scarf on my wet head, I urgently knock on the door. The viola comes to an abrupt stop.

Oli opens the door a second later. A blue light glows from inside her room, but I can't see what it is. She steps out, shutting the door behind her. "Yes?"

I'm at a loss for words. I don't know why. "It's very late" is all I can manage.

She grins. "I agree. It is late."

"Must you play your viola now? When the moon is out?"

"When the moon is out?" She laughs. "You do know it's always out? It doesn't hide away during the day—"

"I know." Frustration creeps up my neck. "Can you please be quiet? It's been a rough day, and I would like some silence."

Oli leans against the doorframe. "Oh yeah, I saw. Your freak-out in the arboretum. *And* you yelled at Frank, too. The poor bastard."

"How did you know I . . ." I shake my head. "It doesn't matter. Just, please . . . I would like to have a quiet night. Please?"

"All you had to say was *please.*" Oli stares at me, a teasing smirk on her face. Perhaps I knocked a bit aggressively.

"Also, I apologize for knocking the water out of your hand earlier. It wasn't my intention."

"All forgiven. Like you said, you had a rough day. By the way, you weren't at dinner. Did you have something to eat?"

"I did."

"Good." She sighs and looks around the dim hallway. "So, Frank tells me that you'll be leaving before the ceremony. We'll be handling the planting ourselves."

I rub my neck. "I have places to be."

Oli nods. "Well, we'll be sure to take care of your sister's ashes. Is there anything you'd like to say to her before she's planted?"

"What do you mean?"

She holds up a finger. "Wait right here." She disappears back into her room, closing the door behind her. I gaze at the dreamcatcher on her handle rocking back and forth. She comes back out with a sheet of paper. "Write to her. I'll make sure it gets planted, too."

I blink, taking the paper. "Thank you. That's oddly kind of you."

She laughs. "Why would it be odd?"

"I don't know." I look her over. "You seem a bit antagonizing."

"Me? Antagonizing?" She feigns shock and bats her dark lashes. "Is it because of my scary skin? Or my tattoos?" She rolls up her sleeves, revealing the inky art decorating her arms.

"Or maybe it's my fangs?" She curls her lip, showing off her teeth.

I'm mesmerized for a moment, gazing at her sharp canines. "No, it's not that—"

"My mother was a witch. Me father a gargoyle. Hence the abomination before you."

The ugly word takes me out of my trance. "I'd never call you an abomination."

She grins. "I see. You're rich *and* kind."

"Who said I was rich?"

Her eyes fall on my silk gloves, and then they trail up my body to the golden locket around my neck. "Lucky guess."

I tuck my locket into my robe. "I'm . . . I'm not rich."

Oli grins even wider. "Whatever you say, princess."

"Princess?" I squawk.

She chuckles. "I only jest, Miss Saika." She turns the handle to her door. "We should get to bed. I have ashes to plant in the morning and you . . ." Her eyes scan down my body, but then she quickly looks away, her cheeks blushing a dark violet. "You have a letter to write."

"Why are you—"

"Good night, Miss Saika. And thanks for the show."

"The show?"

The door shuts gently behind her, and I'm left alone in the dark hallway, wet and a bit disheveled. It's only once she's gone that I finally look down at my robe and see why she had looked so embarrassed. The tie on my robe had loosened.

I run to my room. I've never slammed a door so quickly in my life.

CHAPTER FIVE

Fiona, I have to apologize to you.

I couldn't sleep last night. Frank's offer echoed in my mind. Eventually, I rolled out of bed and found solace in the gentle swing on the veranda. I'm not sure what time it is. It's still dark, but I've been out here for hours, curled in a knitted blanket. Beyond the distant mountains, a thin flicker of grayish-blue light bleeds into the dark sky. It's almost daybreak. And Frank's offer still hasn't left my mind.

Would you like to work for Ash Gardens, he asked. *Until you have the courage to plant your sister's ashes.*

He makes it all sound so simple.

It's going to rain again. The air is getting heavier, damper, but it feels nice on my flushed skin. The first drop of rain hits the veranda. And soon it pelts everywhere—the ground, the steps. Droplets spray, and a cold mist coats my face.

I don't remember the last time I sat in silence like this, feeling the chilly air clam my skin. Perhaps I never have.

The swing is comfortable. Pillows rest at my back as I kick my feet. I gaze out to Frank's land. It's vast, without any buildings or structures disrupting the view. It's nothing like the city.

In your last days, Fi, I wish I had slowed down more. I panicked, knowing that your time was coming to an end. I spent so much time worrying about how to hold on to you that I must have tricked my mind into thinking I'd never lose you. I've cheated Death once before. I thought I could do it a second time.

It's such a silly thing, thinking one can command Death. That's a power that no witch, great or small, could ever possess. I can't try to pull you back, Fi.

Which is why I must apologize to you. Because now, I'm faced with an option to hold on to you for just a while longer. And in the simplest of words, I can't let you go.

The front door creaks open, and Frank steps out holding a book and blanket. He looks surprised to see me. "Saika."

"'Morning, Frank."

He sits on his large rocking chair beside the swing. He sighs greatly when he settles back, and I repress a smile. Such a show of exhaustion is something Nana used to do. "You're up quite early," he comments.

"I could say the very same to you."

"Ah." He rocks back in his chair. "Every morning, I sit out here to see the dawn of a new day. It's comforting to know that it's a chance to start over. Anything is possible." He glances at me, drumming his paw on his book. "Speaking of which, I was certain you'd be well off by now."

"I thought about it." I gaze out at the dark clouds masking the sunrise. "But your offer won't seem to let me go."

"What did you decide?" he asks.

I look away. "I don't have anywhere else to go. And I'm tired. So"—I meet his eyes—"I'd like to stay for as long as you'll have me."

Frank smiles. He reaches over and extends his paw. I shake it, the silk of my gloves sliding against his soft fur.

"Welcome to Ash Gardens, Miss Saika."

News of my employment trickles through the house by breakfast time. Words of congratulations greet me, and I do my best to accept them with a cheerful attitude. Despite my apprehension, I've decided to stay, and the guilt sits like a rock in my stomach.

"What's your job, then?" Oli asks across the table as she butters her toast. I can't bear to look her in the face after embarrassing myself last night.

"She'll be helping you around, Oli," Frank says. "She's a capable witch, aren't you, Saika?"

I swallow the dregs of my tea. I nod, still not looking at Oli. "I can help with whatever you need."

"I think it's a great idea!" Evette's face brightens as she speaks. "We needed another witch around here."

"Hilde and I aren't enough for you, E?" Oli raises her brow. "Besides, I don't think we need any extra hands. We get along just fine."

"Olivie, please." Hilde sits at the end of the table. She lights her smoking wand, her plate of food untouched. "Of course we need the help. You're stretching yourself too thin."

Oli rolls her eyes. "I wouldn't have to if a certain Architect helped out with chores—"

"I'm going to stop you right there." Hilde blows her smoke away from the table. "No."

"Hilde's old," Morose quips. "She can't be working herself to death."

Hilde stares daggers at Morose. "Watch it, demon."

"*Anyhow,*" Frank interrupts. "Saika, we welcome you at Ash Gardens. If there's anything you need, let us know. We'd all be happy to help."

"Thank you, I will." I dig into my eggs, not feeling very hungry.

"Now," Frank addresses everyone. "We have a ceremony tonight. The electricity is still out, but we'll make do. We can . . ." He stops suddenly. "Damn it all," he mutters and loads a plate with pancakes and sausages. "I'm sorry. I'll return shortly."

He runs out of the dining room, but no one even bothers to pay him any mind.

I blink, watching the dining room doors shut behind him. "Why did he just run out?"

"Ignatius," they all answer in unison.

Frank forgetting to send up Ignatius's meals is an everyday occurrence then. It's unfair to Frank. He does so much, and yet he has to acquiesce to Ignatius's demands.

Meal duties are shared, and everyone has a job to do. And yet this Ignatius, this recluse elf, is excluded.

Did Frank give him the same offer he did to me? Like me, did Ignatius come to Ash Gardens for a burial, but never had the courage to do it? So now he stays, taking advantage of Frank's hospitality and good nature.

"What does Ignatius do to earn his keep?" I ask.

Forks and knives clatter to a stop. Everyone's eyes settle on me. I look at their bewildered faces, choosing to skip over Oli's.

"What do you mean?" Evette asks.

"What does Ignatius do to earn his keep?" I repeat. "We all

have a job to do, but he's resigned to his room. I haven't even seen him since I've been here."

"And you won't," Oli says. "He doesn't leave his room."

"Just like a city witch, not minding her own." Morose takes a sip of his coffee. He looks at me with a dead stare. "Our deals with Frank are private."

"Well, they aren't, really." I point at him with my fork. "We know that Frank has you take trips to the city to sell produce, does he not? And Merry, you grow the produce."

Morose keeps quiet, but Merry nods his head. "That's right."

I continue. "Hilde, you are an invaluable asset to Frank. I recognize your work around the house. You can't mistake the detailed craft of an Architect witch."

Hilde grins. "You are correct."

"Phil . . ." I glance at the empty space at the end of the table. Food shifts around the plate, but never gets eaten. "That *is* you down there, isn't it, Phil?"

A fork levitates in the air and waves.

I hum. "I'm not sure what Phil does, to be honest."

Oli laughs. "Neither do we."

"Evette, you're an exceptional cook. And baker," I say, and she beams at the compliment. "You make delicious meals for the bereaved."

Evette nods, light emanating around her head. "I do. I also care for the fruit trees and grow flowers in the garden."

"I've seen them. They're absolutely lovely."

Her light grows brighter. "Thank you, Saika."

"What about me?" Oli asks. She leans on the table, her chin in her hand. "You're so very astute. Can you tell me what my job is?"

I cough, suddenly becoming very interested in the greasy

sausages on my plate. "You're a factotum," I say, eyes forward.

"What did you just call me?" Oli's voice rises. Evette's wings flutter nervously beside her. "The hell is a fack-a-dumb?"

"Factotum," I correct. "It's not a bad word. It's like a jack-of-all-trades. A handyman—"

"She's calling you a janitor!" Morose bursts into a fit of laughter.

"I am not!" My face burns. "I'm saying you're very good with your hands." The table grows quiet, and I panic. "You're an asset to the house. You fix things. You're a fixer."

Oli slowly swallows a mouthful of pancake, scowling the whole while. Then she smiles, and the table erupts into laughter.

I find nothing funny. I wish I could crawl underneath the table.

"Everyone is in a good mood, then?" Frank asks as he saunters back in.

"Oh yes." Oli glances at me. "We're watching Saika eat pancakes for breakfast with a side of foot."

"Oh." Frank sits down. He looks worriedly from my face to my plate.

I sigh. "Not literally, Frank."

"Well, it's nice to hear you all getting along." He finishes off the rest of his plate. "Now, about tonight, our ceremony is for a witch from the city. She's widely known and loved, but her family asked for a small ceremony. She's leaving behind a husband and a son. Hilde, can you construct something for them?"

Hilde blows out more smoke and enchants the cloud away. "Absolutely."

"Evette, she was known for her strawberry pies. Perhaps you can make one of yours?"

Evette beams. "I have just the recipe for it."

"And Saika." Frank turns to me. "Could you play a song for them?"

"Me?" I ask.

"You're a Music witch. The piece you played for me the other night was . . . it was transcendent. Do you think you can do the same for the bereaved tonight?"

I look at everyone's faces. I finally brave a glance at Oli, and her face is a bit scowled.

I answer Frank. "Of course."

"You'll do great." Frank turns his attention back to everyone else. "Now, remember what I said: Be kind. Be hospitable. Be caring."

"You hear that, Oli?" Morose wags his brows.

She blanches. "What are you on about? I care for the bereaved plenty."

Morose laughs. "Oh, we all know how you care for the bereaved."

A dark purple blush colors Oli's cheeks. She tosses her fork down. "Oy, listen here, you fucking donkey-faced goat—"

"That's enough." Frank's voice booms, stilling everyone in their seats. "This is the exact behavior I'm talking about. Be kind to the bereaved, but also be kind to one another. Please, for my sake." Frank gets up, dismissing himself from the table. "Oli, a word, please."

Breakfast ends, and when I begin collecting dirty plates, Hilde stops me.

"Don't you worry about this." She takes the dish from my hands and juts her chin toward Oli. She's standing on the threshold of the dining room, speaking adamantly with Frank.

"I think you need to get acquainted with your new boss." Hilde grins.

I approach Oli and Frank, catching the tail end of their conversation.

". . . don't think you understand exactly who I am. You never said we couldn't be ourselves," Oli whispers, but loud enough for anyone passing by to hear.

"I'm not saying that, Oli, and you know it. I don't want you taking advantage of our patrons."

"Who said I'm taking advantage? Maybe they're helping me. Have you thought about that?" She stops when she sees me standing behind Frank.

He turns around and startles to see me there. He glances back at Oli. "We'll speak of this later." He then greets me with a smile. "Saika, just the witch I wanted to see. Oli is going to show you the grounds this morning."

Oli groans. "Frank, I've got errands to run."

"And she can help with that later. Go on." Frank rubs Oli's shoulder. "Saika needs to get acclimated to the area. And Saika, about tonight. The family enjoys the classics. But I don't want to color your impressions. Just play whatever you feel is right." He gives Oli another hearty pat, and she makes a show of falling forward. "I'll see you two at lunch."

Frank walks off, and Oli's stare bores into my face. "So, you're a Music witch?"

"I am."

"And you're working here now."

"I am."

She folds her arms. "What about the ceremony? Is that not happening anymore?"

"It is," I answer. I think about what to say and how to say it. "It's just . . . it's been postponed for a while."

"I thought you said you have places to be."

An explanation stops itself on the tip of my tongue. "Why does it matter? I'm here now."

Her eyebrows rise. She walks out of the dining room. "Well then. I guess you're like the rest of us."

I don't know what she means by that, but I follow her through the kitchen to the backyard.

Outside, Merry tends to his plants. I spot Evette plucking apricots from the trees. Phil floats behind her, holding up a basket to catch the fruit.

"So this is Ash Gardens." Oli picks a few cherries from a nearby tree. She walks backward down the path, chewing and talking, and I can't help but stare at her fangs.

"You've met everyone. The cherubs. Hilds. Evette. Phil, who follows Evette around like . . . well, like a ghost."

I watch Evette talk to Phil, even laughing, as she drops another apricot into the basket.

"Does Phil speak?" I ask. "I've never seen an actual ghost before."

"According to Evette he does . . . in his own way, but I've never heard him say anything. He doesn't even eat. He just likes to pretend—" She trips backward, falling flat on her back.

Loose carrots tumble down the dirt path, and Merry is sprawled beneath Oli. He squirms, trying to get clear of her.

"Please, watch where you're going, Oli." Merry groans, holding his head.

I hurry to help him up. "Oh, you poor thing. Are you alright?"

Oli stands to her feet just fine, wiping the dirt from her black pants. "You're so small, Mer. Can't you wear a bell or something?"

I roll my eyes. "You were the one walking backward."

"Damn it, I've dropped me cherries." She scans the garden using her hand as a visor.

Merry pats my hand. "Thank you for helping me up, Saika." He turns to get the basket of carrots that he'd dropped, but Oli has already picked them up and placed them back in the basket. "Oh, that was quick."

"Yeah, well, you owe me a few cherries, Mer."

He heaves the basket of carrots. "I'll bake them in a pie."

Oli grimaces. "No offense, but you're lousy in the kitchen. You and that grumpy demon you call a brother."

"Hey, now." Merry laughs. "That's unfair. I think we've gotten better at baking."

Oli chuckles. "No, you haven't."

She shows me the rest of the backyard—all the fruit trees and vegetable gardens. I slow to a stop when we near the entrance of the arboretum. The glimmers from the portal twinkle like tiny stars.

Oli stands beside me. "This is the heart of Ash Gardens. The arboretum." She walks up and places a hand on the trunk of a sycamore. "This is where we plant the ashes. It's a blend of natural and enchanted trees to keep it sustained. A give and take. Like they nurture one another."

It makes sense, from what Frank told me about Kye. She liked magic and non-magic existing together. The arboretum seems like a representation of that.

"There's so much magic coming from here." I'm still in a bit of a trance. "It's a little overwhelming."

I feel her eyes on me. I wonder if she's going to bring up how I ran out of the arboretum the other day, blubbering like a baby. Instead, she walks away.

"Well, Frank trusts me to care for it. And it's an important job." She stops as if she wants to say something else. "It's tough work, but it's rewarding. Ash Gardens is special. We don't even get paid to be here. Our work covers our stay. We love it that much." She looks at me. Her face stern and suspicious. "So I'll ask you this once. Are you sure you want to work here?"

I furrow my brow. "Yes."

"And you think you're powerful enough to handle the tasks? Hilde says you use a wand."

I hesitate to answer. I wish I could've kept that bit of information to myself, but I suppose I've been careless. "So what if I use a wand? I can do anything you ask."

"Why?" She folds her arms. "What are you trying to prove?"

"I'm not trying to prove anything."

"You can be anywhere. With your fancy gloves and head-wraps. I don't want you wasting our time."

My hands ball into fists. "I'm not. Frank asked me to be here. I accepted. I don't understand what your issue is."

Her dark eyes scan over me. "Fine. Let's do our first task of the day, shall we, princess?"

I square my shoulders. "Lead the way. And stop calling me *princess*." I finally blink after she walks off, my eyes feeling dry yet teary.

She directs me across the yard through the manicured paths, and I ignore Merry's curious stares.

We stop at a small, dilapidated barn. The paint and wood are chipped and worn away. One of the hinges on the barn door is broken. When Oli opens it, the door pitches forward.

It's completely dark, save for a few strips of sunlight breaking through the rafters. A trilling screech echoes from inside, and it freezes me to the ground.

"That's Beelzebub." Oli looks at me smugly. "She's a dragon."

"A dragon?" My voice shrieks. "What on earth is a dragon doing here?"

"She belonged to Frank's wife. Bee spends her days in the barn. She never comes out. But she lays eggs that Morose sells at the market. She's been giving me trouble lately, so I haven't been able to get close to her nest."

I'm still a bit frozen. I remember to breathe. To blink. "And what would you have me do that you haven't tried already?"

Oli leans on the door. "Well, I could do it myself, but I'm far too busy. And Frank hired you to help. So, help."

"What about Hilde?"

Oli laughs. "Hilde? You heard the woman. Achy bones and all that. She's too old to be battling a dragon." Oli steps forward, looking me in the eyes. "Is this something you can do, Saika?" she croons. She stares down at my silk gloves. I hide them behind my back.

"Of course, I can do this."

"Great!" she chirps. "Wait here."

I take a deep breath, steeling myself against the screech that echoes again from inside the barn.

Oli returns a moment later with a giant butchered piece of meat poorly wrapped in newspaper. "You'll need this, then."

She plops the meat into my arms, and I buckle under the weight. I gaze down at the blood seeping through the newspaper. I give Oli a bewildered look. "Why would I need this?"

"Beelzebub gets a bit huffy if you come near her. This keeps her busy."

The blood from the meat reaches the front of my bodice. "Um . . ."

Oli pauses, watching the frantic expression on my face. "You don't have to do this, you know. You *can* leave. You can do what you came to Ash Gardens to do. Plant your sister's ashes."

A fresh cut whips across my heart. Absolutely not.

I grit my teeth and stand up straight, showing that I have no problem holding this massive chunk of meat. "Frank asked me to stay and help, so that's what I'm doing."

"If you insist." She steps out of the way to allow me inside the barn. The sunlight behind me slowly begins to fade away. I turn back to see Oli closing the door.

"Oh, Bee doesn't like sunlight." She smiles. "And we wouldn't want her getting out. Good luck. Call if you need help."

Oli doesn't wait for a reply. The door slams shut.

And I'm standing in the dark. Beelzebub screeches from the rafters.

I close my eyes and take a deep breath.

I set the meat on the dusty ground and fidget for the wand stuck in my boot. I don't want to waste the star's power on any more enchantments, but this is important.

"I cannot see. I have no sight. Turn this darkness into light."

My locket warms, and the tip of the wand flicks on. A splotch of blood stains the midsection of my dress. I groan. I'll have to change now.

"Here, Beelzebub. I have your breakfast," I call out. My boots shuffle through the straw on the floor. I hear scuffling to my left, and when I bring my wand up, a long yellow tail whisks just out of sight into the darkness.

My breath seizes, and I freeze again, waiting for the dragon to crawl back out or pounce or swallow me whole.

But instead, Beelzebub waits farther back in the darkness, her tail thumping against the wood of the rafters.

Finding my courage, I toss the meat toward the center of the barn. It lands with a dull thud, and Beelzebub screeches loudly. I cast my wand higher, and on the edge of the light, a leathery claw snakes forward and sinks into the meat. It drags it back into the darkness.

Beelzebub tears into the paper, eating the meat and morning news all at once. I have to act quickly before she finishes. I scan for the eggs.

The light from my wand sweeps over the barn. I shuffle through the scattered hay on the floor. And then I see hay precariously piled high in the corner of the barn. A nest of large cream-colored eggs lies on top.

Placing the end of my wand between my teeth, I lift my dress and hurry to the nest. I try to be silent, but have you ever tried to sneak around in big, clunky boots? It's nearly impossible.

Luckily, Beelzebub is far too busy chomping away at her breakfast to hear me.

The stack of hay looms over me, and my foot sinks in when I try to climb. I teeter to the side.

Damn it. I need a levitation spell, Fi. I think I used one once. I just don't remember what it was.

I give my wand a twirl. *"The earth at my feet, head in the sky…"* The light from my wand peters out.

"No, come on." I give the wand a shake. The light zips back and forth in the darkness, catching the attention of red, glowing eyes.

Beelzebub's jaw isn't hungrily chomping anymore. Her low growl fills the barn.

My voice squeaks. "Oli?" I call out toward the barn door. No answer.

Panic swells in my stomach. My hands tremble as I twirl my wand. "Damn it, what is that spell?" I wish you'd answer me, Fi. I need help.

Your silence, though expected, is heartbreaking. I bite my lip, thinking hard.

"Fine." I wave my wand again. *"Earth at my feet, head in the sky, um . . . take my body and allow me to fly!"*

My feet burst from the ground, and my body soars up. I land clumsily in the large nest on top of the hay, dropping my wand in the process.

A terrifying screech fills the darkness. My wand lands near the cluster of eggs. It's too far. I'm defenseless.

"Oli!" I look toward the barn doors, but she doesn't come sweeping through to save me.

Beelzebub screeches again. I leap forward, the hay scratching at my palms and knees, and scoop up my wand. I place the end between my teeth again and collect as many eggs as I can. They're quite large, so I'm only able to grab three.

Beelzebub announces her arrival with another screech, and she lands in the nest with a thud. Her wings whip large bouts of air over me, and I fall back. I look up at her, taking in her leathery yellow skin, her red eyes, her long yellow neck.

Beelzebub extends her webbed wings. I tighten my grip on the eggs.

She screeches one last time, this time so loud it beats on my eardrums. I cower for a moment, but then I see an opportunity. Beelzebub's eyes are closed as she roars, so I move quickly. I hop out of the nest and slide down the hay while holding my dress in place.

Sunlight outlines the broken barn door, and I run toward it. Beelzebub screeches again behind me, but I push forward and break out of the barn in a single bound. I slam the door shut behind me.

Oli isn't out here.

No, she's drinking coffee in the kitchen—laughing and

talking with Hilde. Her eyes widen when I come through the back door, and they both grow quiet.

"I hope these eggs are worth a fortune," I say, fuming.

A smile flicks on Oli's face. "Did you have any trouble?"

She waits for a break in my resolve. She wants me to break down, to claim that I never signed up for this sort of labor. She knew what she sent me in there to do, Fi. She knew how dangerous it was yet said nothing. Is this some sort of test? A battle of wills?

She stands there, waiting for me to admit that I was weak. Never mind that I called her name twice to save me.

I give her a cheap smile. "I told you I could handle it. So I did." I shove the eggs in her arms.

Hilde watches us, amusement etched on her face. "Wow, three eggs? That's more than you've ever gotten, isn't it, Oli?" Hilde grins. She fans out the skirt of my dress. It's marred with dirt and something black that I must have rolled in. "Love, you're all dirtied up." She wipes at the blood on my bodice. She gives Oli a scornful look. "Shame on you for sending her in there."

Oli looks extremely unapologetic, but she says otherwise. "I apologize, Miss Saika, for not giving you a proper warning. You've mussed up your dress."

"It's nothing that a change of clothes can't fix. Now, do you have any other asinine tests you'd like me to complete?"

Hilde chuckles beside me. "Well, Oli?"

Oli grins. She crosses her arms. "In fact, I do. Go get changed. We're heading to Rose Woods."

CHAPTER SIX

Oli waits for me outside, her broom resting across her shoulders and her dirtied work boots laced up her shins. I meet her in front of the veranda, wearing a clean dress.

She rolls her eyes. "You changed into that? You're hardly dressed for labor."

"This is all that I have." I fan out my gray smock, wondering what is so wrong with it.

"And you wonder why I called you *princess*? When you're wearing silk gloves and gold jewelry and fancy headwraps and dresses—"

"Why does it matter what I'm wearing? I can move around just fine." I stomp off the veranda. "Now, are we going to Rose Woods or not?"

Oli falls silent. Ideas and decisions running through that thick head of hers, I'm sure. She finally relents and shakes her head. "Okay, fine. If you insist on coming, get your broom. We'll be harvesting wood today."

"Oh." I rub the back of my neck.

She settles over her broom. "Why are you just standing there?"

"I don't have a broom."

"Why?"

"Well, if you must know, they're very expensive—"

She laughs, and a muscle twitches in my eyebrow. "Not always. If you want one of those fancy brooms, sure, it'll cost you. But for a regular old broom?" She knocks on her broom handle. "Poor witches fly on used brooms all the time, you know."

I step away. "I'll walk."

"You can't walk to Rose Woods." She pinches the bridge of her nose and thinks for a moment.

She shimmies up the broom. "Get on. I'll account for the weight."

"I haven't co-ridden since I was a girl." I awkwardly saddle behind her. "Are you sure this is safe?"

"Yep, hold on." She kicks up her heel, and the rear of the broom bounces. I yelp louder than I wish I had and cling on to Oli. My hands firmly grip her chest, but I remove them quickly.

She pulls my hands around her waist, and my face feels on fire. "You have to hold on. Just because I saw your chest doesn't mean you can hold on to mine."

"You *did* see something last night!" I pull completely away, and she falls into a fit of laughter. "What did you see?" I demand.

"Nothing, I promise." She looks over her shoulder and smiles. "Now will you just hold on to me?"

Her feet push off the ground, and we take off. My arms crush her midsection. She gives the slightest groan, and I ease my grip. It's been such a long time since I've flown on a broom. I've forgotten how to balance myself.

Oli takes the reins. She enchants the broom to carry more weight, and we sail through the clear blue sky.

"Beautiful day for flying," Oli shouts over the wind whipping in my ear. Her puffy hair blows around like a typhoon, and it tickles my nose. With a wave of her hand, it ties itself up.

The city is incomparable to this view, Fi. The mountains in the distance are like sleeping giants. A train chugs through one of the tunnels, plumes of dark smoke rising in the air.

Rolling green hills pass beneath our feet. The wide river shimmers in the late-morning sun. And as we soar, I become less aware of why we're up here and where we're going.

Flying is an act of freedom, Fi. I didn't realize how much I've missed it. Or how much I missed the air kissing my face. A sweet ache simmers deep in my chest. I never thought I would fly again.

I blink away happy tears.

I'm glad I wipe them away, because Oli glances over her shoulder again. "Are you alright back there?"

"Peachy."

"Just don't know you to be so quiet."

"I'm taking in the sights."

"Ah." She nods. "Well, take one last good look. We're here."

Rose Woods approaches us silently and quickly. One moment it's a tiny dot in the distance. The next, we're faced with the edge of the trees, standing like an intimidating wall.

When we land, my legs feel like jelly. Oli raises her brows at me as I get my bearings. Something is calculated in her head, but she doesn't say anything. She pulls a map out of her back pocket and sets it on the ground. I hover near her, trying to make sense of the lines and circles she's drawn on it.

"I was over here yesterday," Oli explains. She points to an area on the map that had been circled then crossed off with an x. "We have to be careful where we harvest. There are a few creatures who still live in this forest, and they need the trees just like we do."

My eyes are fixed on the map. Many areas have been circled and subsequently crossed off. Nearly half the map has been plowed through already. "That's a lot of areas you've covered. Why does Frank need so much wood?"

"Underneath the ground in Rose Woods are deposits infused with magic. It bleeds into the foliage and trees. And Frank needs enchanted wood."

"Why?"

"He just does," she snaps. She folds up the map and sets off farther into the woods.

Message received. I won't bring it up again.

Unfortunately, that means that we walk in silence for some time. My feet ache, and I'm reminded that these are the same boots that I used to walk to Ash Gardens. My joints are aching, too, but I don't want to complain.

We enter an area cluttered with tall oak trees. The strong, earthy scent seizes my senses. The air feels lighter and electric, much like the arboretum.

Oli comes to an abrupt stop and consults her map. "This should be good. No wildlife around."

She drops her broom and immediately gets to work. She settles into a squat. Her hands move, guiding the air around us. The magic energy shifts. Tremors roll beneath our feet as a tree suddenly tilts, switching left and right until it's plucked from the ground. Before it falls, Oli creates a cyclone of air to lay it down gently.

It's amazing to watch her, but I realize I'm standing here gawking. "You never picked a sector of magic either, then?" I ask dumbly. Of course, she didn't. She's a Nature witch. I knew that already.

Oli looks back at me, wiping the sweat from her forehead.

She gives me a look that's hard to decipher. I feel like an idiot, words bumbling out of my mouth before I can catch them.

"I don't mean anything by it. In an advanced world, witches tend to hone their magic in sectors fitting for society. Nature magic doesn't seem like . . ." I swallow, feeling small from her silence. "It doesn't seem practical."

She exhales and takes off her jacket. I stare at the tattoos on her purple skin. There are many of them, running from the back of her hands, over her arms, even up to her neck. At first glance, I notice a depiction of a whale on her forearm. On the back of her shoulder is an image of a scantily clad sailor woman with big breasts and a cinched waist.

She drops her jacket on the ground. "Why the hell would I want my magic to fit society? Fucking lot it's done for me."

"I didn't mean—"

"I lived most of my life on the sea. Seems like it'd be more *practical* to be a Nature witch when you're surrounded by water. It's not like I can enchant the tides with a song, can I, Music witch?"

"Well, not with that attitude," I mutter. She rolls her shoulders back, and I can't tell if that made her smile.

"Music witch," she repeats under her breath and shakes her head. "What a privileged sector of magic. I'm curious what you plan to play for the bereaved this evening."

I haven't even thought about it. I'll have to think of something. "You and I both."

She looks down at the oak on the forest ground. "Let's get back to work. It's probably been a while since you've enchanted natural elements. So I'll harvest the trees, and you can enchant them into planks."

I blink, dread filling my stomach. I shouldn't be using the

star for any more enchantments. I have to conserve energy. "Do you have an axe?" I ask.

"An axe?" She looks floored, and I would have found it funny if I weren't so embarrassed. "Use an enchantment."

"I need my wand to cast enchantments."

Oli groans, her frustrated cry echoing toward the sky. "Then use your wand."

"I forgot it at home." I inconspicuously slide my wand farther down my boot. "I didn't know I'd be needing it. But if you have any other tools, I can still help."

"What the hell . . . ?" Oli mutters. She takes out a folded burlap bag from her pocket. She fans it open and rummages inside. Her entire arm disappears when she digs into the bag, and I realize belatedly that it's enchanted. Like the packing spell that I used for my suitcase, except her enchantment isn't shoddy.

She pulls out an axe. I feel like a reprimanded child. And Oli drops the axe into my hands like a disgruntled adult. "Here."

It's a lot heavier than I thought.

She notes the strained look on my face and sighs loudly. She waves her hand, and the axe becomes lighter. "Thank you," I mutter.

She returns to the trees, squats once again, and continues harvesting.

I look down at the massive oak before me. How am I supposed to cut this thing down to size by myself? When I glance over at Oli, her body is taut with concentration. The air has shifted somehow. Her playfulness has turned icy. I fear she thinks me incompetent. I'm not. You know I'm skilled, Fi. But the star hanging from my neck is waning. The light is dying, and if it goes out . . . I don't know what I'll do.

On the other hand, I also agreed to help Frank. He's offered to let me stay here, knowing how much I'm a coward, and all he's asked me to do is help with a few chores. I can do this much for him. I'll just use the star this one time.

I squeeze the pendant hanging from my neck, and it warms my fingers. While Oli's back is turned, I pull out my wand, give it a twirl, and whisper, *"I have no strength, I have no speed. Give me power for what I need."*

I slice down, the axe light in my grip, and cut the thick trunk completely in half. The sound reverberates through the woods, and Oli stops. She looks back at me.

"Did you say something . . . ?" Her mouth hangs open as she glances at the split wood then back at me, still holding on to the axe. "Oh."

"You tend to underestimate, you know." I prove my point with another swing of my arms. The wood cracks in half.

She chuckles and turns back to her task. "I'll overestimate from now on."

We spend the remaining morning cutting down trees. Despite my use of enchantment, it still wreaks havoc on my body. I'm exhausted by the fifth tree, but I can't let Oli know that. I wish we'd just get what we need and go back. But Oli powers through, pushing us farther and farther into the woods.

We stop for a moment while she consults her map again, and I catch my breath. We've cut down eleven trees. She wipes sweat from her forehead. Her billowy hair has fallen out of its bun and gathered around her shoulders. She sweeps it back up with a wave of her hand.

"I think if we move farther east, we'll get into more uninhabited land." She moves on without waiting for me. The chopped wood lies on the forest ground.

"Are we just leaving this here?"

"We'll be back for it," she calls over her shoulder. "We gotta keep moving before the storm rolls in."

"Storm?" I glance up through the branches. The sky has dimmed. Gray, wispy clouds float by. It was such a beautiful day a few hours ago.

Oli moves deeper into the woods with determination. We find our harvesting spot, and she settles back into her position. She expertly carves more oaks from the ground. She does the first one quickly, the large trunk landing at my feet. She doesn't falter, moving on to the next one.

I don't understand. We have so much wood already. We should go back to the house. It feels like we're harvesting too much wood.

She notices I haven't moved and stops. "What are you waiting for?" she asks. "We have a storm to beat."

"Right . . ."

She returns to her work, and I raise the axe to begin chopping. But when I strike down, the axe gets wedged in the wood. I try yanking it out, but I have no strength left.

"Oh no." I open my locket, and the star is pulsing. It settles into a dimmer glow.

"What's wrong?"

I glance up, and Oli is staring at me. Her eyes lock on to the chain in my hand, and I clasp it shut.

"Don't you think we have enough wood?" I ask. "Frank has more than he needs for the house. Besides, spring is nearly over, and it shouldn't be as stormy anymore. Why do we need this much?"

"Do you always question everything?" she scoffs. "Why can't you just do your job?"

"I don't understand why we're killing ourselves over this. We're harvesting more than we could possibly use."

"It's called hard work. And if you don't want to do it, then you can leave."

Fire rages in my belly. "I'm no stranger to hard work. Who do you think you are? To speak so plainly—"

Oli turns her back. She rips another tree from the ground with gusto. "Just walk back to the house then."

An argument itches the tip of my tongue. I've worked hard, Fi. We've been raised to become nothing less than winners. I was the top of my class. I excelled in my studies. I graduated with the highest of honors.

And when the world of academics became too much for me, and your death upended my life, I traveled the world.

I sailed the seas as a cabin girl. I trekked mountains and mined caverns in search of something to fill the void that you left in me. And I did it all without relying on enchantments. I honed my own skills. I searched for meaning for myself, and it wasn't a life for a slacker. I worked hard. Harder than I ever had to get to this point. It took so much courage to lay down my adventures and finally fulfill my promise to you.

It took so much work for me to finally come to Ash Gardens.

Oli continues to harvest and ignores my existence. She's moving faster. Her muscles flex across her back as she tears tree after tree out of the ground. She's ferocious. She doesn't care to cushion the trees as they fall anymore. She lets them drop where they are, thudding on the ground.

Seeing her this way, I can make out her gargoyle side. Her round, dark eyes slowly become smaller, sharper. Her fangs elongate just slightly. It's a bit unsettling.

Wood snaps in the distance. A doe comes into view, and a wobbling fawn trails behind her. They scurry closer. They stop when Oli grunts particularly loudly. The doe scampers away, but the fawn stays, curiosity pulling it toward us.

"Oli, wait," I call.

"Just go back." She tears at a tree snug in the ground, not even bothering to look at me.

"No, stop!"

She pulls the tree free, and it teeters backward. The fawn stands petrified, sensing danger, but unaware of the tree falling its way.

I don't know what comes over me, Fi. I dive forward, attempting to scare the fawn away, but I trip over my aching feet, and I slide into the grass.

The fawn wobbles off, but I'm left on the ground. The tree finally snaps backward, falling quickly.

Oli sees me, shouts an expletive, and enchants the tree before it crushes me. She levitates it out of the way and places it on the ground.

She rushes over to me. "I'm sorry. Are you okay?"

"I'm fine." I'm lying. I was already sore and exhausted. The fall only made it worse. Oli helps me up and scans me over. Her big black eyes have returned to normal.

"I wasn't paying attention. I get so focused on what I'm doing . . ." Her attention is whisked to something in the grass. I wonder what she's looking at until she bends down and picks up my wand.

My heart lodges in my throat.

She looks at me. "You said you forgot your wand."

"I lied."

Oli squints at me. "Why?"

The first drop of rain falls onto my lip, and I wipe it away. I don't know what to say.

Oli sighs. "I don't care about your wand. Just don't lie to me about it."

She doesn't understand, Fi. I don't need the wand to help with my enchantments. I can't make any enchantments without it. But I remain silent, and Oli looks lost—rightfully so.

Rain dances over us, falling quicker and harder. She gives up trying to make sense of it all and hands me my wand.

"Let's head back."

She takes out her enchanted burlap bag, and I watch as she moves her hands. The ground shakes again, and the wood we've just harvested rolls together. It brightens as all the harvested wood levitates from the ground. Plank by plank, the wood disappears into her enchanted burlap bag. She doesn't even falter under the cold rain.

It's quite amazing, to be honest. I've never seen Nature magic be used in such a way.

We board her broom, and we lift toward the sky.

"What about the other wood we harvested?" I ask her as we fly over Rose Woods.

"You want to get home, don't you?"

We fly in silence. Dark storm clouds drift behind us. It's drizzling now, and it's getting into my eyes. When I try to wipe the rain off my face, I teeter on the back end of the broom.

Oli grabs my wrist and places it firmly on her stomach. My face heats when my chest presses against her back. She still doesn't say anything, and neither do I.

When we land, Oli hops off her broom quickly and snatches it up without waiting for me to get my bearings this time.

"I have to talk to Frank." She runs into the house, leaving me standing in the rain, clutching my wand in my hands.

CHAPTER SEVEN

By the time the storm settles over Ash Gardens, the ceremony is already underway.

I was invited down to the arboretum, but I decided to stay in my room until the ceremony was over. From the window in my bedroom, I watch the bereaved family walk out from the arboretum underneath black umbrellas.

The tops of their umbrellas bumble through the vegetable garden as they speak with one another. Crying. Consoling.

A line of people heads toward the house for the ceremonial dinner. I take a deep breath. Time to go down.

I'm dressed in my same smock from earlier. I did my best to scrub out the dirt stains, and I doused my silk gloves in sudsy water and hung them to dry. They're still a bit damp when I slide them on.

I tilt back the mirror that stands in the corner of my room. Dear stars, I look ghastly. I don't even recognize myself, Fi. I'm not the perfect little girl from grade school anymore. Our mother would have a fit if she ever saw me like this.

She'd be angry at my plain clothing. She'd question why I'm always hiding my hair under a headwrap. The fabric is tied securely in a bun at the back of my head. She'd want my tight black curls to be loose like a crown around my head. Her heart would break at the length of my hair now.

I touch my reflection and startle when I hear a playful knock at the door.

"Saika, it's Evette. Dinner will be soon. Frank asks that you come down, please."

"I'll be right down."

I glance back out the window where the last of the bereaved family leaves the garden. I suppose it's time.

Evette's orbs of yellow light fill the house. They bob toward the ceiling like tiny lanterns caught in a net, gently swaying and drifting into one another. It sets the foyer in a dim light, where family members gather in small groups, speaking among themselves in swarms of black.

I excuse myself through the small crowd and make my way into the parlor. I find Frank among the throng. He's speaking with a man with a monocle and top hat. They seem deep in conversation, and I don't really want to interrupt.

Instead, I acknowledge the family and ask if there's anything they need. Then amid sniffles and conversation, I hear . . . laughter.

Giggling is a more accurate word. I follow the sound to the lit fireplace. Children are gathered on the rug. They're enraptured by a storyteller, but I can't see who it is. When I come closer, I see Oli kneeling before the mantel, dressed in all black. Her puffy black hair has been parted and plaited into two braids.

She's grinning widely, focusing on a young boy in the front row. She taps his nose as she tells a story. "And that's when we blew the trumpet. We had to raise anchor! For war was beginning . . ." She delivers the line gravely, and the children are sucked in.

I stand back, watching her entertain them with a pirate's tale. I wonder if she was a pirate herself. She has spent time at sea. And only a pirate would have that many tattoos. Perhaps that's why she doesn't mind working herself to death. Or working during torrential rainstorms. She's used to a pirate's life. She certainly swears like one.

I haven't spoken to her since this morning. I frustrated her, I know. I'm sure she can't stand the sight of me now.

"Saika, is that you?" Someone taps my shoulder. It's a woman wearing a mourning veil. She lifts it, and my eyes widen.

"Marionette?" I gasp. Our childhood friend, Fi. Well, using the word *friend* is pretty generous. I haven't seen her since graduation. She holds her arms out in a hug, and it'd be rude if I refused.

"What are you doing here?" I ask her.

Her eyes are red and rubbed raw from crying. "For Julianna's planting ceremony. Is that why you're here?"

I blink. Until now, I hadn't even thought about the dearly departed. Frank mentioned that she was a witch from the city, but the city is so large. What were the chances that I knew the deceased?

"Oh, Marionette, I'm so sorry." I hug her again, meaningfully this time. "I had no idea that Julianna had passed on."

Marionette nods. She dabs her eyes with an embroidered handkerchief. "She'd come down with something and never recovered. It happened so quickly." She stops and looks at me. "Now that I think of it, hadn't Fiona passed the same way? She fell ill but then got better, if I remember correctly?"

My chest feels awfully tight. I strain a smile. "She did. She recovered for three years, but then got sick again. She died peace-fully." I'm impressed with how well I can recall your demise with-out falling to pieces. It could have to do with the fact that I'd rather die than allow Marionette to see me break into tears.

"Oh, I'm so sorry, Saika." She pats my hands, and I try to hide the stains on my silk gloves. "How about that, then? We both lost our elder sister to fate." She swallows her emotion and looks away. "I wish I could reach through time and prevent this heart-ache for us both."

I release a heavy sigh. "Some things, such as death and birth, need to take their natural course. It's best we don't interfere."

"I suppose you're right." She looks over at Oli, still entertain-ing the children. "What do you make of that woman? She's pur-ple. And are those fangs?"

"Those are fangs. Her name is Olivie. And she's a witch, em-ployed by Ash Gardens."

"A witch?" Marionette is amazed.

I hum. "A Nature witch." Oli picks up a toddler and balances her on her back, parading her around the room while other chil-dren vie for her attention. "She's quite skilled."

I feel Marionette's gaze on my face. "So, what are you doing here?" she asks. "I heard you'd gone into the Limestone Mountains after you left your parents' house."

After I left? That's a very kind way of putting it. "I went to many places. But I work here now."

"Oh." Marionette blinks. "I surely thought after graduation, we'd never see you again. You'd set out into the world, enchant-ing entire concert halls with your music. Or hosting wild, fabu-lous parties like your mother."

"I think at a point of time, I might have. But Fiona got sick. And it shifted my life into perspective."

Marionette nods. "I see it has. You seem"—her eyes rest on my stained gloves and my wrinkled dress—"well traveled."

I ignore her jab and notice the piano at the end of the room. Frank must have peeled off the cover. The fallboard is already lifted. The white keys gleam under the light of the fire.

"Might you play us something, Saika?" Marionette asks. "For old times' sake? I'm sure Julianna's husband would adore it."

"How can I say no?"

Honestly, Fi. How can I?

Marionette clears her throat, and I'm instantly reminded of her strong, grating voice when she addresses the crowd.

"Attention, dear family and our precious friends. An old friend of Julianna's will play a song to her memory."

My face flushes with heat, and I hurry over to the piano. I settle myself as the room crowds closer with more bodies and chatter. I become acutely aware of Oli, sitting, again, before the fire with the children, watching me intently.

Frank moves into the parlor, followed by a buzzing dot of yellow and Merry and Morose. They're still shirtless, but at least they have the decency to wear black bow ties and slacks.

Marionette pushes her way to the piano, Julianna's husband and son in tow. She parades them to the front to get as close to me as possible, fussing with the son's tie.

"You are all in for a wonderful treat," Marionette announces again. "Saika was the top of our graduating class. And she's one of the best Music witches you'll ever meet." She turns to me, and I feel like melting into a puddle. "Whenever you're ready."

In other words, *Play now.*

My eyes flick over to Frank, and he gives a gentle nod. He's like a mountain in a sea of mourners. His presence is a comfort, and I close my eyes.

And I play.

Some part of me is grateful to Frank. I've prepared a centuries-old ballad. One that I've practiced so often that I could play it in my sleep. Frank mentioned that this family fancies the classics, so naturally my choice gravitated to a ballad about a young elf yearning to impress the daughter of a wicked king. The elf goes through a series of impossible trials to prove himself, but he ultimately fails at the end. He doesn't win the king's approval, but the princess takes matters into her own hands. She kills her father and becomes free to marry her beloved elf.

It's a story of intense romantic love. It's beautiful. And now that I know that this song is for Julianna, I know her romantic soul would love it. It's the perfect song to play.

But the first note I play is wrong. It sounds like something else entirely.

I don't know this song, but I continue, following the dance of my fingers on the keys. And your face comes to my mind, Fiona.

The conversation I had with Marionette flares in my skull. She talked so casually about you.

Now that I think of it, hadn't Fiona passed the same way? she said. *She fell ill but then got better, if I remember correctly?*

My hands stab at the keys, playing out my anger. Shards of my heart shoot from my chest, impaling everyone in the room.

Feel my anger, I want to scream. *Feel my hurt.*

How about that, then? Marionette's voice continues. *We both lost our elder sister to fate. I wish I could reach through time and prevent this heartache for us both.*

Marionette doesn't know where that road leads. She doesn't know how much it costs to bring someone back, Fi. She isn't willing to do it.

But I am. I did it. I did it for you.

Your voice surrounds me like a high melody, blending into a minor chord, and descends into the dark. *What did you do, Saika?* you ask me. *What have you done?*

My heart is so heavy. It swells with relief because I see your face again. I'm able to hear your voice. But you're angry with me, Fi.

I brought you back, if only for a moment. And I would gladly do it again. I will never regret giving my life to the cause of healing you. I would walk this world barefoot, glass at my heels. I would drag the heaviest ship across a dry, barren land if it meant you were here again. Alive. With me.

We cry together. Fiona, there is nothing I wouldn't do for you. As long as I have breath, you will *never* be a distant memory. You are my sister. And I will keep you with me. Forever.

My hands end on a resounding chord. I press my foot down and let the note sustain through the room.

It's quiet. It's much too quiet. I should have played another song.

"My, Saika . . ." Marionette's arms suddenly wrap around me, squeezing the life out of me.

The room erupts in applause. Weepy eyes and exuberant cheers cement me in my seat. Julianna's husband approaches me—the man in the top hat—and he greets me with a firm handshake. Mist clouds his eyes.

"Thank you. You've . . . you've captured my emotions greatly."

Marionette hugs me again. "Somehow you've gotten better." She laughs, wiping away tears. "Best Music witch I know!" she announces and encourages everyone to give me another round of applause.

"If everyone can transition to the dining hall." Frank's voice rises above the noise. "Dinner is ready."

Everyone moves out like slow-moving cattle. My eyes meet

Frank's, and he gives me a nod. He mouths the words, *"Wonderful job."*

For some reason, Fi, that expression of praise does more for me than a room full of cheering people. Through the departing crowd, I scan for Oli. I thought I'd find her among the throng of children pushing and shoving out of the room, but she isn't there. She must have left during the performance.

I stay seated well after everyone has gone. My stained silk gloves ghost over the keys again.

I thought I had fumbled it. I led with my heart when I was trying so hard to yield. I thought Frank would be furious. I thought that perhaps, maybe, the entire thing sounded horrible.

But it was how I felt. It was how I wanted everyone in the room to feel. And now that I got it out, I feel so much lighter.

The door to the parlor opens, and Hilde strides in, wearing an obsidian-black dress. It's made entirely of lace, and it clings to her body.

She put on a red lip tonight, her silver hair is slicked back, and a thick braid lies over her shoulder. She's carrying a large box.

"Oh, Hilde, allow me." I rush up to help her and place the heavy box on top of the piano. "Great stars, what's in here?"

"Would you like to see?" She smiles. Her misty white eye glints from the light of the fireplace. She pulls off the lid, and the walls of the box fall flat.

It's a wooden house.

It has two levels. Chipped paint on the side of the house reveals bits of red brick underneath. Shutters are broken on the top level, and vines creep along the shingles. But the house doesn't look decrepit. It looks lived in and loved.

And in the front yard are wooden figurines of two small girls, one chasing the other.

I reach out my hand to pick it up, but Hilde stops me. "Don't."

"Oh, I'm sorry."

"Allow me to explain first." She picks up one of the figurines, and I finally see the face painted on it. She has a red bow in her hair. "It's Julianna."

I look down at the shorter figurine, portlier in stature. "That's Marionette." And suddenly, I realize why this house feels so familiar. "This is their childhood home."

"It's my gift for the bereaved." She puts Julianna's figurine back in place, in front of Marionette, who's chasing her. "I get a read on the immediate family and construct a keepsake for them. It's usually a beloved memory shared between the grieving and the departed. In this instance, Marionette and Julianna shared a love of their childhood home. So, I created a model of their house. And when Marionette feels sad, and she wants to hold and feel Julianna again"—she hands me Julianna's figurine—"she'll feel her."

I hold tiny Julianna, and I gasp. It's overwhelming. Intense love swallows my heart, and my chest grows tight. It feels like caressing hands on my shoulders. Arms snuggled around my waist. A kiss on my forehead. It's too much. I set the figurine down.

Hilde chuckles. "And now you see why I told you not to touch." She wraps up the house again, lifting the flaps and placing the lid back on.

"How—how do you do that?" I can't stop blinking, my heart racing. "The house may be an architectural enchantment, but what I just felt is not."

"It isn't." She points to her white eye. "I don't only read emotions, I see them, too. Which is why I stay upstairs during ceremonies. It's too much for me when all the bereaved are here. It gives me a headache." She waves her hand.

I blink, still not understanding. "But . . . how . . . ?"

"When I met with Julianna's family, their emotions bombarded me, like they normally do. But someone stuck out to me." She taps on the box. "Marionette. Her emotions ran deep and were raw. A memory from their childhood presented itself to me. And I knew what to make."

She heaves the box back in her arms. "Everyone is different, and they don't always need a gift. But I think Marionette needs this one."

"How did you enchant the figurine to give Julianna's love?"

"It's not Julianna's love. It's mine." We step out of the parlor into the foyer, and I take the other end of the box.

Chatter and noise echo from the dining room.

"Marionette doesn't need Julianna's love. She just needs to know that she *is* loved. And I have much to give."

We place the box on the settee near the front window. "I don't have a coven," she explains. "I haven't for many years now. I don't have much of a family anymore, either. So when Frank first asked me to design gifts for the bereaved, I was a bit confused. But when I infuse my love into these gifts, I realize why Frank has me make them for the bereaved. It's helping me as much as it's helping them."

I blink, understanding now. "How insightful of him."

"You aren't any different." She smiles. "That ballad you played filled the entire house. I could feel it all the way on the fourth level. Frank asked you to play for a reason. And I think you know why."

This revelation shouldn't hit me sorely, but it does. As if I were being played by a puppeteer, I am nothing but a lifeless doll. Frank is the grand master, pushing me to enact his secret plans.

Hilde raises her brows. "I'll leave you to your emotions then.

Please make sure Frank gets this. I think I'll faint if I go in there right now."

I smile. "Of course."

She leaves, giving me a pinch on the cheek before she goes. I sit on the settee, watching the rain lessen out the window.

The doors to the dining room open, and Frank comes out, searching for something. He sighs with relief when he sees me sitting beside the big box.

"Thank goodness. I didn't think Hilde would have been done in time. The storm is easing up, so we're ending dinner now . . ." He stops and finally notices the pensive look on my face.

"Are you alright, Saika?" he asks.

I gaze up at him. "Funny how you ask. Wouldn't you know already how I'm feeling?" I regret the words as soon as I say them. But Frank doesn't give any indication that he's offended.

"I think what you played tonight was excellent. You have a talent, and I thought the world deserved to hear it as well. I'm sorry. I didn't mean to offend—"

I hug him firmly. He freezes at first, his paws out to the side, but then he relaxes. He hugs me back, and I feel enveloped in his furry arms.

"Thank you," I whisper. I stop crushing him, although I think that's impossible to do. "I'll see you in the morning."

I bid him farewell and only glance back once I ascend the stairs. He gazes up at me, holding Hilde's box with ease.

"Good night, Saika."

Once I return to my room, the heaviness from the day suddenly drops on me. I plop on the bed, my face buried in the pillows.

It's quiet. The rain and wind hitting the windows is soothing.

And in the quiet, I think I hear the longing note of a stringed instrument.

Oli is playing her stars-forsaken viola again. At night, *again.*

I'm exhausted, though. As much as I want to pound on her door and tell her to stop, I lie stationary.

Rain and wind smack against the windows and jolt me awake a few hours later. It's pitch-dark. And downstairs, I hear a thundering crash that shakes the entire house.

CHAPTER EIGHT

I fumble in the dark hallway until I bump into Oli. She's in her pajamas, holding a lit candle.

"What was that sound?" I ask. Panic strains my voice.

"I don't know. It has to be the storm." She blows on her candle, and the flame grows brighter. We hurry to the steps.

We find Evette fluttering down the dark stairwell, yellow light trailing behind her. "It came from the kitchen!" she yells.

We reach the foyer and rush through the dining room to the kitchen. Evette pulls open the door, and wind whips us backward. I grab on to Oli so we don't blow away, and she catches Evette in her hand. Her candle is extinguished.

Evette sets up orbs of light, and we finally see the destruction before us. A tree has crashed through the back wall of the kitchen. Rain pours through the ceiling as the storm's violent wind blows everything into disarray. Shattered dishes and glass litter the floor. It's absolute chaos.

Oli and I stand there, watching in horror. Morose and Merry hover near the ceiling. Long planks of wood buckle under the weight of the collapsing kitchen ceiling, and the cherubs are trying to hold it up, but they're too small. It's not enough.

Frank gazes up at them, looking helpless. He turns around, fear etched on his face. "Oli! Saika!"

Oli moves into action. She circles her arms and levitates the tree out of the kitchen. Her bare feet step over the wet debris and shattered glass on the floor. She doesn't even wince.

Frank's voice reaches me like a distant call, as if he were miles away. "Can you help her, Saika?"

My eyes shift from Frank to Oli as she braves against the harsh winds and tosses the tree outside.

"Saika?" Frank pleads.

"We can't hold it, Frank!" Merry calls down to us. When we look up, even Evette has her back against the ceiling, trying to stop it from falling.

"Take cover! It's gonna break!" Morose shouts. The ceiling suddenly snaps, and the walls of the kitchen buckle. We brace ourselves, but it never drops.

Hilde glides into the kitchen, wearing a frilly nightgown with a matching bonnet. Her hands are outstretched, holding up the ceiling with ease. "I need planks of wood!" she yells.

"Of course," Frank yells back. "Saika, come with me. Evette, you, too."

We run out into the storm. The wind beats upon the house, and Oli is still out there. She creates a bubble of calm air over the massive hole in the kitchen. Even though she's getting doused in rain, she's unmovable.

"You gotta hurry, Frank," she calls out.

"This way," Frank yells, and we run to the shed. Evette is quick to bubble light once we get inside. There are stacks of wood piled together. "We need to get all of this over to Hilde. Saika?" He looks at me expectantly.

"Oh, yes, of course." I pull my wand out of my boot. "Um . . ." I hate having a crowd. And I don't want to use an incantation in front of them.

Then again, the use of incantations is an unheard-of practice for a witch. Perhaps this will go unnoticed.

I raise my wand. I can't stumble now. The enchantment Oli cast in Rose Woods comes to mind. I take a deep breath, and an incantation comes to me.

"There's a storm, and it's no fun. Condense this wood so we may run."

The shed shakes, and the planks of wood tremble. They rise up, folding over until they merge into one solid block. Frank drops on all fours and heaves the wood across his shoulders. His knees buckle when he stands. "Come on," he growls through gritted teeth.

We run back to the destroyed kitchen. Oli and Hilde are still fixed in their positions, warring against nature to keep the house standing.

Frank drops the dense block of wood in the kitchen, and the floor rocks.

"Thank you, Frank." Hilde levitates the wood toward the ceiling, and Merry and Morose finally move out of the way.

"Everyone, shield your eyes," Hilde calls out. Frank towers over me and Evette, shielding us with his body.

A bright light blooms in the kitchen, and then darkness swallows us whole. It's starkly quiet. The silence becomes loud and tinny.

"It's safe," Hilde says.

We open our eyes, but it's pitch-black.

Evette releases orbs of light, and we see that the ceiling and back wall are intact once again. I can make out the scorch marks where the new wood joins with the old. The half-circle windows that used to be above the sink have changed designs. What was once clear glass is now a stained glass of red and pink roses.

The stress drains from our shoulders. We're safe. And the storm is no longer raging inside the house. But we're left with the terrible aftermath. Rainwater, broken glass, and splintered wood is scattered across the floor.

Oli finally comes inside, dripping wet and exhausted. As she limps, blood trails behind her bare feet.

"I can't express how grateful I am to you all. Because of you, Ash Gardens still stands." Frank looks around the kitchen, but his attention settles on me for a moment. His eyes squint in confusion. Now that the rush of adrenaline is gone, does he find it strange that I use a wand and incantations to enchant?

Oli interrupts, cautiously stepping farther into the kitchen. "Ah, it was easy, Frank." She hoists herself onto the counter. Merry wraps a towel over her shoulders.

"Goodness, you're bleeding, Oli." Evette flutters over and tends to her feet.

"This storm is unlike any that we've had before." Hilde turns to Frank. "What's happening?"

"I don't know." He gazes out the double doors, where the storm continues to rage. "Perhaps the magical energy from the arboretum is attracting the storms?"

"That's not it at all," a voice says.

We glance back to see a short elf standing by the kitchen door. He has a black, grubby beard and pointy ears sticking up from his nightcap. His striped pajamas are wrinkled and a smidge too big for him. This must be Ignatius. I never thought I'd actually see him.

He focuses on Frank, as if none of us are gathered with him.

"I told you that we needed more wood. The storm is going to destroy the house."

"I know," Frank answers him. "I told Oli to collect more wood, but the storm was starting. She needed to get home."

"Since when does Oli shy from working in the rain?" Morose asks.

We look at Oli, but she only stares at me. Words position themselves on her tongue, possibly accusatory. I am, in fact, the reason why we didn't bring the rest of the wood home. I pressured her to return. If anyone is to blame, it would be me, and Oli has every right to say so.

But she doesn't. She looks away from me.

I step forward, glass crunching under my boot. "It was my fault. I assisted Oli this afternoon to harvest wood, and we returned early because of me."

Ignatius rolls his eyes. "Frank, you should've had them go back."

"Why does it matter?" I ask. "The threat has passed. The kitchen has been fixed."

Ignatius groans. "The threat *hasn't* passed." He speaks to me as if I'm a nuisance unworthy of his time. "The ceiling and the wall are fixed, but the structure at the back of the house is still broken. If it doesn't get fixed now, the house will collapse."

"That was all the wood we had." Evette looks at Hilde. "Can you construct some more wood?"

"You all don't seem to understand how architectural enchantments work. I don't know how to work with raw materials. I'm not a Nature witch. I don't know how to harvest wood."

I've only been here a few days, and I've already fumbled so much. This is my fault, and I intend to fix it. So, despite knowing exactly how much of the star I have left, I make a decision. A foolish decision in hindsight, but a decision all the same.

I walk outside into the storm. Oli's wide eyes are seared into my mind as I shut the doors behind me. I won't change my mind now.

With my wand in hand, I stomp into the backyard, cold rain slipping down my back. It's a shame to see the garden in such disarray. The fruit trees have been uprooted and torn to the side. Thankfully the sycamore trees edging the arboretum and its arbor are still standing strong against the storm.

The barn where Beelzebub dwells rattles in the wind. Poor Beelzebub. She's probably frightened in a corner somewhere inside.

Rain pelts my eyes, and I glance back at the house. Everyone is huddled, peering out the glass to see what on earth I'm doing. Frank's large silhouette stands out above everyone else.

I suddenly understand Oli's drive to complete her tasks. I see why she doesn't want to disappoint Frank. The shame from botching our task earlier makes me wish I actually had worked myself to death. If this house were to fall, if Frank were to lose Ash Gardens because of something I did, I would never be able to live with myself, Fi.

I don't want to disappoint Frank. I don't want to disappoint any of them. They deserve the best I have to offer. They deserve every bit of me.

I touch the locket around my neck. This old star has helped me so many times. Hopefully it will help me again.

I twirl my wand toward the slain tree, the one that caused this entire mess. My wand trails over to the uprooted fruit trees. The energy in the air burns my skin, but then I realize that it's coming from my locket. It's glowing hot against my collarbone.

"The situation is dire, and I wish this storm would flee. We're in trouble now and need the wood from these trees."

The disassembled fruit trees wobble into the air. The massive tree takes a bit more energy, and I can feel the enchantment waning. The locket on my neck grows cold. "No, please . . ."

I plant my feet and become a conduit. The power from the star flows through me and into my wand. My neck feels aflame as the trees meet together in the sky.

They merge like the enchantment I've done before, but it's grander. Brighter. My locket heats, and my fingers burn from the handle of my wand. It's cooking me alive, but I won't let go.

The transformation finishes, and the block of wood falls to the ground with a heavy thud. I slip back into the wet grass. My head hits the ground, and I see stars.

Frank runs out in an instant. "Saika! Are you alright?"

I cradle my head in my hand. "I'm fine. Tell Hilde the wood is ready."

Frank is hesitant, but he calls back to the house. "Hilde!"

Hilde comes outside. Merry hovers beside her, holding an umbrella over her head. She immediately gets to work, raising the chunk of wood toward the back of the house. She spots the broken structure and works her magic.

I turn away from the bright transformation, and suddenly I feel Frank's wet, furry paw in my hand. His eyes are squeezed shut, waiting for Hilde to finish.

I squeeze his paw a little tighter, and we wait until the back of the house is fixed.

We're bombarded with thanks when we come back inside. Everyone is happy and relieved, except for Oli, I notice. She's still drenched and sitting on the counter, but her feet are now properly bandaged. She stares at me grimly, looking from my face to my locket and then belatedly to my hands.

My silk gloves are ruined. They're riddled with holes and black burn marks. I don't have another pair.

Frank insists we head to bed and allow him to clean up the kitchen, but none of us acquiesce. It takes us mere minutes to sweep up all the debris and broken glass. All without the help of Ignatius, who slinks back upstairs after he realizes the threat is over. He doesn't even care to help clean up.

Neither does Oli. She sits on the counter, bandaged feet propped up, and delegates the cleaning—at which Morose kindly invites her to shut it.

Once the last of the water is mopped up, everyone retires to their rooms. Merry and Morose go up first. Morose complains about the darkness, and Hilde gives us all candles to take upstairs.

She levitates Oli off the counter so she doesn't have to walk.

Evette flutters around them, beaming like the sun. "You're flying just like me, Oli."

Oli grumbles, looking back at Hilde. "This is humiliating. I can walk just fine, Hilds."

Hilde raises her brow. "Sure. I haven't practiced levitation in some time, and you're quite heavy. You want me to place you down?" She waits, but Oli doesn't speak. They move out of the kitchen. "That's what I thought."

I follow them out, but Frank stops me.

"Saika, can I speak to you for a minute?"

We wait until they all leave, and he rests against the counter. He gazes up at Hilde's architectural work. He nods, approving the new design, and turns back to me.

I feel my heart beating, blood rushing to my face.

"Earlier, in the shed," he begins, "you used an incantation to enchant the wood. And then again out there." He points out the window, thinking hard. "And you use a wand. I could be wrong, but those are tools that non-witches use to cast enchantments. Is . . . is that a normal practice for witches?"

I swallow. "No, it isn't."

He nods. "Right. Witches are innately magical, I thought. They have no need for spells or even wands. Is there any reason why you would—"

"It's just something that I prefer," I lie. I don't know why I do. If there's a time to be honest, it's now. Frank hasn't shown himself to be unforgiving or not understanding. But the lie comes out quicker. Easier. "Rest assured; I can generate my own power just fine. I'm interested in spells, you see. Like Kye."

"Oh. Then it begs the question: When you aren't using your own power, where *do* you draw it from?"

I exhale and unhook the chain from my neck. The locket is stuck to where it was searing my skin. I wince when I peel the chain from my chest.

When I open the locket, translucent dust rises from the shell and disappears. Fear rocks my heart. It's gone, Fi. It's all gone.

I clear my throat. "When I was younger, my sister and I found a fallen star. I've only had just a piece of it, and it's fueled my enchantments for the past two years. But now it's gone."

I finally look at Frank. His yellow eyes widen, his mouth agape. "You had a fallen star?" he asks. "And you used the last of it to save Ash Gardens?" His voice is soft and reverent.

Ash Gardens was far from my mind in the heat of every-thing. I used the last of the star to save him. To save everyone who calls Ash Gardens home.

"I did."

He wraps me in a crushing hug. His clothes and fur are soak-ing wet and cold. "That is a kindness I haven't seen in such a long time."

He releases me, resting his heavy paws on my shoulders. "Thank you, Saika."

"Frank, I . . ." I should tell him the truth about my power. I should tell him now.

But if he knows I no longer have a power source, he'll know that I'm useless as a witch. I'd be forced to have your ceremony, Fi, and be put on the first train out of here. Even now, I'm still such a coward.

"I can still be an asset to Ash Gardens. I can still assist Oli on her tasks." How I'll keep up with Oli's intense work practices without enchantments, I do not know. But I'll find a way. I don't want to have your ceremony, Fi, and head back to an unfulfilling life. I can't do it.

"On the contrary"—he strokes his mane—"if you're up for it, I have another job for you."

I blink. I wasn't expecting that. "What about Oli?"

"I think she handles on her own pretty well. And this is a very important job. What do you say?"

Oli's icy stare burns my mind. "If you think it's best."

"I think it is." He pats my shoulder and heads out of the kitchen. "We'll speak about it in the morning then."

When I get to my room, a candle sits by my door along with a little suede bag. A note is attached to the drawstring.

> *To replace your ruined pair.*
> *—Oli*

I empty the contents of the bag. It's a pair of brown leather gloves. They're durable. And much more suitable for labor than my silk ones. I slip them on and admire them in the candlelight. They're the right size.

I glance across the hall. Before I can think too much about it, I knock on Oli's door. I hear clattering inside, and I suddenly remember that she injured her feet.

She answers the door, leaning on a cane. Her eyes widen when she sees me.

"Oh, I'm sorry. I didn't mean to interrupt anything." That strange blue light is still emanating from her room, but she closes her door so I can't peek inside.

I wonder if someone is in there with her. There were a lot of attractive witches at Julianna's ceremony. Any one of them could be in Oli's room right now.

But Oli chuckles. "You aren't interrupting anything." She glances at my gloved hands. "Do you like them?"

I raise my hands so she can see them on me. "I do. They're wonderful. Where did you get them?"

"They were a gift but felt a little too fancy for my liking. I thought you'd like them."

I detect the subtle jab but ignore it. "Well, thank you anyhow. How bad are your feet?"

She lifts her left foot. "This one is worse than the other. It might take some time for them to heal, though. Hilde's tea only works on minor ailments."

I shake my head. "Well, what on earth were you thinking? Walking over sharp wood and broken glass without any shoes. Didn't you stop to think about yourself?"

She grins, her fangs twinkling. "Oh, you're one to talk."

"I'm not sure what you mean."

She tilts her head. "That stunt in the backyard. Had to play hero, didn't you? You just ran out there to gather more wood. I could've done it. Or Hilde. But no, you—"

"Unbelievable," I scoff. "You could've done it? The witch with the bloody feet? Or Hilde? The witch who keeps telling us over and over again that she *only* does architectural magic. Who else could've done a thing about it?"

Oli falls quiet. It feels a bit nice, reveling in her silence, thinking I've won.

"It cost you, didn't it?" she asks. She points to the burn mark on my chest. "What happened to your fancy locket?" Her eyes trace back up to mine. "You know, I notice things, too. You don't fly. You use a wand . . . and that plump lady at the ceremony said you were the best in grade school. Now why would the best witch need a wand? That's for witches who can't focus their power."

I swallow. "What are you getting at?"

"I heard you. In Rose Woods. You used an incantation."

Silence falls over the hallway. I can distantly hear the rain pattering against the window at the end of the hall. She stares at me, but I don't flinch under her gaze.

"Are you really a witch?" she asks.

"Of course I am."

"But you don't have any internal power," she surmises and taps her heart for good measure. "You're not really a witch."

"I am."

"Where do you get your power from then?" she asks.

"I'm not telling you."

"Let me guess. Your locket?" She squints, analyzing my body. I want to cover up. "And judging by how hard you pushed yourself out there, I'm guessing it's done for?"

Damn her. Must she continue to be right? Is this how it feels when I analyze others? It's very annoying.

"No, I don't have it anymore."

"Oh." She chuckles in surprise and leans on her cane. "Look, maybe I owe you an apology, yeah? I didn't know you were power deficient. Were you born that way?"

"What? No." I shake my head. "And if anyone should be apologizing, it's me. I ruined your harvest today. I didn't know how important that wood was going to be. I should've been more truthful. I'm sorry."

"Does Frank know you can't cast enchantments anymore?"

Guilt floods my stomach. I shake my head.

Oli sighs. "Well, I think you should be honest with him, too. He's not as mean as he looks."

I will tell Frank. Eventually. "He's assigning me to another job. But I can still help you around the house."

She waves. "No, just do what Frank tells you to do. You'll be better off there. You'll find fewer ways to annoy me."

I knew I was upsetting her earlier, but hearing her admit it only makes me sink in my teeth and fight back.

"Well, who said that you didn't annoy *me*?"

An amused smile lights her face. "What?"

"Running around like the world is some big joke. Calling me *princess* and *lazy*—"

She laughs. "Hey now, I never called you lazy."

"You implied it. And that's most annoying. I'm a hard worker. Maybe not as hard as a fool who works herself during the heights of a raging storm, but a hard worker nonetheless. You annoy me, too."

Oli stands still, mouth agape. Then she laughs, her voice ringing sweet like light and fresh air. She pushes her voluminous hair out of her face and eases up her left foot.

I frown. "I don't understand what's so funny."

"Damn it all, Saika." She finally looks at me, smile still fixed and tears glistening in her dark eyes. "I like you."

This shuts me down completely. My head spins, untethered from my body. What did she just say, Fi?

And if that's not bad enough, she continues. "I think you're beautiful. And you speak funny." She chuckles.

My eyes have gone dry. How I wish you were alive, Fi. Then you could tell me what to say to that.

"*But*"—Oli raises her finger—"that's all there is to it. It's fun to tease you."

Well, look at that. Complimented and utterly crushed in one breath.

"Why are you telling me this?" I finally remember to blink and tell myself that the tear cresting my eye is from being dry.

She shrugs. "Sometimes people get the wrong idea about me. So, if you're gonna stay here, then it's only fair that you know that I like to tease. Nothing more." She extends her hand to me.

I stare at it. I can finally see her hand tattoos up close now. They wind around her fingers and wrist like snakes. She wears a plain silver ring on her left hand.

I shake her hand and give her a tight smile. "Nothing more."

"Good." She hobbles back into her room. "Then I'll see you in the morning."

She closes the door, and I finally exhale. I stare at my new gloves and make a fist, the leather tight against my skin.

CHAPTER NINE

It's the fallen star all over again. It burns my hands, but I still hold on to it. You're beside me this time, giggling and clutching my arm. It's strange because you appear as a little girl, and I'm your older sister instead.

"Take it, Sai," you say to me. "And let it heal you." And, oh, how the sound of your voice is like warm sunlight on my face. Aching, and present, and reviving.

I want to talk to you, even if only in my dreams. But you disappear. And I wake up.

The sun crests the distant mountains and streams through my bedroom. The storm has long since passed. All that remains are old raindrops streaking down the windows.

I hold the locket between my fingers. The star is gone, Fi. And even after a good night's rest, I don't know how I feel about it, really.

We found this magical item together. It's the last thing shared between us. And now it's gone.

I exhale as I get up, and my back tweaks with pain. That's new. In the morning, my joints are normally stiff, but when I stand up, my knees feel weak. I sit back on the edge of the bed and massage my legs. I don't know what's going on.

I push past the pain and get dressed. Frank wants to speak to me this morning.

He isn't in the parlor. Or the library. Or the dining room.

He's actually in the garden. Merry tells me so when I come into the kitchen. In the light of the day, the kitchen's changes are much more apparent. Even with limited resources, Hilde did an amazing job fixing it. The light shines through the colorful stained glass above the sink. Detailed designs are grooved into the corbels above the cupboards.

Merry and Morose flit about the kitchen as they cook. Thankfully most of the pots and pans weren't touched by the disaster last night. Morose hovers before the stove, where he grumbles and flips sausages.

"I hope you like angel gruel," he says to me.

"Angel gruel?"

Morose laughs, and Merry swats his arm. "It's not angel gruel. It's angel *food*. Our mama used to make it for us. It's a heavenly grain that angels eat for breakfast."

Merry places a pot on the stove, and I glance inside. The contents are ominously gray, gritty, and bubbling. Oli said they didn't do well in the kitchen. It's a wonder they're still on meal duty.

"Well, it smells delicious." I smile tightly. "I can't wait for breakfast." I make my way out to the back, but Merry stops me.

"Wait, Saika. I wanted to ask you something." He glances back at his brother, who is still frying the sausages.

"Go on and say what you gotta say. I don't care to listen." Morose glances over his shoulder.

Merry shakes his head. "Anyway, I wanted to know if you'd like to join me and Evette for a book club meeting?"

"How delightful." I glance between him and Morose. "But why are you whispering?"

"Well, it's sort of a secret club. We have a picnic and talk about what we've been reading. We have snacks and wine. Morose gets a bit huffy because he's not invited anymore."

I chuckle. "Anymore? Great stars, what did he do?"

"Well—"

"I did nothing but get falsely accused of eating all of Evette's strawberry cake," Morose answers. He jabs a spatula toward Merry. "No one said anything to that glutton Phil about his share."

"Phil doesn't eat!" Merry yells. "I know it was all you. Besides, all you did was complain about not having any pictures to look at."

"Bah!" Morose waves and turns back to his sausages.

Merry looks back at me, brows raised. "Do you see?"

I chuckle. "I see. I'd be delighted to join you. Though, I have to admit it's been years since I've read anything."

"Oh." Merry smiles and goes back to his bubbling pot on the stove. "Your company will be more than appreciated."

I continue outside, hearing Morose and Merry bicker behind me.

"Oh, first Phil can join and now Saika?" Morose huffs. "How is that fair?"

"Morose, your sausage is burning."

It's a bit jarring, leaving that encounter to face the terrible damage from last night. The ground is upturned where the fruit trees used to be. The trellises that the tomatoes and cucumbers grew on are broken and toppled over. The garden beds and flowers are decimated.

The arboretum still stands strong, which is a relief. The magic from the sanctuary still dances in the air, electrifying my skin.

Frank rises from the cellar, heaving two large buckets of liquid. It's strange seeing him without his cardigan or suspenders. He's wearing a dirtied flannel instead. A bandanna is wrapped around his head to keep his fur out of his eyes.

"Do you need any help?" I call as I make my way over.

He startles when he sees me. "Oh, 'morning, Saika. And no need. I think I can manage."

I join him on his trek up to the barn, walking beside him and feeling severely overdressed for a day of grueling work.

"Did you sleep well after a night of excitement?" I ask.

We reach Beelzebub's barn, and he grunts when he sets the buckets on the ground. He wipes his paws on his jeans. "Not a wink." He exhales. He touches the barn door, and the wood is splintered from the storm.

"Last night took more from me than I thought. The house is fine, but there's still much to fix. We'll have to pause ceremonies until we're painted and polished again." He procures a wide paintbrush from his back pocket and dips it in one of the buckets.

It glitters in the morning sun. When he brushes it on the door, the paint on the wood darkens, and the splintered pieces fuse together.

"A witch from the market sells this elixir. It can fix about anything. It's saved us so much time and money," Frank explains.

I nod when I see my wavy reflection in the murky liquid. What a work of magic. I roll up my sleeve. "If you have another brush, I can get right to work."

"Saika, that's not necessary."

"Then I can see if Bee has laid any more eggs—"

"Oh no. I . . ." He blinks and looks at me, confused. "I forgot what I was going to say." His eyes search me, looking for an answer.

"Well, you did mention that you had another job for me."

The light returns to his eyes. "Oh, yes! Follow me." He sets his brush down, and we head back to the house.

We cross through the kitchen and head up the stairs. We stop on the second level. I'd forgotten how short the ceiling is. Frank makes a poor attempt to make himself smaller as we go down the hall.

He knocks on a door on the left side. It swings open to Ignatius smoking a pipe, which is odd, isn't it? It's so early in the morning. His hand rests on his suspenders.

"You were supposed to be here earlier," Ignatius says to Frank. He looks unimpressed when he sees me. "Come on in. I guess you forgot."

Ignatius's room, like mine, is spacious on the inside. But while I only have a bedroom, he's equipped with a small kitchenette, complete with a sink and counter and cupboards. Seems a bit unfair.

His furniture is appropriate for his elvish size, so when I sit on his sofa, my knees nearly touch my chest. Frank wisely chooses to stand.

Books litter every inch of Ignatius's room. From the hardwood floor to the short ceiling. They're sprawled over the floor near my feet. They're even spilled on his bed. It makes me wonder where he sleeps.

A desk sits near the front-facing window; it's covered with papers, quill pens, and more books.

But the most interesting thing in his room is the matte-black cauldron inside the kitchenette. He must concoct potions, then.

Ignatius hops onto his desk chair. He sets down his pipe after one last puff. His face hardens when he looks at me.

"So, you're gonna work with me then?" he asks.

"I am?" I look over at Frank.

"I told Ignatius about your star."

"You mean the one I no longer have?"

"But you are familiar with its power. You can tell Ignatius everything you know about fallen stars. And spells. I saw you out there, Saika. Your impromptu spells are powerful. You don't have to be a witch to see that."

My attention unwillingly flicks back to the cauldron. "Even if I tell you everything I know, how will it be of any use to you? You aren't witches. You can't do enchantments."

"Not without a power source. You said yourself that the star granted you enough power that you didn't even have to use your own. Non-witches, beasts like myself, can cast enchantments if we have the right tools."

"Right . . . I suppose." I feel Ignatius's eyes on me. He's been staring me down, puffing on his pipe.

"Is this what you do all day then?" I ask him. "Locked in your room, playing with magic?"

"*Playing*," Ignatius spits out. "Don't you know how much I saved your life—everyone's life—last night?"

Frank moves between us. "Enough."

Ignatius settles back in his chair. A moment of silence passes. Frank looks unsure how to proceed without tripping off any more land mines.

"How *did* you discern that?" I ask, tilting my head to see Ignatius around Frank's body. "Can you predict the future?"

"You make it sound as if I'm some two-bit carnival swindler."
Ignatius stands to his feet. "I read and infer the magical patterns
of the natural world. I study the earth, the air, the mountains
that produce the same magical components that exist in *your*
body." He jabs a finger at me. "I do real, honest research. Not like
some oblivious magical hag who doesn't even understand how
enchantments or spells *work*."

I glance up at Frank. "Why am I here listening to this vitriol?"

"You have invaluable information and experience, Saika," he
says very gently. I'm not sure if it's said just to contrast Ignatius's
harshness. "And I haven't been completely honest with you,
either."

"You don't have to tell her." Ignatius inspects me.

"No, I want to." Frank keeps his eyes on me. "The storms at
Ash Gardens aren't behaving normally. They're happening more
frequently. And last night was the worst we've ever seen."

"Why is that?"

Frank looks away, but Ignatius answers. "We don't know, but
that's what I'm trying to find out. The house keeps falling apart,
and predictions can only get us so far. So when I say we need
materials for the repairs, Frank *has* to listen to me or else Ash
Gardens *will* fall."

Frank hasn't said a word, so he must be telling the truth.
"Why do you need to know about fallen stars?" I ask.

Frank pulls a chart from the desk.

"Hey!" Ignatius yells.

Frank unfurls the chart. It's a map of stars and constellations
beneath an illustration of long, thick trees. "A star parade is coming our way."

Ignatius rolls his eyes. "And one of the stars will fall in Rose
Woods."

"Oh."

Oh. That's all I can say, really. *Oh.*

A fallen star. Here? A powerful token. A host of incalculable magical power that drastically changed my life. Your life, Fi.

"That's an awful lot of power for just . . . what? Repairs for a house? A garden?" I feel like I'm shaking. "It's a *fallen star.* It has the power to change fate, you know. With it, you can cure sicknesses, and move entire mountains and seas, and . . ."

You can even resurrect a life.

Frank finally joins me on the sofa. It dents where he sits, and I lean forward.

"Saika, it's not just about repairing the house. Something is amiss at Ash Gardens. I'm not sure if it's the magic from the arboretum or if this old house is just finally breaking down. But with this star and with the help of Ignatius and his research, we could possibly right what has been broken."

I stare between them. They just want to use it to fix their home. There's nothing wrong with that. I sigh. "What would you like me to do?"

"You can help Ignatius draft incantations for the house. He's a bit swamped with research, between keeping the house from falling and figuring out exactly when the star will fall. If you can give him insight on how to use a star, it would be most helpful."

"I'll do what I can."

Frank sighs with relief. "I'm not sure if I'm a firm believer in fate. But I think you're meant to be here, Saika. Your help could save this place. And, by saving Ash Gardens, save me."

If I can be honest, Fi, losing the star felt like a piece of me crumbled away. The piece of me who reveled in my excellence at casting enchantments. The piece of me who was proud to be a witch.

But it also feels like I've regained something. I don't have to worry about conserving power anymore. I am a bit excited, I'll admit, to prove myself without using any enchantments. By removing my power, I could finally see what I could do without *any* help.

Now, there's a new star to tempt me, and I wish I'd never heard about it.

But Frank needs help. And I would never turn my back on him in his time of need.

"I think I'm meant to be here, too."

He pats my knee and stands from the couch. I nearly shoot up with him. "You two have much work to do. I'll bring up your breakfast then."

"If those idiot cherubs are cooking, I'll skip for today," Ignatius says.

I suddenly remember the angel gruel Merry had boiling on the stove. "Actually, I second that idea."

Frank laughs. "You two don't know what you're missing." He stops at the door. "Saika, one last thing. I ask that you keep this job to yourself. No one knows about the state of the house or the star. I don't want them to worry."

I nod. "Of course, Frank. You have my word."

Ignatius groans and jots down a few words on a pad of paper. He stares back at me.

"You're doing this on purpose, aren't you?"

I shrug. "I don't know what you mean."

He grinds his teeth. "What's the most powerful enchantment you've cast with a star?"

"You know, I don't really remember. Perhaps my tea was too cold, and I needed to warm it up?"

He fixes me with his stare again. "How did you find the star then?"

"I . . ." The memory trickles in unwillingly. The image of you and me, Fi, running in the meadow behind Nana's house. The star parade vanishes as quickly as it came. We see a bright light shooting downward instead of away with the rest of the stars. At first it looks majestic, a soft white light bowing toward the earth. Then it plummets, its trail thinning like lightning until it strikes the ground. Harsh wind nearly blows us flat on our backs.

Curious and giddy, we run toward it in the high grass. I remember the ends of your blue scarf flapping in the wind as you run. You loved wearing that scarf. You would've worn it with every dress if our mother would've let you.

We finally find the star in a large crater. It burns hot and white. As we get nearer, we choke on black gas rising from the star. I keel over, coughing profusely. You take the blue scarf from around your neck and hold it against my face.

You gift me your scarf, yet you take on the brave task of venturing into the crater to pick up the star. It burns you, but the star cools down after your touch. It's a lot smaller than I thought it would be. It fits in your hand.

You hold up your pinky, and I hold up mine. And we swear. This moment. This power. This secret. It's ours to share. And we'll never tell a soul about the miracle we've witnessed together.

Saika, what have you done?

My eyes blink from being dry. My hand reaches up and fiddles with the end of my blue scarf. Your blue scarf.

I focus on Ignatius and clear my throat. "I was young. It was such a long time ago, I hardly remember."

Ignatius relents. "Fine. If you won't tell me, then just sit there and keep quiet." He turns around in his chair and pulls a book off the stack on his desk.

I gaze over his room, my hands over my knee, as I assess exactly how much this space is a pigsty. I don't see how anyone could focus in here.

"So," I begin.

"No." He picks up his pipe again and swiftly lights it.

"You don't know what I was going to say."

He blows smoke into the air. "I don't want you cleaning up my room. It's fine the way it is."

I stand. My knees crack when I do. Damn it, I don't know what's going on with my body. Ignatius eyes me curiously, and I speak to interrupt the silence. "Ah, I see now. You're a fortune teller, *and* you can read minds. You and Hilde ought to have a club."

"I'm not a fortune teller. I read and infer patterns—"

"Okay, yes. Whatever you'd like to call it." I cross my arms and peer around his room. "How did you know about the storm, again? And the house almost collapsing?"

He chuckles. "You want answers, but you won't give me any of yours? You arrogant witch."

"And you've been a crotchety old elf. Unkind. Unpleasant. Of course I don't want to divulge my innermost secrets with you."

"Old? I'm hardly two hundred years old."

I shake my head. "Look. Perhaps we got off on the wrong foot. Frank would like us to work together, but we can't go on like this. Why don't we properly introduce ourselves?" I hold out my hand. "Hello, my name is Saika. I'm a Music witch, and I'm new here at Ash Gardens."

Ignatius looks at me with a dead expression. He slowly removes the pipe from his mouth and blows smoke toward me. "I know who you are. I saw you walking up that first day. Bumbling about in the rain."

"Why does everyone think I was bumbling?"

"I don't need to know any more about you."

I step away to take a better look at all of his belongings. "Then I'll just infer and make my own patterns about you."

I stop at a shelf near the kitchenette. It's filled with antique relics of such high quality. A bronze compass in a locked case. An artisan-crafted dish holding a lone thick-banded ring. It's studded with diamonds and an orange gemstone in the center. It looks far too small to fit Ignatius's pudgy fingers.

"Ah, what's this? Did this belong to your mother? Or your nana?"

It's only in my hands for a second. Ignatius, light on his feet, makes his way over, jumps up, and plucks the ring from my hand.

"Alright, fine." He stomps back over to his desk. He tosses the ring in the bottom drawer and slams it shut with his foot.

"I knew the storm was coming because I noticed the patterns of the clouds and the behavior of the birds over Ash Gardens. And as for my magical research . . ." He leans over his desk and brings out a ledger, holding it up for me to see.

"I keep record of all of the storms we've had, the rain, how frequent, and the severity of damage caused by each storm. The severity of the storm correlates to the severity of the damage. Doesn't take a scientist to realize that, right? Right." He closes the ledger. "I predicted it was going to be a bad storm last night. The damage was going to be catastrophic. I told Frank to harvest enchanted wood ahead of time so we'd be prepared. But you made sure we didn't, remember?"

I ignore the warm flush on my cheeks. "I apologized for that. And I fixed it, didn't I?"

He hops back in his chair. He turns to his book. "You got lucky. But I guess dealing with magic, luck is the highest currency there is."

I bite the inside of my cheek. "Thank you for saving our lives. I'm sorry if I hadn't said it before."

He doesn't say anything. He continues reading.

"And . . ." I sigh. "We found the star behind my nana's house."

He picks his head up, but he doesn't turn around. He inconspicuously picks up a pen and writes. "Where does she live?" he asks.

I laugh. "You may think I'm joking, but I honestly don't remember. I was just a girl. But she lived in an entirely different country, if that helps."

He scribbles on his pad, but still doesn't look back. "Go on."

"Well, it was my sister and I who found it. About midday, perhaps . . ."

I tell him the story, walking the length of his room, back and forth. He doesn't look at me the entire time, and honestly, I think I prefer it that way. Finally telling someone else the story feels a bit freeing.

And if I'm not looking at Ignatius, I'm just telling this story to myself in a messy, crowded, dusty room full of books. I'm not breaking my promise to you, Fi. It's still just our secret. It's still, and will always be, just you and me.

CHAPTER TEN

It's been a few days, and Oli's feet are beginning to heal. At least enough so that she's mobile and isn't sequestered in her room all day.

Ordinarily, I'd speak to you every day, Fi. I've never gone this long without addressing you.

I've been exhausted. I get called to Ignatius's room early in the morning. I've forgone having breakfast with the others and instead spend it with Ignatius and his mountain of dusty books. And it seems being on research duty means that I'm exempt from meal duty as well. I should be happy about it. But I couldn't help but feel a bit guilty when Morose questioned it in front of everyone at dinner last night.

Frank merely said that Ignatius and I have an important task and left it at that. Everyone returned to eating, but that didn't deflate that horrible feeling I had. I want to do more to assist the house. I'm tired of reading mind-numbing texts all day. So, this morning, I'm seeking to change that.

Before daybreak, I get dressed and quietly head downstairs. It's still dark, but when I pass the windows, I catch a glimpse of dawn encroaching on the mountains. Outside, the air is brisk, and the sky is slowly bidding farewell to night.

I take a deep breath and head toward the barn, nervously holding my empty locket between my fingers. Hopefully, Beelzebub is asleep so I can get in and out without waking her.

It's daybreak when I finally emerge from the barn. My heart is pounding, sweat lining my forehead, but in my arms, I'm carrying the last eggs from Beelzebub's nest. I managed to snag four dragon eggs right from underneath her. *Four!*

A silly grin on my face, I gaze up at the blue, cloudless sky. I did it, Fi. Without an enchantment. I was capable of doing something on my own.

Although, Beelzebub did wake near the end and sent a hurl of fire my way. I managed to save myself just in time. If I had moved any slower, they would've had to plant my ashes alongside yours, Fi.

"What's all this?" Oli's voice, smug and light, greets me when I enter the kitchen carrying the eggs. She's still using her cane, favoring her left foot. It's still bandaged. She fills a pitcher of water from the cistern tap. "Having fun with Bee out there?"

"I wanted to help in some way other than reading all day." I settle the eggs on the counter. "And you should be resting." I turn off the water.

"I can work just fine." She reaches for the pans hanging above the stove. Her cane clatters to the floor. She freezes with her left foot hovering, deciding whether to pick up the cane or get the out-of-reach pan.

I stand back, arms crossed. "Go on, then."

She grumbles, hopping on her right foot to pick up her cane, then goes back to reaching for the pan. "It might take me longer to cook, but I'm tired of taking it easy. I need to get the rest of our harvest from Rose Woods. I need to fix the generator. Frank's been bustin' his little wolfy tail doing repairs when I should be—"

I stand on my toes and grab the pan she's been failing to get. "Then allow me to help. You hurt yourself defending the house. You should be resting." I release the pan to her. "So I'd like to have your meal duty today."

She ignites the stovetop, her face fixed in deep thought. "You can't. Frank says you have an important job." Her tone is devoid of malice, but I still feel a touch of guilt.

"I've been reading dusty old books for the past couple of days. I need something else to do." I move to the icebox. It's nearly empty. "What happened to all of the food?"

Oli shrugs, picking up chicken eggs from the counter. She cracks a few and whisks them in a bowl. "This is all we have left. The storm destroyed the garden. We haven't been able to send off any more produce with Morose, but thanks to you, we'll have Bee's eggs to sell at the market."

She pours the whisked eggs onto the sizzling pan, then nods her head toward the cupboard. "If you're gonna stand there, get out the loaf of bread. It's a bit old, but we can eat it today before it molds."

I do as she asks, and when I hand her the bread, she purses her lips. "So . . . you've been reading these past couple of days?"

She doesn't look at me, as if she's ashamed to be asking. "That's what Frank's got you doing?"

"In part," I answer her. "It's a bit more than that."

She nods, thinking to herself as she flips the eggs. "I see."

She's quiet this morning. Quieter than I know her to be. I haven't been helping her with chores around the house. And perhaps she's feeling a bit stressed with her workload.

"I'd like to do your meal duty today," I offer again. "You're still healing and have loads to do. Allow me to take at least one thing off your plate."

Oli chuckles. She sets down the spatula. "You know, how can I refuse such an offer?" She looks me up and down. "You sure you can handle this? Breakfast, lunch, and dinner on your own?"

"Of course."

She raises her brow. "Well then." She pulls an apron off the hook near the stove. She takes one hobbling step toward me and gently turns me around.

My breath stills when her arms wrap around me, and she pulls the apron tight across my torso.

"Frank is allergic to bananas." Her breath tickles the back of my neck. "Merry doesn't like raspberries, and Phil won't eat a thing that has broccoli in it."

"But Phil doesn't even eat." I turn around, and she's grinning much too close to my face. Heat rises up my neck, but I remain cool. She's a shameless flirt. I won't fall prey to her teasing.

"We accommodate everyone. I'll see you at breakfast."

She heads out of the kitchen but then pauses before the double doors. "Saika, whatever it is that Frank has you and Ignatius doing, is it dangerous?" she asks. Her teasing facade from just a moment ago is gone. Worry looks foreign on her face.

"It isn't. I promise."

I'm not sure if she believes me. She exhales. "Alright then. Looking forward to brekkie. Make something good." And with that, she leaves.

I hate keeping my job a secret from everyone. Frank only wants to protect them, I know. And he doesn't want them to get involved. But I think they'd want to be involved. I'm sure Oli would jump at the chance to help him.

A bit later, after I complete a whole batch of omelets with onions, cherry tomatoes, and toasted bread, and also find a few frozen sausage links in the icebox, Frank comes into the kitchen.

He's surprised to see me, and he stands lost in the middle of the kitchen. "Now, what did I come in here to do?" He scratches his head.

"You like to make yourself coffee in the morning."

"Oh, right." He gazes at the spread on the counter. "What brings you down here so early?"

"I gathered the rest of Bee's eggs, and I took Oli's meal duty. She's still on the mend, although she doesn't act like it."

"Quite an eventful morning then." He glances at the hem of my dress and I look down. It's been marred, singed black from Beelzebub's fire. Damn. Now, I'm down to only one dress.

"The help is appreciated, Saika, but I'd prefer if you spent your time with Ignatius." He glances at the jar that used to be filled with coffee beans. There's only enough for a few more cups. "Running out of coffee, then," he mutters.

"That's not the only thing. We're running out of everything. I can do more than researching with Ignatius—"

"No, Saika. You need to—"

"This is important, too, Frank." I stand before him. "I know you want us to focus on our research, but this house and everyone in it is important, too. We can't go hungry while pursuing answers."

He sets his empty coffee mug on the counter. "I suppose you're right. We'll talk about what we should do during breakfast today."

I take his mug and begin making him one last cup of coffee.

We meet for breakfast, and I'll admit, it's a bit dismal compared to the other meals we've had at this table. I feel their eyes when I set the food out. Hilde voices what they're all thinking.

"How nice of you to take over Oli's meal duty." She smiles and fans her napkin on her lap.

"I thought Saika wasn't meant to cook," Merry says.

"Yeah," Morose seconds. "Oli doesn't need charity. Her arms aren't broken."

Oli throws a spoon across the table, and it hits his naked, hairy chest. "It's called being kind, you ogre."

Morose's mouth twists in a frown. "You ill-begotten demon spawn. Call me an ogre one more time." He stands on his chair. "And I'm gonna—"

"Tucking hell, do what?" Oli smiles, teasing him with her sharp fangs. "Kick me in the shins?"

"Oh, I'll do more than that—"

"Morose, stop it." Merry grabs his brother's shoulder and forces him to take a seat with a surprising grip. He looks at me. "Thank you for breakfast, Saika."

"It was no trouble at all." I glance at Frank. He still hasn't touched his food. He rubs his temple with his paw. "Are you alright, Frank?"

He shakes his head. "I'm fine. There was something I was supposed to say . . ."

"It's alright, I will." I pat his arm and address everyone else. "We have to talk about our resources. After the storm damaged the garden, we aren't able to grow any more food. Isn't that right, Merry?"

He nods. "It'll be some time before the ground is ready to grow anything again. The soil is still too wet, and we keep getting this blasted rain. I'm not sure if it'll dry up again."

"And the fruit trees have been here for years," Evette adds. "It'll be some time before we can plant new ones."

Guilt floods my stomach. "I'm sorry for using them for the enchantment, Evette."

She waves her hand. "No, Saika, don't apologize. You did what you had to. We'll grow more."

"But we counted on selling that produce." Morose rubs his chubby arm, sore from when Merry yanked him. "We have a few things left at the stand, but once they're sold, that's it."

"You'll have to stretch that money as much as you can. In the meantime, Frank"—Hilde turns to him—"I think it may be time to charge for the planting ceremonies."

"Absolutely not." Frank's voice booms across the table. We stiffen in our seats. "I won't do it. That's not an option."

Hilde is unperturbed by Frank's tone. She takes out a cigarette and lights it. "Only a suggestion. If not, there might not be an Ash Gardens to even host ceremonies."

"I just . . ." He cradles his head. "I'm sorry. I'm not feeling too well. I think I need to lie down." He leaves the dining room, and we hear the heavy doors from his wing swing open and shut.

Oli picks off a piece of mold from her bread. "He's been actin' a bit strange, hasn't he? Is he gettin' sick?"

"I'm tellin' ya. He's getting old," Merry suggests, and Hilde fixes him with a stare.

"Getting older doesn't equate to sickness. He's got a lot on his shoulders. I can feel it."

Oli stands to her feet and grabs her cane. "Well, the generator's still busted, but I'll do what I can to get it to work. Hilde, I know your expertise is limited—"

Hilde puts out her cigarette. "No, it's fine. I'll take a look at it and see what I can do." She points her cigarette holder toward Morose. "I have some healing teas you can take to the market to sell, too."

"No one wants your disgusting grass tea."

"Just take it, you oaf," Hilde retorts.

Breakfast is over, and everyone heads to their duties. I, on the other hand, feel helpless.

"Wait," I say. Oli is the only one who stops. Hilde and Morose leave the dining room. Evette and Merry head out to the garden to salvage what crops they can.

"What should I do? There must be something."

Oli rubs the back of her neck. "Don't you have some reading to do?" She takes her cane and sees herself out.

There must be something else I can do. I can't go up to that suffocating room and read until dusk.

Then an idea hits me. I know how I can help.

I get up from the table, but I suddenly feel a hand grab my wrist. I yelp and yank it free, but then I realize it's only Phil. I thought he followed Evette out to the garden.

"Goodness, Phil. You nearly gave me a heart attack."

He doesn't say anything.

I glance at his plate at the end of the table. All of his food is still there. "Did you enjoy breakfast?" I ask.

Silence.

I feel his hand again, this time gentler. He pats my arm, but I'm not sure what it means. I don't have time to play charades.

"I'm sorry, Phil. There's something I must do. We'll have to discuss this later."

Phil lets me go, and I hurry up to my room.

I catch Morose before he heads out for the city. He's loading up his bag with some salvaged crops and Beelzebub's eggs. I try not to gush over his adorable ivy cap or the matching vest over his naked chest. "Don't you look handsome."

His face reddens. "What do you want?"

I hand him a tiny pouch, and it jingles in his hand. He opens it immediately. "What's all this?"

"I had some travel money stored in my suitcase, and I forgot about it."

His eyes widen, ogling the silver coins inside the bag. "You just *forgot* about all this money. Who forgets about this?"

"Please, Morose, get everything we need for Ash Gardens. Food. Supplies. Fruit tree saplings for Evette and Merry. Coffee beans for Frank."

Morose gives me a playful punch on the arm. "First Bee's eggs, and now you're showering us with money. You might not be so bad, Your Majesty."

I feel like Frank, hurrying to assemble Ignatius's cold breakfast on a tray. Frank didn't get a chance to send it up to him this morning. Ignatius must be starving, and if he says anything about my cooking, then this tray is going upside his head.

I take a short break on the second platform to catch my breath. I've been running around this house all morning—the fatigue must finally be getting to me. The joints in my arms and knees feel sore. They click and grind as I move.

I continue to the second level, but my boot catches on a raised plank of wood, and I go tumbling forward.

The tray flies out of my hands, and the plate of eggs and sausage crashes on the floor. I've also done a good job banging up my shin.

"Damn it," I whisper and rub the sore spot on my leg. What did I trip over?

The top step of the stair is poking up. The wood is splintered and broken. That wasn't there before.

I make quick work cleaning up the spilled breakfast. One of the sausage links has rolled over to a darkened corner of the hall. When I pick it up, I notice a brown paper package lying there on the runner. It has the weight and feel of a book.

"Is this my breakfast, then?" Ignatius asks.

It's odd seeing him so far from his room. He's puffing on his pipe, his white button-up shirt rolled up his stubby arms. He shakes his head at the destroyed breakfast on the tray. "Good thing I wasn't hungry."

"I had a little accident." I point to the warped top step. "Wonder how that got there."

He peers at it boredly. "Things like that appear all the time. Just have that purple witch give it a fix." He heads back to his room. "Don't forget me at lunchtime."

"Wait," I call out, and he actually stops. "This book. Did you drop it here?"

I hold up the book, but he doesn't bother to look at it. "You think I'd let one of my precious books leave my room?" he asks. "If you're gonna do research, then let's go. If not, stop wasting my time."

"You go on. I have some things to do today."

I hear his door slam down the hall.

I tear off the paper packaging. The book is actually a journal bound with ribbon. Glossy peonies and vines are illustrated on the front. Whoever created this did so with lots of love.

I flip to the title page. "'Records of Dragons, Beasts, and Mythical Creatures and Their Relationship to Magic. A documented assessment and research by . . .'" My eyes widen. "Kye?"

Curiosity beckons me, and I flip to the other pages. There are sections upon sections of notes. They're well organized. Kye had remarkable penmanship.

There's mention of dragons from all different countries, but I stop when I see Beelzebub's name. She has a section all to herself.

This is amazing. More information on Beelzebub means I could possibly tame her. It could mean a way to gain more money and sell more eggs. This may save Ash Gardens.

Kye had written a list of Beelzebub's attributes:

- *Hails from the North*
- *Fire-breathing*
- *Naturally cold-blooded but able to adapt to different climates*
- *The color of ripened lemons*
- *Scaly skinned*
- *Four legs*
- *Venomous tail*

I pause. I read it again.

Venomous tail. Venomous tail? My eyes bulge.

I could've been killed by Beelzebub. Did Oli know this? Bee could have poisoned me.

Beelzebub is a Northern dragon, Kye writes, *but her size suggests otherwise. She should be more than three times her current size, but she hasn't grown in all the years I've known her. Her wingspan measures roughly twenty feet.*

In the thick of it, she felt much larger than that.

Because she's from the North, Bee enjoys dark spaces and prefers to dwell in caves. Her diet consists of butchered pig, cow, and lamb. Bee personally likes lamb over everything else.

In another subsection, Kye details mating and procreation. Her eggs. This is what I'm looking for.

And when I'm done reading, I wish I never had.

I gently close the journal, and I stand in the hall, thinking to myself.

Saika, what have you done?

I look up, and a bowler hat floats before me. "Phil?" I ask, and he nods.

"Did you place this book here?"

He nods again.

I stare down at the cover. At breakfast, he was trying to tell me something, but I wouldn't listen. "You were trying to tell me about Beelzebub." I glance back up at him. "Thank you. I know what I have to do."

I hurry back downstairs and run to the backyard.

The cellar door is open, and I hear Hilde and Oli bickering

about the generator—Hilde's voice low and condescending, Oli's much higher and irritated.

I find Merry and Evette tending to the garden, on their hands and knees salvaging whatever plants they can. Despite the unfortunate scene before them, they're laughing and talking. They seem much more approachable, so I go to them instead.

"Oh, Saika!" Evette beams. "What's wrong? You look shaken up."

"I'm fine. I just have perhaps a strange question. Where can I find butchered lamb? It's for Bee."

Merry and Evette exchange confused looks, but they still help me find the outdoor icebox where Frank stores all of Beelzebub's food. They don't ask any questions when I heave the bloody meat onto newspaper.

I head up to Beelzebub's barn alone. Kye's words ring in my head.

Beelzebub's species prioritizes community and love above everything else.

I reach the barn and release a shaky breath. Yes, Beelzebub has a venomous tail. But if I do this right, I may never see it.

I open the barn door. It's dark, but I step inside anyway. The door slams behind me.

Northern dragons have mating seasons, and they choose their partners for life. If a dragon is separated from their horde, like Bee, they will adapt to reproduce asexually. Once this process begins, their goal is to build a colony of their own. They seek to create a community.

I was so careless, Fi. I wanted to help Ash Gardens so desperately that I didn't even realize what I was doing to Bee.

Tears prick my eyes as I walk toward the center of the barn. It's foolish to come here unprepared, I know. I don't have any power to save myself if Beelzebub hurls another ball of fire my way. But I needed to come now. I needed to see her.

"I'm sorry, Beelzebub," I call out into the darkness. Then I hear her. A long screeching cry that echoes into the rafters.

I set the bloody lamb on the ground and take a step back. I call up to her again. "I had no idea that you were trying to build a family, and we just kept taking your eggs from you. We took away your family. No wonder you became so angry." I place a hand over my heart. "Truly, Bee, I'm so sorry."

She doesn't screech or roar. Her wings flap, and a slight breeze rushes over me. She wooshes down from the rafters and lands with a heavy thump. She sniffs toward me, possibly sniffing out the lamb.

"I'm not here to take your eggs, Bee. I won't. Not anymore."

Beelzebub is a kind, gentle creature, Kye had written. *Once trust is established, she will become docile and playful. Like a dog with very large, sharp teeth. Sometimes, I sit with her in the barn, and I'll read to her. She'll set her head at my feet and breathe gently. How I love that Beelzebub.*

Beelzebub comes closer. She chomps through the wrapped meat on the ground and finishes it quickly. Her red eyes glint in the darkness.

"I'm sure you miss Kye very much." I reach out my hand. She steps forward, and I feel the heat from her breath.

Then her heavy head rests against my palm. Heat emanates through the tough leather of my glove. "You're a good girl, Bee."

And this time she doesn't screech. In fact, I feel her purr.

CHAPTER ELEVEN

There's something wrong with me, Fi.

Over the course of this week, I've been extremely exhausted. More than I normally am. My joints ache, and I'm slow getting around the house. I could be stretching myself too thin.

I've been pouring myself into research with Ignatius. I've recorded all the incantations I've ever cast. I've explained to Ignatius in great and excruciating detail how I used a portion of the fallen star to fuel my enchantments.

He asked what happened to the rest of it, and I clammed up. I don't think I'm ready to divulge that information. I may never be ready.

I think Ignatius realizes that, so he's tasked me with reading even more volumes of text about potions and spells. Topics we learned in grade school, Fi. I already know about the magical anatomy of a witch, and how we are able to cast enchantments from our own power. Or the way the earth inherently has magical properties, and we share parts of our DNA with it.

I've learned all of this before, and I'm bored to tears. When I thought I'd be reading again, I hoped it would be something fun like when we would read lore and high legends to each other. But

I fear Ignatius is only giving me menial tasks to keep me busy and appease Frank.

My only saving grace is Kye's journal. I've learned more about Beelzebub and other beasts like her. Every morning, I go out to feed her, and I'll spend just a few extra minutes by her side as she eats, reading Kye's words to her. She hasn't laid any more eggs, and I wonder why that is.

To ease my anxious mind, this morning I've decided to run myself a bath. My body is exhausted, I need something to relax it. There are some lavender petals left, and I sprinkle them in the water.

I get undressed but pause when I catch a glimpse of myself in the mirror. The skin around my neck, right under my jaw, is getting looser. My stomach drops as I further inspect my body.

Age spots have crept up from my hand onto my forearm. When I unravel my headwrap, tufts of black hair unravel with it. And when I analyze the puff of hair in my hand, I see strands of white.

I don't understand what's happening, Fi. My body is ailing me more than normal. Now my hair is turning white and falling out even quicker. It feels like it's all happening so much faster. I don't know what's changed—

My locket glints in the mirror's reflection. I lift the empty locket. The star.

The star must've been keeping me together more than I thought. So when I used the last of it, it expedited the curse.

Blood rushes in my ears. Without the star, my time may soon come to an end.

But all isn't completely lost. The star that's going to fall in Rose Woods. Frank only needs it to fix up Ash Gardens. Perhaps he could part with just a portion of it to help sustain me. At least just a while longer.

The warm water envelopes me when I sink into the tub. It's fine. I'll be fine, Fi. I'll find a way to fix this. I always do.

I top off the bath with hotter water, but when I try to close the tap, the handle doesn't move. I pull again. The handle breaks.

"Oh, stars."

Water rushes into the tub. But before it spills over, I'm able to pinch the valve and finally turn it off. It wreaks havoc on my joints, but at least it's stopped.

I sigh when I look at the broken handle and flex my withered, age-spotted hand. Things have been falling apart in the house lately. Wood splintering on the floor. Wallpaper peeling. I think I even saw some mold in the hallway the other day.

The star is powerful, Fi. We should be able to fix Ash Gardens with it, and also help me. I just need to ask Frank.

After my bath, I find Frank on the veranda. He sits in his rocking chair, reading a book and drinking a glass of iced lavender tea. I can smell it when I pass by him. He's wearing reading glasses and looks deep in thought.

He glances up when I sit in the swing beside him. "'Morning, Saika."

"'Morning, Frank." I'm holding a few books I've taken from Ignatius's hoard. "I can't stand to spend such a nice morning in that elf's stuffy room. I've brought my work down here if that's okay with you."

Frank smiles. "Of course. It gets a bit lonely in the mornings, so I welcome the company."

I pick up the first book. An anthology by an old, famous witch who lived centuries ago. I read the first line over and over again, then close the book.

"I don't seem to know my own strength," I say, and Frank

lifts his head from his book. "I broke the handle on the tub this morning. I'm sorry. I'll fix it."

"Oli will probably get to it before you do." He removes his glasses. "But now that you're here, there's something I've been meaning to ask you."

Oh, good. This could be a great segue to ask him about the star. I didn't know how to open up that conversation.

"Of course." I set my books to the side.

"Are you responsible for the food and supplies that Morose brought from the markets?"

"I am. I had a bit of money left from my days of traveling. It wasn't much, but I think what Morose got with it should last us for a few weeks. At least until we get the garden running again. Now we can continue hosting ceremonies."

"That was very kind of you." He doesn't look particularly happy. "I wish you hadn't, though. Bee should be laying more eggs soon, so you won't have to spend any more of your money."

"Actually, Frank. I don't think we should be collecting Bee's eggs anymore."

"Why not?"

"Well, I . . ." I rummage through my books until I find Kye's journal. "Phil gave this to me."

Frank's eyes widen. "Phil did?" He holds out his paw. "May I see it?" I gladly hand it over, and he grins, running his paw over the cover. "I haven't seen this in years."

He flips through the pages. "Oh, look at her penmanship," he gushes.

I chuckle softly. "Your wife was a remarkable witch. She's very learned and inquisitive. Her findings about beasts and dragons were most helpful. I don't know why Phil gave it to me specifically, but maybe he knew I'd find the passage Kye wrote about Bee. It's where I learned that she reproduces to create a family. We're taking her babies away from her every time we sell her eggs."

Frank pauses. He glances up at me. "I had no idea."

"I don't think Kye would want us treating her beloved Beelzebub this way."

He closes the journal. "Once we have the star, it'll fix the problems with the house. With the garden." He glances down to the journal. "I hope Ignatius soon figures out when it'll fall."

I've heard this kind of talk before, Fi. Frank is holding the star in such high esteem, as if it'll be the answer for everything. But I'm no better. Even now, knowing what I know, I'm still hoping to use the star to fix my own issues.

My decaying body is my penance for partaking in taboo practices. Perhaps I should allow nature to run its course. I'll keep falling apart, much like Ash Gardens, until I'm nothing but dust.

"You know, once we have the star and the house is fixed, I won't need extra help at Ash Gardens anymore." Frank taps on the journal. "Have you thought about your sister's planting at all?"

I haven't thought about your burial for a couple of days, Fi. Your ashes still sit as a reminder on my bedside table. I've been so preoccupied with collapsing kitchens, and stars, and my aching body, that I've forgotten the reason why I came to Ash Gardens in the first place.

But there will come a time when everything will be bright, and perfect, and rosy again at Ash Gardens. And you will be the only thing that remains. You and your ashes and the arboretum.

I won't have an excuse to delay anymore. I won't have anything else preoccupying my mind.

I look at Frank. "I've thought about it, yes."

He pats my arm. "My offer will never change. You're welcome to stay for as long as you'd like." He stands up with a grunt. "Might I hold on to this journal for a bit? I'd like to read some of my wife's words."

"Of course." I smile. "For as long as you'd like."

Frank chuckles, collects his empty glass, and heads back into the house.

I push myself on the swing. I'll find another time to ask him about the star. And it's possibly a good thing that I wait. He'll question why I need a piece of the star, and then I'll have to tell him the ugly truth about my curse. And he'll know I lied about my power.

I look down at my leather gloves. I'm not ready for him to hate me, too.

My body slants back in the swing. It rocks me gently. The lavender from my bath still coats my skin and weighs heavy on my eyelids. The breeze kisses my face and cools me down.

My body is so tired. I'm so tired. The books will be there once I wake from a moment of rest.

It's a strange sensation when you're asleep, and you're aware that you're sleeping, yet you can't stop the events tossing you around in your dream. I'm aware that I'm not awake, Fi, but I'm still very much afraid when I find myself in darkness and cold rain pours over me.

I'm shivering, and when I turn around, I see Ash Gardens. The house is under a massive storm. I don't know if everyone is safe, so I try to run, but a tree springs up and blocks my path. I run again, but I'm met with the same obstacle.

Over and over again, I'm thwarted by trees, and they surround me. And when I finally look up, I see vibrant and colorful leaves. Cool wind laced with magic hits my face. I'm in the arboretum.

A buzzing sound nags my ear, and it startles me awake. A tiny dot of yellow light circles around my head and lands on my nose. I chuckle. "Afternoon, Evette."

The dot doesn't answer. Instead, it zips away, heading down the veranda steps.

"Wait, hold on!" I laugh. I collect my books and follow after the light. The dot waits for me at the bottom of the steps, but when I get near, it takes off again.

"Evette, you're going too fast!" I hike up my dress, laughing giddily. The dot flutters away, and then comes back. It spirals around me before diving toward the back of the house.

I'm running so fast that I collide with a wall. I fall flat into the grass and tweak my back.

The wall groans in pain, and I realize that it's Oli, sprawled on the ground beside me. She rubs her head. "I just got that damn bandage off. You want to break somethin' else?"

"I'm sorry. I didn't see you. Evette was . . ." I've lost sight of the light. It's gone now.

I'm slow to stand but still offer my hand to Oli. She glares at me before conceding and allowing me to help her up.

Oli dusts dirt off her bottom. "Must be nice frolicking during the day."

I roll my eyes. "I was not frolicking."

Oli laughs, skipping circles around me. *"Oh, Evette, wait for me,"* she sings. *"I'm so slow and clumsy. I can't keep up."*

It would be a foolish attempt to hide my grin, so I nudge her shoulder. "I don't sound like that."

She chuckles. "Whatever you say. Now, if you don't mind, I've got some real work to do."

With an unnecessary grunt, she picks up a bucket of that glittering elixir. Some part of me feels like she's flexing her shoulder muscles just to get my attention. I roll my eyes.

"Do you need a hand?" I ask.

"I'm fine. The front steps just need a bit of touching up. Besides, they're waiting for you back there." She nods toward the backyard. She walks off, and I watch her round to the front of the house.

Oli has been working from sunup to sundown, tirelessly. The electricity is still not working. The entire generator needs to be replaced now. I fear that Oli is overextending herself because she can't fix it all. She'll tire herself out one of these days.

In the backyard, the garden beds are bare, but the top layers are finally dry. The trellises have been reconstructed, and the pathways between the garden beds have been redefined. Though, it looks emptier without the fruit trees.

Merry and Evette are sitting on a tanned blanket in the grass.

"Saika!" Evette waves her arms. I come over to see their spread of cheese, strawberries, and scones, all complete with a bottle of wine. Evette sits on a small stack of books.

"What's all this?" I ask with a delighted smile.

Merry sits neatly, holding out a glass of wine for me. His naked chest shows off his freckles, and they're light brown in the sunlight. It brings out the earthy color in his eyes. "Book club."

I join them on the blanket, and Merry makes some room for

me. A saucer filled with scones hovers in the air, is extended toward me.

"Thank you, Phil." I pick one off. Ever since he gave me Kye's journal, I've been thinking of a way to thank him. I just don't know how you show gratitude toward a ghost. "This all looks so wonderful. I wish I had brought something to read."

"Don't worry," Evette says. "We mainly use this as a way to talk."

"Besides, it looks like you have plenty to read." Merry glances at the books cradled in my arms.

"Oh." I set them aside. "Those aren't for play. More mind-numbing than entertaining." My research with Ignatius is a sticky topic, and I don't feel like talking about it. I slide the books behind my back. "What about you two? Any interesting reads?"

I reach for a red book that Evette has chosen for seating, and she flies up.

"No, wait," Merry says, but I've already opened up the book. It's a collection of lore and high legends. Merry's face is as red as a tomato. "I know it's a bit juvenile, isn't it? Mor always gives me grief because I still read them."

"No, are you joking?" I gasp. I flip through the pages and marvel at the high-quality illustrations of towers and castles and monsters. "This is the exact kind of thing that I'd love to be reading. What's your favorite legend?"

Merry lights up. "I'm so happy to hear that, Saika. Well, I adore the legend of the Raboo Pirates. It's a cautionary tale of greed and power and adventure. I loved it as a kid. I still do."

"Oh, yes. The Raboo Pirates. My sister adored that tale as well." I gaze down at the book. "How fascinating. What about you, Evette?"

She sits now atop the breadbasket, legs dangling and

kicking lazily. "I'm not too familiar with legends, but I love hearing Merry talk about them. Personally, I enjoy reading about histories. There's one that I really like, but Merry doesn't like to hear about it."

I frown. "Why not?"

"Well, it's about creation and the history of beasts, fae, and witches," Evette explains. "When I think about our place in the world and how infinitesimal yet large it is, it makes me feel . . . insignificant? But in a good way. This corner of the world is mine to impact and brighten up, even if it doesn't reach the other parts of the world. And I think that's beautiful." She stops, and she glances at Merry. "But when I talk that way, it messes Merry up in the head."

"I just don't like hearing about all that cosmic talk," Merry grumbles, sounding like a record of his brother. "Growing up, we were forbidden to talk that way. We couldn't talk about creation or . . ." His eyes widen. "Death," he whispers.

Evette smirks. "Come on, Merry. You can call Death by his name."

"Are you mad, Evette?" he asks, genuinely afraid. "You dare not speak his name or else he'll be listening and watching you."

Evette placates him with a smile. "Okay, Merry. I won't."

I blink my dry eyes. "Oh, Merry. I had no idea you were so shaken up by . . . well, you know who." I rest my hand on his shoulder. "If it makes you feel any better, lore states that only powerful relics and an ancient spell can summon . . . you know who. You can speak his name. Nothing will come of it."

Merry shakes his head. "No, I know better. You don't say the name. You don't touch him. You don't even look him in the eye lest you fall over dead. Our mama taught us better. I'll be safe, thank you very much."

How funny is that, Fi? Summoning Death is as easy as speaking his name, according to Merry. If only he knew . . .

"Okay, Merry. I won't say his name, either." When I flip his book closed, I notice an inscription on the inside cover.

From your mama,
To my joy, my heart, and my blood.
Merry, Mellow, and Morose.

I pause. "Mellow?" I ask, and the sound of his name is as if I called Death himself.

Merry glances at Evette, and she nods. "It's okay, Merry."

He takes the book back and holds it in his lap. "He was my brother. *Our* brother," he corrects himself. "We're triplets, you see. Morose and I. Mel always sort of kept the peace between us. He kept us from arguing most of the time."

Merry smiles sadly as he thinks back. "He'd sit and listen to me ramble. He was about the only one who could make Morose laugh. He was the best of us, but . . ." He stops, and Evette hovers onto his knee. "I'm alright," he says to her.

Merry looks back at me. "He died in a pillagin' raid. We were delivery cherubs. We'd bring supplies all over town, and we just happened to be at the wrong place at the wrong time. A group of bandits came into town, and we were gonna fly away, but Mellow wanted to stay and help. He . . . uh . . ." Merry sighs. "He just didn't make it."

It's quiet for a moment. Mellow sounds a bit like someone I know, Fi. Always so selfless, you were. Trying to help me to your dying days. Even now, beyond your death, your phantom arms are reaching through the void to help me.

"I'm so sorry, Merry. He sounded like a mighty fine cherub."

"Oh, the best," Merry says with a deflated laugh. I hand him a cloth to dab his eyes. "Morose may seem like he's hardened, but he isn't. He's the softest of us all. Mellow being gone really did a number on him. He wasn't always so angry, you know. He's gotten a lot better since being at Ash Gardens."

I pat Merry's shoulder. "It seems we've all lost . . ." I'm sensing a pattern. "We've all lost someone. Or something." It could be a coincidence. Hilde losing her coven, Frank losing his wife, Merry and Morose their brother, me a sister.

It's a sensitive topic, and although I wish to ask Evette if she's lost someone, too, I don't. No need to open fresh wounds just for the sake of discovery. Instead, I offer a round of fresh strawberries, and I ask them a rousing question about a book they wish they could read all over again.

We only get a few minutes into our discussion when we hear the back doors fly open, and Oli rushes out. She bends over, gasping for breath.

Evette flies up. "Oli, what happened?"

"Ceremony." She regains her breath and stands upright. "There's a ceremony today. Right now. The family is pulling down the road."

"What?" Evette immediately begins packing up the food. "Why didn't Frank say anything?"

"He forgot!" Oli yells. She pushes her hair back from her forehead. "I'm sorry. I'm sorry. Frank hasn't been much help. Let's just . . . Hilde'll greet them, but she can only be around them for a bit. Merry, I want you to direct them and for fuck's sake, put on some pants."

"Right away." He chuckles and helps Evette pack up the picnic.

"Frank is still getting dressed and bumblin' about," Oli

continues. "I don't know what's going through that beast's head. Evette, can you whip something up?"

"I can. But we hardly have enough food as it is. To make a feast for the bereaved would use most of the food we just got."

It falls silent. We all look at Oli, wondering what we should do. She thinks it over only for a second before coming to a decision. "Use whatever you need. We'll figure it out. I'm heading into the arboretum to find a planting spot."

Evette zips up. "Come on, Phil. Carry the food inside." She flies off without a word.

Merry and I are left folding up the blanket. He glances over at me. "Never a dull moment at Ash Gardens. You should probably go get dressed, too."

I glance down at my gray smock. It's been dirtied and stained, but I've done my best trying to keep it clean and presentable. "This is all I have."

"Oh." He blinks. He picks up his books and chuckles. "Don't let Hilde hear you say that."

CHAPTER TWELVE

The next couple of moments happen in a whirlwind. I do very little to make myself look presentable. I wash up my face, spot clean my dress, change out my headscarf, and head down to greet the family of witches in the foyer.

Hilde's still here, and I suppose Merry isn't ready yet. How long does it take to simply put on a pair of pants?

Hilde's eyes widen when she sees me. Her eyes ghost over my frumpy dress, and I'm sure she doesn't even need her gift to detect my embarrassment.

"Hello, I'm Saika." I shake the hand of the first witch I see. She's much older than the other four witches in her party.

I learn that the young man with her is her son, and he's brought his wife and their young daughter. The old witch also brought her daughter, who looks about the same age as me. The deceased is the patriarch of their family, and he'd been married to the old woman for the past forty-seven years.

I express my condolences as Merry finally flutters down the stairs in his best slacks and vest. "Welcome to Ash Gardens," he greets them. "If you can follow me, I'll show you to the parlor."

The family shuffles out, and I follow them, but Hilde stops me. "Are you sure you can handle this?" she asks, voice lowered.

"I don't know what's wrong with Frank, so yes. I'll be happy to step up."

Hilde raises her brow, and further inspects my gray smock. "Are you sure about this dress?"

"What's wrong with it?"

"Oh, Saika." She spins me around, humming to herself. "Twenty-eight. I'll say thirty-six," she mutters.

"Excuse me?"

She grins, but her white eye suddenly flashes and pain laces her face. She rubs her head. "Don't mind me. I should head upstairs. Too much emotion down here."

"Did you get a feel from the family to make a gift?"

Hilde smirks at me as she ascends the stairs. "Please, child. It's what I do."

Merry's voice trails from the parlor, asking questions of the bereaved and offering refreshments. He's not used to this act. But he's buying time for Frank. What the hell is he doing?

I knock on Frank's door. The embossed image of him and his wife is starting to corrode. I wonder how long that's been there.

The door opens a moment later. Frank is still in his pajamas.

"Frank, what is going on?"

He holds up his paw. "I'm not feeling well, Saika. It's taking me some time to get ready. I'm . . . not all there right now."

"Clearly." I try to enter his wing, but he blocks the doorway. I gaze up at him. "Let me help you."

"I need you to help them." He gestures toward the parlor. "I promise, I'll be out. Just give me some time."

"Frank, I can't just—"

"Please, Saika. Thank you." He ends the conversation and shuts the door. The sound echoes through the foyer.

I'm left standing there. I lift my hand to knock again, but

I stop. I don't know what to do. I can't lead this stars-forsaken burial.

I hear a loud sigh, and I gaze up the steps. Oli sits at the top, dressed in a black pressed shirt and slacks. Her hair is tied up and away from her face. Her shirt is partially buttoned, displaying the tattoos on her chest and neck. She buttons the rest as she stands up and comes down the remainder of the stairs.

"Let him sit in there." She fixes the cuff of her shirt and straightens out the twist in her pant leg. "We'll handle the ceremony then."

"Do you think you can handle this?" I ask.

"I can do just about anything. What's that thing you called me? Ah, yes, a fack-a-dumb."

My face heats. "I said *factotum*. It means—"

"It means I'm good with my hands. I remember." She grins, and all the moisture in my mouth dries up. "Are you ready? How do I look?"

She had just been in the arboretum. Some of the magic from the trees still surrounds her—I can feel it. She smells like earth, and lavender, and the first drops of rain. Her face is flushed from running around, but she cleaned up nicely. Without her hair on her shoulders, I can finally see her thin face and pointy ears. The rosy color on her purple cheeks. Her round, obsidian eyes and full lashes.

She has a loose hair poking from her bun, and I tuck it back. She smiles softly at me, and blood thuds in my ears.

"You . . ." My mouth is incredibly dry. "You look fine."

"Good. So do you."

I watch in amazement how Oli greets the family. She uses her full name, smiles widely, and assures them that their loved one's ashes will be deeply and expertly cared for. After their refreshments, the family is invited outside for the planting ceremony.

As they walk out, Oli comes to me. "I need your help, please, with the planting."

"I'd have to go inside the arboretum?" I ask.

Oli gives me a deadpan look.

I nod my head. Right, no time for fear. "Yes, of course."

"Don't worry. It's not as scary as it seems."

During my time here, I think I've gotten familiar with the sight of the sanctuary and all the deceased planted within. Perhaps seeing a ceremony firsthand will ease the idea of you . . . of you finally getting your resting place, Fi.

As we journey through the backyard toward the arboretum, Merry flutters beside me. "Where's your brother?" I ask.

"He's tired from the day at the market. He's finally sold everything from the stand. Uh-oh." He stops, and I follow his gaze toward the entrance of the sanctuary. Oli helps the widow through the portal, and she disappears. Her son is next, along with his wife and daughter. The widow's daughter is last. She steps close to Oli, who says something with that slick smile of hers, and it makes the daughter laugh. Oli's hand rests on the small of her back as they both disappear inside.

"What's the matter?" I ask, although my voice is shaky.

"Frank isn't gonna like it if Oli doesn't keep her hands to herself."

"She's just being kind, that's all." Merry looks at me curiously, an amused smile on his face. "Shouldn't you be helping Evette in the kitchen?" I leave him behind and enter the sanctuary on my own.

I don't know if it's because of the absence of magic in my own life, but entering the sanctuary, the air feels thicker with enchantment. It's almost suffocating. I feel like I can't move.

Gentle hands touch my arm. I open my eyes, and Oli stands before me, concern on her face. "Are you alright?" she whispers. "Just take a deep breath."

I exhale, possibly louder than I should. "I'm alright."

She searches my eyes to see if it's true. "Okay."

She turns back to the family. "This is the heart of Ash Gardens. The arboretum sanctuary. If you follow me, I've picked the perfect place for your beloved Edgar."

We follow Oli deeper into the arboretum. The bereaved daughter walks beside her, chatting idly. She presses her hand on Oli's arm here. A chuckle is thrown there.

I turn my head. I don't know why Oli asked me to come. She seems to have everything handled. Clearly.

The widowed mother begins to trail behind. She tells us to continue ahead even though Oli makes it clear that we'll wait for her.

The woman looks over at me. "I have this nice lady to keep me company. I'll be right behind you."

They reluctantly walk forward, and the woman extends her elbow. "Won't you help an old witch?"

I accept her arm. I'm glad she offered to walk slower. I was getting just as winded as her.

"I'm surprised that you've been married for over forty years. Your Edgar must have kept you youthful."

"Oh, he did." She smiles.

It's helpful having someone to concentrate on as we walk. We pass through the kaleidoscopic, colorful trees. They're all uniquely different, and it makes me wonder about the souls planted. Who were they? What did they like to do for fun? Did they leave behind a family who still mourns and loves them?

"Frank has made something special here," the woman says. "No one really thinks of caring for the dead after they're gone, yet he's made a place where they can still live."

"His wife was actually the one who came up with the idea."

"Oh, I know. I was a patron of Ash Gardens years before. When my youngest son passed." She stops to take a deep breath. And so do I. We keep walking.

"Frank could've let this dream die with his wife," she continues. "He's not a witch. Yet, he's made an effort to keep Ash Gardens a reality."

"He works very hard. I'm sorry that he couldn't join us today. He's a bit under the weather."

She shakes her head. "Not a worry at all. We all need to listen to our bodies when it's time to rest."

"So, did you know Frank's wife?"

We pass a small oak laden with green and orange branches. And we stop for a moment to look at its peculiar star-shaped leaves. Then we continue on.

"I've only heard about Kye through Frank. Such a sad way to go," she says.

I've never actually given thought to how Kye passed. "I'm afraid I don't know that story. How did she die?"

"Oh, well"—she grunts when we step over a large root sticking from the ground—"from the sounds of it, Frank's wife lost herself in the end. She was plagued by voices and thoughts that weren't her own. Eventually, she just couldn't take it any longer."

I stop. "Are you implying she ended her own life?"

"Frank never told me in such plain words. I only assumed

from what he'd told me. Perhaps you should ask him yourself to know the full truth."

We continue walking. "Perhaps I will."

I can't imagine asking Frank such a thing. I nearly bit off Marionette's head when she mentioned your death, Fi, and you went peacefully in your sleep. A violent passing, such as what she's implying, cannot be discussed over morning coffee.

I'll simply wait for Frank to tell me himself when he's ready. If he's ever ready.

We reach the planting site, and Oli and the family wait for us patiently. The old woman brightens up when she sees the area.

Oli grins. "I recognized you when we met earlier, Miss Greta. And I knew exactly where to plant Edgar for his final rest."

The bereaved son's eyes widen, and he looks at his sister. "Our brother. He's here?" he asks Oli.

She nods. She points to an elm tree with pink and blue leaves. "He's right over there."

"*Oh.*" The word sounds like it's been lodged in Greta's soul. She gazes at the elm and hums softly. "Hello, my son."

A soft breeze blows through the clearing, and a few pink and blue leaves rustle toward us. They dance above Greta's head before blowing away.

I smile, despite tears clouding my vision. "Looks like he heard you."

Greta wipes her eyes. "Looks like." She turns to Oli. "I'm ready to send my husband home."

With misty eyes, Oli steps up to the plot of soil she prepared earlier. I've never seen her cry before.

"We're joined today by the family of the Linguist witch Edgar," Oli begins. "Though his body is gone, may his spirit live on at Ash Gardens."

The bereaved son hands her a jar of light, glittering ash. Oli looks at me. "Saika?"

I come to her side. She speaks to me softly. "Can you pour the ashes in while I enchant the ground?"

I'm a bit confused, but I do as she asks. Oli circles her arms in a fluid dance as I pour the ashes into the ground. Oli enchants the dirt, the soil sifting and tumbling over and over. She fills in the remaining soil after the contents of the jar are empty.

I step back, and Oli finishes her enchantment. The soil is packed tightly above the ashes. She enchants water from a nearby bucket and feeds it to the ground.

After she's done, we step away and allow time for the family to speak to Edgar's resting place.

"Thank you for helping," Oli whispers beside me.

"Why did you need me, though? Seems like you could've handled this by yourself."

She glares at me sharply. "How could I? We need two people to plant. One to pour the ashes, the other to set the ground. It has to be done at the same time or the enchantment won't work. And Frank knows that. I don't know what the hell is wrong with him lately."

She scans my face for a moment. "I also just wanted you here. You calm me for some reason," she mutters. I grin, and she rolls her eyes. "Oh, don't let it get to your head."

Dinner isn't ready when we get back to the house. The family settles in the parlor, and the covered piano beckons me. Greta is busy regaling Oli with a story about her husband when Frank finally walks in.

His mane is brushed and groomed, and he's dressed in his finest maroon cardigan. "Good evening, everyone." He goes around the room, introducing himself and apologizing profusely for coming so late. I watch Oli's stern face as he talks with the family.

She looks irritated, but she moves her attention to the granddaughter. She's a small girl, sitting before the fireplace, and Oli joins her. She engages her in rousing conversation, and the little girl giggles. The bereaved daughter joins them a moment later, sitting much too close to Oli.

Oli tells a joke that makes her laugh. She rests a hand on Oli's thigh.

Next thing I know, I'm sitting at the piano and peeling back the cover. I play the first tune that comes to mind.

It breaks up the conversations in the room, and they all look my way. I play a jaunty tune, hitting the keys lightly. "I'd like to play a song for you, Miss Greta." She makes her way over to the piano, watching me endearingly. "This is for you and Edgar."

I play a love ballad. One about wanting and desire. The melodies ring out from the piano, connecting us all with the feeling of yearning and hope. I want to show Greta that even though her husband is gone, the love she has for him will keep her alive. Therefore, he will never be gone. His memory will only grow.

The ballad isn't very long. It's over within a few minutes, and when I play the last chord, light applause fills the room.

"That was just lovely." Greta squeezes my hand.

Evette hovers by the door. She's changed, too, into more fitting attire for a ceremony. She's wearing a pink dress that sways when she moves. Her hair is slicked back into a low puff. "Dinner is ready. Please, follow me."

The family moves out, and Frank stops at the door after they've gone. He looks back at us, me still sitting at the piano flexing my wrists, which ache from playing, and Oli sitting on the rug before the fireplace.

"Thank you both. I'm indebted to you for this night."

"It was our pleasure," I say.

Oli lays herself flat on the floor. "Whatever, Frank. You owe me a day off."

He chuckles, gazing down at her. "Take all the days you need, Oli." He shuts the door behind him.

Once he's gone, Oli groans and folds her arms across her face. "Thought this damn day would never end, fucking hell."

I rest my elbow on the fallboard. I'm exhausted as well. "I thought you did very well today. I've never seen you so professional."

"Not bad for a fack-a-dumb then?" She grins, still shielding her face with her arms. "Frank is actin' funky. I couldn't let the ceremony go to shit."

"Still . . . I think you do a fine job running things."

We sit in silence, the fireplace crackling in the stillness.

"Still no enchantments, then?" she asks.

I glance down, and she's staring up at me from the floor, the glow from the fire illuminating half of her face.

"No, still none. Why do you ask?"

She raises her brows. "You're a Music witch who doesn't enchant when she plays. How impressive."

I smile, mindlessly tapping on the fallboard. "Well, I'm glad you liked it. You left the last time I played. I thought I'd offended you somehow."

Oli shakes her head. "No, quite the opposite, actually. It was too much for me."

"Too much how?"

She wags her finger lazily. "Nah. I keep quiet about my secrets, thank you. Another time maybe?" She yawns loudly.

"What about a secret for a secret then?" I ask. She nods,

amused. "Okay, well. I don't cast musical enchantments. Even before I used up my power source."

Oli frowns in confusion. "But you're a Music witch."

"Truthfully, I taught myself how to play for my sister. And I haven't had my power for quite some time, so I continued to play music without magic. I don't know for certain if that still qualifies me as a witch or not."

Oli yawns again. "Who am I to judge?" Her words drag as she speaks. "I'm only half a witch." Her eyes close. "It takes so much energy to do just one enchantment. Maybe that's why I'm always tired. The house needs so much work, and I don't want to let poor Frank down. I'm just . . . half a witch."

She falls silent.

"Oli?" She doesn't answer. "Olivie?"

I get down on the floor with her, and she snores lightly, her arms crossed over her belly. I chuckle. "What a child."

I take her by the arm and lift it across my shoulders. She wakes up, just barely.

"I'm fine . . . ," she mumbles.

"Of course you are," I grunt. Her full weight leans against me, and I'm hit with her scent again. Like the lavender petals from our bath. "You've been overexerting yourself, you grump. You need to rest."

I'm not as strong as I used to be, Fi. She's heavy, and I can't carry her upstairs all by myself.

Thankfully she moves her feet and helps me along. We reach the threshold of the parlor, and we bump into someone coming into the room.

It's the daughter of the deceased. Her eyes lock onto Oli. "Hello." She waves sheepishly.

Oli has enough sense to wake up and stand on her own two

feet. "Jeannie." Her voice is devoid of any drowsiness. How convenient. "Are you alright?"

"Oh, yes." Jeannie folds her hands, swaying back and forth. "Dinner is wonderful. That light fairy—"

"Her name is Evette," I say. Oli smirks at me.

Jeannie looks mortified. "Right, of course. I know she has a name. Anyway, she's done such a great job. It's just, I ate before I came. And I want to thank you for speaking to my niece. You made her feel better about all of this. Your pirate stories were comforting for her . . . and for me. I was wondering if I could take you up on that talk you promised earlier. You said you understood how it felt to miss someone who was such a big part of you and . . . that's how I feel about my father."

I look at Oli. That sobered her up. She mindlessly rubs the silver ring on her finger. "I think right now you should be with your family. They'd understand you more than I ever could."

Jeannie squints, formulating something in her head. "I see. Well then, I thank you for your service, and I bid you both a good night." She turns sharply and heads back to the dining room, back to her family, where she belongs.

I feel Oli's burning gaze on my face. "What?" I ask.

"Nothing." She tosses her arm back over my shoulder. "As you were. Carry me up to my room then."

I pry her arm off me. "You seem pretty awake now. You can walk yourself."

Oli laughs. "Oh, come on. It was so sweet of you. Here, would it help if I pretend to be boneless again so you can play hero?"

"You were pretending?" I squawk.

Frank comes out of the dining room. "Oh, Saika. I'm glad I caught you. Can I speak to you for a moment?"

I glance over to Oli. Her smile wanes. "Okay, fine. I get it. I'll walk myself." She playfully punches my arm. "Thank you for your help today."

"Of course."

She waves good night to Frank, then enchants a small ball of fire in her palm and ascends the dark stairs.

Frank hands me Kye's journal. "Thank you for allowing me some time with my wife again. If only by the company of her words."

"I'm glad they were a comfort to you."

He sighs. "I also want to apologize for earlier. I just wasn't myself. I don't know why I've been feeling so sick."

"Maybe we should visit a hospital in the city?" I ask, but Frank is visibly disgusted by the idea. "Or we could send for a doctor?"

"I'll be fine. I've been so worried about the star and the house and our food."

Right, our food. I wonder if he knows that the bereaved family is eating up what we had saved to last us the next couple of weeks.

"Frank." I sigh. "Just tell us the next time you aren't feeling well instead of dealing with it alone. Please?"

He nods. "I will."

We bid each other good night, and I grab a candle to lead me back upstairs to my room. Across the hall, I stop to look at Oli's work boots by her door and the dreamcatcher on the doorknob. It's a bit strange, seeing her with a dreamcatcher. She doesn't seem like the superstitious type.

Then again, I don't know much about her.

That bereaved vixen mentioned something about Oli that even I didn't know about her. She's lost someone, too. Someone who had been a huge part of her.

At first glance, I can't imagine Oli caring about anyone besides herself.

But that's not entirely true, is it? I've seen how she treats Evette like a little sister. I see how she reveres and respects Hilde. How she yearns for Frank's approval.

She's kind and compassionate to the bereaved. She's professional when she needs to be. At ceremonies, she finds the children and entertains them with stories so that the most horrible day of their life isn't *so* horrible.

When I think about it, I realize that Oli is actually quite kind.

I glance down at my leather gloves before I go to my room and shut the door tight.

CHAPTER THIRTEEN

Frank decided to wake early in the morning and fix all of us breakfast.

It's an entire spread of eggs and pancakes and jams and toasts and sausages. He sits at his place at the head of the table with a wide grin. "Good morning, everyone. Please, come sit."

I'm a bit hesitant, and when I glance at Oli and the cherubs, they're cautious, too. Evette flies into the dining room behind us. She halts at the sight of the table.

"What is this?" she asks.

"Hilde feels a bit run-down, so I'm taking her meal duty today." Frank stands. "Last night, I fell ill. In fact, I've been feeling ill for some time now. I thought I could recover on my own, but after last night, after forgetting about scheduling a ceremony, I . . ." He places a gentle paw on his chest. "I'm sorry that I neglected myself and Ash Gardens, and in turn, all of you had to take on my role. I'm deeply sorry."

"Oh, Frank, no," Evette counters.

"We'd do it again," Merry adds.

We join Frank at the table, and I notice that Oli hasn't said a word.

"Thank you for making this today, Frank," I say. "*Are* you feeling better? Have you decided if you want to send for a doctor?"

Oli had been scooping eggs onto her plate, and she snaps her head up. She looks at Frank. "Do you need a doctor?" she asks with concern.

"No." Frank shakes his head. "Everything is fine, I promise. Saika is just a little worried. I'm feeling much better today."

We eat breakfast in idle chatter. Evette talks about the family from last night. Merry praises Oli's ability to handle things under pressure.

"Hey, Oli," Morose calls across the table. "I saw that the deceased had a daughter." He cups his chest with his hands. "And she had a pair of nice, round—"

"Morose!" I call.

Oli stares daggers at him. "You degenerate." She sucks her teeth.

"Is she still upstairs?" Morose wags his brows. "Just couldn't help yourself, could you?"

"Morose, enough," Frank calls.

Morose finally stops, but he smirks at Oli.

She doesn't say anything, and for some reason, I wish she had, Fi. Had that grieving woman found her way up to Oli's room last night seeking some kind of comfort?

"Moving on." Evette shakes her head. "Frank, this meal was very kind of you to make. But after last night, we have very little. Saika was able to help with food last time, but we don't have the money to sustain us for too long. What are we going to do?"

Frank looks undisturbed, and he explains with a calm tone. "It's going to be fine. I'll take care of our food problem. Soon, we'll have everything we need to keep Ash Gardens running. I just ask that you all be patient in the meanwhile."

"What do you mean by that?" Oli asks.

"All in good time." Frank cuts into his pancakes.

It's a bit tense getting through the rest of breakfast, and by the end, I nearly fly out of my seat to corner Frank in the kitchen. He's at the sink, scrubbing away at a plate.

"What's going on with you?" I ask. "You seem awfully chipper considering you've just thrown a lavish breakfast with our reserves."

Frank calmly turns off the water and looks at me with a smile. "He's found the date," he whispers. His tail wags slowly. "Ignatius knows when the fallen star will hit Rose Woods. It's only in a couple of weeks."

I blink and step back. "That's so soon."

"Saika, now that we have a date, it makes . . . it makes me feel like I can breathe again." He stares out the stained glass window. I follow his gaze to the arboretum.

"I promised Kye that I wouldn't fail her dream. I told her that I'd do everything in my power to keep Ash Gardens afloat. It's very . . . auspicious that this star is coming when it is." He looks at me. "And that you came when you did."

His wet paw rests on my shoulder. "You've been an amazing asset to Ash Gardens. I know that your work isn't over yet. You and Ignatius still have to create the spells to fix the house and the gardens. But it means so much that you're willing to be here and see things through. Thank you, Saika."

Frank's heavy arms wrap me in a hug. When he steps back, he dabs at his eyes. "Forgive me for being so emotional." He chuckles.

"No." I swallow thickly. "It's fine. It's always my pleasure to help you, Frank."

What Frank said is true.

I go to Ignatius to confirm that he has, in fact, found the exact date of the fallen star. He rambles on about his research and how he deduced it, and he seems fairly confident. There will be a star falling from the sky in a little less than three weeks.

Ignatius stresses how important it is that I finish concocting the spells to help the house. And I realize that after just a moment of sitting in his stuffy room, I can't bear to sit there any longer.

I seek a different place to write. I wander the halls. I sit on the stairs. I find a comfy seat in the library. I sit in my favorite place on the porch swing. No matter where I go, pen and paper in hand, I can't think of any spells. I can't write. I can't focus.

Ultimately, I come back to my room to sit at my desk. I stare at the blank pages I promised I'd fill with spells.

I've never done this before. Whenever I needed an incantation, I'd come up with one in the moment, and it would work. I've never sat down and thought of an incantation for later. And what's worse, without our star, there's no way for me to actually test it out.

I never wanted to become this type of witch—obsessed with knowledge and looking for answers.

Fi, do you remember when our father would come home from work, and he'd hole himself away in his study? He always fussed about learning more, doing more, creating more. Architectural enchantments take a lot of work, he'd tell us. Which proved a deterrent for me. I never wanted to spend my days cramming myself with knowledge just for the sake of a job.

It's why I chose art. It's why I wanted to surround myself

with music and those who loved it as well. I didn't need a lesson on how music made me feel. I could just feel it.

I suppose that's how my incantations work. It's what I need in the moment. There's little thought behind the words I string together. It just comes to me. Perhaps that's the difference between witches and non-witches. We don't need to know how the magic works. Because we *are* the magic.

Besides, in three weeks, we'll have the star to fuel the enchantments, so why does it matter if I write adequate spells or not?

I lean back in my chair and wonder if Ignatius is yet again giving me mindless tasks to keep me occupied. I mean, he deduced the date of the star without an ounce of my help.

Frank's gratitude, though appreciated, feels misplaced. I don't think I've done a single thing to help Ash Gardens. Not where it matters. And isn't that the whole justification of my stay?

Your planting is inevitable, Fi. This I know. I just . . .

My throat aches when I think about it.

I need to make a stricter plan for myself. I need an end date for my time here at Ash Gardens. After all, I don't plan on being here forever.

Once we've obtained the star, and the house is fixed up, and the garden is thriving again, then . . . I'll honor your wish, Fi. I'll lay you to rest in the arboretum. I'll even leave a spot next to you so we can grow together one more time. I think you'd like that.

A yawn escapes my mouth. My body is still breaking down, so I'm getting tired more often. Even sitting at my desk is hurting my back.

I settle into bed with Kye's journal. I'll just read a few pieces of her findings, and then I'll get back to work.

. . . A thud clatters against the hardwood floor. I jolt up and glance around my room. I must have drifted off again. It's dark outside my window, and the bedside lamp is on.

It's on? Oli must've finally fixed the electricity.

Another thud echoes on the floor. The noise is so very loud, but it's not coming from my room. It sounds like it's above me. And the only one up there is Hilde. I suppose Phil, as well. Evette told me he dwells in the attic. What a ghost does in a room of his own, I could not tell you. I'm sure he doesn't sleep.

Well, Phil eats, if only as a masquerade. Perhaps he sleeps as one, as well.

The noise echoes again, and I've had enough. Hilde needs to quiet down. I half expect to find Oli in the hallway when I open the door. The thudding is getting louder and more insistent. I thought she'd find it a nuisance, too, and seek to shut it up.

But she doesn't come out. I suppose I'm on my own.

As I follow the sounds up to the fourth platform, I realize that I've never been to Hilde's level before. I've never seen her room, or Phil's, for that matter.

The thumping noise ceases abruptly as I step onto Hilde's level. There's a short, narrow hallway. Although, it's a bit peculiar.

Photographs hang along the walls, suspended from the ceiling and displayed on shelves. The frames are uncoordinated. Some are silver and some are gold. Circular and rectangular. Big and small.

I take a moment to peruse the photographs, quietly shopping for information. The first ones I see are very old. They're wrinkled and distorted, and they only appear in black and white.

I see a loving couple, a man and woman, holding a tiny baby.

The mother is dark-skinned and young. She has a sharp jaw and catlike eyes just like Hilde. It's uncanny.

I follow the photographs, analyzing the images of that same baby growing into a healthy little boy. In the scenes that follow, he's happy and bright-eyed. Many of the photos capture him wedged in a hug from his mother. As I move to each new one, I realize I'm reading the timeline of this young boy's life.

His first day at school. His performance at some kind of dance recital. There's another one of him onstage, dressed as a schoolgirl for a play.

As he gets older, the photos colorize into a dull sepia. His parents slowly disappear, picture after picture, and they are replaced with his friends. His company increases, and he's surrounded by more and more people at parties, and graduations, and ceremonies. His countenance looks fallen, but I can't honestly tell. There don't seem to be any close-up photographs of this boy. I wish I could get a better look at his face.

I've come full circle, rounding out the hallway, and stop at the large frame nailed on Hilde's door.

It's a portrait of the boy from the shoulders up. His tight black curls have grown past his shoulders, and he's wearing a ceremonial cap and gown. The hammer symbol for Architect witch is embroidered on his robe. He's finally smiling wide and joyously. The light that I saw in him as a boy has returned. His face is tastefully done in makeup. His full lips are matted in red lipstick, his eyebrows arched and sharp. And his milky left eye shines through the glass of the frame.

I reach up to touch her face. "Oh, Hilde."

The ceiling thumps again, and it stirs me from my relentless prying. I hurry back to the steps before Hilde catches me snooping around her door, giving her graduation portrait one last glimpse before I ascend the stairs in search of that sound.

I stop halfway up the steps. There isn't another platform. There isn't even a hallway. At the top of the steps is a lone door with deadbolt locks.

The sound thumps again, and it's much louder this time. The steps shake beneath my feet.

I run up the remainder of the steps. "Phil? Are you in there? What's going on?"

I bang on the door, and to my surprise, it gently blows back. I don't know if I should intrude, but I step inside anyway. "Phil?"

It's pitch-black. Cool air breezes over my face and sends chills down my spine. "Phil, what is that noise? Is everything alright?"

I take another step and hear wind whistling from above.

Out of the canvas of black, a shimmery silhouette appears in front of me. I yelp and nearly fall back.

"Phil?"

He doesn't answer. Instead, he directs my attention to the ceiling of the attic. When I look up, more wind coats my face. And I see why. There's a massive, gaping hole in the roof. Outside is the twinkling night sky. Then I see what's been causing the thumping sounds.

A chunk of wood falls from the support beams and clatters to the ground. The sound echoes in the empty attic.

"What is this? What's going on?" I search for Phil again, but he isn't there.

Then an unfamiliar voice whispers in my ear. It tells me "Wake up."

CHAPTER FOURTEEN

I wake with a start. My heart is racing. My neck is severely cramped. I move my legs, and Kye's journal shifts in my lap.

All of that was just some horrible dream. It didn't feel like it, though. It felt alive. It felt real.

I leave my room, and it's getting dark out. I suppose I've missed lunch. What's left of the early evening sun glances through the windows as I head to the fourth level for what feels like the second time.

To my relief, there isn't a hallway filled with photographs of Hilde's life. Instead, it's only a small platform with a chair and an end table beside Hilde's door. Not a photograph in sight.

I feel a bit calmer. If my dream was wrong about this, then it must be wrong about the attic. The roof isn't collapsing. It was all a horrible dream.

But I need to be absolutely certain. I continue to the top level. The stairs creak as I move. And at the top is a lone door, like I had seen before in my dream.

Before I get to the top, I hear my name. "Saika?"

Hilde is at the bottom of the steps. She's wearing her night-gown, a sleep mask pushed up onto her forehead and her hair under a silk bonnet.

"'Evening, Hilde."

"I knew I heard someone creeping around these steps."

"I wouldn't exactly say 'creeping.' I was just . . . um . . ." I don't really know what I was doing. Was I just going to knock on Phil's door and ask to see his room?

Hilde notes my silence. "Come on down. Phil doesn't like visitors."

I meet her on her level. She opens the door to her room, and notes of lilac and eucalyptus float from inside. "Come on in," she calls over her shoulder. "I have something for you."

Her room is filled with framed art and knickknacks. There are shelves of curios, and colorful tapestries hang from the walls. Incense burns on top of the mantel near her bed. A rose-patterned sofa sits before the mantel. And like Ignatius, she has her own kitchenette with jars of loose-leaf teas sitting on the shelves.

She has a wide wooden dressing screen, and a mannequin stands beside it wearing a simple light blue dress. It seems very plain for Hilde's taste.

She strips the mannequin and hands me the dress. "Try this on."

I blink. "Hilde, you made this for me?"

"Seeing you wear that same old smock day in and day out, darling, I couldn't stand it." She juts her chin toward her dressing screen. "Go on. You can change behind there."

"Thank you," I mumble. I go behind the dressing screen and begin to change. I'm not wearing my corset today, so there are places that sag that shouldn't for a woman my age. Hopefully, the dress will hide it. I don't want Hilde asking questions.

"So." Hilde's voice is muffled behind the screen. "What's got you in such a fuss this fine evening?"

I slip the dress over my head. It swallows me and bunches at my feet. "I'm not in a fuss. I was only looking for Phil."

I come out from behind the screen, and her eyebrows shoot up. "Heavens," she chuckles. "I'll have to take it in quite a bit."

She directs me to the front of her sofa, then heads across the room to her sewing machine and comes back with a ball of pins. "So, why are you looking for Phil?"

I'm so worried about her getting too close and seeing my aging body that I nearly forget to answer. "Oh, I . . ." I think of an excuse. "I wanted to thank him. He gave me an old journal from Kye. I learned a lot about Beelzebub. Kye really loved that dragon."

She pulls the dress by its side seams and sets a pin in the fabric. "I never met Kye. I didn't even know she kept journals."

"She researched monsters, and dragons, and beasts. It's actually very fascinating. Beelzebub and I have become closer because of it. I'm thankful for it. And I'm thankful for you doing this, Hilde. I didn't think anyone would notice that I only had one dress."

"Of course. Everyone needs a new dress every now and then. Knowing that you prefer simplicity, I made sure that I didn't embellish it. But I couldn't help but choose this wonderful sky blue for you."

"Why's that?"

Hilde smirks at me. "It's Oli's favorite color."

My face becomes aflame, and I look away. "I don't know what you're implying."

She laughs. "Fine, neither do I." She pins the unfinished collar, and thankfully changes the conversation. "So, when's the last time you had something new for yourself?"

It's a simple question, but one I don't really have an answer for. The moment you got sick, Fi, I had no desire for new and shiny things. "It's been some time," I answer. "I've been traveling the past couple of years so I only had a few outfits to pack light. Besides, having multiple outfits seems excessive."

Hilde laughs. "I'd beg to differ." She begins pinning the hem of my dress. "You need to get dressed, Saika." She stands up and looks into my eyes. "It brings you back to a sense of self again. Own who you are and where you belong in this world. Because you *do* belong here. And you deserve to look like royalty every day. Because it's all a gift, isn't it, darling?"

"What's a gift?"

"Life. Especially after seeing how fragile it can be. You're broken for some time, yes. But then you pick yourself up again."

To be honest, I don't think I've ever accounted for the way I look since you've passed on. You're gone. Clothing and appearances seem so very trivial compared to the chasm that broke open my heart. I've only done what I could manage. I covered up any part of me that I couldn't bear to deal with.

My hair is thinning and falling out in small clumps. So, I wear a headscarf.

My hands are withering, and dark spots are sprouting up my arms. So, I got used to wearing gloves.

My breasts are sagging, and loose skin gathers at my stomach. Now, I wear a corset.

So, no, I haven't thought to wear anything that suited me. I only wore what kept me together.

She finishes pinning the rest of my hem.

"You pick out the fine linens, Saika. You pick out the extravagant fabric, and you wear them. You buy the expensive tea or the book you've always wanted. You eat the pie you've always wanted to bake, because after knowing how precious life is, those little moments start to feel quite damn big."

I swallow, watching her, feeling like a child getting a lesson from a school teacher. But this lesson isn't like the ones we used to get from our mother. It's gentle, like it's peeling back a film that I've cocooned myself in.

"Thank you, Hilde," I tell her.

"I enjoy doing this. So thank *you*."

She moves to pin the long sleeve of the dress but pauses when she sees the age spot on my skin. I snatch my arm back. "The sleeves are fine, I think."

She looks at me curiously. Her white eye flashes, and I'm not sure if she's reading me or not. "Okay. Go on and change. I'll finish the dress later."

I go back behind the dressing screen, and I hear the sound of a kettle filling with water. When I finish changing and come out, she's pouring two mugs of tea in her kitchenette.

"You seem like you need this." She hands me a hot cup of tea. The water sparkles when I stare into it.

She takes a sip and settles down on her sofa. "It's enchanted. A healing concoction with just a little mood enhancer."

I join her on the sofa. I sniff the tea, and it smells earthy and light. I take a sip, and it tastes strongly of dirt, or perhaps grass, but the aftertaste is that of a honeysuckle. It's an enigma of disgusting and sweet that has me drinking more.

"Are you feeling better?" I ask. "Frank mentioned you were a bit run-down from yesterday."

"Ah, yes." She lifts her mug. "Thanks to this heavenly elixir. Last night there were so many emotions I couldn't think straight. And it wasn't even from the bereaved family. It was from all of you, running around while Frank hid away."

"I wouldn't say 'hid away.' He wasn't feeling well."

She gives me a deadpan look, her white eye glinting. "I suppose. He sent up an entire spread for breakfast and lunch. He must be in a good mood now."

"He claims so." I take another sip of the tea. It's starting to grow on me. "You said this was a mood enhancer?"

She nods. "It helps ease a troubled mind." She fans her long nightgown over her legs and the sofa. She's poised, yet relaxed, like she's waiting for someone to take her photograph.

"Do you often have a troubled mind?" I ask her.

"Oh yes. Times where I can hardly sleep. Memories and feelings keep me up at night sometimes. A little tea cures just that. But it can also cause some strange dreams." She chuckles.

"I've been having strange dreams myself." I don't know why I say that. The tea is slowly working through my body. My eyelids blink one at a time, and my arms and legs feel like noodles. My head, therefore my thoughts and brain, feels detached from the rest of me. Which is why I believe I continue to explain.

"I keep seeing odd things. Like you, for example."

Hilde is still, but her perfectly sculpted eyebrow arches up. "Me?"

"Just now, I had a dream where I saw your entire life. From beginning to end. I saw your parents. You . . ." I stop. My eyes fall on a small portrait sitting on her mantel. My blood runs like ice in my veins.

It's not hanging on her front door like in my dream, but it's her graduation portrait. She's grinning widely, looking as if she finally found herself.

"I saw you as a child. And when you got older, you finally came home to yourself again."

I glance back at her, but she's staring at her graduation portrait.

"You're right." She sets down her mug. "Growing up with my gift, it was hard trying to place what emotions were mine, and what emotions were everyone else's. It often felt like I was only a vessel to be used by everyone else. That portrait"—she points to the one on the mantel—"was made the day I chose to become an Architect witch. And also the day that I decided to live my life as exactly who I needed to be. And I found the real me . . . and her name was Hilde. And she . . . *I* . . . am everything that I've ever wanted."

"That's beautiful, Hilde." The tea makes me bold, and I ask a question. "What happened with your Architect coven? Did they not accept you?"

"They resented me for a completely different reason. It was because of this." She points at her white eye. "I'm an only child, so I didn't grow up with a large family. But I loved my coven like they were my own. Using my gift, I'd see someone hurting, and I'd try to help them. *Fix* them." She shakes her head. "Over time, they came to not appreciate my efforts, and in turn, I felt them slowly removing themselves from me. I felt outcast. And then, one day, I made a mistake.

"I read my coven leader. He was a very important man, and like important men, he was always busy. I'd heard great things about him. And when I finally met him, I read some . . . horrible emotions from him, to say the least. There were a few women in our coven who would give off intense waves of fear every time he came around. I became flooded with visions of him and these poor women."

Hilde stands up and goes into her kitchenette. She comes

back and tops me off with more tea. "The coven didn't like it when I spoke up about it," she continues. "My coven leader denied everything, and they all treated me like I was a troublemaker. I was promptly kicked out for false accusations."

She sits back down with a huff and rolls her head back. "Anyway, he died a few years later, and *then* all of these women came forward about him. They said that I was right all along. But the deed was already done. I didn't care to come back to the coven. I didn't care to be an Architect witch anymore. By then, I was already on my own journey, experimenting with turning my architecture into art, and crafting healing teas, and finding more pieces of Hilde."

I haven't blinked the entire time she's been talking. I don't know what to say in a moment like this, Fi. Pithy words won't give any reprieve to someone who has faced such an injustice.

"Oh, Hilde" is all I can say.

She shrugs. "Years down an endless river, Saika. It's simple. I didn't mean as much to them as they meant to me. But it all worked out. Ash Gardens was looking for an Architect witch, and here I am."

"I don't think you made a mistake. You were right to speak up and do what you thought was right."

"Righteous actions still have consequences. It cost me a family and years of solitude." She looks down into her mug. "But I didn't care to pay the price. It all worked out."

I know how it feels to be cut off from a family. I know how it feels to have love and watch it be torn away because you made a decision you thought was right.

A power, a force, greater than anything that I've ever known, reached through our twisted lines of fate, Fi, and snapped the cords. Now, I'm a wandering witch. I'm untethered. And unbound. Much like Hilde.

"Anyway, that was such a long time ago. Frank has created a space where I can be myself, and I can use my gift for so much more. I can give the love that I've always wanted to give."

When I smile, my face feels droopy. My eyelids are heavy. "If it's any consolation, I feel your love immensely, Hilde. Even more than from my parents."

I lift my mug to take another sip, but it's empty. Have I drunk two whole mugs of tea already? My head feels woozy. My stomach does, too.

"Thank you, Saika." She looks at me inquisitively. "So, your dream was right about me. Maybe there's something your other dreams are trying to tell you."

I blink slowly. I hope not. They've been more like nightmares.

My stomach rolls. My head feels like it's spinning. I place the mug down. "I . . ." I hold my hand over my mouth. "I don't feel too well."

"Oh." Hilde waves nonchalantly. "It's just the tea. You'll feel better soon."

I stand, resisting the urge to vomit all over Hilde's woven rug. "Thank you for the tea. And for sharing so much with me. I need . . ." I close my eyes to fight the urge again. "I need to go."

I hurry out of Hilde's room, her voice trailing behind me. "Of course, dear. Come back anytime."

I hold myself together. I'm able to get down the flight of steps to my level. I speed past my room and head straight to the bathroom. I know it's disgusting and unladylike, Fi, but I throw myself onto the floor and vomit into the toilet.

I wake up some time later in my bed. The stiffness in my neck and joints has gotten better. I flex my fingers, and they aren't as achy as before. Hilde's tea must have worked.

Through bleary eyes I peer out my window—the clouds are dark and low. I hope there won't be another storm tonight. We can't handle another disaster.

I pull the blankets over my groggy head. Hilde's words settle over me.

Maybe there's something your other dreams are trying to tell you.

If my dream was right about Hilde, then it must be right about everything else. It could also be my anxiety. I've been fretting over the house collapsing so much that it was bound to find its way into my dreams.

I don't understand why. We're going to get the star. We'll fix up the house, and Ash Gardens will stand strong once again.

So why am I still anxious?

"Still a grump, I see."

I snatch the blankets off my head to see Oli sitting in the armchair beside the front window. A dinner tray sits atop my desk with toasted cheese bread. Steam rises from a bowl of tomato soup topped with a dollop of cream.

"You missed dinner."

My brow furrows. I fix my headwrap to make sure it's still on. "What are you doing in my bedroom?"

She whistles softly. "Aye, this is the thanks I get for scooping you off the bathroom floor. By the way, you broke the tub handle, didn't you?"

My face heats. I can only imagine the state I was in when she found me. "Thank you for bringing me to my room. And to answer your question, yes, I did break it. It was an accident. I plan to fix it—"

"I fixed it already." She rests her hands on her lap, and I realize what she's been holding. She holds up Kye's journal. "A book about beasts?" she asks, amused. She thumbs through the journal. "You think there's anything in here about Frank?"

"That's not funny." I sit upright and fix my twisted bodice. "I don't think she'd analyze her own husband."

"You didn't know Kye. She was a very curious witch. No question was too intimate."

I watch her scan through the pages. "You knew Kye pretty well then?"

"Well enough." She continues to examine the journal.

"This may be an insensitive question, but how did she die?"

Oli glances up. She snaps the journal shut. "In her sleep. It was peaceful according to Frank."

That widowed witch, Greta, mentioned Kye's wandering mind. She wasn't herself in her last days. Frank hasn't been acting like himself, either.

"Why do you ask?"

"I was only curious—" I stop to cradle my throbbing head. Seems that tea hasn't cured everything.

Oli smirks. "Ah, you're in pain? That's what happens when you down *two* mugs of Hilde's grass tea." She laughs. "I didn't think you had it in you."

My mouth twists in a frown. "She said it was a healing tea with a touch of mood enhancer."

"A touch?" Oli chuckles. "Getting relaxed with Hilds sometimes has consequences. I've never had more than one cup me-self."

"Oh, so you didn't think to warn me?"

"How was I supposed to know you went up there?" She laughs, but then her lips thin into a line, and she picks up the journal. "Actually, I wanted to ask you something." She comes to my bedside.

I don't want to seem prudish and push her away, but all I can think about is what I must smell like. The last thing I remember, I was clinging to the side of a toilet.

If I smell terrible, Oli doesn't show it. She sits on the edge of my bed, concern on her face. She hands me the journal.

"I'm worried about Frank. He hasn't been actin' like himself."

"I know."

"No." Oli stops me. "Even before you came. He'd been getting distant. He never forgot anything, but now . . ." She rubs her forehead. "It was understandable at first. He'd forget to bring Ignatius his dinner here and there, but now it's every day. He's forgetting about ceremonies, for fuck's sake. It's like it's getting worse."

I fall silent. I don't know what to say.

"This job, or task, or whatever it is that Frank has you doing, are you sure it isn't dangerous?"

"Yes—"

"Are you certain?" Oli presses. Her black eyes search mine. "Frank used to tell me everything, but now he's so shut up, it makes me nervous. I just want to make sure he's okay."

My breath stills, but I nod. "I assure you. It isn't dangerous. In fact, it's actually really good. If Ignatius and I do our job right, Ash Gardens will want for nothing. Everything will be good again."

Oli swallows. She stands to her feet. "Right. That's what Frank keeps saying. I wish he'd understand that when it concerns the future of Ash Gardens, he should include the *people* of Ash Gardens."

"He doesn't want you all to worry."

"But that's what a family does. We worry, but we worry together." She pinches the space between her eyes. "Whatever, I'm sorry."

"It's fine." My voice sounds so small.

She sighs. "Anyway. There's your dinner. Frank's made another delicious spread."

Oli doesn't wait for a thank-you. She heads out of my room and gently closes the door. It's only once I look out the window and gaze into the dark sky that I see it's beginning to rain.

CHAPTER FIFTEEN

We've completely run out of money.

And we've spent the remainder of my travel funds. We've resorted to foraging in Rose Woods. Oli has hunted a few deer for meat. Morose has also been trying to sell some of Hilde's grass teas at the market.

Beelzebub, bless her soul, has been getting on just fine, even though we've been dipping into her food. We've cooked up the few pieces of lamb and pig that should've been for her.

On the plus side, it hasn't been raining as often, so the soil for the garden has finally become dry enough to plant.

Oli mentioned to me that she was running low on the elixir that helped fix up the house. I was surprised when Ignatius actually listened to me, and we researched how to make the elixir ourselves.

It only took us a few days to concoct it, but it was missing something powerful for fuel. It was a long shot, but I took off my locket and dipped it in Ignatius's cauldron.

I thought that there might have been some powder residue left from the star. Ignatius screamed profanities at me, but he stopped when we saw the elixir begin to bubble and shimmer.

We were successful, and in good time, too.

Ignatius senses a big storm making its way toward Ash Gardens.

I've given it some thought, Fi. I don't have any more money, but that doesn't mean I don't know where to get more.

I fear it's time I try reaching out to Jonathan again. If I talk with him, I wouldn't have to face our parents. That is, if they'd even want to see me.

I should've written sooner. The moment I decided to come to Ash Gardens, I should have told him so he knew that I hadn't forgotten about you. I'm working toward completing my promise.

If I write to him now requesting my portion of money, he might think ill of my intentions. He may even tell our parents that I've resurfaced, and that I've requested the sight of money before my own nieces.

It's not that I don't wish to see them, Fi. You know I do. I had to flee after you died because I loved your children *too* much. Every time I looked at them, I saw your face in theirs, and it rent my heart in two. Their laughter, sweet like jingle bells, reminded me sorely of yours. I recognized your brilliant mind shining through theirs. In their play, I witnessed your silly nature. I had to get away.

I plan on returning home, Fi. I promise I will. Ash Gardens just needs a bit of help.

Hiding behind pen and paper gives me a sort of confidence. I'll write to your husband. And if he disregards me, well . . . then I'll know I'm not welcome any longer.

And if he answers, well . . .

I'll invite him and the girls to your planting.

At my desk, I get out a fresh sheet of paper and decide to use a quill pen. I take a deep breath. And finally, I write.

> *Dear Jonathan,*
>
> *It's been over two years since we've seen or heard from each other. And for that, I'm sorry. I'm sure the girls have grown unrecognizable by now. I didn't mean for it to be this long or for me to be as distant as I've been. It's just . . .*

I exhale. I write on.

> *It's just that I've been a coward. I've scoured far and vast countries, even briefly journeying to the sea, in search of something that Fiona's death took from me. I couldn't function as I was before. I needed to search for something—some hopeful meaning of life in the face of death. This isn't an excuse. I could've written to you. I could've written to the girls. I was selfish to seclude myself and leave you all to fester in your own grief without so much as a helping hand.*
>
> *But I write to you now to announce my arrival. I've returned, in a manner of speaking. On Fiona's deathbed, I swore that once she passed, I'd fulfill a final request for her. I'd lay her to rest. And I'm at the location of her choosing. I should've completed my task already, but like I stated before, I'm a coward. And in my delay, I*

found that her choice of final rest has a few issues that could be resolved with, well . . . money.

I hate to ask you this after years of silence, but I request the money that Fiona had set aside for me before she passed. If it's still available. Once I receive it, I will finally lay her to rest. And if you should choose, I invite you and the girls to be witnesses of her final resting place. I'd even invite my parents, but I know how they feel about me. I know how you all must feel about me.

An unholy thing. A cursed thing. A wicked thing.

I pause, fearing my tears will stain the page. I wipe them quickly and shake my cramping hand.

If you choose not to come, I completely understand. But the offer still stands if you happen to change your mind.

Please, give the girls all of my love.
Your sister, Saika

I wipe the cresting tear from my eye and fold up the letter.

When I finally find my land legs and make my way downstairs, I find just the man, or cherub, that I'm looking for. Morose walks toward the front door, weariness weighing upon his shoulders. His poor wings are flitting uselessly behind his back.

"Morose!"

"Yeah," he answers back, but he continues out the door.

I roll my eyes as I run across the foyer. "Can't you wait for just a second?"

"I'm already late. I gotta make the train." He does a little hop off the front steps, and his wings carry him to a basket on the ground.

I stumble to a stop when I notice what's inside. "Where did you get those?"

Morose heaves the basket, hovering with great difficulty. "Frank gave 'em to me." Bee's eggs shift in the basket. "Why do you want to know?" he asks.

I blink my dry eyes. "No reason. Um, once you're in town, can you see that this gets posted?" I hand him the envelope.

I hope he doesn't pry, but of course he does. He eyes the envelope, turning it forward and back. "Who's Jonathan?"

"Never mind that. Can you do it? Please."

He places the letter in his loincloth. "It'll cost you."

Typical. "What would you like?"

He scratches the scraggly hair on his chin. "Take my meal duty."

"Fine. It's not like we have much to cook anyway."

"Not true." He pats the basket. "These babies will catch a pretty price." He heaves the basket up his forearm. "See you later." He zips up into the air, toward the station.

I watch him go, witnessing yet another time we've taken Bee's family from her. I turn on my heels in search of Frank.

He's in the garden, on his knees and planting seeds. He sees my shadow approaching, and he glances back with a smile on his face. The absolute nerve.

"Good morning, Saika." He stops when he sees my face. "You're angry."

"How could you, Frank?" I ask. I try to keep my voice down, but I'm livid. "After what I told you about Beelzebub, you still took her eggs anyway."

He sets down his trowel. "What are you saying? What's this about Beelzebub?"

"We had a conversation just days ago. We're selling off her attempt at a family."

Frank stands up, wiping the dirt from his knees. "I'm sorry, Saika. I didn't know."

"How could you have forgotten? You promised that we'd stop. If I'd known that you'd attempt to fix our food issue like this, I'd—"

"I don't remember us having that conversation." He looks at me, fear in his eyes. "I'm still not feeling exactly myself. The past few days have felt more like a blur. I'm sorry." He holds his paw over his chest.

My rage takes a dousing hit. I hold my head. It's beginning to ache. "Frank, I think you should consider the option of . . . of letting Beelzebub go."

"No." His voice is stern. "Why would you suggest such a thing?"

"She's lonely, Frank. She's reduced to producing her own family, and when she does, they get taken from her. She spends her days in isolation. No one to talk to. No one to listen to. Kye wouldn't want this."

"You don't know what Kye wants." Frank's eyes glisten when he stares at me. I'm fastened to the ground with fear, but I keep my head high, my gaze unwavering.

"I won't let Beelzebub go. She belonged to Kye. I . . ." He blinks, and his eyes mist. "If she knew I released Bee, she'd never forgive me."

My hand braves the space between us, and I touch Frank's chest—right over his heart. "Frank, you know that Kye is gone . . . right?"

Frank moves past me in a huff. He goes inside, and the back doors shut with a hefty slam.

Later that day I enter Ignatius's room, and a musty odor hits my nose. It's an ungodly smell mixed with the bitterness of Ignatius's toxic smoke. He's pacing the floor. He looks significantly more disheveled than when I saw him last. The skin beneath his eyes has darkened. I'm noticing more gray hair in his beard and mustache. He's relentlessly puffing at his pipe as he mulls over some writing on paper.

"Goodness, you need some fresh air in here." I open the window above his desk, and a gust of wind blows into the room.

Papers from his desk get swept to the floor. "Oh, I'm so sorry." I kneel in a hurry to pick them up.

As I'm gathering the loose documents, my hand comes across a tattered piece of parchment. I glance over it and recognize a symbol on the center of the page. It looks like a scythe. But before I can inspect any further, Ignatius snatches it out of my hand.

"Why are you always making a mess?" he grumbles.

"Always? Name another time." I pick up the rest of the papers. "On second thought, please don't."

He sets his things back on the desk and settles a horseshoe paperweight over them. I notice the one with a scythe is discreetly placed at the bottom of the stack. I'm not sure if my mind is playing tricks on me. I'm fairly certain I saw the image of a scythe, Fi. A scythe.

It's not completely impossible in our line of spell research to come across any works that deal with the entity Death. But only the truly desperate and foolish seek out Death willingly, as we both already know.

After being bottled in this room for who knows how long, it's only a matter of time before Ignatius begins to look into things he shouldn't. And judging by the state of his room, his hygiene, and his tired eyes, I think he may need to finally take a step back.

"Why don't you give yourself a break?" I ask. "You're falling apart worse than the house."

"I don't need a break." He sits back at his desk and resumes his studying. "What do you want? Why are you here?"

I drop a stack of papers on Ignatius's desk. But he's unamused. He pulls the pipe from his mouth.

"What is this?"

"Spells. All spells to help the house. And the garden. I have spells for the splintering wood on the steps. I have spells for the mold in the hallway. The leaky faucets, the peeling wallpaper. Everything that could possibly go wrong with the house. I have a spell for it."

"Okay, what do you want from me?"

"More meaningful tasks. What research are you inundated with? I can help." I reach for a piece of parchment on his desk, but he's quick to snatch it up.

He glares at me. "And you are certain that these spells will work?"

"Well, I haven't tested them yet."

"Then test them."

I scoff. "I've used a star myself. I think I know how to use its power to—"

Ignatius turns back to his work. "If you don't know for certain that the spells will work, then it seems your task isn't finished." He slides my papers full of spells back to me. "Now, leave me alone. I have to figure out when this big storm is coming." He pauses, appearing both bored and annoyed with me. "And when that purple witch harvests more lumber from Rose Woods, don't mess it up again."

Blood pricks my lip, I'm biting it so hard. No wonder Frank used to grumble about this damn elf. He's insufferable, Fi!

"What are you waiting for?" he continues. "Get back to work."

I snatch the papers back. "Fine."

I leave his room and slam the door behind me.

Stars, I'm aggravated, Fi. First, Frank sells off Bee's eggs. And now this.

I thump my head back on Ignatius's door, exhaling loudly.

Times like this, I wish I had my power. All of this would be so much better if I never lost it.

My power . . . my wand. I open my eyes.

I search my boot, but it isn't there. The last time I remember having it was the night of the storm. I used it in the garden. It must still be back there.

I hurry down the steps and don't stop until I've made it to the backyard. The warm glow from the setting sun cascades over the bare garden. In the strips of light falling over the arboretum, translucent glimmers sparkle in the air.

Before the sun officially sets, I search the grass for my wand. I don't remember picking it up, and if anyone else had found it, they would've told me. It has to be here somewhere.

I get down on the ground, searching blindly in the waning light. The sun is setting too quickly.

The sound of the cellar door bursting open catches my attention. I poke up from the ground like a meerkat.

Oli comes out of the cellar in the midst of a coughing fit, fuming to herself. "Fucking hell!" she yells. She throws a wrench to the ground. "Damn it!"

"Olivie?" I call.

It looks like her anger melts away. "What are you doing out here?" She coughs again, making her way toward me.

"I'm searching for my wand. Have you seen it?"

Her eyes grow wide. "No, I wouldn't have the faintest idea."

"You know where it is." I stand up.

She grins. "I do not."

"Come on, Olivie."

"Since when have you called me Olivie?"

"I don't know. Just give me my wand."

"I don't have it." She laughs, pulling a familiar stick of wood from her boot. "But I do have one that I *found*."

"That's mine. Give it back!"

"Nuh-uh." She lifts the wand out of my reach. "Magic word, Saika. Come on. You know all about magic words."

"I won't plead for things that are mine." I cross my arms. "Why do you have it anyway?"

Her smile relaxes. She holds the wand between her hands. "I was trying to fix the generator and a few things in the house . . . but it didn't work. Things are breaking around the house faster than I can fix them. I thought the wand would help."

How odd. The wand should have worked for a witch like Oli. "I suppose you don't need it then. Give it back."

She snatches it out of reach again, a teasing smirk on her lips. "No, I found it."

I see. She wants to play a game, Fi. Fine. I'll give her a game.

I step forward, placing a gentle hand on her forearm. "I suppose the wand didn't work because you're already a *powerful* witch, Olivie." My voice becomes soft. Breathless. "You don't have any need for a silly trainer's wand, do you?"

My hand slides up her arm, and Oli freezes. Her mouth hangs open as she watches me press against her.

But . . . then she laughs.

An outright guffaw. She doubles over, holding her sides. She tucks the wand back in her boot. "Did you think that was going to work on me?"

My neck and ears turn flaming hot. "Give me back my wand."

Oli grins, her eyes trailing over me from top to bottom. "Fucking hell, Saika. How do you plan on getting it back?"

I tackle her, and we fall into the grass. We tussle on the ground, my hand searching for her boot. When I find it, I grasp the end of my wand, but Oli seizes my wrist. She pins me down in the grass, heaving and laughing the whole while.

In the scuffle, her face gets dangerously close to mine. "You need lessons in getting what you want, Saika. That was so . . . so terrible." Her lips brush against my cheek, and I freeze.

"Olivie," I whisper her name. She stares into my wide eyes. "Stop. Please."

My hand rests on her side, and for once, actually for once, she looks stunned.

She hops off me. "Saika, I'm sorry. I've crossed a line." She stops when she sees what I'm wagging before her face.

My wand.

She checks her boot, and a grin spreads on her face. "Oh, you fucker—"

"What's wrong?" I raise my brow. "Do I still need lessons in getting what I want?"

She offers her hand to help me up. "That was a sneaky move."

"As if you gave me any choice." I chuckle, handing back the wand. "Here. I'd like to try something."

"Are you sure?"

I lift my empty locket. "I can't use it anymore anyway. But there are some spells I'd like to try. Can you help me?"

We spend the next few moments in the garden, the sun long gone to rest, and fireflies come out to greet us. I tell Oli what incantations to say to revive the garden. She waves the wand and says my spell exactly, but we come to a problem, Fi.

The spells aren't working. Oli enchants a small fire from her hand to give us a bit of light. I scan the papers, all the incantations I've written over the past few days. I don't understand why they aren't working.

"Maybe it's me," Oli suggests. "I'm not a full witch, so maybe my power isn't good enough."

My eyes snap up at her. "You are one of the most powerful witches I know. It isn't you. There's something wrong here."

"You think I'm powerful?" she asks. Her mouth lifts into a smirk.

I roll my eyes. "Please. That's your big takeaway?" I consult my spells again.

"Saika," Oli says, and I look up from the papers. "Thank you for doing this. It seems like you're working hard to help Ash Gardens and it means a lot." She rubs the back of her neck. "To me."

"I couldn't do it without you. I don't have my power, so I need you." I smile.

She looks away to the house. "Frank still doesn't know about your power?"

"I haven't told him, no. I'm afraid to."

"He seems scary. But he'll understand. I think you should just tell him."

"Oli? Saika?"

Oli lifts her fire toward the arboretum. Frank emerges from the arbor, closing his cardigan over himself.

"Frank? What are you doing in there?" Oli asks.

Frank disregards her and looks directly at me. "Are you working on spells? You're supposed to be with Ignatius."

"That elf practically kicked me out of the room. But it's fine." I show him my list of spells. "I need to find a way to make sure these spells work. And I can't do it on my own."

"I didn't want anyone else involved. Why can't you test the spells yourself?"

I look at Oli, and she nods. I exhale. "Frank, I don't have my power anymore."

He blinks. He looks between me and Oli. "What do you mean?"

"It means without a power source, I can't cast enchantments. That's why I need Oli's help to test the spells."

"Why didn't you tell me before?" he asks. He scrunches up his face and holds his head in pain. "We can talk about this later. I need to lie down."

"Frank." Oli steps forward, holding the light up to his face. "What were you doing in the arboretum? It's late."

He finally looks at Oli. "I was visiting Kye. She . . . she wanted to see me." He folds his cardigan over himself again. "I'm sorry for the confusion. It's been a long day. I'll see you both in the morning."

He walks past us and heads back inside the house.

Oli lifts the fire toward me. "What in the absolute hell was that?"

I blink, staring back at Oli. Finally telling Frank about my power went as well as I hoped, but I fear that's the least of my worries. Frank isn't himself . . . but Oli may be able to fill in some blanks.

Oli rubs her head. "Did you see the way he looked at me? As if I wasn't there?"

"Oli." I say her name to get her to focus. "Before Kye died, did she behave strangely? I was told that she wasn't herself."

"Who told you that?" Oli asks. "No, she was perfectly fine. It was just one day she was alive, the next she . . . she wasn't."

"Were you two close?"

"Not really. I only knew Kye a few months before she passed. The only one who would really know about her is Frank, and, well . . . Phil. They used to be real chummy. At first, I thought she was talking to herself, but then I found out he was a ghost."

Phil. He'd know more about Kye. I wish I knew how to communicate with him.

"What's going on in that head of yours?" Oli asks.

"I'm worried about Frank, too. And for some reason, I feel like it's connected to Kye."

She points her fire toward the arboretum. "He said Kye wanted to see him. I wonder if he's seeing her apparition again. Like he used to after she died."

I shrug, exhaling deeply. "It's not uncommon. When my sister died, it took me months to stop hearing her."

"Well, what can we do for Frank?"

I look toward the barn. Our spat about Beelzebub earlier rings in my head. Frank is having a little trouble letting go. I think I should help him.

CHAPTER SIXTEEN

An entire day passes before Frank realizes Beelzebub's absence. And when he does, all of Ash Gardens is awakened with a loud, thunderous roar.

"Absolute nonsense!" Frank's voice reaches all the way up to the third level, where I'm jolted awake. "I can't believe such a thing!"

Doors slam, shaking the house from Frank's powerful rage.

Robed in my pajamas, I hurry downstairs. I meet the cherubs on the way. They fly beside me as we bumble down the stairwell.

"What in the hell is going on?" Morose calls.

"Frank's going to tear the house apart!" Merry yells.

We reach the end of the stairwell and cross through the foyer into the library. Frank is inside, tossing furniture and books. A lamp crashes to the floor.

Oli is already there, trying to get through to him. "Frank, it's alright!"

"Bee's gone!" he yells. He paces the library, and his massive stomps shake the room. "It's not alright! Not in the least!" His paws ball into fists and slam into the bookshelf. Dozens of books and curios fall, crashing onto the floor.

"Frank!" Oli takes cautious steps toward him. He flails his arms back, nearly nipping her face. She ducks just in time. "You have to calm down!"

I enter the room, stopping on the threshold. "I released Beelzebub."

Frank suddenly stops. He slowly turns, facing me. Merry and Morose cower behind me. Oli steps out of the way as he comes toward me. His bushy brows crowd over his yellow eyes.

"*You,*" he says, his voice low and gravelly. "You did this, Saika?"

I square my shoulders. "I had to. Frank, you've been forgetting more every day. Beelzebub wasn't being properly cared for. Kye isn't here to—"

Frank's fist slams through the wall, and everything grows silent. His chest heaves before me. I pause, my breath shallow as he slowly removes his fist from the wall.

I swallow. "I'm sorry, Frank. I didn't have any malicious intent. I was trying to help you."

Frank steps even closer, and I'm fastened to the floor. But he walks right by me. His rage and disappointment nearly choke me as he passes by.

He exits the library, and Merry and Morose flutter out of the way. Frank goes to his wing, opens his doors, and calls over his shoulder. "I wish not to be disturbed today." The doors slam shut behind him, echoing throughout the entire first level.

It's silent for what feels like a millennium. The first one to speak is Hilde, who strides into the library, smoking one of her long cigarettes and eyeing the disaster. She puffs smoke into the air.

"We'll need more wood, then?" She analyzes the hole in the wall. "I have to fix that, too, I suppose."

"I'll go to Rose Woods today, Hilds." Oli steps up. "I'll get you wood."

"You got rid of Bee, Saika?" Merry asks. "Why?"

They all look at me, and it's quiet for a moment. I don't know how to respond, Fi. I thought Frank would eventually be grateful. I took away the burden of releasing Bee. She was wasting away in there. It was a matter of time before he had to.

I should have expected Frank to be angry. I removed one of the last things connecting him to Kye. But Beelzebub was suffering. I stand by my decision, though it's hard to face everyone now. Judging me with their curious eyes.

"I helped her." Oli faces everyone. My heart skips a beat. The attention shifts to her. "We needed to. We don't have the money to keep feeding her."

"We would've if she kept laying eggs," Morose says. "That was our last chance for money."

"That was the issue." I finally find my voice. I step forward, cautious of the mess on the floor. "I've been reading Kye's journal. When we were selling her eggs, we were selling Bee's attempt at a family. It wasn't right."

"So?" Morose asks. "Who cares about Bee's happiness?"

He's met with a room full of protests. "That's not a kind thing to say." Merry shakes his head.

Morose flutters up to me. "The fact remains that we don't have any food. We don't have any money. And you just released any hopes of that."

"How much did you get from the last dragon eggs?" Oli asks Morose, and it diverts his attention from me.

He shrugs. "I've only sold one so far."

Oli exhales as she picks up an armload of books. "Push to sell the rest today. What's done is done."

Everyone moves in silence to clean up the library. I want to go to Oli, and speak to her, but for some reason, I just can't find my voice.

●

I'm still frozen in silence as I cook breakfast. As promised, I take Morose's meal duty, so I brave the cooking all on my own. Evette finally comes down, and she meets me in the kitchen.

"You missed all the fun." I ignite the stove.

She gathers leaves from a glass jar. She sets out a few mugs and puts a kettle on the fire.

"No, I didn't. I don't like to see Frank when he gets like that."

I raise my brows. "You've seen him in that state before?"

Evette nods. "I came to Ash Gardens a few weeks after Kye died. Frank would wander the halls at night. He'd swear that he saw her walking about. Oli would try to calm him down when he couldn't find Kye, but he wouldn't listen. He'd get violent. Smash things. Throw things." Evette looks up at me. "We all handle our grief in strange ways."

"We do."

"Is it true?" she asks. "You released Beelzebub?"

"It was time. She needed to be free."

"You don't have to explain." Evette sits on the counter. She swings her little legs over the edge. "I'm actually glad. I felt bad for taking her food just so we could eat. She always seemed so lonely in there."

I nod. "Yeah. Terrible thing. Being lonely."

The kettle whistles on the stove, and Evette is quick to remove it. She makes tea for everyone. "I know exactly what you mean."

Breakfast is tense. I knock on Frank's door, but he doesn't answer. I leave his tray on the floor and return to the dining room.

The silence is insufferable. I wish I could dash to my room and hide under the blankets until this horrible feeling passes. I wish there was something I could do to ease this tension.

Once breakfast is over, and everyone disperses to do their tasks for the day, the idea hits me.

Before Morose heads outside, I follow him out to the foyer. I notice Oli knock on Frank's door. She's holding his tray. "You have to eat." Her tone is hushed. "Come on, Frank."

He still doesn't answer. Oli sighs and puts the tray back where she found it. When she glances over, we meet eyes, hers a bit misted.

"Oli," I begin, but she wipes her eyes roughly and heads up the stairs.

When I step out onto the veranda, Morose is massaging his chubby legs before he takes off.

"Morose," I call. "Are you heading to the city now?"

"If you're asking about that letter, I sent it already."

"No, I just . . . I feel horrible about this morning."

"You should."

"I deserve that." I sigh. "To make amends, I'd like to help you today. I can sell the last of Bee's eggs. If you're having trouble, that is."

Morose looks at me strangely. "You want to do my job?"

"I think you deserve a day off, don't you?" He looks at me, contemplating. "You wouldn't have to spend your day haggling. I'll do it for you. In fact, we can all go down to the market for a day out. I fear we all need it."

Morose bites his lip in thought. "Frank won't like it."

"He's sequestering himself today. He'll hardly notice we're gone."

Morose stares at me. A small smirk spreads on his face until he bends over, laughing. "Okay, okay, Your Majesty. You're something else, you know that?"

I didn't think he'd agree so easily, Fi. I'm so happy that I reach down to hug him, but he fends me off with surprising strength. "Sorry, sorry."

It takes some finagling, but I manage to round the house up in just a few moments. I entice them with a day in the city under Frank's nose, after the tense debacle this morning.

Oli is the last one to convince. When I come down our shared hallway, I hear the light strings of her viola. After I've gathered my cloak from my bedroom, I knock on her door.

The viola comes to a stop, and she opens the door with glassy eyes.

"Hi."

She smiles tiredly. "Hello."

"Fancy a day out?"

She glances at the cloak draped over my arm. "What do you mean?"

"We're all going into the city with Morose. I'm going to sell the last of Bee's eggs so we can get some money. It's the least I can do."

"What about our jobs?"

"Day off." Her hand is on the doorframe, and I touch her wrist. Surprisingly, she lets me. "We need some space to breathe after this morning. You deserve it, Olivie."

She looks away, the purple skin on her cheeks turning a deep violet. "I'll meet you downstairs," she mutters.

Frank's breakfast is still outside his door when I come back down. I'm tempted to apologize, but I've been in this situation before.

After crossing a line like this, I have to remind myself it's for the best. Frank just needs some time to reflect and calm down. In time, he'll be fine.

Like you were, Fi.

I come out onto the veranda, and everyone looks at me expectantly. I grin. "She said yes! She's coming with us."

They all cheer, and I laugh. "I didn't think it'd be that close of a call."

"I was certain Oli was going to say no." Merry's wearing an ivy cap and vest like his brother.

"She never misses a day of work," Evette adds. "She's worked in full typhoons before. I'm surprised she said yes to you."

"I'm not." Hilde smirks. She's hidden beneath a parasol, dressed in delicate lace and long silk. She's chosen to wear her silver hair in a bun today.

Oli comes out of the house wearing all black—loose, dark pantaloons and a black sleeveless shirt with a form-fitting vest. She rolls her eyes when everyone cheers at her arrival. "Enough. Let's make this quick."

Our winged friends take to the sky. Hilde brings out a polished broom and side-saddles elegantly. She scoots up, and a floating bowler hat saddles behind her. "Hold on, Phil," she calls to him, and they take to the air.

Oli nudges me with her broom. "I guess you're with me."

I ignore the warmth in my cheeks as I saddle behind her once again. The broom jolts when she enchants it, and this time, she takes very little time to get us airborne.

In the sky, our housemates breeze through the air. Hilde flies ahead of us, still holding on to her parasol, enjoying the soft wind. Merry and Morose fly like bumbling bees, occasionally knocking into each other. Evette is a circle of light flowing through the air in a mesmerizing dance.

To give Oli more space, I slink farther back on the broom, but the balance throws us off. We wobble, and she glances back.

"What are you doing?"

"Nothing. I'm sorry." I scoot up to where I was. When she turns forward again, I catch a glimpse of a smile on her face. "There's something I wanted to ask you."

"You want to know why I lied?" she asks.

"You didn't help me release Beelzebub. In fact, you were against the idea."

That night, Fi, I told Oli about Beelzebub's eggs and her loneliness. I told her that Frank agreed to stop, but he'd forgotten. I was worried that he'd forget again. And he'd keep forgetting.

Oli agreed but was adamant that it wasn't my place to make that decision for Frank. And she was right, I suppose. But Frank needed me to do this for him. I wish someone would've made a decision like this for me when I needed it. In time he'll understand.

So, after we went inside that night, I came back out and released Beelzebub on my own. And she looked happier than I've ever seen her, twirling into the air and soaring away into the night sky.

But Oli wasn't there.

"Why did you lie?" I ask.

"Shared blame lessens the guilt. They may look nice, but these people can hold a grudge."

"You didn't have to do that, though."

"I know I didn't."

We reach the train station quickly. I'm a bit bummed, reminded of the fact that what took me hours to walk when I first arrived at Ash Gardens only took us mere moments with flying.

We land, and everyone takes a minute to fix themselves from the tussling wind. Hilde doesn't need it. She's prim and proper when she lands. Oli, however, has hair sticking straight back like it's frozen.

"Nice hair," Morose snickers.

Oli fluffs out her curls to their original cloudlike form. "At least my hair is on my head and not my back."

Morose shrugs. "Hey, ladies love a man with a little body hair."

"Please, you're an infant with stubble."

Morose charges at her, but Merry holds him back. "Get off me, ugly," Morose snaps.

"That's hurtful," Merry says.

I shake my head. "Morose, you have the same face." I pull him off to the side. "Day off, remember? Let not our temper get the better of us."

"Fine." Morose sniffs, still staring up at Oli. She sticks out her tongue as we continue into the station.

I give Oli a deadpan look. "Really?"

"What?" She laughs.

"Good behavior, please. I don't want to be detained because you two can't be nice to each other."

"I'd never hit a baby." She laughs again. I stare at her, and she lifts her hands in surrender. "Okay, fine. I'll be good."

We take the inbound express, and our party settles into a four-seat compartment. Merry and Evette flutter to the window and gaze out to the mountains. Morose settles beside them. The three of them take up only one seat.

Hilde strolls in, holding her folded parasol like a cane. Oli and I take the remaining seats. Then Phil's floating hat enters the space.

"Oh, Phil." I stand up. "You can have my seat."

"It's okay," Evette says. "Phil doesn't need to sit. He's fine just being there. Right, Phil?"

I glance at Phil's bowler hat, but he's silent. I suppose that means he's fine. How on earth does Evette communicate with him? I'd like to find out so I can ask a few questions

No. Today is supposed to be a day off. A fun day. I won't worry about Frank. Or Kye. Or her journal. Or strange dreams. Or stars.

The train starts up, and we move forward. I sit beside Oli.

"Giving up your seat for a ghost?" she asks.

"What?"

"Nothing. It's just . . . it's nice. Unnecessary. But nice."

I roll my eyes. The compliment feels like a trap. I fold my hands in my lap and glance down to my leather gloves.

I feel compelled, so I tell her, "Thank you."

CHAPTER SEVENTEEN

It takes an hour to reach the city. I stare out the window the entire time, watching the countryside die away, and the city bleeds in with its many buildings and structures that block the sun. When we depart the train, I stop outside the station, taking in the enchanted buildings. They're taller and wider than thought structurally possible. The people—witch, beast, and fae—roam about in their fancy clothes. Clouds of stuffy perfume trail after them as they pass by.

We follow Morose and head deeper into the bustling streets. The city hasn't changed much, Fi. People are still rude. They're still in a fuss over the most menial things. They're still always in a rush and bumping your shoulder when you don't move fast enough.

Morose leads us toward South End, and the towering buildings begin to dwindle. The glass and mosaic architecture morphs into dirt-stained brick and concrete, housing storefronts with barred front windows. We've never ventured this far in the city before, Fi. Our childhood townhome is safely secluded in the north, away from unseemly types. Our parents forbade us from ever crossing city lines, and we listened.

So entering the market, witnessing strange witches selling interesting wares, feels like I'm breaking a rule. They call across the streets to each other, laughing and swearing. It feels like I'm defiling our parents' wishes, even though I'm certain they couldn't care less about their failure of a daughter or where she spends her time.

I've always envisioned South End to be desolate, and grimy, and crawling with shifty eyes and hands. I even left my handbag at home for such a reason. But Morose turns us away from this area, and we cross the avenue into the thick of the market.

Tents of all sizes and colors flood a wide cobblestone street. Smoky incense, and food, and grease fill the air.

I feel a bit silly gawking. Hagglers fight for dominance underneath a bright orange tent that's selling beaded jewelry and scarves.

We pass a market stand full of curios and old keepsakes. I stumble to a stop when something catches my eye. A small wooden music box. I pick it up, turning it over in my hand. And my heart aches just a bit. The white paint is faded, and the lock is broken.

"See something you like?" Oli's voice startles me.

"This music box reminds me of one I had as a girl. It belonged to my sister, and she passed it down to me. We shared a love for music."

Stars, that was complete lifetimes ago, Fi.

It's strange how grief works. I was content, walking these strange cobblestone streets, but then here you are. You lurk everywhere. You're in my thoughts. You're in my heart, so I cannot help but to find you everywhere.

"Are you alright?" Oli asks. She looks at me keenly, almost braving a hand to my shoulder, but she stops herself.

I place the music box back on the table with the rest of the piled knickknacks. "Yes, I'm fine."

I continue, following Morose and everyone else to Ash Gardens' yellow tent down by the water's edge. The canal flows through the entire city. Water trolleys give passage from South End to all the way up north. I stare at the water, the sun reflecting and hurting my eyes. A horn from a nearby water trolley suddenly blows, and I jump.

Morose chuckles. "It gets loud down here. Be careful." He ceremoniously unzips our four-post tent and opens the stand. A large wooden sign hangs on the front. It reads: Wild, Organically Produced Produce.

Great stars, who wrote that sign?

And in smaller but still very large lettering, it reads: Psst, We Have Dragon Eggs.

"Perhaps we shouldn't advertise the produce right now?" I ask. "At least, until we get something growing in the garden."

"Oh, right." Morose hops behind the stand. There's a loud clatter, and he suddenly pops back up with a hastily constructed sign. "Made this yesterday." He slaps it on.

Now it reads: Wild, Organically Produced Produce . . . Never Mind.

I sigh. "Nice, Morose."

"The seeds we planted are taking some time to grow." Evette looks to Merry. "Maybe we can find some kind of elixir for the garden?"

"Sounds like a great idea," Merry agrees. "Morose?"

Morose huffs. He settles them with a few copper coins. "That's all I'm giving you. Make it work."

They set off into the maze of tents like excited, helpless children. Evette pulls at the air, and Phil's floating hat trails after them.

Morose sets up Bee's three eggs on the stand. "Well, this is the last of it."

"Did Frank choose you to work the stand, or was it your idea?" I ask.

Morose crosses his arms. "You don't ever stop prying."

"It's only a question. Come on, Morose."

He sighs. "It was Frank's idea. He thought spending some time away from my brother would help me . . . get out some of my anger. And arguing with people down here lets me blow off some steam."

"Maybe you should go get something for yourself?" Oli says to Morose. "Spend a few copper pieces. You work so hard, Morry."

He eyes Oli suspiciously. "Why are you being so nice?"

"I can also dress you up in a cute little outfit to attract patrons. Do you want that instead?"

"Fine." He looks at me. "Don't let these fools take you for a spin."

"She'll be fine." Oli places her arm over my shoulder, and I tense up a bit. "I'll stay and make sure she doesn't muck up."

Morose seems content with the idea and flits off, scratching his bum as he disappears into the crowd.

Once he's gone, I suddenly realize it's only me and Oli left at the stand. "Where did Hilde get off to?" I ask.

"She's got things to do. People to see." She positions herself in front of our tent, stretching her arms over her head, and yawns. "Alright. Where are all the patrons?" She scans the market while shielding her eyes from the sun.

Oli takes off her vest and flexes her toned, tattooed arms. She faces me with a grin. "So, you're gonna sell all these eggs for our little Morry? You were so against it before. Why the change of heart?"

"Well, Beelzebub is gone. And we already have the eggs here." I pick at the loose threads on my gloves. "Do you think Frank will forgive me for what I did?"

Oli leans on the stand. "I don't know. Either that, or he forgets the damn thing ever happened. We go through this whole mess again."

"Maybe I should've listened to you, then. What was I thinking?"

"You were doing what you thought was right, even if Frank hates you for it. Besides, you did something that all of us had been thinking about for a while. Bee needed to be free, but no one would've said anything to Frank about it. Sometimes he can be stubborn. He needs a strong hand to help him see his own foolishness."

"Hmm, sounds like someone else I know." I smile. Oli rolls her eyes. I continue to pick at my gloves. "Evette told me about Frank . . . after Kye passed. You tried to help him when he'd lose his sense of reality. You've always looked out for Frank, haven't you?"

Oli looks away. "He was there for me. I'm indebted to him." She pauses, then forces a smile onto her face. "Like making sure you hold to your word and sell these eggs. Have you ever done anything like this before?"

She grins at me, but I note the despair in her eyes. She doesn't want to talk about Frank. I understand. For her sake, I'll play along.

"Why do you and Morose think I'm some princess who's never lifted a finger? I have, you know."

"Ah." Oli chuckles. "When you were gallivanting around the world? Your various harrowing adventures, eh?"

I nod. "Exactly."

Oli smiles, leaning forward. "Oh, I'd love to hear about even *one* instance where you—"

"Excuse me."

We turn to see a young elf girl approaching the stand. She has long braids that blow in the wind, revealing her pointed ears. She's holding a small satchel.

"Are you selling dragon eggs?" she asks.

"We are." I greet her with a smile. "Are you interested in purchasing one?"

The girl nods and steps up to the counter. "But I don't know much about raising a dragon."

"Oh, well, I've recently read lots about dragons and all sorts of beasts. This particular dragon is a Northern dragon. Yellow skinned, and they have a venomous tail, but if you treat them right, you won't have any issue. Let's see . . ." I think back to Kye's journal. "Ah, if they're anything like their mother, they'll love lamb. Their favorite meal. They *do* breathe fire, so just keep a watchful eye for hay and other flammables—"

"Saika," Oli interrupts me gently.

I follow her gaze to the young girl. She's standing there, petrified.

"Now that I've thought about it, I don't think I'm ready," she says.

"Hey." Oli hops to the front of the stand. She squats to look the young girl in the eyes. "All of those things my friend said are true, but she forgot to mention something else."

Oli places a hand on the girl's shoulder. "This dragon is fiercely loyal. And loving. They'll love to hear stories about anything. They'll be gentle, and kind, but only if they have a gentle and kind owner. Is that something you can be? From the looks of it, it seems you are."

The young girl nods. "I can be those things."

"Then, that's all that matters." Oli smiles at her. "Just be the best owner, the best friend, you can be to this dragon, and I promise you, they'll love you just as you are." Oli picks up an egg, and she hands it to her. "What do you say?"

The young girl smiles. "Thank you. How much?"

"Ten silver pieces."

My eyes widen. We're only selling them for six.

The girl reaches into her satchel, and she drops ten silver pieces onto the counter. "Would that cover it?"

I glance over at Oli. I hand back two silver pieces. "Just for you, dear."

She grins widely, cradling her new egg. "Thank you so much." She scurries off, happy as can be.

"That's pretty cruel, you know?" Once she's gone, I collect the eight pieces of silver. "How could you take advantage of her that way?"

Oli hops back over the counter. She smirks, seeing me pocket the coins. *"Just for you, dear,"* she mocks. "You only gave her two silver pieces back."

"We need money."

Oli laughs. "Oh, so it's fine when you do it, but when I do it, I'm a scoundrel."

"Yes, exactly."

I watch her set the two remaining eggs on the stand, pushing them forward to entice any wandering eyes. "You have a way with children, you know."

Oli glances back. "What are you on about?"

"Honestly. It's amazing to witness sometimes. At ceremonies. Just now. You know how to speak to them."

Oli leans on one of the metal posts supporting the stand. "Well, children get overlooked sometimes. Doesn't hurt to give 'em some attention."

A moment later, we get our second patron. A university

student wanting Bee's eggs for study. After questioning him about his intentions and making sure he wasn't going to mistreat Bee's offspring in any way, I allow him to purchase an egg.

I even make a poor attempt at haggling. And it's quite embarrassing.

He doesn't want to pay ten silver pieces when he knows he could go somewhere cheaper. I counter with nine, and he says no. I drop to seven, and he still won't budge.

Oli offers a voucher for free produce when we grow some again. He agrees, although reluctantly. He pays seven silver pieces (and one copper piece) and makes off with the second egg.

Once he leaves, Oli turns to me and laughs. "What was that?" she asks.

"It wasn't that bad."

"That's how you haggle?"

"It was my first time."

Oli blinks at me. "Have you ever dealt with money before?"

I tilt my head. "Well, I . . . um."

"Oh . . . my goodness. You haven't, have you?"

I cross my arms. "Well, it's true that when I traveled, I never worried about money—"

"Oh, so you're rich?" Oli asks. She nods her head. "I get it now. This makes so much sense."

"I'm not rich."

"Rich people never say that they're rich." Oli holds back a smile as she analyzes me. "It's fine. I finally see why you're so sheltered."

"Me? Sheltered?"

"Sure." She leans on the counter. "I can read you like a book. Let's see, you took off from home to explore the world, is that it?

Mom and Dad gave you some money so you could 'find yourself' because, obviously, you can't do that here in the city. No,
you have to venture out far and wide, partaking in adventure and
putting yourself in various perils so you can find the true meaning of life. Only now, you've run out of money, and you've come
running back home." She grins at me. "Am I on, or what?"

I blink at her, my mouth feeling dry. "You've read me to
rights."

"Ah, I'm good." She raps her knuckles on the counter. "I don't
understand then. Why are you suffering here at Ash Gardens?
You could have left us long ago."

"I think I've come to love Ash Gardens, in a way. I wouldn't
think of leaving any of you right now. Not like this."

Oli looks away. "Well, once you've done the deed . . . planted
your sister's ashes, I mean—"

"I knew what you meant."

"Do you plan on going back home to Mom and Dad? Resume
your polished, rich life?"

"There's not really anything to go back to."

Oli tilts her head, pondering. I don't feel like explaining myself. I move on.

"Well then. What about you? You have your whole life decorated on your skin." I direct my gaze at her tattooed arms and
collarbone. I feel comfortable enough to peruse her tattoos now
without feeling embarrassed. She has inked markings threading
up her arms. Across her chest, hiding underneath her shirt, is a
name scripted in a fancy font.

"You told me you've spent time at sea, but it's also written
here." I point to the inky black waves on her forearm. I skip past
the whale and trail down to a three-lined dash around her wrist.
"Hmm . . . three-lined dash. You were a first mate?"

"Captain," she corrects. "I'm a bit hurt that you haven't heard of me. You said that you sailed the seas for a spell."

"I don't think I would call my time at sea 'a spell' really. I sailed for only a week, or two." I chuckle.

"Only a week or two?" Oli feigns shock. "I had no idea. Don't I feel like a fuckin' idiot? I thought you were a seasoned sailor—"

"Alright, alright, okay," I intone, shaking my head. "So, you were a famous captain then?"

Oli grins, falling back into a memory. "Oh yeah, I had my time of infamy. Witch and beast alike would come from all over if they had a monster that needed slaying or some relic that needed to be uncovered. Feels like a lifetime ago."

"I see." I analyze more of her tattoos, wondering now about the significance of the monsters she had inked on her skin. My eyes trace up, noting the black petunias blossoming on her purple shoulder. "Petunias. A symbol for inner turmoil over something you've lost. Or someone."

I don't know why, but my hand touches the top of her shirt, tipping it down just a bit to see the name written on her collarbone. She stops me immediately, placing a gentle hand on top of mine. Her silver ring gleams.

"Saika, stop." But it's too late. I've already seen the name. She looks at me softly.

"Who's Henley?" I ask.

"Excuse me, I'd like to buy an egg." A familiar, kind-faced woman stands at the counter, and it's like my nerves have been doused with ice-cold water.

The woman is holding an armload of sunflowers. Your favorite flowers, Fi. "Madam Saika?" She laughs uncomfortably. "I can't believe my eyes. It feels like I'm seeing a ghost."

My eyes widen. "Lorna. What on earth . . . What are you doing in South End?"

"Master Jonathan likes to keep these sunflowers year-round," she explains. "His wife's favorite, as I'm sure you know." Concern suddenly crosses her face. "He needed something to lift his spirits after receiving that strange letter from you. Your parents had told everyone that you were dead. They said that blasted curse finally made its claim. Master Jonathan thought your letter arrived posthumously."

Oli's attention snaps toward me. "What is she talking about?"

My hands shake. Our parents told everyone I was dead? Do they really think so little of me that they'd rather have a dead daughter than a cursed one?

My hand covers my mouth to stop a sob from embarrassing me. I swallow the despair and smile, although my eyes mist over. "No, Lorna. I'm very much alive." My hands shake as I roll a dragon egg over to her. "Now, you wanted to buy an egg?"

"It's for the girls. They wanted a dragon." Her eyes light up. "Oh, Master Jonathan and the girls would love to see you."

"Actually, Lorna." I lean closer, and I don't think she means to hurt me, but she cowers away. Right. I should keep my distance. I stand back. "Please, don't tell Jonathan that you saw me. I don't want to create any problems within the family. Can you keep this meeting between us?"

Lorna blinks, not fully understanding. She nods anyhow. "Oh, of course, madam. Mum's the word. They won't hear a peep out of me."

I smile. "I appreciate your discretion."

She pays for the dragon egg (I charge her extra), and she dips her head in a bow. "I hope you return to your former health, ma'am." She waddles off, and I give her one last wave.

I feel Oli's eyes the moment she leaves, but when I look at her, she turns away. We're both silent, afraid to question each other.

Thankfully, Hilde bursts into the tent a moment later, smelling of lilac and eucalyptus. Shopping bags float behind her and settle themselves on the ground.

"Oh, I needed this day, Saika. How did you know?" Hilde asks.

"I'm glad. . . . Where, um, where did you go, Hilde?"

"Oh, I traded with some artisans. I was able to get more herbs, a few new dresses, a polisher for my stones, and ingredients to make more grass tea. You've been cleaning me out, you know."

It's the only thing that's been helping my ailments. It's disgusting, but it's a temporary fix until I get a piece of the star.

"By the way, Saika, look at this." She digs into one of her bags and pulls out a long piece of red taffeta. "You can wear it on your head or over your shoulders. Whichever you prefer."

"It's beautiful." I hold the stiff, shiny fabric between my hands. "I wish I had something to wear with this."

Hilde's eyes light up. "Oh, I just thought of the perfect dress for it. Leave it to me." She places the fabric back into her bag, and when she stands up, she finally notices how silent we are. Her white eye flashes. "Oh, something happened between you two."

"No," I say quickly.

"Nothing happened, Hilds." Oli rubs the back of her neck.

But when I look back at Oli, she turns away. She can't even look me in the face.

CHAPTER EIGHTEEN

The star parade will be here in a week, Fi. And Ignatius's room is filthy.

I have to sit on the floor because his sofa is littered with tomes and letters, and a few underpants, which I'm too embarrassed to even bring to his attention. I'd say something, but he's been transfixed on his research.

I finish the book I'd been reading and set it aside. I stroll up to Ignatius, who is reading madly at his desk.

He pauses. He actually looks me in the eyes for the first time this morning. "Have you changed clothes?" he asks.

"No."

"You're wearing a different dress."

I glance down at my blue dress. "Hilde made it for me." I'm surprised he's even noticed. I've been wearing my new wardrobe for a couple of days now.

"On your travels, you know, gallivanting into the city, and trying on new dresses, and getting prim and proper, did you happen to test out your spells?"

"You know I haven't." I sigh. "You see, I don't have—"

"You don't have your power," he finishes without missing a

beat. "Not my problem. Find a way to test the spells and leave me alone." He turns his chair so that he doesn't have to see me.

If you have nothing nice to say, then don't say anything at all. Isn't that the way it goes, Fi?

But that doesn't mean I can't take my choice words for Ignatius, then throw them in an empty space where none would be offended. I leave his room and choose the hallway outside his door, and unfortunately, the wall is the victim of said verbal beating.

"Of all the boorish, pig-brained . . . miscreants!" I yell to the air. "He's slovenly. Unkempt. How dare he? How dare he think I'm some thoughtless girl who is only interested in pretty, frilly things. He doesn't know me at all. Does he, Fi?"

I freeze. I realize I've said your name out loud. I've never done that before. You know, in all my time speaking to you in my mind, I don't think I've ever envisioned you here, actually listening to me. I think you've just become another part of me, another half to my soul. The shape of your memory, your thoughts, my love for you, formed your voice for me.

There's an armchair in the hallway, and I stop to envision you there. You're sitting in this pea-colored chair, and you make some remark about how ugly this color green is. You think it looks like vomit, and I laugh. Can you imagine our mother hearing you speak that way? She'd have a heart attack. But you wouldn't care, Fi. You enjoyed dancing on the strings of our mother's patience, and I loved the melody it played.

I can see you staring out the window from this ugly chair. The puff of your hair circles around your head, perhaps a jewel or flower pinned in that beautiful black cloud. Sunlight falls on your dark brown skin, and it highlights your honey eyes, and it all sets the mere image of you as simply . . . golden.

You smile, and my heart aches because you and Nana had the exact same smile, lines creasing from years of laughing way too often.

And I ask you, "What should I do?"

You understand my dilemma. I'm no use to Ignatius. I've no power. I can't enchant using the simplest of spells.

I could leave Ash Gardens. I could go back to your husband. Or . . . without the star, I could simply forgo everything and start anew. Continue having adventures until this curse claims me like our parents said it has. Like Oli said, I don't have to be here.

But you've asked me to plant you here. You insisted.

"Why?" I ask you. "Why did you choose Ash Gardens as your resting place, Fi? Why did you choose me to do this for you?"

You don't answer. Naturally. And I can't conjure up a response for you. Not one that wouldn't make me unravel at the seams.

I hear a creak, and when I look toward the stairwell, a bowler hat floats in the air.

Stars, did he just witness me having a lapse of reality?

"Phil." I smile. "'Morning. Pleasant day so far?"

No answer.

I don't know how to have a conversation with a ghost, but I try my luck. "Are you happy, Phil? I found what you wanted me to find in Kye's journal. I've released Bee. And now Frank is angry with me."

This elicits a response out of Phil. He continues walking up the steps. His hat suddenly pauses, and I wonder . . .

"Would you like me to follow you?"

He walks on. I guess I'll take that as a yes.

The steps creak ahead of me. His floating hat is the only indication that Phil is leading the way. After passing the third and fourth levels, we get to the top of the stairwell, where we're met with his bolted door.

Phil steps forward, but his hat hits the door and falls to the ground. It rolls to my feet, and I catch it.

"Phil?"

The locks move, clicking one by one until the door finally opens.

"So, you can walk through walls. Never knew that was a real thing. I believe this is yours?"

Phil takes his hat and places it back onto his head. He steps aside to allow me farther into the attic.

I've been curious since learning that Phil dwelled up here. What does a ghost do with his time, and with a whole room to himself? And I stand in the attic, having my answer.

Phil's space has high ceilings that come to a point and exposed beams. Cobwebs cluster in the rafters, and it's a bit drafty. I shiver as I step inside, eyeing the shelves filled not with books, but with vials of liquid. There are jars with shimmery substances and weird creatures in stasis. Boxes are stacked along the walls and over the dusty floor, making the space feel much tighter than it actually is.

Phil moves along the cluttered floor, demonstrating where to walk. The attic smells damp, and I cough from the dust. No wonder Frank set him up here. Anyone with a voice would've complained.

There's no bed, but there is a large oak desk with tattered old books piled on top. "You know, I'm glad you've invited me up here. I've been wanting to ask you something. It's about Kye. I'm sure it might be a bit hard to talk about her. I know she was your friend."

He doesn't say anything, still. But he walks off and disappears between two mountains of boxes. I hear rustling, and he comes back out carrying a box labeled Phil.

He sets it on the floor and begins rummaging through it. Curious, I stand beside him, peering in. It's filled with hats, watches, newspaper clippings, and then I finally see what Phil is trying to retrieve. A photo album.

The book hovers as Phil pulls out the chair from the desk. He sets the album on top of it.

"For me?" I sit down, fanning my dress over my knees. "Such a gentleman."

The desk looks just like Ignatius's. Ancient texts about beasts and potions and spells. This must be where Kye worked. There are more journals up here. My eye catches one labeled Potions, Pig Noses, and Pixie Dust. He has dozens of journals that she's written.

I crack open the photo album, and the pages stick together. The first photograph is of a man. Athletic in build, handsome spectacles, and a bright smile. It's a professional photograph with a white backdrop. The man is kneeling beside a dog who's licking his face.

"Is this you?"

Phil's hat tilts forward and back.

"Oh, Phil. You were so handsome. I'm sure you had many interested suitors."

The following pages are photographs filled with people. Phil and his dog are in every single one. I skim through his life. I witness his graduation from school and learn that Phil used to be a Research and Agriculture witch. From the looks of the photos, he fell in love with a kind-faced man from school. There are many photographs of their wedding celebrated in a field decorated with lanterns. All types of fae and witches were in attendance.

"This looks so beautiful." I continue, going deeper into Phil's life. He used to live in the city, the northern side like we did, Fi. His husband was also a witch, and it seems like they worked together, judging by the photographs of their matching white lab coats. The green insignia stitched on their sleeves is of a book surrounded by stalks of wheat.

"Research and Agriculture? You're a very smart man, Phil. Well, ghost."

Flipping through the pages of the album, I see that Phil had lived a very full life. He'd gone to school. He married the love of his life. He went on adventures with his dog.

But as the photos continue, Phil and his husband are starting to get older. Lines crease their foreheads. Gray hair starts appearing in their beards and mustaches.

And then it's only Phil and his dog.

Phil's bright smile is gone in every photo after that. He's found solace in the crook of his dog's neck, hugging him tight every time he got his picture taken.

And then it's Phil. On the last page of the album, there's only one photo. He's sitting in a chair, aged greatly since the first page. He's staring out a window, looking pensive, and a bit forlorn.

I close the book.

A knot is wedged in my throat. I knew Phil was dead all this time, but I hadn't thought about what it actually meant. He's no longer alive, and neither is the little family he created.

I hand the photo album back to him. "I'm so sorry, Phil. It seems like your life was filled with so much love."

He nods again, and I stand to my feet. "Thank you for sharing your life with me. It must be so difficult to be separated from those you love. Why are you hanging on? Are you enchanting your soul to stay around?"

He retrieves a framed photo from his box. He hands it to me.

It's a picture of him when he was alive, sandwiched in a hug between Frank and Kye.

She was taller than Phil by at least a foot. She had that vibrant orange hair that touched the ground. She was absolutely stunning. "Quite a handsome bunch." I smile. "You knew Kye before she passed then. Did she behave strangely before she—" Phil takes the frame from my hand and promptly walks away.

"Wait, Phil. I'm sorry. I didn't mean to upset you." I follow him through the maze of boxes. He stops by the back wall. He heaves box after box out of the way. Dust kicks up, and I cough.

"Phil, what are you doing?"

He reveals a tarp veiling the wall. And in one swift motion, he pulls it down.

There's a gaping hole in the wall about seven feet wide. It's so massive, I don't see how we could have missed this. Does Frank know about this? Does Oli?

Phil's hand wraps around my wrist, and he gently pulls me forward. He puts my hand up to the destruction. My finger touches a piece of the wood, and it chips like cheap paint. The wood crumbles away, shimmering as it goes.

This isn't normal damage. There's something supernatural at play.

"I don't understand." I reach my hand out. The air fizzles in the way that enchantments normally do, but this feels different. The magic feels stronger, more potent. "Oh, Frank."

Phil picks up the tarp and begins covering up the hole again. I blink as I watch him. Kye's journal . . . he wasn't trying to warn me about Beelzebub. I think he was trying to tell me about Kye. Or Frank. Or this house. I'm not sure which.

"Are you also responsible for the strange dreams I've been

having about the house?" He nods. He hands me the framed picture. "I don't understand. Do you think I can talk to Frank? He's been a hermit for the past couple of days. And I'm sure he doesn't want to see my face right now. I released Beelzebub. He still needs time to . . ." I stare down at the photo of Frank, his furry arms covering both Phil and Kye.

"I'll talk to him."

I offer the framed picture back to Phil, but he pushes it back into my hand. Then he returns the boxes back to their place, as if we were never there to begin with.

I knock on Frank's door, staring at the silhouette portrait of him and Kye. At least in this image, they're still here. Still kissing. Still together.

The door opens, splitting them apart. Frank's eyes widen when he sees me. He tries closing the doors, but I stick out my foot.

"Frank, wait."

"I thought you were Evette with lunch."

"I can go get it if you want." I struggle against the door. I'm sure he's humoring me. He could easily close it if he wanted to.

"No, I'm fine. Thank you."

"Frank, please." I grunt.

He concedes and allows me in. I fall forward into Frank's wing. Everything inside is so large that I feel like an ant.

His room is enchanted, there's no mistaking that. The ceiling is the highest I've seen in the entire house. It's painted with the same turquoise clouds and stars as the foyer. A red-and-gold wool rug rolls from the door into the sitting room, where a chandelier hangs overhead. There's a tall sofa and an enlarged mantel and fireplace.

"You have my attention," he says.

I'm glad to see he isn't disheveled from his time in solitude. His mane is combed, and he's dressed in a sage-green cardigan.

"I'm sorry."

He raises his brow. "Do you honestly mean that?"

I bite my lip. I'm a terrible liar. "I'm sorry, no. I don't."

Frank sighs. "You released Beelzebub," he reminds me. "And you lied about having your power."

"Alright, yes, I lied. I apologize for that. Honest. But for Beelzebub, I can't apologize. You may *think* that I overstepped, but in time, you'll come to forgive me."

"I will?" Frank scoffs. "Why do you think that?"

I fix him with a stern look. "You needed me to do this for you. Frank, I don't know what's been going on, but you need help. I'm worried about you. Your memory is getting worse."

He laughs, and for some reason, it makes rage boil in my belly. "My memory is fine."

"It is *not* fine! You're not fine. This house isn't fine. Ash Gardens isn't fine." I come closer. My voice drops to a whisper. "It is *falling* apart, and you know it. What is happening?"

Frank swallows and steps back. He runs his paw through his mane. "It's not falling apart. It's all under control."

"Don't you see? This is exactly why you needed me to release Bee for you. You're evading your problems. It's not healthy."

Frank walks farther into the sitting room and picks up his tea from the tall coffee table. He takes a smooth sip. "Do you honestly want to talk about evading issues, Saika?" He lifts his bushy brow.

It feels like ice water pours down my back. "That's different."

"Is it?" Frank asks. He sets down his tea. "You're welcome to be here, that will never change. But Saika, you don't have to stay around to watch over me. I'm not an issue you need to fix."

"I'm not trying to fix you, Frank. I'm just trying to help."

He tilts his head. "I *needed* you to release Bee for me, that is what you said. What would ever give you that idea?"

"Because you . . . you just did. You were conflating your visions with reality. Bee, therefore Kye, was burdening your conscience."

"But she and Kye are my burdens to bear, Saika. You didn't need to intervene. I was fine on my own."

"You *weren't* fine, Fiona! You needed me!"

Your presence fills the room, Fi. You stand beside Frank. Both of you stare at me, mouths slightly agape. Your eyes are fixed on me in an unwavering gaze.

I didn't need you to intervene, Saika, your voice ghosts over me.

"I didn't need you to intervene. You have to understand that," Frank says calmly.

"In time," I tell you both, "I hope you'll understand and come to forgive me."

I leave his wing, slowly closing the doors behind me.

CHAPTER NINETEEN

I sit in the grass by the side of the house, chin resting on my knees. The sunset's golden light casts shadows over the house, and how I wish that darkness would just swallow me up, too. Tears drip down my cheek, and I wipe them quickly. Stars forbid anyone catches me like this.

Fi, I was only trying to help. You know that, right? You didn't choose to die so soon. So I brought you back, Fi. I did. I did a good thing.

You didn't need to intervene, Frank's voice floats in my mind. *You have to understand that.*

I groan, pressing my hands on my head. Everyone is so upset with me. You were angry. Our parents wish death upon me. And Frank is . . .

Damn it, Fi. I thought I was finally ready for this. I thought I'd be okay coming to Ash Gardens and laying you to rest. *I'm fine,* I kept telling myself. *Everything is fine. I'm fine.*

But I'm not fine at all. In fact, I'm screaming on the inside, desperately pulling my limbs like a puppeteer just to show everyone else how perfectly *fine* I am.

I cover my face, hiding myself in the crooks of my arms. I'm useless. I'm so useless. Perhaps I should just send myself out to sea on a piece of driftwood. No one would even know I was gone.

Laughter echoes from the backyard. As the sound gets closer, I sit upright, wipe my eyes raw, and fix my disheveled headscarf.

Oli comes around the bend with a tiny circle of light hovering beside her. The sound of their laughter makes my heart flutter.

They come to a stop when they see me lying half bathed in shadows, half in sunlight. I'm quiet when Oli sets her eyes on me. We haven't spoken since our day at the market. We've bumped into each other around the house, in the hall, and we'd hover just for a moment. Wanting to say something, but then deciding to walk away.

"Enjoying the sunset?" she asks. She smiles at me, and it chips a bit of ice from around my heart.

"I am, in fact." It's a delicate act, pretending as if my voice isn't on the verge of breaking.

I'm sure Evette and Oli see my red, puffy eyes. But thankfully, they don't mention it. Instead, Evette floats down to me.

"We just came back from Rose Woods, and Oli is going to help me make some venison stew for dinner. Can you come help, too, Saika?" She folds her hands. Her brown eyes are so big and captivating.

I stand to my feet. "I'm useless everywhere else, but I'll give it a shot."

"Oh, great." Evette chuckles uncomfortably. She flutters away as a circle of light.

Oli analyzes me but remains quiet as we go inside.

Once we reach the kitchen, Evette is already buzzing around and setting out pots and pans for dinner.

Oli washes her hands and looks at me. "I know you fancy those gloves, but you have to wash your hands, too."

I roll my eyes and join her at the sink. A few weeks ago, I

would've been sensitive about my hands. I would've delayed washing them until they all turned away. But Oli heard what Lorna said at the market. She knows that I'm cursed. There's no sense in hiding it.

Oli watches me slip off my gloves. My hands are spotty and withered, and I submerge them in the running water.

"Listen, Saika." She lowers her voice. "I—"

Evette shakes the counter when she slams down an entire basket of lemons. "Thanks to Bee's last eggs, I was able to get some lemons." She flutters away to pull out more ingredients.

I look at Oli. "Is there something you wanted to say?"

She shakes her head. "Later."

Evette comes back and slides the basket toward me. "Here, Sai. You're on lemon-shaving duty. Oli, can you get the meat from the icebox?"

Oli salutes. "Aye, Cap'n."

Evette gets out the zester and shows me how to shave the lemons. It seems like such a ridiculous thing, but Evette takes her time, and it's amazing seeing her work, her focus.

"Frank loves lemon cake," she says. "He's been so down lately."

"That's kind of you, Evette." I take the zester. "I think I understand how to do it. I'll take it from here."

She breaks from her stupor. "Oh, right. Sorry. Sometimes I get so into it." She laughs and joins Oli at the other end of the kitchen.

"Doesn't Phil normally help you with meals?" I ask.

"He does," she answers. She sets a pot on the stove and pours in brown stock. She flutters around the kitchen, picking up ingredients and spices, then sets carrots and onions on a wooden block and directs Oli to chop. "I knocked on Phil's door so he could come down, but he didn't answer."

"Why didn't you just go in?" I ask. I remember her intrusion into my room on my first day here.

"Oh, I would never. Phil likes his space. I try to respect that."

I set the lemon down. "You two seem very close."

"Oh, we are." Light brightens around Evette's face. Oli wiggles her brows, and Evette shoos her away. "No, not like that." She laughs. "I love Phil. He's a good friend. He listens to me."

Oli stops cutting and leans on the counter. "You've never once thought there might be something more?"

"Dust and shimmers, no!" Evette chuckles. "You know I don't see people in a romantical way. Phil is my family. All of you are. And that's enough for me." She picks up the carrots and onions that Oli had been cutting and tosses them into the pot. She sprinkles in seasoning, and the kitchen fills with a savory aroma.

"I still don't understand how anyone could go through life that way," Oli says. "I'd die if I couldn't . . . you know, express myself with someone." She begins chopping another onion.

My ears feel hot.

Evette gives the simmering pot a mix. "Oh, Oli, we all know that."

"Evette!" Oli laughs.

"Oh, was I not supposed to say that?"

"You're supposed to be sweet and innocent. Especially when it comes to me."

"Oli, you make it *so* hard sometimes." She laughs.

I smile, watching them. I'm not sure if this warm feeling in my chest is from them or the stove heating up the kitchen. But as I resign myself to silence and listen to their idle conversation, the stress from the past few days feels like it's melting away.

Frank finally comes out of his room for dinner.

It's the first time he has in days. He's wearing a burgundy woven cardigan, and he actually grins when he joins us at the table. "'Evening, everyone."

"Frank." Evette positively buzzes. "It's so good to see your face again."

"Are you feeling better?" Hilde asks.

Frank nods. "I needed some time to myself after the loss of Bee." No one looks my way, but I still feel a million eyes on me. "Evette, did I smell lemon cake earlier?"

Evette grins, her light shining as bright as a star. "You did. It's in the kitchen. I just need the icing to cool."

He lifts a steaming spoon of carrots and venison. "I thought the lemon tree was torn down."

And used for an enchantment by me. Thank you, again, for the reminder, Frank.

"It was," Evette explains. "But we sold the remainder of Bee's eggs. I was able to get some fruit including some lemons and all sorts of vegetables. They should last us for a bit at least."

Frank hums, turning his attention to his food. We eat in stilted silence. I glance at Oli across the table.

"You know, Frank," she begins, "when we went to the city, I realized—"

"You went to the city?" Frank asks, setting down his glass of wine.

Eyes shift to me. I stiffen in my seat. "We joined Morose on his last trip to the city." I take a sip of wine so small, I'm certain it doesn't even reach my throat.

Frank's yellow eyes widen. "All of you went?"

"We did, Frank," Oli says.

"It was a day of leisure," I further explain. "After the morning you found . . . you found out about Bee."

"A day of leisure?" Frank looks around the table. He wipes his mouth with a cloth napkin.

I'm not sure what his reaction will be. We're all adults, for stars' sake. We should be able to do as we please as long as our work gets done.

But Frank is also a ten-foot mythical beast with horns and sharp teeth. Although none of us came to harm, we witnessed his anger that morning. And I fear I keep testing the limits of Frank's patience.

Unlike that fateful morning, he doesn't rise in a fit of anger.

He takes a thoughtful sip of his wine again. "I'd prefer that you all stick to your assigned jobs." He ends with one last bite of stew and gets up from the table. "Thank you for the meal, Evette. It was delicious."

Evette gets up, hesitant to fly after him. "You haven't had any lemon cake."

"Forgive me. Perhaps I can have some later." He leaves without saying another word. The door to his wing opens and shuts with a resounding slam.

Morose tosses a napkin on the table. He glares at me. "This is all your fault, you know."

"Hey," Oli interjects, but Morose continues.

"No, I'm allowed to speak my mind. All she's done is speak hers since she's got here. We've been having terrible weather. The kitchen nearly collapsed the house. She ruined our entire garden, not to mention all of the fruit trees—"

"Saika didn't ruin anything. The storm did. And she isn't responsible for the damage it caused," Oli says.

"But everything was fine before she showed up, wasn't it, though?" he counters. "Now, everything has turned to dung."

"Morose," Merry snaps. "That's enough."

"No. Morose is right." I blink my dry eyes. "The garden isn't yielding anything. We don't have Beelzebub. We don't know how long we'll last like this. And that's not even mentioning the house. It's . . ." I pause. The words *falling apart* lie on the tip of my tongue, but I glance down to Phil's place setting. His bowl of stew is untouched.

"Is Phil here?" I ask.

"Oy, she's got the attention span of a fruit fly," Morose quips.

Evette answers me. "No, he still hasn't answered his door. Maybe he didn't want to come down today?"

That's strange. Phil never misses a meal.

"What were you saying?" Hilde asks, bringing me back to the present. "About the house?"

I blink, trying to think quickly. "The house is . . . special to Frank. I don't want him to lose Ash Gardens. I don't want any of you to lose your home."

"We just need to keep working hard, right?" Merry asks. He looks around the table for approval. "We'll keep planting until something grows."

The issue with the garden can't be solved with sheer perseverance. It needs powerful magic. It needs a star. And Frank is waiting for this miracle to come.

I realize that Ignatius could be wrong. What if the star parade doesn't come? What will we do then? We need other solutions just in case. And I don't think Frank is preparing for that.

I stand from the table. "That's a good attitude, Merry. Just keep trying to do what you can." I take my leave, going upstairs to my room and shutting the door tight.

The sky turns black outside my window. I hear one pitter, then a patter, and soon a shower of rain hits the glass of the window. I lie on my bed, cradling my nauseous stomach. I just drank two mugs of Hilde's grass tea. I hoped I would've gotten used to its side effects. The healing magic rejuvenates my body, but I wish it would work on my heart, too.

The emotional turmoil from today alone is sending me into a spiral. I'm haunted by the idea of the house crashing down on us. I'm haunted by Frank's anger and his secrets and his receding memory.

I'm even haunted by memories of you, Fi. My heart seeks comfort in you and in your voice. I think about the advice you would give to clean up this mess.

Well, for starters, you would never have lost your power to begin with. You'd fix all of Ash Gardens before you even had your morning tea. You'd make this right, Fi.

I shouldn't have stayed this long. I should have just fulfilled my promise to you and went on my way.

Or better yet, I should never have come here. I could have returned your ashes to Jonathan and continued wandering the world, broken and hopeless and seeking something for myself.

I shouldn't have left your groom and children.

I shouldn't have been cursed.

I shouldn't have tried to save you, Fi . . .

No. You shouldn't have gotten sick. Then none of this would be happening right now. I wouldn't be feeling so contrite and angry and alone.

Instead, I speak to you in my mind, but what can I do with silence, Fi? I speak to you, as a friend seeking a confidante. But I'd be better off yelling my frustration into the sea, where the waves would carry my anguish to oblivion.

I'm such a fool. Babbling about my day is one thing. And venting about a certain purple-skinned hallmate is another, but you can't give me actual answers, Fi. And it's not fair.

I groan and look up to the vaulted ceiling. I need someone here. I need a friend.

A knock sounds at my door, and it sends me into a panic. I wipe my face dry and answer.

It's Oli, carrying a tiny plate of frosted lemon cake.

"You missed dessert." She grins. "You zested the hell out of this thing. It's only right that you try it."

I chuckle. "How can I say no?" I take the plate and place it on my desk. When I turn around, Oli is standing in my room.

"It's been a bit chaotic at Ash Gardens, eh?" She holds her arms behind her back, gazing around my room, then sits on the edge of my bed.

"Ever since I arrived." I smile cheaply.

Oli furrows her brow. "That damn cherub doesn't know what he's on about."

"He does, though." I sit at my desk and run my hands down my tired face. "I don't even know what I'm doing anymore. I've been alone ever since my sister died. So I've been carrying all of my thoughts around with no one to tell them to." No one except you, Fi. "I feel like screaming. Or getting pissed. I'm not sure which."

Oli laughs. "My, Saika. Such language." She feigns shock. "Did you learn that on your travels?"

I look over at her, smirking. "Possibly."

"While I don't have any alcohol on me, I do have an ear. Two of them, in fact." She leans back on my bed, crosses her legs, and pats the space beside her. "It sounds like you need to talk it out."

Against my better judgment, Fi, I pick up the plate of lemon cake and join her on the bed. Our knees touch, and she grins when she looks up at me. "I had no idea it would be this easy to get you into bed."

I stand up. "You ruined it."

"Ah, come on." She laughs and pulls me back down. She doesn't have to try very hard. She rests her hand on my knee. "I've been wanting to talk to you, Saika. I wanted to apologize for that day at the market."

She pulls down the collar of her shirt just enough so I can see the inked name. "I haven't heard Henley's name spoken in such a long time. It threw me off. I got scared. And honestly, I don't think I'm ready to talk about it yet."

"You don't have to. I apologize, Olivie. I crossed a boundary. I shouldn't have pulled down your collar. I shouldn't have touched you."

"No." Her cheeks blush a dark violet. Her hand hasn't left my knee. She draws circles with her thumb, and it tickles a bit. I could move my knee, but I don't. I sit still, transfixed on her circling thumb. The curve of her wrist and the matte-black ink on the back of her hand.

I think about what she said in the kitchen earlier. *I'd die if I couldn't . . . you know, express myself with someone.*

When was the last time Oli expressed herself with someone? There haven't been many ceremonies, so she hasn't had anyone in her room for a while. Is she just bored and our whole friendship is still a game to her? A tease, as she so lightly put it before.

It grows too quiet, and she looks at me from under those dark lashes. Her chin slightly tilts, and her eyes flick to my lips.

But the spell breaks, and I don't know what causes it. She

shifts slightly back so that we aren't touching anymore. "I'm sorry. I said I'd sit here and listen. Tell me what's on your mind."

I blink rapidly, sitting back as well, trying to get my bearings. "Right." I finally eat a spoonful of lemon cake. It's sweet, and I savor it for just a moment. "Well, you heard that lady at the market. What she said."

"I did. So, you're cursed? What happened?"

I swallow. "Well, it's a bit of a heavy story," I begin.

I've never thought of myself telling the full truth to anyone, Fi. I've always imagined our lives—our beginnings and your end—belonging solely to us. No one else needs to know about it. They wouldn't feel the way we felt. They've never been desperate or foolish enough to try to change the course of their fate.

But I've learned after my stay at Ash Gardens that we aren't wholly unique creatures. I have to remind myself that relaying our story isn't an embarrassment. It isn't the hubris of witches with seemingly endless power who run headfirst into the fact that we are, indeed, powerless. And the only absolute in this life is that there will always be Death. And there is no controlling him.

And I realize that when I think back on it, our story begins and ends with him.

"My older sister, Fiona, was an adventurer. She was daring, and inventive, and creative. She frequently went seafaring. She wasn't as infamous as you were, but she went on many voyages." I exhale, long and deep. "Our parents didn't agree with her line of work. She'd venture into far-off lands, but when she started bringing home treasures and artifacts, well, they began to change their tune. She was free to do as she pleased. She never picked a sector of magic, either. If she was interested in Languages, or Science, or Music, she'd dabble in it. And our parents let her. I wasn't so fortunate. They made me choose, so I picked Music.

But as one last slight to them, I learned to play instruments and learned sheet music on my own without enchantments. They didn't really care for that, but Fiona loved it, and that's all that really mattered to me."

Here it is, Fi. The hard part. My chest tightens just a bit.

"She went on a journey to the Limestone Mountains. It's a very dangerous place. Adventurers would fall over dead if they misstepped. Fiona assured us that she took every precaution before she went. But she and her fiancé returned just days later. Jonathan was badly hurt, and Fiona . . . she wouldn't wake up. It was strange seeing her so still, when I've known Fiona to be lively and joyous. Here I was waiting at home, anticipating her tales from the mountains, but instead she came back . . . silent. I don't think I really understood the severity of her state until the Medic witches exhausted all of their options. And when I heard the words *She's going to die* . . . all reasoning simply eluded me. I was going to get my sister back. And I didn't care what would become of me.

"I was desperate, so I looked into answers not suited for a young girl. And I found one. I knew exactly who to summon to bring Fiona back."

Oli blinks, eyes wide. "Saika . . . you called Death? How? You'd need a powerful source—" She glances at my empty locket. "Your power source."

"When we were girls, Fiona and I witnessed a star fall from the sky and we kept it for ourselves. Fiona advised that we hide the star away. With a power this grand, she thought it would be better if we waited until we needed a miracle. So we hid it away. But Fiona was going to die. I needed a miracle."

The memory of breaking into our father's study rises in my mind. I pick the lock to his forbidden texts and find the one about

Death. I seclude myself in the safety of my bedroom. I sit the star on the floor and recite the ancient spell to summon him. My voice trembles as I read the foreign language, and for a moment, I think I must've said something incorrectly. But then thick smoke fills the room. I cry out to Death, and the anguish is so tight in my chest it feels like my lungs might burst. I'm holding your life in my hands, Fi. I'm not going to mess it up. I will bring you back.

"Death came instantly as a bright light in my room, and I turned my face away. I knew not to look directly at him or touch him. So I bowed, and I pleaded for Fiona's life. But it was more weeping than actual words. I was desperate, and Death heard me. I was willing to do absolutely anything for her to wake up. Death accepted, but I was asked to give something else in return. My power. My youth."

I take a deep breath and slip off my gloves. Oli doesn't react when she sees my withered, age-spotted hands. She remains quiet.

"Fiona was angry when she woke up. She was okay with dying. Can you believe that? She didn't want me to intervene. She was at peace. And then, our parents found out what I'd done, and they were wroth with me for dealing with Death. They banished me from their household and their estate. They gave my portion of the trust entirely to Fiona. Everyone hated me." I chuckle sorely, a few tears falling from my eyes. "I was only trying to help, and it worked. I saved my sister. Death gave Fiona three years. It was enough time for her to finally get married, and she gave birth to twin girls who look exactly like her."

I mindlessly pick at the cake on my plate. "And she finally came around to forgiving me. We spent the last year of her life together. The deal was slowly ending, so her sickness returned, and she spent the majority of her days in bed. I lived with her and her husband until the very end. I got to see my nieces grow. And over that time, my power slowly drained. I couldn't cast enchantments anymore. And now my body is breaking down and aging faster than ever. I'm not sure when Death will collect on his end of the deal. But I don't mind waiting it out. I don't regret saving Fiona's life. And I don't regret being cursed."

Oli's knees press against mine. I look up and she's scooted closer. She touches my cursed hands, but I snatch them back. "You don't have to be around me. No one wants to be around a curse."

She takes my hands anyway and slides our fingers together. I finally feel her skin on mine. "I'm not afraid to be around you." She brings my knuckles to her mouth, and my body freezes.

She holds my hands against her lips and looks me in the eyes. A million things run through my mind, Fi. She gazes at me with that same look again. Her dark, round eyes taking all of me in as if I'm the only thing that matters in this moment.

"I think what you did was brave. And it was brave for you to tell me. You aren't a curse, Saika. Not to Ash Gardens, or to Frank. Not to me."

She kisses my knuckles, and the next thing I know, I'm crying. Oli welcomes me into her arms, and I fall into her. She grips me tight. I sob into her neck, smelling her lavender skin and rain-scented hair.

"It's alright, Saika," she whispers in my ear. "It's alright." She rubs my back, humming the melody that she usually plays on her viola at night. I close my eyes, and I relish the feeling of her warm body.

I was so afraid to tell someone else our story, Fi. I thought if they knew the truth, they'd hate me. They wouldn't want to be around me. But they still do. I spoke the truth, and the world didn't end.

CHAPTER TWENTY

It's another dream. I'm pretty certain because I feel my soft, puffy hair resting on my shoulders. Wild and beautiful zigzagged curls frame my face. When I look down at my hands, I'm not wearing my gloves. My hands are smooth and brown. No loose skin in sight.

I'm standing in a field of tall grass, barefoot, and in a red dress that flows in the wind. This field looks familiar. I've seen it before. I think I've stood here before.

It's the beginning of the day. Sunlight pours on my face, and I feel the reviving heat from the sun.

I remember this. We were playing in the field behind Nana's house. We were so young. So free.

Wind tickles my back. I feel your presence behind me. "Do you remember this, Fi?" I turn around, and the smile drops from my face.

Ash Gardens is in the distance. It's standing, but not for long. Dark storm clouds swirl over the house. Lightning strikes the attic, and the wood crumbles. Rain pelts the windows and shutters. Wind rocks the house, and it teeters forward and back.

My heart lodges in my throat. "Wait, no!" I hike up my dress to run, but a hand catches my elbow.

It's a man, dressed in a tailored shirt and vest. A black bowler hat sits atop his head. "Saika, don't."

"Phil?" My voice breaks. Thunder crashes over the field, and I jump. My body is shaking. "What's going on? Are you really here?"

"I am. I needed to talk to you, and I didn't know how else to get your attention. I don't know how long I can keep this form."

Thunder crashes again, and the ground begins to shake. The entire back of the house cracks apart, the wood and beams split open. It's all so loud. The wind. The rain. The thunder. I can't focus. The destruction sends me back to the night the kitchen got destroyed. It shakes me to my core. I don't know what's a dream and what's a memory.

Phil's cold hands gently turn my face to look in his piercing blue eyes.

"You have to focus. Listen to me. That storm, the destruction you see, *will* happen. Ash Gardens is going to fall. It's only a matter of time."

"I can stop it. The star is almost here."

"The star will not matter. You have to tell Frank. Tell him that it's hopeless. His debt will be paid."

"I don't understand. You aren't making any sense."

Phil runs his hands through his perfectly coifed hair. He looks back to me, hair mussed, and desperation in his eyes. "This is all my fault. I shouldn't have shown Frank how to . . ." His body fades in and out. He falls to his knees and clutches handfuls of grass.

"Phil?" I kneel beside him.

He becomes solid again and holds his head. "It takes a lot of power to enchant my soul this way," he mutters. "It's difficult to keep up, but I have to tell you . . ." He groans in pain, releasing a shuddering breath.

"I put the notion in Kye's head for the ash arboretum. I helped her with her research. But then Kye began to think . . . she thought she could hear them. She thought she could hear the deceased."

The ground shakes again. Another part of Ash Gardens falls to the ground. The storm is growing, slowly bleeding over to us. It's getting louder. Angrier.

"The voices of the dead clouded her mind," Phil continues. "She thought enchanting the dead through the arboretum was a remarkable discovery. And then this world wasn't enough for her. She wanted to join them.

"She didn't tell Frank what she was planning. He found her unresponsive in their bed. He came to me, begging for some way to bring her back. I felt responsible for setting her on this path. So, I offered Frank a way to bring her back."

My eyes well with tears. "Phil, you didn't . . ."

"Were you any different, Saika?" he asks. "I see you, you know. Your power is gone. Your body is not that of a young lady." He struggles through labored breathing. "I can feel your cursed energy." He places his hands over mine, and they become bony and withered again. Spots sprout on my skin.

I rip my hands away, and they turn back to normal.

"I sought you out because you understand the consequences of dealing with Death. You can speak to Frank in a way that I can't. He stopped listening to me a long time ago."

Phil disappears for a second before coming back. He groans. "You have to talk to Frank. You have to tell him. The star doesn't matter. The spells do not matter. There is no escaping Death. He will come."

I feel the first drop of rain. I look back to see that Ash Gardens is no longer standing. It's been reduced to a pile of rubble. Storm clouds blanket the sky. The sun hides away as rain showers over us. Phil falls over, his face tight with exertion.

"My soul must move on now," he whispers. "I'm sorry, Saika. I wish I could have done more for him."

"Don't, please." I hold on to his hand and squeeze it tight. Tears burn my eyes. "What about Evette? You can't leave her."

He smiles dreamily. "Oh, sweet Evette. Please, tell her I said thank you."

Rain falls on his face, and I wipe his wet bangs from his eyes. "Phil, please," I cry. "Don't leave like this."

He stares straight ahead. A small smile crosses his face. "I see him," he whispers. "I see Gerard. Oh, you handsome devil." His eyes shift over to me. He grins. "It's time for me to go, Saika."

"No, Phil, I won't—"

"Wake up."

***

My eyes open, but I stay still in bed. I glance out the front window. Dawn. It's quiet after the noise of my dream, but this silence is somehow louder.

That couldn't have been a nightmare. It felt too real.

I lift my head, and my eyes land on something sitting on top of my desk.

Phil's bowler hat.

I swallow, rubbing my tired eyes. I can't deal with this, Fi. I can't.

I rip the blankets from my body. I didn't ask for any of this. I didn't ask to come here. I didn't ask to be the person to carry out your final request, Fi. I'm going to pack my things, right now, and set off. I'll forget all about Ash Gardens and Frank,

and Phil, and Evette, and Merry and Morose, and Hilde . . .
and Oli.

I pause, hovering over my open suitcase.

I slam my bag on the floor. No, I need to talk to Frank. And I
don't care what time it is. He *will* speak to me.

Using an oil lamp, I sneak out into the dark hallway and continue
downstairs. It's only when I'm standing outside Frank's door that
I contemplate what I'm doing.

But I've come too far now. I can't back down.

I knock softly at first. No answer. I take a deep breath and
knock harder. "Frank, I know you're in there."

I hear a clicking sound, and the door opens. My heart pounds,
seeing the dark outline of Frank's head, horns, and shoulders
towering over me. Once the light from my lamp touches his face,
I feel a bit calmer.

"Saika? It's barely day. What's going on?"

"It's Phil. He's moved on," I tell him.

Frank blinks. "How do you know?"

"I saw him." Before he can say anything else, I hand him the
framed picture of him, his wife, and Phil. "And he has a message
for you."

Frank sighs and steps aside. "Come on in."

Stepping inside, I see a sole candle is burning in his sitting
room. Steam rises from the tea he has placed on his coffee table.
"Did I wake you?" I ask him, already knowing the answer.

Frank walks through a wide archway into his kitchenette. I
hear him pour another cup of tea. "I've been up all night. I hav-
en't been sleeping," he calls out.

I hop up to reach the sofa. Frank sits across from me in an armchair. He offers the large cup of tea. I take it, having to hold it with both hands.

Frank sighs, running a paw over his tired face. "What happened with Phil?"

"He told me everything." I settle back into the sofa, my face stern. "I know about Kye. I know what you did to bring her back."

His eyes widen with understanding, as if the weight of his past actions suddenly falls on him. "Saika, you have to know I didn't mean for any of that to happen. I just wanted to see her again."

"I understand, Frank." I set the tea down. "In fact, I may be one of the only people in this world who would understand. How long did Death give her?"

"One year." He pauses as if he's piecing the memory back together. "It should've been longer but calling on Death proved disastrous. Phil used an ancient relic to summon him, but it wasn't enough power. Death sought more, and he took Phil's life. And it worked. Kye came back." He taps his paw on the arm of the chair.

"Phil sacrificed his life to get her back, and still, Death only gave her one year. It wasn't fair. She didn't understand what she was doing. Her death was a mistake."

"But it wasn't a mistake, Frank. Kye chose to die—"

"She didn't choose!" His voice booms, echoing in his front room.

I swallow.

He exhales a shaky breath. "She wouldn't have chosen to leave me that way."

I fold my hands in my lap. We sit in silence for a moment, stewing in the tension until it fades.

"Frank, Phil wanted me to tell you that the star won't fix the house. It won't help Ash Gardens. Your debt will have to be paid."

"Did he now? He doesn't know anything."

"He does. Stars, Frank, I didn't know that Death was coming to claim Ash Gardens. What was the deal for your arrangement? What did he ask for in return?"

"All of me," he answers. "Everything that I hold dear. I used to pride myself on my strong mind and wit. And Ash Gardens, this house, is my most prized possession. But I willingly gave it all up because it meant I could have Kye again. Our year together passed quickly, too quickly. I had to watch her die a second time, and Death has been trying to collect on our deal ever since. Storms began to constantly brew this side of the mountains, threatening to destroy the house. But I'd always find a way to fix it. I looked for witches who could do repairs and take care of Ash Gardens. Kye worked so hard to create the arboretum. I can't bear to see it all fall apart."

"Who else knows about this?"

"No one." He stands up and crosses the room. He opens a large door into his bedroom and comes out a moment later holding a stack of torn parchment. He hands it to me.

"Damn it, Frank. You took this from Kye's journal."

"I'm sorry."

The section heading reads: Mythical Beast, Classification: Rare.

Frank's name is surrounded by question marks. There's a rather elementary illustration of him. His eyes are bright yellow. His fur is reddish brown. His teeth are sharp, and his horns intimidating. Below are listed characteristics: omnivore, loving, incredibly kind, loves sweaters, selfless, can recall any memory with striking precision.

"You can recall any memory?" I ask. "Why didn't you want me to see this?"

"You know that my mind is waning. I realized some time ago that whenever the house breaks, so does a piece of my mind. And there's nothing I can do to fix it."

"Surely Ignatius and I can find some way to restore your mind."

"No, Ignatius can't know about this. No one can know. We've all lost someone or something, Saika. And they've helped me with my grief as much as I've helped them. I could never face them if they knew I revived Kye."

He sinks back into the armchair and places his head in his paws. "I thought I'd be free from this, but I'm still being haunted by her memory. I feel like I'm seeing her all over again. I hear her call my name from the arboretum."

My chest feels tight as I watch him fight back a sob. I hop off the sofa and kneel before him. I place my hand on his knee, and he looks at me through misty eyes. "Frank, you and I are alike in more ways than you think."

I peel off a glove, and I show him my withered hand. "I never told you exactly why I don't have my power anymore. I called upon Death, too. And he brought back my sister." Tears crest my eyes. "And she was angry with me for it."

Saika, what did you do? I was at peace! You didn't need to intervene!

I close my eyes, letting that memory wash away. "Over time, she came to forgive me. But by then, her time was up. She left willingly, and Death is collecting on our deal. My power. My youth. It all belongs to him now. But it doesn't have to be the same for you."

"Saika, I fear I'm too far gone now. My only hope is to save Ash Gardens. What's done is done."

"No," I snap. "I've used a star once before. It brought back Fiona." I hold up my locket. "It restrained my curse and powered my enchantments. I'll come up with a spell. And when the new star comes, we'll use it to fix Ash Gardens, and we'll use it to fix you."

He sighs and looks at me sadly. "And what about you, Saika?" he asks. "Will this star be enough to fix you, too?"

I look away. I had thought about asking him for a portion of the star before, Fi. But to heal the house and his mind against the power of Death, there won't be enough for me.

My throat tightens. When Death comes to collect, I won't have anything to save me. I blink back tears and gaze up at his kind face.

"I'll be fine." I smile. "You once said that you believe you've been put on this earth to love. Well, I believe I was put here to help. And I want to help you, Frank. You've done so much for me. For Hilde. The cherubs. Oli. You've been there for everyone else. Allow me to be there for you."

I don't realize I'm crying, but he pulls out a handkerchief from his pocket and dabs my eyes. "You're an incredible witch, Saika. And an even more incredible friend." His soft paw caresses the side of my face. "Thank you."

CHAPTER TWENTY-ONE

The past couple of days have felt like a whirlwind. The morning Phil moved on, I was the one who broke the news at breakfast. Frank was there, sitting at the head of the table with his head down.

It pained me to unload something like this on everyone, especially seeing the look on Evette's face. Or the realization settling over Merry and Morose. I told them that Phil was at peace, and he wanted to join his husband once again. I relayed Phil's final message to Evette, stressing how much he loved and thanked her for her friendship. It cushioned the blow a tad, but it left a dark cloud over the house that I've yet to see go away.

The only one who didn't have a reaction was Ignatius. Upon hearing the tragic news, he simply said, "Phil was already dead." And he returned to his work without missing a stride.

Phil may have been dead, but he was alive to us. To Evette. And no one knows exactly why his spirit lingered for so long. No one knew who Phil really was, and I want to tell them. But Frank still wants to keep everything to himself. And I don't want to break his trust.

To prove my loyalty to Frank, I've been dedicating my time

and energy to spell research. I've resumed my mornings with Ignatius, despite bad-mouthing his habits. I'm on the hunt for an enchantment that will restore Frank's mind. The problem is, I could concoct all the spells in the world, but I still don't have any power to test them out.

So, I hoard the research, writing it all down in a handmade pamphlet to test out once we have the star. I won't let Frank's mind, or this house, turn to ash.

This morning, I get up quite early. After all of those vivid dreams, it's been hard to stay asleep. It's Evette's turn for meal duty, and I'd like to help her.

When I come into the kitchen, the morning sun shines through the stained glass windows. A clay mug sits on the counter, and a name is painted across the rim: Phil. The tips of two fluttering wings peek out of the top.

Evette doesn't move when I come closer. I pick up the mug, but she only turns away, trying to dig herself farther inside.

"I'd say 'good morning,' but it doesn't quite feel good, does it? So, morning, Evette."

Her voice is low, but she answers back. "Morning."

"Did you sleep in here last night? You're still in your jammies." She's also wearing a tiny silk bonnet decorated with pink strawberries.

Evette looks up at me. She rubs her puffy eyes. "He's gone, Saika. I know he was a spirit. But he was my best friend. My first friend, after . . ." She swallows. "Do you know why I came to Ash Gardens?"

"No, I don't think I've ever heard the tale."

Evette hugs her knees, looking off to someplace distant. "I'm from a fairy borough in the east. It sat on the River Heille. It was known to flood, but we've always set up precautions. Anyway, I went on a solo journey to have some time to myself. My family had been irritating me, and I needed to get away . . . but when I came back home, the entire borough had been flooded. Everyone. My entire family . . . I'm the only one left, Saika."

"Oh, Evette."

"I worked in the city for a while after that. But I felt so alone. I saw an ad for Ash Gardens needing a chef. I always loved cooking with my mama. And when I came, I met Frank, and Oli, and everyone else. They greeted me with open arms, and it made me *so happy* to be around loving people again. I was so happy . . . and then I met Phil." Her eyes glaze over. "I don't know if it was his silence, but the first time we sat together, I finally stopped and processed everything that had happened to me. And I just cried." She looks up at me. A globing tear hangs from her lower lash. "It was the first time I actually sat, and cried, and grieved about everyone and everything that I lost. And I talked for hours. I swore. I yelled. I screamed. And Phil sat there, listening to every word." She wipes the tears from her cheek. The light glowing around her face pulses and becomes dimmer. "I understand that he had to move on. I do. I just wish there was some way I could have thanked him, too."

I hold out my hand, and she flutters onto my palm. I wipe her eyes with the pad of my finger. "Feel how you're going to feel. Cry as much as you'd like to cry. And when you want to speak to Phil again, do it. Write to him and thank him. Write him letters upon letters, telling him about your day. Tell him what you had for breakfast. Some small part of me feels like he's still listening."

Evette touches my finger and then flies up to my face. She

hugs my cheek with her full body. It's still a very strange sensation, but one that I welcome all the same.

"I'll give that a try. Thank you, Saika."

"It's just some advice that was given to me long ago." I smile. "Go on, get dressed. I'll handle breakfast this morning."

Evette flits off. I'm left in the kitchen, thinking about the words of comfort I've given her and contemplating if I should have. Speaking to you, Fi, is about the same as Evette finding a confidant in Phil. Except, he was actually *there* and listening. I don't know if I've doomed her to prolong the inevitable. One day, she will have to let him go, and move on.

And that scares me because what does that mean for me?

Breakfast is quiet. Hilde hasn't come out of her room since Phil moved on. She's been having her meals in solitude because she can't be around Evette's intense emotions.

All I can manage for breakfast are a few eggs and some slices of old bread with the last bit of berries and preserved jam. The meal is over quickly, and I'm a bit glad. Everyone feels so down and forlorn, and I wish there was something I could do to lift their spirits.

We're all feeling a loss. So, perhaps, that's why I settle on a distraction. Before everyone can depart from the table, I stand up. "I think we all need a celebration."

I'm met with bewildered faces, naturally.

"For what?" Oli asks.

"For life. Our life. We are still here. We are still able to . . . to have fun."

"Didn't think you knew how to have fun," Morose says.

"I do, *Morry*." He doesn't like that one bit. "I think we ought to dress in our finest clothes, bring on the music, and have a feast."

"I don't mean to sound rude, but feast on what?" Merry asks, holding up his empty plate. "We have no food."

"I'll worry about that. I'm hopeful for the future. It's a bit bleak right now, but it won't be always. I'm certain of that."

Evette gleams. "I love this idea! I think Phil would've wanted us to have a celebration. Thank you, Saika."

I look at Frank, who hasn't said a word. "What do you think?" I ask.

Frank polishes off the rest of his eggs. "If you'd like to have a celebration, then I won't stop you." He silently gets up and leaves the dining room. Oli and I share a worried look.

I clap my hands together. "Okay, that's two *yay*s and one apprehensive *yes*. We're having a party!"

"Hey, I didn't vote," Morose says.

"It doesn't matter. We're having a party."

I gather everyone's dishes and pile them in the kitchen as they head off to do their jobs. I run the water to begin washing the dishes, but when I pick up a plate, it slips through my fingers. It crashes on the floor. My hand has locked up and gone stiff.

"Oh my." Oli comes into the kitchen. "Bit clumsy this morning?" She enchants a cyclone of air to sweep up the shattered mess.

I turn off the running water. "My hand." The joints are stiff on my right hand. They won't move.

Oli watches me, then she takes my hand. I don't think I'll

ever get used to her touching me this way. "Hand's a bit locked up?" she asks.

"I need to finish cleaning up breakfast."

She goes digging in the cupboards until she comes out with a jar of green ash leaves. She pulls one out, and it glitters in the morning light. "It's enchanted." She wraps the leaf around my hand, then closes her eyes, and the leaf glows brightly for a split second before turning back to normal. "Keep this wrapped."

The leaf begins to warm, and magic energy coats my hand, massaging my joints. "What is it?"

She moves to the sink and begins washing the dishes. "Hilde likes to keep it secret, but it's one of the ingredients for her healing tea. Ash leaves from Rose Woods."

She rinses off a sudsy dish. "In fact, I have to go there to get wood for this storm Ignatius sees on the horizon. Care to join me?" She smiles. "You can tell me all about this fancy party."

"Of course."

You would think I've grown accustomed to sharing a broom with Oli, but I've yet to ride with her without fumbling like a teenager with a crush. I'm still cradling my arthritic hand, so I can't hold on to her from behind.

So, she directs me to the front of the broom and saddles behind me. My ears feel aflame when she tugs me back into her arms. "You alright up there?" she croons. Her voice is like fire in my ear.

I nod. "I'm fine. Just fine."

We touch down in Rose Woods in mere moments, settling into an area crowded with trees. Deer scurry off when they hear us trampling through. Oli walks ahead, reading her map. "Gotta find more of these damn trees to harvest," she mutters.

I trail behind her, still holding my wrapped hand. "I don't think you'll have to do this for too long. In a few days, I think our luck will turn around."

Oli folds up the map and looks back at me. "How could you know that? Did Ignatius share his wisdom of prophecy with you?"

"No, I just have a feeling. I think we'll have a lot to celebrate."

"Hence the party?"

"Hence the party."

She opens her map again, and we continue walking. "I'm not too sure. In all of my time at Ash Gardens, we've never had an issue this bad or for this long. There's no food *and* no money. We're running out of places to harvest in Rose Woods. I'm being asked to cut down in inhabited lands."

"No, Frank wouldn't want you to—" Oli looks back at me, and I stop. "He asked you to do that?"

She leans against a tree and folds her arms. "I need to ask you a question. And please, I want you to be honest with me." She looks at me. "What's going on with Frank?"

"Nothing."

"Cut the shit, Saika."

"What? He's feeling just fine. He's . . . he's fine."

"You said that your job with Ignatius wasn't dangerous."

For once, I can speak with confidence. "It's not."

Oli bites her lip, thinking for a moment. She crumples the map in her hand. "What's he having you and Ignatius do? Is it just spells for the house? Why the secrecy?"

"I've sworn to Frank that I'd keep our dealings private. And as I assured you last time, everything is fine. Frank is not in danger."

"Are you?"

I blink. "I'm sorry?"

"Are you in danger?" Oli repeats flatly. "You've been busting your ass trying to help Ash Gardens, but look at you. You're fucking falling apart." She points to my leaf-wrapped hand. "What's going to happen to you, Saika?"

"Oh, I'm fine." I smile.

"Phil died, and it's like you don't care."

"Phil was a spirit. It's natural. He just went on."

"He died," Oli corrects. "You said he visited you in your dream, and he died. You witnessed it. That's gotta . . . Are you sure you're alright?"

I suppose I haven't thought about it like that. I witnessed Phil's second death. I think I've been so concentrated on Frank and his problems that I haven't thought about what it meant for me. I've had trouble sleeping. I've been afraid to, because somewhere in the darkness of my mind, I'm afraid to dream again.

"I think I'm tired, Olivie."

She swings her broom around. "Get on. Let's go rest, then."

Oli's arms cradle my waist, and I lean back against her as we fly. I close my eyes as wind ghosts over us. We land a few moments later in a shady grove. The sound of trickling water entices my sweaty face. It's coming from the creek just over the bank. A tall willow tree sways in the wind, its long leaves breaking off and landing in the sparkling water.

"Ah, so this is where you disappear to when you're gone for hours."

Oli laughs. "No one knows this is here. Well, except Evette. But still, don't go telling the others." She goes underneath the tall willow and sets down her broom and bag. "I'm going to go dip."

"Dip?"

"A little splash?" Oli reaches for the hem of her shirt and pulls it over her head. She laughs when I completely turn around. "Oh, don't be like that. You can fancy a swim with me."

"I haven't done that since I was a girl."

"You still are a girl."

I turn around, and she's pointing at her chest. "At least, you still are, here. At heart."

I'm well aware that she's trying to point at her heart, but all I can see is her tattooed chest and her breasts sitting comfortably in a brassiere. I read Henley's name again, and to my embarrassment, she continues stripping.

She pulls down her pants and I see that her tattoos aren't limited to her arms and chest. They look like chaotic works of art, spanning down her torso, over her legs, and even down to her feet.

She catches me staring and grins wickedly. "Do you see something you like?"

I furrow my brow. Wait, is this still a game, Fi? I thought my moment of vulnerability the other night would've done away with the teasing.

"I'm joking." She chuckles. "Look, you can rest here then. The willow tree always gives me the best naps." She rubs its velvety leaves. And then she's off, running toward the small cliff hanging over the creek. She jumps off and gives a hooting shout before she's drowned by a massive splash of water.

She's ridiculous, Fi. Utterly ridiculous. But it's not like I can get on her broom and fly back home. My face is so hot. I fan myself to cool off.

"This cold water feels so nice, Saika!" Oli's voice echoes.

"I'm fine here, thanks!" I lie on my back and gaze up to the sunlight filtering through leaves. I watch a cluster of birds fly overhead. They glide in a loop until they set off, disappearing.

My eyes feel droopy. The wind kisses my flushed face. Shade from the tree cascades over my eyes. A yawn escapes my mouth. I'll just rest my eyes. Only for a moment.

Finally, a dreamless sleep. A peaceful one, too. After running myself ragged the last couple of days, my body has melted into the ground. The ash leaf wrapped around my hand has turned to . . . well, ash. I flex my hand, and it feels loads better. But I know this is only a temporary fix. It'll just keep getting worse until I'm nothing but dust.

I finally sit up. Oli isn't back. Her black clothes are still thrown on the ground.

I hear splashing coming from the creek, and I take a leisurely stroll over. I stand at the edge of the small cliff to see Oli, floating in the clear water. Her eyes are shut. Her black hair floats in a circle around her head.

I sit down, swinging my legs over the edge. "How relaxing," I call.

She peeks her eye open, holding up her hand to the blinding sun. "The princess has awakened, I see."

The water looks cool. After that nap, my back is drenched with sweat. "Can I ask you a question?"

Oli closes her eyes and folds her hands over her stomach. "Sure."

"Are you going to harvest the trees like Frank asked?"

She's quiet for a moment, drifting aimlessly in the water.

"Nah. Frank's off. Never thought I'd see the day I question his judgment. I'll get wood someplace else. Why do you ask?"

"I don't know. When I first came, I thought you'd always do what Frank asked, no judgment."

"At a point in time, I think I would have. I owe him my life." She continues drifting in meandering circles. "I wouldn't be here if it weren't for him."

"I see." I look down to my gloveless hand. My aged skin looks like leather in the sun. "I feel that may be the same for everyone at Ash Gardens. You've all helped me, too, I think."

Oli opens her eyes and grins. "Even me?"

"Of course you. I told you the ugly truth about me, and you didn't run off. That's more than I can say about my own family."

She freezes the enchanted water, keeping her in place, and stares up at me. "Why would I run off, Saika? I like you."

I blink, looking down at her. Her eyes haven't left me. I feel a bit stuck, Fi. I'm afraid. The truth knocks on my heart, and I want to tell Oli everything about the curse. I want to tell her that liking me is a fruitless action. I'm not sure how much time I have left.

But when I gaze down at her beautiful black eyes in the sun, rational thought leaves my mind, which is instead filled with her beauty. Her kindness. Her ability to make everything feel okay. So instead of closing this door, I kick it wide open and utter five little words. "I like you, too, Olivie."

For a second, I don't think she heard me. She's quiet, and the air around us goes still. But then in the next moment, Oli is circling her arm, and enchanted water spirals up from the creek. It rushes toward me, and before I can run away, it swallows me. It pulls me from the cliff, and I come splashing down into the creek. A cushion of water softens my landing, but I'm still sputtering when I stand to my feet. I nearly slip again, but Oli is quick to catch me.

"You are such a child!" I cough, but Oli is too busy laughing. She pulls me into her arms.

Her wet hands cup the sides of my face, and in the next moment, her soft lips press against mine. I'm stunned in place. My neck and face are aflame. I reach up and hold on to her, fearful if I let her go, I might drown.

She breaks away and gives a chaste kiss to my forehead before standing back and taking all of me in. "Damn it all, Saika." She says my name so sweetly, it aches.

"Oli, what are you . . ." I feel a cold, wet breeze over my scalp. I touch the top of my head. My headwrap is gone. "No . . ."

I push Oli away and clamber toward the bank of the creek.

"Saika, wait!"

I jump up from the water, but my soaked dress nearly drags me back in. My joints crack as I flop onto the grass. I heave my heavy, wet dress and run toward the willow tree.

"Saika, stop!" Oli calls. She sounds closer than before. I glance back and trip over a tree root sticking up from the ground. I tumble forward, and Oli is on me in an instant.

"Damn it. Stop running, Saika. Stop!" She grabs me, but I shake her off.

"Stop, Oli!"

Oli freezes above me. She's clutching my soaked headwrap in her hand. "You don't have to pretend, alright?"

My chest is heaving so much, it feels like it's on fire. "I understand. You like to tease. You like to play. But I can't take these games anymore."

"I'm not teasing." She kneels before me. She enchants the air, and it dries the headwrap quickly. She hands it back to me.

"Saika, I'm not playing when it comes to you. I never was."

I quickly tie the fabric over my wet head. "You . . . you said you like to tease—"

"Well, that wasn't a lie." She chuckles brokenly. "It *is* fun to tease you because . . . because I like you."

"I'm no one special, Olivie. By the next ceremony, you'll find someone else, someone better. You don't really like me—"

"I don't want anyone else." She holds my hand firmly. "When I would bring someone to my room after a ceremony, it wasn't so I could bed them. I was lonely, Saika. They were hurting. I was hurting. But when I'm with you, I'm not. You make me laugh. You make me want to be better, and have fun, and live. So, yes. I think I do like you. A lot, actually."

I have to look away before I melt into a puddle of tears. "How do I know this isn't a trick?"

Oli sighs. She fiddles with the silver ring on her finger. "Can I show you something? Something I've never shown to anyone. Not Hilde or Evette. Even Frank."

I look at her warily, but concede with a nod.

She dries all our clothes and gets dressed again. We settle beneath the willow tree. I sit on a thick root, and she sits on another. She takes the silver ring from her finger and places it on the patch of grass between us.

"I think you'll enjoy this."

A cloud of smoke leaks from the ring. Faint blue light emanates, and it slowly takes a form. It shifts from a large mass into the small frame of a boy with slender shoulders. He has wild, puffy hair, similar to Oli's, and glances around with round, doll-like eyes.

He smiles a toothless grin and carries a viola in his hands. He waves silently, looking as if he sees someone beyond our sight, and Oli smiles sadly at him. She waves back. He laughs noise-lessly, and I watch Oli gaze upon him, soaking up his presence.

He fits the viola to his shoulder and begins to play. The sound is soft at first. The notes float around us, taking us away and fold-ing us into his melody. It's angelic. It's heartfelt. And hearing it makes me wish you were alive, Fi, so I could show this to you. I wish you could hear this, too. And suddenly, the knowledge of that fact, that you'd never hear such beautiful sounds again, makes my throat ache. And I sit, watching this little boy play as a tear falls from my eye.

His song crescendos, and I recognize the melody. I hum along, for I've heard it in my sleep. I've heard it play across the hall softly in the wee hours of the night. It's beautiful, and I don't want it to stop.

The blue light slowly fades until it disappears back into the smoke. When it all dissipates, I look at Oli. Her eyes are misty.

"That's my son. That's Henley."

I pick up the ring and analyze the silver band. I'm speechless. I don't know what to say.

"Long before I found my crew and became a captain, I was just a young girl," Oli begins. "And like most girls living in the city, I wanted to make a name for myself and become an adven-turer. So, I signed up for the first crew leaving port. The captain was an older man, and he took a shine to me. He told me sweet things and knew how to make a naive young girl feel special. I was young, and I was stupid. And he took advantage of that." She closes her eyes. She exhales.

"I was eighteen when I gave birth to Henley. And oh, did he hang the stars in the sky." Tears well up in her eyes again. "He was such a bright, beautiful boy. He loved music. He taught him-self how to play the viola, you know? The boatswain showed him a thing or two, but Henley was a damn genius. He made art with it. He'd perform for the crew when he learned a new song. One of the witches on board knew a timekeeping spell, and I was able to hold on to one of those moments."

I hand back the ring, and she places it on her finger. "And I'm so glad I did."

"What happened to him?"

She scratches her head. "Well, by the time he was eight, I was a captain of my own crew, and we sailed into dangerous waters. We were warned that there was a creature who roamed at night. He'd entice you through your dreams by playing strange music. He called himself the Phantom Piper. Fucking ridiculous name. Anyway, we weren't afraid of him. We'd handled worse things before.

"That night, Henley slept in the berth deck with the rest of the crew. I remember waking up in the middle of the night and hearing a flute outside my cabin. I ran out onto the deck. The fog had set in, so I couldn't see a thing. But then I saw him . . ." Oli's voice goes soft, as if she's reliving the nightmare. "Henley was standing in the shrouds, his eyes closed as if he were still sleeping. His viola in hand. I called for him to get down, but he couldn't hear me. That strange flute would play a note, and then Henley would respond on his viola. They went back and forth, I didn't understand what was happening. The next moment I knew, my first mate was shaking me awake, and I realized we'd been attacked in our sleep. Half of our crew had been slain"—her voice strains—"including Henley."

"I spent weeks hunting that damn thing down. I used every favor I had, contacted every witch I knew, to find the bastard. I didn't care that my enchantments weren't powerful. I wanted to hunt him down and kill him with my own hands. And I did."

My eyes widen.

"Odd thing was," she continues, "it didn't really feel like I did. All I could think about was Henley. Killing that monster didn't bring him back. I didn't know what to do with myself. Life lost its meaning. We made port in the city, and I saw an ad for Ash Gardens. Frank was in need of a Nature witch to care for the house. I didn't even think about it. I gave my ship, my treasures, everything, to my first mate. My first few weeks here, I was so angry at everyone and everything. But Frank still allowed me to stay. He met me at my level to heal and to grieve Henley. And learn not to be so, so angry."

I kneel before her and wipe the tears from her cheeks. "I'm so sorry, Olivie."

"I don't want you to feel sorry. I want you to realize that I want to be honest with you. I'm not playing you like some game, Saika. I trust you with my pain. I trust you with my heart. It's all I can give to you."

I cup her face with my hand, and she leans into it. "That's more than enough."

She cradles the back of my head and pulls me forward. But instead of kissing my lips like I thought she would, she kisses the top of my head.

Her forehead rests on mine, and we sit there for a moment. Breathing. Aching. Healing.

CHAPTER TWENTY-TWO

Tomorrow night, the star will fall in Rose Woods.

Being honest with Oli at the creek felt like I'd been carrying a weight, and I finally set it down. Though I wish I had told her the truth about my impending demise. But doing that would mean revealing the star prematurely, and Frank still wants my discretion.

I wish you were here, Fi. That way I could talk to you about my feelings of love, and desire, and you'd give me the wisdom that only older sisters can give.

Even in your absence, I think I can conjure some advice that sounds like you: *Love fully. Speak truthfully.*

That about sums it up, right, Fi? Still doesn't help me, though.

I yawn and stretch my aching back. Out the back window, sunlight is slowly creeping over the arboretum. It's sunrise. It's a new day.

Before I step away to get dressed, I catch a glimpse of Frank in the backyard. He's in pajamas, standing outside the arboretum. He looks like he's talking to someone, arguing more like it, but no one else is out there. He paces back and forth, then scratches his mane. He disappears through the arbor's portal.

"What's going on now?"

I throw on a robe and head down to find out.

When I get outside, the morning air has a chill bite. The grass is still wet from last night's rain. I reach the vine-wrapped arbor and release a shaky breath. I enter the arboretum.

That familiar sensation of magic coats my skin. The air buzzes when I walk inside. I exhale, trying to get my bearings. The feeling is so intoxicating. It's like wading through water, and it's difficult to breathe.

I have to ground myself and take a deep breath. When I open my eyes, I see a small spruce. It has striped white-and-gold leaves. The colors spiral all the way down to its trunk.

"Hello. Don't mind me. Just passing through." I walk deeper into the arboretum, my hands to my sides and robe fastened close. "Frank?" I call out. "Frank, where have you gone?"

Through a cluster of trees, I catch a glimpse of reddish-brown fur and tall horns. It slips between the trees.

"Frank!" I call. I pull up my nightgown and hurry after him. The forest ground is uneven, and my slipper catches on a few fallen branches. A rogue twig lashes across my ankle, and I stumble forward.

"Damn it. Frank!" I break into a sprint. "Frank, stop!"

I finally have full sight of him. His pajama shirt flaps in the wind as he runs. Dirt kicks up on his light blue pant legs. "I'm coming!" he calls out. "I'm coming!"

My heart pounds. Who is he talking to?

We run through the arboretum, passing through the colorful trees. Frank suddenly drops to all fours, and he sprints. There's no way I can keep up with him now.

Luckily, I don't have to. I see where he's heading. A massive hickory tree sits in the center of the arboretum. Its orange leaves fan out over the surrounding trees. Frank runs up to it and finally stops. His chest heaves as he catches his breath.

He places his paw on the shaggy, splintering bark. He pets it affectionately. "I'm here," I hear him say. "Kye, I'm here."

I stumble to a stop a few feet behind him. My heart is still pounding in my ears and blood rushes to my face.

"What do you want from me?" He kneels before the hickory and lifts his arms. "I hear you, my love. What is it? What do you want me to do?"

It's silent. Kye's leaves are various shades of orange. The wind blows through them, and they dance. A few break off and shower over Frank's head. He sits back on his legs and exhales.

"Frank," I call.

He snaps around, hope in his eyes, but he's disappointed when he sees me. "Saika, what are you doing here?"

I'm cautious as I come closer. I fold my robe over my nightgown. "Just taking a morning stroll. What about you?"

He scratches the back of his head. "I know how it looks. But I heard her. I know I did. She's calling me."

"I believe you." I kneel beside him. I pluck the orange leaves from his fur. "What's she saying to you?"

He blinks, staring distantly. "I don't know. Just . . . my name. I don't know what it means." His eyes trail over to me. He looks so frightened. I hold his paw.

"Well, next time she calls you, come get me. I'd love to meet Kye." I smile warmly. "But for now, we're both in our pajamas, and we've gotten messed up from all this dirt."

He slowly stands to his feet. "Right. Right, let's get dressed." He gives one last glance at the hickory. "I'll see you soon, my love."

I offer my arm, and we walk back to the house.

I lead Frank into his bedroom, still holding on to his arm. Similar to his other furniture, his four-poster bed is the largest I've ever seen. Frank plops on the edge.

"There you are." He has a decanter filled with water by his bedside, and I pour him a glass. "How are you feeling?"

He takes the glass. "I'm sorry to put you through so much trouble."

"It's no trouble. I just want to make sure you're okay. Why don't you rest today, hmm? I'll bring your meals to you."

He sits back in bed, and I help him lift his legs. "Yes, I think that might be for the best. There's just something . . ." He gazes up at me. "There's something I need to tell you, but I'm . . . I can't remember for some reason."

"Don't worry. I'm sure it'll come back to you."

After I leave his wing, I close his double doors and release a weighted sigh. What the hell was that? It rained last night, but I didn't hear anything break. I should just check around the house to be sure.

I go level by level. I inspect the kitchen, the parlor, and the library. I look through the halls of the second and third level. Except for a few broken pieces of wood and peeling paint, there's no damage big enough to make Frank have such a lapse in memory. At Hilde's level, I stop on the fourth platform and gaze up to Phil's room.

On my way up, wood peels from the steps. It splinters when I step on it. I bend down to touch it, and the chipped wood crumbles like dust.

Phil's door pushes open with ease, and a gust of wind chills my skin. My eyes widen at the sight before me.

It's like I've seen in my dream. A gaping hole in the roof. The early morning sun cascades broken bits of light through the darkness. Particles of wood chip away from the walls. My mouth dries.

I hurry down to the second level, careful not to wake anyone with my clomping footsteps.

Ignatius isn't happy to see me so early in the morning, but I don't care. I push my way through into his room. "The house is falling apart."

He yawns. "I know."

"No, I mean actively. I just came from the attic, and the roof is crumbling." My chest heaves. "Are you certain that the star will come tomorrow night?"

"Do you think I'm some kind of fool?" He snaps. "Of course, it is. I know about the roof. The top level's been falling apart for weeks."

"Why haven't you said anything?"

"It's breaking down slowly. There's nothing we can do about it. Regular magic won't fix it. We'd need the star."

"So, we aren't in danger then? At least right now?"

"You think I'd still be here if we were?"

His cauldron sparkles from the elixir we've made. I fill up a bucket. "Well, there's a few spots around the house that need fixing. I'll go do that."

Ignatius waves me off and settles back on his sofa, face down. I stop to look at him before I leave. "You know, we're having a celebration. It'll be fun. You should get out of this dusty room and get fancied up. Maybe give that mustache and beard a trim and join us. We'll have food, and company, and many reasons to celebrate."

"We don't have any food."

"By then we will. Once we have the star, everything will be fixed."

He snaps his head up, eyes red and tired. "You didn't tell them about the star, did you?"

"No." For such a little elf, he can be scary. "So, what do you say? Are you going to join us?"

He drops his head down again, and he answers, his voice muffled by the cushion. "No."

The wallpaper near Hilde's level is peeling the worst, so I start there. I take a bit of the elixir and touch up the warped wood coming down the stairwell as well. I feel a bit frantic, my nerves jumbled and a mess, as I work my way down the steps.

I stop on the third level. Oli is standing on the platform, dressed in her pajamas with arms crossed. A scarf is tied over her hair. She grins. "I thought a mouse was scurrying along the halls. What are you doing?"

I try to hide the elixir behind my back. "Oh, it's nothing. I was doing some housework."

"How kind of you." She meets me on my step. I pin my back against the wall as she crowds closer. But she takes the bucket I'm trying to hide. "Good morning," she whispers.

"Good morning," I respond.

She steps back. "Why are you up doing this—" She suddenly fumbles forward and goes crashing onto the platform. The elixir splashes everywhere, and the wood instantly soaks it up, becoming lacquered.

"Oli!" I rush down to her.

She sits up and cradles her foot. "Fucking hell!" She glares at the last step. The wood is warped, and it's splintering on the edge. "I just fixed that step yesterday. What the hell is happening?"

"Are you alright?"

She rotates her foot. "I rolled my ankle. It's a bit sore, but I'll be fine."

I chuckle. "You know, you have more foot injuries than the average witch."

She hums. "Laugh now, but you're gonna have to take care of me."

"I will not." I laugh.

"It's true. That's what happens—"

"Oli!" Evette's voice travels up to us before we see her. She flutters from the stairwell, her eyes wide in terror. "Oli, there's a problem."

"I'm fine, Evette." She laughs. I help her stand on her feet. "Just a bit of hurt pride."

"What?" Evette looks confused. "No, there's a family coming down the way. A family of witches."

We both stiffen. "What?"

"They might be here for a ceremony. Frank didn't say anything about it."

Oli groans. "He must have forgotten . . . again. Okay, have Hilde greet them when they come."

"What should we do about food?" Evette asks. "We only have enough food for the party."

Oli takes a long, deep breath and invites Evette to try. "It's fine, Evette. All that matters is the arboretum. We'll perform the ceremony and offer whatever food we have." Oli looks at me. "I know it was for the party . . ."

"It's fine. Evette, use whatever you need."

"Are you sure?" Evette asks.

"Yes. Go on. We'll be down in a bit," Oli says. Once Evette zips off, I help Oli limp to her room.

"Are you sure you'll be alright?" I ask.

She plants both feet on the ground without a wink of pain. "Do you know who you're talking to?"

"Ah, yes. The Great Captain Oli. How could I forget?"

After I get dressed, I'm quick to hurry out of my room again. Coming down the stairwell, I hear Hilde's voice echo up from the foyer. It's followed by a man's voice, thick with an Eastern accent. Something about it feels familiar.

I cross the second platform, but stumble to a stop. A little girl laughs, and it's like jingle bells ringing in my ears. And I'm swept away into a memory.

Come on, Saika, you laugh. *It'll be funny. Do the face.*

Once our mother turns her back, I do "the face" as you so affectionately call it, and you giggle. Your laugh is so unique. It reminds me of jingle bells, angelic and melodious.

I step down the remaining stairs into the foyer. And I see you, Fi. But you're a little girl again. How can that be? Your skin is much lighter than I remember. Your curls aren't tightly coiled, but are like loose waves, and a ribbon ties them back into a long ponytail.

You meet me at the bottom of the steps, and I kneel before you so I can look in your eyes, but they're different. They're hooded and more deep-set than I remember. Your nose is flatter, too.

I blink, and suddenly there are two of you. You're both wearing black, frilly dresses. I don't understand what's happening.

"Saika," a man calls from across the foyer.

I look past you to the man dressed in a black suit. He's carrying a bouquet of sunflowers. He hands them over to Hilde and rushes to me.

He falls to his knees and crushes me in a hug. Everything hits me at once.

Jonathan's oak-smelling cologne. His stubble scratching my cheek. Your girls, Fi, looking at me like I'm a stranger.

Jonathan sits back, and he's sobbing and holding me by the shoulders. "Goodness, look at you!" He laughs and hugs me a second time "I never thought I'd see you again."

Reality suddenly sets in, and I finally hug him back. "Yes, I'm here. I'm not dead."

He lets me go. "Some part of me never thought you were. But your parents, they insisted—"

"Jonathan." I glance up at Hilde and Evette, then back at him. "How did you know I was here?"

"Lorna."

Damn that housemaid.

"She told me she saw you at the market in the city. I didn't believe her at first, but after that letter I received, and how Fiona spoke about Ash Gardens before she died . . . I simply looked for a red door." He chuckles.

I try to stand up, and he's quick to help me. He even pats me off and helps fix my crooked headscarf. He's sickeningly sweet, that man. No wonder you loved him so much, Fi.

"It's so great to see you." I look at your girls. "All of you, really, but *why* are you here?"

He looks genuinely confused. "You invited me. For Fiona's planting ceremony."

The shock rocks me to my knees. "Oh, I didn't know you'd be coming so soon." I didn't know he'd be coming at all.

"I spoke with the owner yesterday. A fellow named Frank. He said everything would be set."

So, this must be what Frank forgot to tell me. Damn. I can't turn Jonathan away. He was so happy to see me. I have to see this through.

I suppose you're having your planting ceremony today, Fi.

I clear my throat. "Well, Frank is feeling a bit down today, but we'll handle everything for the ceremony."

"We?" Jonathan asks.

"Oh, yes. I guess I didn't include that in the letter. I work at Ash Gardens."

Hilde steps in. "Saika isn't ready yet for the ceremony." I look down, and I'm wearing my old gray smock. "If you follow our chef, she'll direct you to the parlor for some refreshments."

I watch them walk off, Evette leading the way and asking them about life in the city. Once they're gone, my knees finally give out, and I collapse on the bottom step.

Hilde is quick to come to my side. "Come on, you can't go boneless now." She helps me up, and I lean on her. "Are you alright, Saika?"

I don't answer her. I only look at her, and her milky white eye searches me. She sighs. "I see. Well, just because you don't feel alright doesn't mean you can't look alright. Come with me. I have a surprise for you."

I'm quiet as I follow Hilde up to her room. Lilac and eucalyptus incense greet us when we walk through the door. She pulls a stylish ottoman to the center of the room. "Sit, darling."

I do as she says. My mind feels like smoke, and my vision is hazy. That can't really be Jonathan downstairs. He hasn't really come with your girls, Fi. This must all be a joke.

Hilde swiftly lights a long cigarette and studies my pensive face. "Are you ready for this?" she asks. "Are you ready to plant your sister's ashes?"

My hands feel clammy. I had always planned to do it, Fi. I didn't plan to live out the rest of my days with your ashes decorating my shelf. Your final request deserves to be honored. And the more I sit, and think on this, I realize that I am. I'm ready.

I look up at Hilde. I nod.

She blows smoke from her mouth. "Good." She disappears behind her dressing screen and comes out pulling a mannequin displaying a red dress. The top is taffeta in a wraparound bodice with a sparkly tulle skirt. There's also a set of elbow-length silk gloves that matches it perfectly.

"Come." She holds me by the hand and directs me to the long mirror near her bed. She holds the dress over me. "I put that fabric to good use. Isn't it just divine?"

The deep, rich red complements my brown skin beautifully. "Hilde, I couldn't possibly—"

"Please, darling. It's for you. When I heard about the party, I knew you would need a fancy dress to wear. I had to work fast, but I think I churned it out flawlessly. What do you think?"

I turn around and grip her in a hug.

She grunts, but then it turns into a chuckle. "You're welcome, Saika."

When I pull back, she dabs at her eyes. She draws on her cigarette. "Now, I still have leftover taffeta. I can help fashion it on your head if you'd like."

That fabric is rich, and I think it would pair nicely with this dress. But when I plant you, Fi, I don't want to hide who I am. I'm not ashamed of the consequences of saving your life.

"Actually, Hilde, I know you've done so much. But can I ask one more tiny favor from you?"

"Always."

"How good are you at cutting hair?"

CHAPTER TWENTY-THREE

I come down the stairs a few moments later, hanging on to the banister for dear life. It's been such a long time since I've worn heels. I admit, they match the dress like Hilde said, but I'd much rather be wearing my boots right now.

I take timid steps crossing the foyer into the parlor. My head feels so very cold. When I enter the parlor, it feels like I'm walking into an entirely different place. The curtains are drawn closed, and twinkling orbs of light fill the ceiling. More hang from the frames on the walls. Soft chatter greets me when I step inside.

Merry and Morose are dressed in matching vests and pants with colorful stitching. They're speaking with Jonathan while the girls play a hand game before the fireplace. They remind me so much of us as children, Fi.

Merry and Morose finally notice me, and their mouths drop.

Jonathan looks back, and he grins at me. "Oh, Saika. You look stunning."

Merry blinks. "More than stunning, really."

I run my red silk gloves over my shaved head. It's soft to the touch.

"So, that's what she's been hidin' under them things," Morose says, swirling wine in his glass. Merry elbows him in the side.

"It's fine, Mer. Thank you. All of you."

Jonathan looks down at his black suit. "I wish I had known to dress more festively. I certainly would have."

"We planned to have a celebration of life tomorrow," I explain. "But I think that's what we should do for Fiona."

They raise their glasses.

"Can I speak with you for a moment?" Jonathan asks. He pulls me aside, speaking in a hushed tone. "Saika, I realize that this was all so sudden. I didn't mean to cause you and the staff so much trouble."

"It's fine. This actually has happened before. So, I think we've become professionals." I laugh.

"Well." He pulls out an envelope from his inside jacket pocket. "This is yours."

It's addressed from the bank. "Jonathan, I didn't—"

He holds up his hand. "Fiona never spent your portion of the trust. She didn't think it was fair for your parents to punish you the way they had, and neither did I. I'm sorry we didn't speak up more back then."

I take the envelope. "Did you tell them about the ceremony?"

He looks away. "I did. Your parents just need time."

"They've had all the time in the world. They'll never allow me back into the family."

He holds my hand. "You will always be a part of ours." He looks at the girls giggling and clapping their hands together. "I'd love for you to come back home. We all miss you."

Evette enters the sitting room. She's gotten changed, too. Her gold dress looks like an extension of the beaming light surrounding her body. Her short, tiny curls are defined and pinned to the side. She's followed by Hilde. Her white dress, like many of her others, has a long train, but this one shimmers like stars when it moves. It's captivating to watch.

They all group together—Evette, Hilde, Merry, and Morose—gushing over their outfits and laughing. Stars, they all look absolutely amazing. They didn't have to join me for your ceremony, Fi, but they dressed up and came anyway. And isn't that what a family does?

But I also know that Ash Gardens was never going to be permanent for me. Once I plant your ashes, Fi, that's it. The star falls tomorrow, and we'll fix up Ash Gardens, and I'll heal Frank's mind. And I'll be free to leave. I'm fortunate that Jonathan is here now, offering a place to stay in the midst of my dilemma.

Truly . . . truly fortunate.

I swallow and look at Jonathan. "Thank you. There's something that I must see through tomorrow night, but then after that, I'm all yours. I'll be ready to come home."

"Oh, good." He beams. "The girls are going to love that. They're a bit shy right now, but I believe once you're back, they'll really—"

He stops talking when he realizes I'm not paying attention anymore. It's a bit hard to. My attention is stolen away by the purple witch standing in the threshold of the parlor.

She's wearing a matte-black suit, and she grins, fangs twinkling as she fixes her cuff links. Her voluminous hair is divided into two sections and braided neatly back. A few loose curls frame her face. Vibrant red trim runs along the lapel of her jacket and hem of her pants. I glance down to my red dress then over at Hilde, who smirks at me. "You're welcome," she whispers.

I clear my throat and look back at Jonathan. "I'm sorry, what were you saying?"

His mouth is slightly agape. His eyes shift from me to Oli, then back to me. He grins. "Nothing. We can talk about it later."

Oli addresses the room. "Hello, good . . . late morning, early afternoon, everyone." She finds Jonathan over by the window. She stops when she sees me, a grin slowly blossoming on her face.

She limps a bit when she walks over. "Hi, you must be Jonathan." She extends her hand, and he shakes it readily. "Welcome to Ash Gardens. I'm sorry we've had a delay this morning. The owner, Frank, needs some time to himself. He's not feeling right."

"As long as I'm here with my sister." He rubs my arm. "It's alright."

"Well, the weather is looking great, but we should hurry. There'll be a storm brewing later."

"Oh, of course."

Oli looks back at Evette and the cherubs. "You can follow them, and they'll lead you to the arboretum. I'll be right out."

They all file out of the room, and I fall in, but Oli holds on to my arm. "Whoa, hey. Wait. Are you alright?"

"What do you mean?"

Oli holds me by the shoulders. "We're about to plant the ashes of your sister . . . Fiona."

It suddenly clicks, what she's asking. "Oh." I blink. "Oh, yes. Olivie, I'm fine."

"You say that a lot, you know."

I pat her hand. "I mean it this time. I'm fine. Fi's been waiting so long, her ashes are collecting dust—" My eyes widen. "Her ashes! I've left them upstairs—"

I nearly run off again, but Oli holds on to my arm. "Saika, I've taken care of it. I've set out a planting spot and gathered her ashes. When I found out who the ceremony was for, I wanted to make sure everything was okay."

I hold her cheek in my hand. The red from my glove contrasts against her purple skin. She closes her eyes at the touch. "Thank you," I whisper. "And you look wonderful."

"Hilde has such great taste, doesn't she?" She opens her eyes. "And you are beautiful, Saika. Honestly to die for."

"Please, we don't need anyone else dying."

"Ha." She grins. "You made a joke about death."

I lean forward and kiss her lips. She hums against me. "I'm also really liking this look." She rubs the back of my head. It sends shivers up my spine, and I close my eyes at the sensation. And damn Oli for noticing.

"You like when I rub your head?" she asks with a smirk.

"I don't," I lie. "It's just cold."

She kisses me again, her finger caresses the fuzzy stubble, and I feel like I'm melting against her. She laughs when we break apart. "Okay," she chuckles. "You like your head rubbed. I'll keep a note of that."

It's difficult, but I push away from her. "We need to go. They're waiting for us."

We meet everyone outside before they cross into the arboretum. It's so sweet to see them all together, here for you. I only wish Frank was better and that he could join us, too.

"Thank you all for coming out for my sister's planting. It means so much to me."

"Oh, Saika, we wouldn't miss it for the world," Evette says.

"Come on, love." Oli holds out her hand, and we cross into the arboretum first.

Jonathan and the girls come in second, and I watch their eyes widen at the colorful trees. "Oh, this is amazing," he says.

Oli holds on to my arm, and she limps along. She gives Jonathan the history of Ash Gardens. She tells him about Kye and Frank and all the ashes that are planted in this magical forest.

Jonathan walks beside us. "Fiona is going to love it here," he tells Oli. "She had gotten sick, and she knew her time was coming." He glances at me as we walk ahead. "So, she wanted to prepare as much as possible. She heard about Ash Gardens and thought that it was the perfect place to be laid to rest."

"And we welcome Fiona." Oli gives my arm a comforting squeeze as we continue.

We reach a clearing surrounded by natural evergreens. A plot of land has already been dug up. And beside the hole sits your jar of glittering ashes, Fi.

We surround the site. Evette and the cherubs follow us, but Hilde gently pulls them back to allow us space.

Oli lets go of my hand and shuffles forward. She stands by the hole and faces us. "Friends, today we are joined by the family of the great and adventurous witch Fiona." Her voice carries through the clearing, loud and strong. "Though her body is gone, may her spirit live on at Ash Gardens."

My palms sweat as Oli picks up your ashes. She looks at me. "Are you ready, Saika?"

Jonathan's hand touches mine. He smiles at me. "Go on, Sai. It's okay."

I take a deep breath. I begin to walk forward, but I stop. I slip off my silk gloves and hand them back to Jonathan. He startles at my withered and spotty hands. "Can you hold these for me?"

"Of course."

Oli holds out your ashes, and I take them. I hold the last pieces of you in my hands. The hands I cursed for you. And I'd do it again, Fiona. Until the end of eternity.

I look up at our family, yours and mine. They watch me with teary eyes. "Fiona . . . Fiona wanted to become something beautiful in her death. Like Oli said, she *was* great and adventurous. She was kind. She was loving. She was bossy at times." I chuckle.

A dark silhouette looms through the trees past the clearing. Frank emerges, dressed and proper in a dark suit. He smiles softly when he meets my eyes. He gives a curt nod and joins Hilde and the others on the side.

"Fiona was my very best friend. She was my first friend. She was my sister." I glance down to your jar of ashes. "I love you, Fi. In life and in death, you will always be my sister."

I turn to Oli, and she begins the enchantment. She circles her arms, and the soil lifts into the air. And together, she pours the soil into the ground, and I finally plant your ashes.

It's quiet, yet everything feels so loud.

The jar empties, and I stand back as Oli packs the soil tight and tops it off with enchanted water.

Oli moves forward. "I invite the family to offer any final words to Fiona."

The girls hold Jonathan by the hand, and they come over. I step out of the way as Jonathan kneels to the ground.

"You don't want to say anything?" Oli whispers to me.

"I've said all I needed to."

We join everyone standing near the evergreens.

"Your sister sounds like a true gem." Hilde smiles.

"I'm sorry she's gone," Morose mutters.

"Thank you." I look over to Frank. I fix his flipped lapel. "How are you feeling?"

"Loads better. I'm so sorry I didn't tell you earlier."

"I'm glad you didn't. I probably would've found another

excuse to avoid it." He wraps me in a hug, and I squeeze him tight. "Thank you for showing up."

Back at the house, Oli directs everyone into the parlor. I pull Evette into the kitchen and speak in a low tone.

"Have you made anything for food?" I ask.

"I have a few pastries out but that's it. We only have enough for a day or two of meals."

"Make it. Make everything you can."

Her eyes widen. "Are you sure?"

"I have our food situation under control. I'll have Morose pick up everything we need tomorrow." I touch the top of my bodice, where my check is secured underneath. "Trust me."

"Okay, I'll see what I can do." She flies off to the cupboards and gets to work. "I wish Phil was here."

"What if I bring Merry and Morose to help?" I ask. Evette gives me a deadpan look. I laugh. "They don't have to cook. Maybe they can help prep?"

Evette gives me a nod. "I suppose that will do."

Before I head out, I call back to her. "Thank you, Evette. And by the way, you look absolutely smashing."

Light radiates from her body. "Thank you, Saika."

In the parlor, I find Merry and Morose with the girls. Merry has his book about high lore and legends and he's showing it to the girls. I hate to interrupt them, but I ask for their help in the kitchen, and they hurry off, leaving me with the twins.

"Hi, girls." I kneel before them. "I'm sorry I didn't properly greet you before. I was caught a little off guard."

One wears a blue ribbon in her hair, and the other wears purple. The one with the blue ribbon speaks first. "Daddy told us you were a little sad. Are you still sad?"

"I am. But it's not as consuming as before. Your mother was my sister. And I love her very much. But she's gone now."

They glance at each other, and the purple-ribboned twin responds. "We don't remember her much."

"It has been a while, and you two were very young. I'm sorry, I used to be able to tell you two apart. Who is who?"

"I'm Riza." The blue-ribboned twin smiles.

"And I'm Azure," the purple-ribboned twin says.

"Ah, yes. Riza and Azure." I wrap them both in a hug. "Fiona named you, Riza, after our nana. She was such a lovely woman."

"What about me?" Azure asks.

"Well, your daddy . . ." I glance back at Jonathan. He's speaking excitedly with Frank while holding a glass of brandy. "He said that the morning you two were born, there wasn't a cloud in the sky. And it was the most beautiful blue he'd ever seen. Azure."

Oli presents a tray of small glasses filled with amber liquid. "Hello, ladies. I'm sorry, but Hilde cleared us out of all the brandy. All I have left is some apple juice. Would you care for some?"

Riza and Azure both take a glass and thank her politely.

"I know planting ashes can sound scary and odd." Oli sits with us. "But at Ash Gardens, your mother is going to grow into a beautiful tree. She may be a spruce. Or a maple. Or a pine."

"Or a willow tree," Azure pipes up. Riza glances at her. "What? We learned about it in school."

Oli smiles. "A willow is such a fine tree. It's one of my favorites, you know. Willow signifies resilience and strength. And from what I've heard about your mother, it sounds like something she'd grow to be."

"It is," I say. "It sounds like her exactly."

A hand touches my shoulder, and I glance up to Hilde. "Can I speak to you a moment?"

"Of course." I stand up, excusing myself as Oli gathers closer to Riza and Azure, offering them a harrowing pirate's tale.

I stand with Hilde near the front window of the parlor. The curtains are still drawn to drown out the sun. But when I peek, I see that the sun is hiding away behind dark clouds. It'll rain soon.

"I have a gift for you."

"Oh, Hilde. You've showered me with gifts." I pat down my new dress. "I think this is enough."

"This isn't from me." She hands over a small box that fits in her hand and takes the lid off.

It's a wooden music box. It has a fresh coat of white paint and silver hearts painted along the top. I pick it up and love rushes over me. It drowns me, and I instantly think of you, Fi. I think about when you first handed the music box down to me.

It plays the most beautiful song I've ever heard, Sai, listen.

You open the music box, and we press our ears forward, closing our eyes and enjoying the sound. It makes me fall deeper in love with music and the magic it holds.

I tighten my grip on the music box. The love intensifies. I wipe the tear from my eye. "How did you know about this?" I ask. "Did you read me?"

"I didn't." Hilde points over to Oli. Riza and Azure sit before her, wide smiles on their faces as she tells a story. They giggle at her, covering their mouths.

"Oli told me about a music box you saw at the market and asked me to make one for you. The love embedded in it didn't come from me. It came from her."

"Oh." I blink, watching her.

"Thank her properly." Hilde winks.

"Hilde!"

She laughs. "It's only a suggestion."

Jonathan looks over at us. "Saika, the greatest pianist I've ever known," he calls across the library. "Might you play a song for us now?"

They all look at me, anticipating my response.

I straighten my shoulders. "Of course."

We gather around the piano, and I pull the cover back. It's been a while since I've played for a ceremony. I didn't think the next time I played would be for you.

I could play one of our father's favorites. The one you liked as a girl and used to dance to before the fireplace. Or perhaps a sorrowful ballad.

But as I sit down, my fingers skim over the keys. Another song comes to mind. And I begin to play.

I see you, Fi. I see your bright smile that's so large your eyes would disappear. We're girls together, staying up late in our shared bedroom. It's way past our bedtime, but our parents do not know we're still awake. You've just retold me the story of the Raboo Pirates, fashioned a scarf over your head, and using a flower as a wand, you declare one day you will be an adventurer, too. Your passion is music to me. It's sweet and uplifting and makes me feel like I can float above any dangers of the world.

I see you as a youth, defending me from Marionette's hurtful comments. You stand your ground, shoulders squared as you threaten to turn her into a toad should she mock me again. The pride that blossomed in my chest feels like an explosion, blood coursing and racing through my veins.

My fingers dance on the keys quicker, playing and sustaining simultaneously.

Then I see you as a young woman. You've made your mark as an adventurer. You've gone to distant lands. You've seen the world. You've laughed, and you've made your dream come true.

But then you didn't return to me. I'm no longer seeing the light. It all bleeds out to darkness. I can't see a thing.

The melody slows. I dance on the minor keys.

An ember burns. A soft light pulsating in the darkness.

A beat.

Saika.

I see you.
Another beat.

Don't forget me.

I can hear you.

I love you.

My fingers fiddle to a stop. I end on a high key.

I love you, too.

I open my eyes to see the parlor crowded with the people who love me. And they clap.

I stand up and take a bow.

Evette flutters through the threshold. "The ceremonial meal is ready," she announces.

Evette sets up more floating lights in the dining room. Candles and vases of sunflowers are placed on top of a lace runner. We come to our seats, and we're met with the aroma of freshly baked pumpkin bread.

On the table are ceramic bowls of mashed potatoes and left-over venison. Evette had roasted sweet corn and carrots.

Conversation is light. We enjoy more wine and cheese once the food gets quickly eaten up. Jonathan and I tell stories about you, Fi. We talk about your infectious humor and your tendency to be sharp tongued.

"Ah, sounds like someone I know." Frank laughs. "You and Fiona must be very alike."

I hide my smile behind a sip of wine. "I'm not sharp tongued at all."

Oli rubs the back of her neck. "You are when you want to be."

"Maybe you rubbed off on her," Evette says. "You two *have* been spending a lot of time together."

Oli and I lock eyes, embarrassment blushes our faces. "What are you on about, E?" Oli chuckles.

"You don't have to lie." Morose blinks slowly. Perhaps this should be his last glass of wine. "We know you two are buggerin' each other."

"Morose!" I gasp.

"Come on, man." Oli laughs. "There're children present." She gestures to Riza and Azure, who are having their own conversation at the end of the table, off in their own world.

"Morose, I think you've had too much to drink." I smirk, shaking my head.

"That's good to hear. Kye and I are happy that you two found each other." Frank lifts his glass. "To Saika and Oli."

"To Saika and Oli," everyone cheers.

I drink, but I keep my eye on Frank as he talks with Jonathan. *Kye and I . . .*

He's never referred to Kye in this manner. As if she's here. As if he's speaking on her behalf.

Evette brings out the pumpkin bread glazed with cinnamon butter for dessert. Frank gets up from his chair while we finish up. "I'll go check on the weather. I want to make sure the rain hasn't started, so our guests can fly home safely."

I finish the last bit of my food and excuse myself from the table.

I find Frank back in the parlor. He's opened the front curtains. The skies have turned gray and dark. He sees me and shakes his head. "We should wrap up soon. The storm is coming in fast."

"I agree." I stand beside him. "Ignatius said a big one was coming."

"Did he?" he asks, genuinely surprised. He turns back to the window. "I miss that fellow. What did he ever get up to? Do you know?"

My brows shoot up, but I do my best to remain calm. "I . . . I'm not sure."

Frank nods. "It was a beautiful ceremony. You did a great job."

"Thank you, Frank. You're a great teacher." I direct him away from the window. "It looks like the storm is moving in fast. Why don't you retire to your wing? It's been such a long day."

"Oh, sure. You all have everything settled, right?" We cross through the foyer toward his door. "I guess I'll go and get a pot of tea ready for Kye."

Ice runs through my veins.

"She always likes having a nice hot cup when she returns

from a long journey." He looks down at me, smiling sweetly. "Do you know when she'll be home?"

I blink away my teary vision. "I don't. But just go on and rest. I'll make tea for her, Frank."

He hugs me and exhales deeply. "You are such a treasure. Thank you."

Once the doors shut, a sob shakes my chest. I can't bear to see Frank this way.

●

I relay the news of the impending storm, and I walk Jonathan and the girls to the front door. The girls have taken a shine to Oli, and they attack her in a hug. Jonathan pulls me aside again.

"I'm so glad that you reached out to me, Saika. I know I didn't deserve it. I was worried about you when you left. I know that Fiona's passing made you . . ." He places a firm hand on my wrist. "It made you forget who you were for a bit. But now, seeing you here and the company that you keep." Tears mist his eyes. "It makes me glad that you are doing so, so well. And I'm sure Fiona would be glad, too."

"Ash Gardens has treated me kindly. But once my job is done tomorrow, I'll be back to the city."

He glances at Oli making jokes with Riza and Azure, tapping their chests and flicking their noses when they look down.

"There's no rush, you know. Take all the time you'd like. The girls and I will always be here." He smiles.

I step out on the veranda, waving farewell to them as they hop on their fancy brooms and take to the sky.

●

I'm still sitting on the porch swing long after Jonathan and the girls disappear from my sight. I finally take off these damn heels and rub my sore feet.

Oli comes out, holding two cups of hot tea. "Here you are, love." She sits on the swing with me and pulls my feet onto her lap. "How are you feeling?"

The storm clouds are so dark it looks like night. The first drops of rain begin to fall.

"I don't know, really."

"Understandable." She sips her tea. Her hand runs from my foot and up my leg. She stops when she feels the fresh welt on my ankle. "How'd you get this?"

"Oh, from running in the arboretum," I say casually, and she looks at me, confused. I blink. "No, I'm sorry. Not running. Walking. Walking earlier while wearing these damn heels. I nearly twisted my ankle like you did." I laugh, but Oli doesn't smile back.

"I spoke to Jonathan. He said that you were returning home."

"Oh, yes."

Oli nods. She takes another sip of tea. "Why?"

"My work is done. There's no more reason for me to be here."

"What's so special about tomorrow night? He said you aren't leaving until then."

I look away from her, crossing my arms. "I can't say—"

"Fucking hell, Saika." She furrows her brow. "I know you're keeping things from me. Even still. Do you not trust me?"

"Of course I trust you—"

"Then why won't you just tell me what's going on?" Her hand rests on my leg again, rubbing over the welt on my ankle. "I'm not gonna pry it out of you. That's not fair. I just want you to trust me."

I close my eyes. "No, you're right. I can trust you—I *do* trust you." I hold her hand. "I'll tell you why tomorrow night is so special."

And I do. I tell her about Ignatius's research. About mine. I tell her about the house and why the same things kept breaking in the house and why she had to fix them over and over again. I tell her about the fallen star. And I tell her that even if the star doesn't come through, I have the money to keep Ash Gardens afloat for a very long time. Everything will work out just fine.

I don't, however, tell her about Frank. I leave out anything alluding to his waning memory and his past sins concerning his wife. Frank is going to be fine. He'll be better tomorrow. I'll be able to use the star, and I'll fix him. I can fix him.

Oli sits back on the swing. We teeter back and forth silently. The rain is getting louder, coming down harder and pelting the roof of the veranda.

"I understand if you recant your feelings toward me," I say. "This is a lot to take in."

Oli chuckles and wipes away a tear. "Oh, come on. Saika, what are you saying?"

"I won't be needed here anymore. Ignatius will have the star to fix everything. The house. The garden. And I mean, you and Hilde are welcome to use the star as well, I'm sure—"

"I don't give a damn about a star. I don't care about this house getting fixed." Oli faces me, a firm grip on my thigh. "I care about you."

My chest tightens. "I don't want you to waste your time with me. I have no power. I can't enchant—"

"Are you just spouting out things I already know? So what if you've got no power. What's that got to do with me?"

"Well, I'm of no use to you."

"I don't want to *use* you, Saika." She presses closer to me on the swing. She holds my face in her hands and speaks calmly, slightly squishing my cheeks. "I want to love you and be with you. For as long as I can. For as much as I can. Do you understand that?"

My face is still a bit squished, so I can't really answer back. But I nod.

Oli sighs. "Good." She kisses me, and I don't think I can ever get used to the sensation of her lips on mine.

"So stay," she whispers.

"Olivie—"

"Please," she begs. Her hand snakes up my arm. "Evette loves you. Hilde loves you. Merry . . . and even that toad Morose." She sighs. "And Frank. Especially Frank. We all want you here. I want you here."

I chuckle, wiping my eye. "I don't know. I may need more convincing."

"Oh, more convincing, you say?" Oli grins mischievously and prowls over me, the swing shifting us forward and back. Her hand slides up my thigh and nestles beneath the puffy tulle of my dress. She seizes me in a kiss again. She pecks me once. Then twice before lightly brushing her lips over mine.

"Stay, Saika," she whispers again. "Please?"

I'm not sure how much time I have left, Fi. But in my last days, I want to spend it with the people I love, and the people who love me. So, I answer Oli with a nod. A tiny movement, but she sees it. She grins.

"It's the end of a ceremony," I say. "Aren't you going to invite me to your room to console me?"

The points of Oli's ears tinge red, and she gasps. "My, Miss Saika. Aren't you forward?" Her hand hasn't left from underneath my dress. She grips my thigh even tighter. "The problem is, you might have to carry me upstairs."

I laugh. "Why on earth would I do that?"

"I've got a busted ankle, right? I need someone to help me to my room." She kisses me. "Get me undressed." Kiss. "And get me into bed." This kiss is longer. Slower.

My hand touches her cheek. It's about as hot as mine. My heart is rattling in my chest. I don't know how I find my voice, but I do. I whisper between our lips, "Okay."

So that night, I help Oli get to her room. I help her shed her jacket. She helps me shed my silk gloves. And under the soft pitter-patters of rain, to each other, we express ourselves.

CHAPTER TWENTY-FOUR

Oli's arm rests over my stomach. Her hair is soft like a cushion under my hand. She breathes slowly. Softly. Her dark lashes flutter just a bit when she sleeps. It's a little endearing, actually.

Her room is a bit like mine, and I'm only able to really snoop around now that she's asleep. She's fond of plants. They're everywhere, from her desk to her bookshelf, to the floor, and hanging over us while we lie in the bed.

Ignatius said there'd be a massive storm. But last night, the wind and the rain were gentle. They knocked against the windows in a soothing lullaby. The rain should have lulled me to sleep the way it had Oli, but my mind is too alert.

All of Oli. All of Frank. All of Ash Gardens weighs down on me. Even you, Fi, now that you've officially departed. I'm too restless to sleep, but perhaps that's good.

Outside Oli's back window, night is slowly turning into day, accompanied by a light drizzle. I suppose I should get up now.

Oli stirs beside me, and I gently pry her arm away. I pull the blanket over her chest so she doesn't get cold. Some loose hairs have been pulled from her braids. I bend over and kiss her head. "I'll be back," I whisper.

I find my dress and gloves on the floor and quickly zip up to get back to my room.

Today, a star will fall in Rose Woods. Ignatius and I will head out to get it. And everything will be fine again. I take a deep breath. Everything will be fine again.

I come into my room, and it's so quiet, I can hear the floor creak as I step. It's odd, looking on my desk and not seeing your jar of ashes there, Fi.

I pick up my pamphlet of spells and skim through it, settling on the last page, where I've concocted multiple incantations that could heal Frank's memory.

The deal is done, but now it's time. Take this star and heal Frank's mind.

It's a bit silly now that I read it again. I'll keep trying, despite Phil's warning. I won't allow Death to claim Frank.

I should check on him. But before I head downstairs, I see a flash in the corner of my eye. I clamber toward the front window.

Oh, my stars, Fi. It's . . . stars. Dozens of them rippling through the dark sky, leaving trails of shimmery white dust.

My hand presses against the cold, wet glass of the window. "It's beautiful . . ."

The star parade passes over the house so quickly, the only thing remaining is its fading trail.

I hurry over to the other end of my room and gaze out the back. I open the window and stick out my head to catch the procession of stars. They shoot over the arboretum.

And I watch as one of the stars breaks from the pack, and slowly, and quite beautifully, falls to the earth.

Wait. It's falling here. Into the arboretum. That wasn't supposed to happen. And it wasn't supposed to happen until tonight. Ignatius said the star would fall in Rose Woods.

He was wrong. He got the prediction wrong!

Not bothering with shoes, I race down to the second level and don't stop until I'm pounding on Ignatius's door.

"Ignatius, answer the door, please! It's urgent!"

He doesn't answer. Even if he were sleeping, he'd answer within a couple of seconds, but it's quiet. "Ignatius?"

I turn the door handle, and it opens.

Ignatius's room is dark and musty. His books are like mountains taking up space on his floor, but it's clear within one scan of the room that Ignatius isn't here.

I go to his desk, peering over his research papers and books. It's all in languages that I don't understand.

Curiosity, and a few parts fear, draws me to the desk drawers that he never allowed me to touch. In the bottom drawer, I find the orange-gemmed ring that once sat on one of his shelves. Underneath the ring are a few photographs, and the first one immediately catches my eye. It's of Ignatius, smiling, which is a rare sight.

He's standing beside another elf with dark, long ringlet curls. They both have their arms around a little boy with a wide grin and chubby cheeks. The woman, presumably Ignatius's wife, holds the boy's chin affectionately. And on her finger is the orange-gemmed ring that's currently in my hand.

Chills run down my spine. "Oh, Ignatius." I flip the photo over and on the back is an inscription: *Jerusa, Nicolas, and I . . . our last time together.*

I blink, flipping the photograph back around. "He lost his family . . ."

A loud cracking sound thunders through the house, and the walls and floors sway.

I pull the shade back on the window. The drizzle is turning

into rain. And instead of the night turning into morning, it's getting darker. Dark clouds roll in from over the mountains.

I need to find Ignatius.

But on my way out the door, I freeze in my tracks. On his sofa, surrounded by blankets, is a large tome with an embossed cover. There's a symbol on the cover that I've seen before. In our father's study, under lock and key where he kept forbidden texts. The texts that I broke into when you fell sick.

"Ignatius, no . . ."

I hear someone rushing down the hall toward the steps, and then Evette's voice: "What was that crash?"

"I don't know." Merry sounds out of breath. "It sounded like it came from the back."

I crack open the heavy book. There's a page marker inside. I swallow when I see the image of a scythe . . . and below are the ancient, forbidden words for a summoning spell. There's a note written hastily in the margins.

It doesn't matter that it's been years, it reads. *I'll give all that I am. Do it for him. Do it for her.*

Tears well up in my eyes. Has Ignatius been lying to us this entire time? He never planned to use the star for Ash Gardens or even for Frank. He plans on using it to condemn himself.

The same way that I've condemned myself.

The same way that Frank has.

With the star, he plans on calling Death.

My feet barely touch the ground as I hurry downstairs. I thought everyone would be well on their way to the arboretum, but I hear a commotion coming from the library.

Frank, clad in his pajamas, is calmly perusing the bookshelf and humming to himself.

"What's going on?" I ask.

Merry and Morose look back at me. "It's Frank."

"He's actin' funky."

"Oh, here it is." Frank picks up a book from the shelf. He walks it over to an empty armchair and kneels before it. "Here, my love. I think you'd enjoy this one, as well."

Hilde walks up to him. "Frank, who are you talking to?"

"Oh, Hilde! So good to see you." He grins.

Evette flutters into the room in a frenzy. "There's smoke coming from the arboretum!"

Oli runs into the library a second later. She startles at Frank kneeling on the floor. "What the hell was that sound?"

"I . . ." I begin to explain, but it's all too much. "Frank." I walk up to him and tap him on the shoulder, and he breaks out of his daze. He looks at me with a loving smile.

"Oh, Saika. Just the witch I wanted to see. Kye, this is Saika." He looks at the empty space in the chair. "She's such a delight. I think you two will get along very well."

I hear gasps behind me. "He's finally lost it . . . ," Morose whispers.

"Frank?" Oli comes up behind me. She furrows her brow, looking from Frank's happy face to the empty armchair. "What's going on?"

"Oli!" he exclaims happily. "Oh, look, Kye. A familiar face. You're all here." His attention seems to broaden, and he takes in everyone in the library. "None of you have had the pleasure to meet Kye. All besides Phil, who . . ." Frank stops to gaze around the room. "I suppose he isn't here right now."

Evette gasps, covering her mouth with her hand.

My eyes go dry, I can't even blink. "Frank, Ignatius lied about the star falling in Rose Woods. It's here. We have to stop him from using it."

Frank laughs. His paws grip my arms. "Don't you see, Saika? It's all fine now. My mind feels complete again. I'm not forgetting anything. Kye is here. We won. We don't need that star anymore."

Oli's voice cuts through my panic. "Saika, you said that the star was for Ash Gardens. What's he talking about?"

"What's this talk about a star?" Hilde asks.

Frank is like a beautiful, heart-wrenching sunset that I can't look away from. My mind draws a blank, and I close my eyes. Too much. This is too much. "It's a long story."

Oli stares me down, arms crossed. "Tell me the truth."

"I can't. Ignatius—"

"We'd all like to know." Hilde steps closer. "Explain."

It wasn't supposed to happen this way. I was supposed to find the star. I was supposed to fix Ash Gardens. I was supposed to heal Frank's mind without worrying any of them.

But seeing Frank now, smiling and doting on a wife who isn't there, is way too much for me. And we're running out of time. I can't do this by myself.

"Ignatius predicted a star falling over Rose Woods a few weeks ago. My job for Frank was to create suitable spells to fix the house once we got the star. But I soon found, through the help of Phil, that the house is much worse than we ever realized. Frank is cursed." I look at him, blissfully unaware that we're even talking about him as he continues to pull out more books for his wife. "His mind, the house, it's all breaking apart."

"Why?" Oli asks. Her face is still creased in a frown, and I hate seeing her this way.

"Frank called on Death to revive his wife. And now he's paying the price for it. We thought using the star would slow it down and fix what's been lost. But now Ignatius is taking the star for himself to commit the same sin that we did."

"What do you mean 'we'?" Hilde asks, but then understanding finally crosses over her face. She covers her mouth in shock. "Saika, your power . . ."

"What?" Merry asks. "I don't understand."

"I called upon Death to save my sister, and as a result, I've lost my power. And I'm losing my youth. But that doesn't matter right now. I have to stop Ignatius from making the same mistake that we did."

"Where is he?" Oli asks.

"He's probably on his way to get the star. It's fallen in the arboretum."

"It must be what's causing that smoke," Evette says.

"Right, then." Hilde whistles, and it shakes the house. Her broom comes flying into the library. "Let's go get that little elf. You three"—she points to the cherubs and Evette—"stay here and make sure Frank doesn't get into any trouble."

Oli, Hilde, and I make it out the front doors and onto the veranda. Dark storm clouds blanket the sky in the near distance. They're almost reaching the house.

"We need to hurry." Hilde side-saddles her broom and sweeps up into the dark, rainy sky.

Oli calls for her broom, and it flies to her hand. We follow Hilde, my arms wrapped tightly around Oli's waist. We bound high over the house, cold rain pouring over us. Dark smoke billows up from the sycamores edging the arboretum.

Oli's silence unnerves me as we fly toward it. "Thank you for helping me," I call. "I'm sorry you had to find out this way."

"You're sorry?" Oli yells back. "Saika, I'm rightly pissed off. You lied to me. You lied to me about Frank."

"It wasn't an outright lie."

"I asked you if your work was dangerous, and you told me no. Multiple times."

"At the time I didn't think it was."

"And when you did? Did you tell me then?"

I fall silent. We dive through the arboretum's entrance, following Hilde. Once we enter, we're covered by the sweet magical air, and the rain stops. Our brooms skim low over the ground as we glide quickly. Oli and Hilde are masters, weaving through the colorful trunks and branches.

"You know how much I love Frank," Oli yells above the rushing wind. "And you didn't think it was important to mention he was falling into the pits of insanity. I could've been there. I could've helped him."

"Frank didn't want you to help. We thought we had it under control."

"Does it look like it's all fucking under control, Saika?" She snaps quickly to the side to avoid hitting a tree, and I'm almost jostled off the broom. I grip her tighter.

"We didn't know that Ignatius would be taking the star to bring back his family."

"Doesn't he know what will happen if he does? Doesn't he know he'll be cursed?"

I clench my eyes shut, thinking about everything I could have done differently to avoid this. "He didn't know. We never told him about our curses." My words are just loud enough for Oli to hear.

She glances back at me, her brow furrowed. "So much for you all keeping your secrets."

"I should've said something sooner. I just don't want Ignatius to make the same mistake."

Oli pulls her broom up, and we soar faster, barreling past Hilde.

Thick plumes of dark smoke cover the trees. As we near the crash site, I'm haunted by memories of our youth, Fi. The memory of burning earth and air so thick it nearly choked us.

I cover my nose, and Oli goes into a coughing fit. "It's the star!" I yell. "It produces a wave of noxious gas!"

Oli wastes no time. While keeping an impressive balance on her broom, Oli twists her hand and surrounds us in a cyclone of air. She creates another one to cover Hilde as well.

Hilde wobbles on her broom, afraid of what's happening, but then she looks over at us and exhales. "Thank you!" she calls out.

We dive deeper into the smoke until it suddenly clears. Our brooms stutter to a halt before a massive crater in the ground. Broken trees surround it; some have fallen in. The grass is black and burned. Little spots of fire are still burning all around.

We hop off our brooms. "Oli, the fires!" I call. And she goes into action. She enchants bodies of dirt to stomp out the fires. Hilde is quick to aid her, though she's moving slowly. She isn't used to enchanting nature, but thank the stars, she is trying.

I walk to the edge of the crater and peer inside. My eyes widen. Ignatius kneels in the center of all the destruction.

His shirt has burned away. His hands are glowing hot and blistering from holding the star.

He's a disaster. Broken. Lost. And desolate. Yet he's smiling. In fact, his shoulders bounce as he begins to laugh. He holds the star above his head and yells into the sky.

"Take it all, I bear my bones. My fears and heart I've gladly shown."

I don't recognize the incantation at first. He's translated it from its original language.

"Ignatius, stop!" I hurry over the edge of the crater and slide down. My dress rips along the side as I scoot through the dirt, trying to reach him.

His voice is overwrought with despair. He shouts, with burns on his hands and chest. I can taste his anguish as he continues to cry out.

"Be it wrong, or be it right, to you I release my breath . . ."

I hit the floor of the crater. I hear Oli and Hilde shouting my name from above, but I sprint forward. "Don't do it!" I scream.

"With this star," he says calmly, *"I unleash its power, to wholly welcome Death."*

"No!" The scream rips from my throat, and I fall to the ground.

The star glows white and burns above Ignatius's head. He cries out in pain as we're consumed in a blinding light. Black smoke and wind whip around us. I pitch my head downward to cover my eyes.

"Saika!" Hilde's voice finds me in the darkness. Then I feel her hand pulling me by the back of my collar. "Come, daughter, come!" she calls. She pushes me onto her broom, and we become airborne, ascending from the smoke.

We circle high over the clearing, and I clutch the back of Hilde's nightgown, struggling to catch my breath. When I open my eyes, I stare down at Oli putting out a fire consuming the surrounding trees.

Hilde and I land. My legs wobble as I thank her.

"Saika!" Oli runs over to us and scans me to make sure I'm alright.

"Ignatius," I choke out. My throat feels like it's crammed with dust. "He's still down there. We have to stop him."

"Stand back!" Oli nears the edge of the crater and circles her arms. The air electrifies as she seizes it. She creates a mighty gust of wind, blowing away the opaque smoke filling the crater.

Ignatius is kneeling before a figure made of light. There's no shape, no form. No voice. It's everything, yet nothing at the same time, and the sight brings me to my knees.

The look in Ignatius's eyes mirrors my own. The way he's pleading with Death is like reopening a deep, fresh wound in my heart. I had been that desperate for you, Fi.

I stand beside Oli on the edge of the crater. "I'm going back down."

Oli snaps. "There's no way you're going near—"

"I need to reach Ignatius. I have to speak to him." I look between her and Hilde. "If he doesn't listen to reason, enchant the ground beneath his feet and move him out of the way."

"Saika," Oli pleads.

I crouch low and slide down the wall of the crater yet a second time. When I get to the bottom, I stand on two strong legs and walk forward, my eyes fixated on Ignatius.

He grovels before Death, his body prostrate on the ground. I hear him pleading, "Please, my son, Nicolas, and my wife, Jerusa. I can't go on without them. I need them back, please. I'll do anything."

"Ignatius!" I call.

He finally looks at me. His eyes are wide, wet, and bloody. "Saika?"

"Don't do this. You don't know the cost of reviving someone you love."

"I don't care about the cost!" he yells. "I'll do it. I'll do it for them."

"What about Frank?" I ask. "He's sick. He needs the star, Ignatius."

"But . . ." He turns his head back toward Death. He keeps his eyes down. "I need them."

Eyes are on me. The full attention of Death is boring into my soul. I'm tempted to look him in the face, but I avert my eyes.

"They're gone," I tell Ignatius. "And to make a deal of this magnitude, you don't realize how much of your life it will cost you. It'll cost you everything."

"Listen to her, Ignatius." Hilde appears beside me, shoulders squared. She takes my hand and squeezes it. "You aren't a witch. Using the star to its full power could kill you."

"We don't know that!" he screams. "I have to try."

I lift my head to the rim of the crater. Oli is up there, positioned in a squat, her arms outstretched. She looks at me, waiting for a signal.

There's no talking to Ignatius. He's too far gone.

I nod at Oli, and she sees me. She circles her arms, and the entire clearing begins to shake.

Ignatius glances down. The ground suddenly rips a chasm between him and Death, and Ignatius falls back.

"No! I will pay the price!" He springs back up, clutching the star in his hand. He bounds toward the light. "I accept the deal!"

Death stands still, welcoming him. Ignatius reaches out to hand over the star.

"No!" I lunge forward, but Hilde catches me.

Oli growls, her roar echoing around us. Her fangs grow longer, her muscles bulge, and her eyes fill with black. The chasm in the crater rips wider, utterly splitting the ground. We all careen back, but Hilde is quick to snatch me up again. We hop onto her broom and sail upward.

Ignatius tumbles down into the broken, uneven ground. The star drops from his hand, and he cries out.

The light surrounding Death begins to fade, wrapping itself into a cyclone of black smoke.

Ignatius scrambles toward Death, bounding on all fours to reach him. "No, no! Come back! I'll do it! I'll do anything! Bring them back!" He lunges forward to touch the fading light.

"Ignatius, don't touch him!" I call, but it's too late.

His hand touches the light, and Death whisks away in a flurry of smoke and light.

Ignatius slumps forward onto the ground. Motionless.

"Oh, Ig." Hilde covers her mouth.

CHAPTER TWENTY-FIVE

We crowd around Ignatius. I'm afraid to step forward. I don't want to see. I hold on to Oli as she slumps on my shoulder. "Fucking hell," she groans. That last enchantment took a lot out of her.

Hilde crouches before Ignatius and turns him over. She checks his breathing, then silently looks back at me and Oli, shaking her head.

"Ignatius . . ." I swallow his name.

"That damn elf." Hilde tears up. "What a fool."

My eyes skim over Ignatius's body, and I feel sick to my stomach. He was a mean elf . . . but he just wanted his family back. He was on a mission this entire time, and he tried to focus on it as much as he could. He gave everything to be with them again.

And I don't think I'm any different, Fi.

"Look." Hilde dries her eyes with the back of her hand. She points to something in the rubble. Something shiny and bright.

"No." I gasp. Oli hobbles over to hang on to Hilde, and I rush to the shining treasure buried in the ground. I fall to my knees to dig it out.

"It's the star!" I quickly examine it. The surface is smooth like glass, and the inside contains a white, wispy cosmos swirling about. It's whole. There are no cracks. There are no blemishes.

It isn't broken. It's still heavy with power.

"We can use this to save Ash Gardens. We can save Frank." I release a shuddered breath.

Our moment of joy is quickly stolen away when we hear Evette's voice, shrill and loud, echoing through the forest.

"Oli! Hilde!" she calls. "Saika!"

We clamber out of the crater, and Evette zips from the trees in a panic. Her light pulses, brightening and dimming when she sees us.

"It's Frank," she says, catching her breath. "The storm is destroying the house, and he won't leave. You have to do something."

My heart hammers as we climb back on our brooms and soar toward the house. Once we break away from the sanctity of the arboretum, we're bombarded with rain and thunder. Lightning cracks against the house. The entire top level is gone. Wood is falling like sheets of snow to the ground.

The wind whips us as we dismount. Merry and Morose are in the garden, looking up at the destruction of our beloved house. "What's happening? What are we going to do?" Merry cries.

"We tried to get Frank out, but he won't listen to us!" Morose yells. He wipes the rain from his eyes. "The bastard is gonna get himself killed."

"I'll get him." I cradle the star in my hand, and everyone looks at me. "Hilde, can you try to hold up the house until I bring him out?"

"I'll do what I can."

I run toward the kitchen doors as Hilde calls out orders to Evette and the cherubs, telling them to bring her all the wood we have from the shed.

It's only once I break into the dark kitchen that I realize I'm not alone. Oli is running right behind me.

"What are you doing?" I shout. My wet feet slip, and I slide into the kitchen door.

Oli helps me up. Her hair is drenched around her face. "Like hell I'm letting you come in here alone!"

"You're drained from that last enchantment. Wait outside—"

"I'm not leaving you." Oli holds me by the shoulders, her voice calm. "We'll find Frank together."

The house rocks forward and back, and we stumble to the floor. I clutch Oli's arm. "Fine. We may need to split up. I don't know how long Hilde can keep this house from collapsing."

Oli looks up at the high ceiling. Dust sprinkles down as the house continues to rock. "You check down here, and I'll check upstairs. If the house starts to collapse, I'll just fly out." She holds on to her broom. "But, Saika, if the house breaks down while we're inside—"

"I know."

"I want you to run out, okay?" she asks. "I know it hurts, but don't die trying to save him. You run."

"Oli—"

"Do you promise?" she presses. Her cold, wet hand rests on my face. "Please."

I nod stiffly. "I promise."

She gives me a quick kiss, and then she's off, running through the dining room. "Frank! Where are you, you furry bastard?"

I run to the library, but Frank isn't there. He's not in the foyer, either. I cross over toward his wing and burst through the doors.

"Frank?" I call out. I scan over his sofa and into his kitchenette. He's a ten-foot beast. Where could he be hiding?

I run into his room, the floor shaking as I do. I lose my balance and fall forward, catching myself on his bedroom door, then I scan over the room. "Damn it, Frank. Where are you?"

"Saika?" a voice calls behind me. It's sweet and calm. Soothing like warm light.

I turn around, and there's a woman standing in Frank's front room. She stands by the mantel, hands elegantly poised over her stomach. She has brown skin, but it's ghostly, as if I could see right through her. The vibrant orange color of her hair is muted, though it flows over her shoulders. All the way down to the floor. She grins at me.

"I've been wanting to meet you for some time." Her voice is a bouncy, singsongy drawl. She steps closer. The house shakes again, but she doesn't waver an inch. "I'm Kye."

This isn't happening. I tear my eyes away from her. "You aren't here. . . . Frank?" I pass by her, running through the front room. "Frank, where are you?"

I stumble back out into the foyer and gaze up the steps. I hear Oli yelling out for Frank. She still hasn't found him, either. This is taking too long.

"Try the parlor, dear."

I glance back, and Kye is following me. She glides across the wooden floor. Her hands are still poised together. I clench my eyes shut. She's not there. I'm not seeing her.

I run off to the parlor, yelling Frank's name. And suddenly, I hear music. Piano keys play softly through the chaos of thunder and rain outside.

Frank is there, sitting before the piano, and his paws press multiple keys at a time. I sigh with relief. "Thank the stars, Frank. Come on, we have to go."

He has a distant smile on his face when he sees me. "Saika,

there you are. I wanted to show Kye that song you played your first day here. It was so lovely, I think she'd enjoy it, too."

I glance behind me to see Kye crossing the threshold and reaching her hands out to Frank. "Hello, my beloved."

"Darling." Frank rises from the piano and goes to her, brushing by me as if I weren't there. "Have you met Saika? She's the newest witch at Ash Gardens."

Kye looks at me, and her eyes are void of color. I turn my head away from her. "Frank, we need to go."

"I can't. Kye is here. She's finally here."

"She's not here, Frank. She's gone."

"But I am here." Kye's voice is sweet. I brave a glance at her, and she's holding on to Frank, staring up into his eyes. "And if he stays, we'll be together. That was the deal, remember, Frank? Our time is up."

I stare at Frank, ignoring Kye completely. "I have the star. I can heal your mind. We can stop your curse before it's too late."

"Saika." Frank releases a frustrated breath and holds on to Kye a bit tighter. "It *is* too late for me. Look around. Death is claiming everything. Seeing Kye right now is my last reprieve before it all goes away. Would you take this from me, too?"

"Frank—"

"Wouldn't you choose the same? If you had no hope, no chance, of reversing your curse?" he asks. "If Fiona asked you to stay, wouldn't you?"

I shake my head. "I wouldn't—"

Saika . . .

The air feels like it's knocked out of me. I stumble back, falling to the floor. I gaze up at the ceiling, searching for you.

Saika, I am here.

My back presses against the wall, and I shut my eyes, holding the star to my head. "It's not real. This isn't real."

Saika . . .

Your voice is like a melody, Fi, that beckons me to listen. "Stop, please . . ."

Thunder clatters outside, and a heavy shake rumbles through the house. I glance up, and the ceiling is splitting apart. Oli's voice is distant, like it's calling through a funnel. *"Saika, where are you? Get out now!"*

I can't . . . I can't move. Images of you dance in my head, Fi. Your voice. Your smile. Your laugh . . .

I look down to my hands and realize I'm still holding on to the star. Frank stands across the room, still holding on to Kye. "I don't want to go, Saika. If I leave, I'll forget all about her."

"Then I'll tell you, Frank." I struggle to my feet, and the room sways. "I'll remind you about your love for Kye every day, every night, if I have to." On shaky legs, I move toward Frank. "There's just something I have to try first."

I grip the star in my hand. My mind empties as it heats up. I pull Frank down by the collar so that we're face to face. I place the star against his head, and it glows bright.

"Saika, what are you doing?" he asks. Kye looks worriedly between us.

Damn. What was the spell? I can't remember. Too much is going on. I take a deep breath. Say what is true. Say what is honest. Say what I need.

"We know the pain. We know the cost," I begin.

Frank's eyes widen, realizing what's happening. "Saika, don't. I don't want to leave her."

"Now fully take this star." I take a deep breath. *"And restore what's been lost."*

The star glows hotter, but before its power unleashes, Frank grabs my wrist and presses the star against my chest.

"Frank, what—"

"Take care of them."

A light blinds us, and my chest is set ablaze. The ceiling finally snaps, and the wood and debris crash down. I fall to my knees, cradling my burning chest and crying out. Then I feel Frank's heavy body crash on top of me, and there's nothing at all. Only darkness.

⬮

"I found something for you."

I set my book down and glare at you. "I'm done with your parting gifts." I go back to reading.

"No, it's a good gift." You laugh. "I promise."

You sit on your bed, pillows propped behind your back. You're gaunt, and your hand shakes when you reach for your bedside table.

I hurry to my feet. "What is it? I'll get it."

"Sai, I'm not made of paper. I can do it." You grab the blue velvet box from the stand. "Here."

I open the box and pull out a golden locket. *Your* golden locket. "Just because you're dying, it doesn't mean I want to keep all of your things."

You roll your eyes. "Just open it."

I already know what's inside. A portrait of our parents,

and I don't really care to see them right now. Even in picture form.

But I freeze when I open the locket. "Where did you get this?"

"After you . . . did what you did. I wanted to see where you committed your *taboo*. And I saw something twinkling from underneath your bed." You grin as you point to the star fragment in my hand. "Looks like Death didn't take it all."

"Fiona, what can I do with this?"

You take a deep breath and invite me to sit beside you. "I am *so* grateful to have a sister who would consult with heaven and hell just to bring me back. I regret my reaction before, and I regret not reaching out to you sooner. This past year with you, living here with me and Jonathan and the girls, has been . . ." You inhale. "It has been perhaps the best year of my life. And you gave that to me. You gave me a chance to be a mother to Azure and Riza. You gave me time to spend with Jonathan, and you gave me time to spend with you."

Your hand grips my wrist earnestly. "You've spent so much of your life catering to mine. But this time, Saika, when I'm gone, that's it. I'm not coming back. So, please, take this star and use it for enchantments. Travel the world. Write music. Fall in love." Tears slip down your cheek, wetting your shirt. "When I die, please, do not die with me."

I release a shuddering breath. "Fiona, what am I going to do without you? Who will I talk to about my life? I have no one."

"Then talk to me. Write me letters. Speak to me in your mind. You are my sister, and our souls will forever be intertwined. In this life and the next. Speak to me. I'll hear you."

I hear you.

I've heard you this entire time.

And now, I ask you, Saika . . . are you ready to come with me? Do you want to be together again?

It's dark, but your voice is light, and air, and everything that's keeping me afloat. More than I want to breathe. More than I want food or water or joy do I want us to be together. Fiona, you are my lifeline. You are my blood. You are the very thing that keeps me tethered to this earth.

But I am not ready to join you, sister. I can't. Not now. Not yet.

I can't see you, but I feel your love. I feel your joy and your pride, and it burns my chest.

Then there's something you need to do, Sai. Lift your hands.

It's dark. My arms feel numb, suspended above my head. My neck and back scream in pain when I move. Once I've finally put my hands down, I touch a solid mass of fur. I hear groaning, and thick arms wrap around me. They curse in pain.

I can't move, and it hurts to breathe. In fact, my chest feels tight whenever I inhale.

If only I had some light, I could finally see—

My palm glows, and it illuminates the darkness. The blood feels hot in my veins. I move my hand over the dark until I see Frank lying beside me. His eyes are closed, but he's breathing.

"Frank, are you alright?"

He groans and nods his head.

I stare back at my illuminated palm. How am I doing this?

Muffled voices call our names above us. I lift my illuminated hand to the wreckage. It's been enchanted to stay in place. The wooden planks, glass, and debris form a protective dome around us.

My back cracks when I stand to my feet. I listen for our names. "We're here! We're down here!"

The frozen wreckage above us begins to crack apart. I hear Oli's muffled voice above it all. "What the hell? How did this happen?"

"I don't know," Hilde's voice supplies.

Cracks of sunlight filter through the debris, and Oli's face is the first one I see.

She exhales with relief. "Oh." She laughs, tears brimming her eyes. "Stay put, love. We're gonna get you out. Is Frank in there with you?"

I glance back at Frank sprawled on top of a pile of rubble. "Yes, he's here. He's okay. We're okay."

We get pulled out quickly. After puncturing a hole through the wall of wreckage, Oli and Hilde come in on their brooms. They startle when they see me and glance at each other.

"What?" I ask.

"Nothing." Oli rushes toward me and kisses me senseless. "We're just so happy you're both alright."

It takes all of us to help Frank balance on Hilde's broom so she can lift him out of the wreckage. I saddle behind Oli, and we rise out of this mess. The storm has passed, and we fly into the cool morning sky.

I look down at the house. It's utterly destroyed. Ash Gardens is gone. All except a tiny dome of broken wood and debris where Frank and I were. "How did that happen?" I ask.

Oli glances back at me. "You mean you don't know?"

I shake my head.

We descend to the ground and dismount. Everyone crowds around us, but they stutter to a stop when they see me. They glance down at my chest.

"Oh, my goodness." Evette holds her hand over her mouth.

I finally look down, and I nearly fall back onto the ground. Oli catches me quickly.

I'm frantic, swatting at my chest. "What is this? Get it off!"

"Saika, love, it's fine." Oli soothes me. Her gentle hand steadies my face. "Just breathe."

I take a deep breath and glance down again. The star is fused into my chest. Bits of brown skin are seared and stretch across the star like ribbon. It's grotesque.

"You just got ten times more interesting," Morose says.

"Are you alright?" Merry asks.

My voice shakes. "I am. I'm fine. But Frank." I search past them to Hilde, who is sitting beside him in the grass. He's awake now, shifting to sit up.

I kneel beside him and pat his mane back. "Frank, can you hear us?"

"I'm okay." He grunts. He glances up at me. "You saved me. Thank you. How can I ever repay you?"

"No need. You saved me first—"

"Well, at least tell me your name so I can thank you properly." He chuckles.

My hands feel ice cold. I glance at everyone crowded around us. I can feel their heartbreak, too. I turn back to Frank with a tired smile. "My name is Saika."

"Oh, what a wonderful name." Frank grins at Hilde. "And you, too, my rescuer. There was another woman. Ah . . ." His eyes settle on Oli. "You all helped me. I can't thank you enough."

"No." Oli kneels before him. "No, Frank, we can't thank *you* enough." Tears threaten to fall, but she refuses to cry. She exhales and looks away to the house.

"He's alive," she says to us. "He's safe. That's what matters."

"But Frank's mind," Evette says. Oli holds out her hand, and Evette sits on her palm. "What are we going to do?"

Oli sighs. "This is the price he has to pay. There's nothing we can do. We can only focus on what we can do. And there's lots." She faces the destruction of Ash Gardens. "We have a lot of work to do if we're to rebuild."

"Oli is right." Hilde rises to her feet. "We made it. We're alive. Let's work."

"Hey, now. How are we going to rebuild this place on our own?" Morose squawks.

Oli musses up his damp hair. "With a couple of witches, a light fairy, and some cherubs. Let's scour the wreckage and see what's salvageable."

They all head toward the house, and I stand to follow, but my knees wobble.

"Saika." Oli comes to me. "Just stay here with Frank."

"I want to—"

"If you say *help*, I swear to Phil . . ."

I chuckle. "Okay."

She tugs on my chin. "I'm glad you're okay."

"You, too." I pull her in for a kiss. "And I'm sorry. No more secrets."

"Sure." She nods and glances at the top of my head. "Then I'll tell you now, I don't care for all the white."

"What do you mean?" My hand reaches up to my fuzzy head. Oli scans the grass for a piece of broken glass. She holds it in front of me, and I see my reflection.

My hair, eyebrows, and lashes have turned snowy white. I glance up at her. She tilts her head and smirks. "You know, actually, it's starting to grow on me." She chuckles, but I fuss at my reflection. She promptly takes the glass away.

"It's fine, Saika. You're here. You're alive. You did well, my love."

I squeeze her hand gently, and she goes off with the others to sift through the debris.

Frank sits beside me, a simple smile on his face. "You two make a very lovely couple."

"We do?" I ask, and he nods. I scoot beside him in the slippery grass and rest my head on his shoulder. "You know, you have someone you love, too."

He blinks. "I do?"

"You do. Her name is Kye. And she's one of the most beautiful witches I've ever seen."

EPILOGUE

Dear Fiona,

It's been a while since I've talked to you. There was a moment last year when Ash Gardens fell that I swore I heard you. I thought I felt you, and as time grows between now and then, I fear I've simply dreamed the whole thing.

I don't know if you really are listening to me. Or if your soul is as intertwined with mine as you had me believe. But I couldn't continue life without giving you one last update. It's something of a downer, but it's an important one.

Frank died last week.

It was painless. He went peacefully, as if falling into a deep sleep. He held a picture of Kye on his chest.

In his last days, Frank spent his time reading, drinking tea, and meeting friend after friend.

We rebuilt Ash Gardens, and it was loads of hard work. Especially being under the architectural tutelage of Hilde now that I've regained power. I basically spent everything I had from my trust, and when that wasn't enough, your beloved Jonathan came like a knight in shining armor. I've gone back to revisit your home, and my, your girls are growing overnight, Fi. They no longer cower in fear because of the glowing star in my chest or the white hair on my head. They've grown to not only trust me, but love me, and that is way more than I could ever ask for.

They also took a huge shine to Frank—he'd introduce himself every time they met, and they never tired of doing the same. The dragon from the egg Lorna bought for them is growing and thriving. And they named him Beelzebub Jr. What sweet, sentimental girls you have, Fi.

I tried healing Frank's mind with the power of the star, but it proved fruitless. My powers may have revived, and my curse placed in a stasis, but I still wasn't powerful enough to reverse what's been done. Eventually, we had to give up and instead focused on making Frank's life as comfortable as it could be.

So, every day I would tell him about his wife. I'd tell him about Phil. And we'd sit out on the veranda. Me in the swing, him in his massive rocking chair. And we'd drink tea and wait for the sun to rise over the mountains. And I'd tell Frank, "Look, it's a brand-new day." Just like he loved to say.

On his last day, I finished telling him the story of his wife and how much she loved her dragon, Beelzebub. I could've been mistaken, but there was a bit of recognition flashing in his yellow eyes.

"Where is that dragon now?" he asked with childlike wonder.

I smiled at him, pushing the fur away from his eyes. "I let her go. She's free now."

Frank sighed, looking blissfully up at the ceiling. "Good, that's good." He looked back at me. "You're a wonderful person. You just came in here and sat with me to tell me stories. How delightful. The way you talk. You remind me of someone." He furrowed his brow. "What is your name again?"

My eyes burned with tears as I bent down to kiss his head. "Don't worry about it, Frank. Just know that I'm a friend. I'll go get your breakfast."

As I picked up my journal to leave, he called out to me.

"Thank you, Saika."

I turned around, and he smiled, waving at me. I stuffed down the sob that threatened to ruin me. I blew him a kiss instead. "And thank you, Frank."

When I returned with his breakfast, he was gone.

I felt guilty for some time, for not writing to you this past year. I felt as though I was committing a sin by not including you in my everyday life. But the fact is, you will never be apart from me, Fi.

You consume my thoughts. Your absence actively shapes and colors my world. My memories of you are folded into my actions.

I think about you when I make breakfast in the morning. Or when I sit on the veranda to drink tea. Or when Hilde dresses me up or when I laugh with Evette and the cherubs. Sometimes imagining your voice or your face is like a dull ache, but other times, it encourages me to live with all that I am.

I will act on my final promise to you. I will live. I will travel. I will write and play music. I will continue to fall deeper and deeper in love with Olivie.

I will wait patiently for our reunion, Fiona, like how I wait for mornings to come. And should you cross celestial paths with Frank, or Phil, or even Ignatius, please, give them an earnest hug and kiss from me. And tell them that I wait for them also.

Now, I sit on the veranda, the purple skies turning into day, and I feel the first rays of sunlight hit my face.

Oli sits beside me on the swing. She has a newspaper.

"Look what Morose brought back last night. The ad printed."

She has the paper opened up to the back page, and there we are. I smile and read it aloud.

"'Losing a loved one can be hurtful. And it can be scary. But you can take that pain and turn it into something beautiful. If you'd like a planting ceremony at the country's largest arboretum sanctuary, come out to the newly rebuilt House of Frank (formerly Ash Gardens). It's just a short way from the last train stop (by flying!). Once you see the bright red door, you'll know you're home. Just ring the doorbell and—'"

"Ask for Oli."

I look over at her, and Oli is grinning from ear to ear. "I think we did a bang-up job, love. The ad is printed. The arboretum is standing strong. And the house is better than ever."

I swing my feet, and we rock forward and back. "I don't know, there's a bit of a creaking sound on this swing. Do you hear that?"

"Oh, come off it."

"What?" I laugh. "I'm just not sure if you installed this swing properly." I dodge Oli's attempt to swat my head with the newspaper. I kiss her cheek instead. "You've done a wonderful job, my love."

"Thank you."

I make myself comfortable, resting my head on her lap. We sway on the swing as she rubs the back of my head. I close my eyes.

"We have a ceremony today. Time to get up, you think?" she asks.

"No, not yet." I open my eyes, smiling as the sun crests over the mountains. "I'm waiting for the sunrise."

ACKNOWLEDGMENTS

Nothing great is accomplished alone. There were many hands that helped *House of Frank* transform from just an idea that I went to bed thinking about to the polished book that it is today. And I have so many people to thank.

This book wouldn't be possible without my sister, Dominique. She allowed me a space to grieve, and subsequently heal, after the loss of our mother. From that time, thoughts were formulated, and deep emotions grew until they bled on the page. Without her support and her love, *House of Frank* wouldn't have gotten to where it is today. Also, I appreciate her best friend, Shirr Joseph, for pushing me to get *House of Frank* done in time for the Pitchfest deadline.

My critique partner, and wonderful kindred spirit of a friend, Ruby Young, helped *House of Frank* shine brighter than I could have ever imagined. She was the first one to read it and gave me encouragement and helped with line edits. All our writing and editing sprints together led to this moment, and I'm grateful for her and for our friendship.

Michelle Restrepo-Ocasio is probably one of my oldest friends and biggest fans. She has stoked the flames for me to chase my dream of being an author. Her enthusiasm and input are so valuable and unmatched. She understands me. She'll sit and listen to me explain an entire book series from start to end (I'm not kidding, we have done this multiple times). She's a wonderful asset, and *House of Frank* would not have gotten to where it is if not for her.

I'd also like to thank my trusted beta readers, who gave me feedback and encouragement on the first draft of *House of Frank*. It helped me more than you know.

I'd like to say a huge, huge thank-you to Rebecca Thorne. She brought Bindery to my attention through her online content and encouraged me to apply. She has a wealth of information, and I'm so grateful for her. Also, I'd like to acknowledge a writer friend, Kelsie Gonzalez. She's an absolute beast when it comes to writing pitch letters, and I had never written one a day in my life. I'm thankful that she took the time to help me.

I've probably told him this more than he cares to hear, but I'd like to express my highest gratitude for Jaysen Headley. I had seen his online content before and thought he was so funny and relatable. Never in my wildest dreams did I think he'd find *House of Frank* in a slush pile and be moved to tears by something I wrote. I'm so happy that this work spoke out to him, and I'm grateful that he chose *House of Frank* to be his first published work.

I'm thankful for Bindery and its founders, Matt Kaye and Meghan Harvey, for opening up Pitchfest and allowing underrepresented writers like me to have a fighting chance in the publishing industry. I'd also like to say a huge thank-you to their editorial partner, Girl Friday, and the wonderful job they did with editing. Jon Reyes, my editor, was an absolute gem and I appreciate all his notes and encouragement that helped make *House of Frank* sparkle. Also, I'd like to acknowledge Barry Blankenship, our cover artist, and Charlotte Strick, who understood *House of Frank* to a molecular level and thought of such neat ideas for the design of the book.

And of course, everyone who took part in making this little

story about witches and grief and posted about it online or spoke about it to their friends. You've made this whole author journey feel just a little bit more real. Thank you. And I'm sure that my mother would be proud of us for getting this far. This is only the beginning.

—Kay Synclaire

THANK YOU

This book would not have been possible without the support from the Ezeekat Press community, with a special thank-you to the Lionbrarian members:

Abby Smith
Amysue Chase
Biblioholicbeth
Bookspokenly
Brett Foster
Cassie Jay
CassidyPage
Dani Paez
Fowzi Abdulle
J. Caddel
Jeffrey Tristan Thyme
Kari Frazier
Katie Krishnamoorthi
Kelly Mead
Katrassidy
LucilaGarciaGray

ABOUT THE AUTHOR

KAY SYNCLAIRE is the youngest of five children and the proud aunt of twelve. Kay attended Philadelphia University (now Thomas Jefferson University) before working in caretaking roles as a nurse assistant and preschool teacher. Kay currently lives in Philadelphia with her sister, who is the coauthor of her 2022 collection of short stories, *The Strange Accounts of Germantown and Other Peculiar Phenomena*. *House of Frank* is Kay's debut novel.

Ezeekat Press is an imprint of Bindery, a book publisher powered by community.

We're inspired by the way book tastemakers have reinvigorated the publishing industry. With strong taste and direct connections with readers, book tastemakers have illuminated self-published, backlisted, and overlooked authors, rocketing many to bestseller lists and the big screen.

This book was chosen by Jaysen Headley in close collaboration with the Ezeekat Press community on Bindery. By inviting tastemakers and their reading communities to participate in publishing, Bindery creates opportunities for deserving authors to reach readers who will love them.

Visit Ezeekat Press for a thriving bookish community and bonus content:

ezeekat.binderybooks.com

JAYSEN HEADLEY is a content creator on TikTok, Instagram, and YouTube known as Ezeekat, who celebrates and curates diverse voices in books, games, and other media. Jaysen is listed in the top 5 BookTok influencers in the world with over 945K followers on TikTok and over 225K on Instagram, as well as nearly 10K members in the Ezeekat book club on Fable. He reads and enjoys a wide range of stories but focuses on fantasy and contemporary middle-grade to adult fiction, with a preference for queer storylines.

TIKTOK.COM/@EZEEKAT

INSTAGRAM.COM/EZEEKAT

YOUTUBE.COM/@EZEEKAT